The End of the World

Rise of the After Lord

H. S. Gilchrist

Dystopian Sunrise Press

Paperback: 978-1-7380611-2-9
Hardcover: 978-1-7380611-1-2
Ebook: 978-1-7380611-0-5

Cover art by G&S Cover Design
Developmental editor Lindsay Ribar
Copy editor Lillian Boyd

1st Edition

Dystopian Sunrise Press
Parry Sound, Ontario, Canada

Author Website: https://hsgilchrist.com
Author Newletter: https://hsgilchrist.substack.com
Linktree: https://linktr.ee/hsgilchrist

For my mom and dad.

PART ONE

Chapter One

"Lord of the After, Keeper of Dreams! Answer the cries of this decaying world! Cleanse our suffering with the fire of Thy eternal grace, O great World Devourer..."

The droning liturgies of the After Cult's morning service seeped into Mica's dimly lit prison cell, pulling her from restless slumber. *Still alive.* She buried her face in the pillow, muffling a scream of frustration. The nightmare that had hammered at her skull all night now shattered into visceral bits of memories: her mother's corpse with its rictus smile, pools of tarry black blood, Pandora slumped over a steel desk with the top of her head blown off...

As the dream retreated, the cold sweats and bone-shaking tremors of drug withdrawal crept in. Rolling to the side of her thin, miserable cot, she threw up the oily broth her captors had force-fed her the previous night. Then she clung to the bed's edge with trembling fingers, a knot of desperation forming in her chest.

If only she could decipher something new from her dreams, something that might hold value to her captors. Maybe then, they'd let her go.

Within their delusions, the Cult clung to the maddening belief that Mica's dreams concealed a gateway to another world. Each day, they forced her to sift through her nightmares, viciously reawakening a trauma she'd spent nine long years trying to forget. Still, the portal remained hidden. Did it even exist? she wondered bitterly. Or was it just another figment of their collective insanity?

She lifted her head, and through watery eyes gazed at the fifty-two fine white scratches etched on the wall opposite her bed: one line for each day of her imprisonment.

How long before their patience ran out, and they killed her?

"And all the ends of this broken Earth shall witness the glory of our God. For He shall emerge from the Dream to devour the old and bring forth the new. Forever He shall reign. Amen."

The final hymn echoed from a distance, resonating through the abandoned factory-turned-church, reaching the makeshift prison cells on the third floor. Mica shivered in the cold air of the windowless room, the thin brown robes they'd given her soaked with sweat and freezing-cold against her skin. The familiar dread was setting in, replacing despair.

The service was over. They'd be coming for her soon.

The minutes dragged on, each more agonizing than the last. Every tick of the unseen clock echoed in her mind, amplifying her anxiety. As the hour approached its end, a loud beep pierced the silence, signaling the completion of her prison cell's security scan. Sick with anticipation, she sat on the edge of her creaking cot, clenching her knuckles tight in her lap. Then, with a soft-but-distinct snick, the door lock released.

When she saw who stood there, the monstrosity who'd once been a man, she made a horrified gurgle in her throat, somewhere between a cry and a groan, and shrank back against the wall behind her bed. This was no ordinary priest.

High Father Holy.

The After Cult's lunatic leader filled the room with his awful presence. A mask of shimmering silver biosteel obscured his true face with the visage of a dimple-cheeked toddler whose rosebud smile moved as naturally as if made of flesh. That mockery of innocence was more horrifying than the bestial masks worn by the other high priests.

And yet the mask was the most human thing about him.

High Father Holy was a mod. The Technocrats had gutted his human body years ago and filled it with their technology. She couldn't even guess how he'd broken free from their control, but like all orphaned mods, he'd left part of his mind behind. The ravages of time on the cult leader's modified form were evident. Without the care of the Technocrats' technologists, it appeared he'd resorted to scavenging, patching himself up with mismatched parts sourced from shady black-market recyclers who traded in the Technocrats' leftovers. This makeshift maintenance was glaringly visible—bundles of wires and tubes snaking into the nape of his neck, pumping the cocktail of stims needed to sustain his life. The rest of his machine body was concealed beneath an austere white robe that flowed to the floor and spilled out to his wrists, but the hands were bare of flesh, revealing skeletal metal fingers.

More than once, she'd overheard the frightened whispers of acolytes discussing the deterioration of their leader's physical state and his growing detachment from reality. She'd only witnessed it herself from a safe distance, during the early days of her captivity when the Cult had forced her to attend their worship services. She'd watched him ranting about the end of the world from his pulpit, his steel fingers clawing at the air in fits of zealotry while the congregation echoed his madness with their cries of exultation.

But sometimes he seemed to lose the threads of his sermons, standing mute and staring into space as if locked inside the abyss of his own mind, or he'd scream incoherently and go on a rampage, tearing apart his surroundings. Once, he'd even ripped the pulpit from the floor and thrown it at his adherents.

During these episodes, one of the other priests would step in and claim that their leader was in communion with the After Lord and no longer in control of his own body. The congregation loved it. The sanctuary would fill with the sounds of jubilation as the fanatical crowd lifted their hands into the air and sang praises to the After Lord.

Judging by the look in his eyes, he was having one of those episodes right now.

"You!" The childish lips of the priest's mask twisted with fury. He lunged at his captive, his arm shooting out, his steel fingers snaring her by the throat and squeezing. "You stole my dreams."

"I don't know what you're talking about!" she choked, the words not reaching her lips as anything more than a gasp.

"Our Lord has withdrawn his favor from me. He no longer speaks in my dreams." His voice cracked, unstable, a child's warble on the edge of tears. "And why should He? We have failed Him time and time again. We put our trust in those with the Traitor's blood, but we were wrong. Lord, forgive us!"

Traitor's blood? What was he going on about? Was this some new delusion?

Terrified, Mica kicked at her assailant, her vision dancing between darkness and light as he pulled her up into the air by the neck. Her hands clawed at his steel grip, trying to loosen his fingers and failing. Panic replaced the pain as her last breath evaporated and her chest burned with suffocation.

"Please, Your Holiness!" an unfamiliar voice called from the darkness.

She heard the frantic shuffle of movement, hands prying her body out of that killing grip. Her throat opened and she sucked in a grateful breath, collapsing backward into the waiting arms of a gray-robed acolyte, his young face a mix of terror, gawkiness, and rat teeth. Mica's eyes focused and fixed on the second newcomer: another masked priest, the one who'd called out on her behalf.

Only high priests wore masks, but she didn't recognize this one: He wore the guise of a serpent over his face, its silvery scales shimmering across the biosteel surface as its nostrils flared and its mouth stretched thin with tension.

"If you kill her, there are no others left to take her place," he reminded his superior, his voice echoing from behind the reptilian visage, the metal distorting its natural timbre.

Mica's heart sank. So the others were dead, then. She'd never seen their faces, only heard their desperate wails from neighboring cells. In the early days, she'd tried calling out to them, but their minds had already slipped away, driven mad by their dreams. Three days ago, the final whisper died out, leaving Mica wondering when her turn would come.

An eerie calm came over the cult leader at his inferior's words, his mania slipping away like a bad dream. "We have fallen off the righteous path, Father Dark," he said. "We will make a sacrifice of her tonight, and when the blood of Revan spills, our Lord will show me the portal."

Sacrifice? The very word sent a deep, cold dread spiraling down her spine. The horrifying images of how they might take her life flooded her mind, each more gruesome than the last.

Mica bolted for the open door. Her heart thundered against her ribcage. The rodent-faced acolyte who'd caught her earlier fall lunged after her with a cry, but caught the hem of his robe underfoot. He crashed forward, mouth agape, and skidded across the dusty floor.

A second acolyte, this one broad and towering, blocked her path. His bearish face was set in a grimace of determination as he tried to wrap his thick arms around her. Mica pivoted and drove her elbow sharply upward, feeling a satisfying crunch as it connected with his nose, the youth recoiling with a howl as she lunged past him.

A perilously narrow hallway opened before her, lined with old crates, rusty corrugated sheets nailed to the walls and broken up by a succession of closed cell doors, including one marked with a long-dried bloody handprint. As she ran, she kicked loose crates into her pursuers' path, gratified to hear their muffled curses as they stumbled over the obstacles.

This wasn't Mica's first escape attempt. The sanctuary downstairs had a front foyer that opened into the streets of Zeta's undercity, an invitation to the disillusioned masses to attend the Cult's worship services. Beyond that, she was certain she could lose any pursuers in the labyrinth of alleyways and half-ruined buildings that made up the city's second quadrant.

"After her!" High Father Holy's voice roared out behind her, a mixture of rage and desperation. "Don't let her get away!"

Her legs shook with terror as she bypassed the stairwell leading down and veered off to a side passage. There, she found a decrepit elevator shaft. The lift was long gone, but cables dangled temptingly. Without hesitation, she began her descent, hoping it would lead her closer to the exit. Two floors down, she paused to listen. The muted sounds of footsteps and frustrated voices echoed from above. She exhaled her relief. Good. They hadn't thought to pursue her this way.

She emerged into a vast, dimly lit storage space, its tall shelves casting eerie, elongated shadows. Here, relics of the past—old machinery, broken automatons, and crates filled with forgotten parts—lay dormant. Mica wove through them, using the darkness as cover.

Exiting the storage, she encountered another corridor. The walls here showcased murals of winged men and apocalyptic scenes, crudely painted in stark colors, while gleaming orbs of light floated nearby, illuminating the artwork with a sinister glow. But what caught her eye was a distant back stairwell with a sign pointing downward: "Sanctuary." Mica smiled.

Before she could move, a loud metallic clang reverberated from the floor above, startling her into action. The acolytes had found her escape route! Their muffled voices grew louder as she sprinted toward the distant staircase. The streets were so close, she could almost taste the stagnant undercity air.

But out of nowhere, just as freedom was within her grasp, a shadow burst from a side-passage. Before she could react, a powerful hand yanked her hair from behind, twisting it until her knees buckled beneath her. It was the larger acolyte, his bearish grasp finally finding its mark.

"We have her secured, Your Holiness!" he called.

"Ow, let go!"

A few minutes later, High Father Holy arrived, walking toward them with a slow, uneven gait—*shuffle, scrape, shuffle, scrape*. He released a sigh that sounded like a soft whistle. "You've done well, Brother." He then turned to the rat-faced acolyte. "Summon our brethren to the sanctuary. Tell them to begin preparations."

"Is this what you did to the others?!" Mica's voice broke as she recalled the tormented wails of those other faceless prisoners and the last three days of silence. "Did you sacrifice them too?" She watched in despair as the acolyte vanished down the stairs to freedom out of her own reach, his gray robes flapping around his ankles.

Father Dark arrived, the mouth of his snake mask curled downward as he regarded his leader, his hollowed eyes betraying a flicker of discontent. "High Father, I beg you to delay the ceremony until tomorrow," he said. "You're not well. Your stims need replenishing. I've found a new supplier—"

"You'd protect her?"

"I protect *us*. We can't afford to make another mistake, not when all our other plans are falling into place. Our efforts in the north are reaching fruition thanks to our new allies, and our influence in the southern undercities continues to grow unimpeded. But all of that will amount to nothing if we can't open the Blood Gate. There are no other chances. She is the only one left."

That the Cult was spreading, infesting the world outside Under-Zeta, left Mica cold with fear, not for herself but for the ones she'd be leaving behind. Reid... Samiel...

"The Traitor's blood taints her. Just like the others, she will fall into madness, and the portal will not open for her." High Father Holy's posture tensed, wreathed with hostility. "Once her life spills out on His altar, our Lord will show me the portal. I will be the one to awaken Him."

There was a pause from the lesser priest, then a tremulous question, full of hope: "Our Lord has spoken this to you?"

"I am His mouthpiece."

"Praise be to the After Lord!"

Mica didn't miss the relief in that proclamation. Acting with new resolve, Father Dark stepped to her side, pulling her free from the stocky acolyte's grip.

"High Father Holy's lying," she said, latching onto the other priest's hesitation. "Your god no longer speaks to him. He told me himself—"

The High Father backhanded her. The strike came out of nowhere, landing on her jaw in an explosion of pain, the impact sending both Mica and her serpent-masked captor staggering backward as the other priest absorbed the weight of her falling body. The remaining acolyte cried out in alarm as he rushed to attend to Father Dark. Blood spilled from Mica's nose and down the front of her robes.

"Deceiver!" High Father Holy's fists clenched, a wrathful energy gathering into a storm around him. The expression on his mask was that of a toddler amid a full-blown tantrum, only with murder in his eyes. "I should kill you now!"

Once more, the other priest intervened, rolling Mica's body behind him defensively as he soothed his mad master. "Remember our Lord's purpose, Your Holiness! If we don't perform the proper ritual before she dies, you might not be able to access the portal. Let the After Lord judge her actions."

"Yes... Yes, you're right." It was the strangest thing to watch the transformation. It was like a light went out in the cult leader's eyes, his shoulders slumping as the fury evaporated, leaving behind an empty, vapid expression on his childish face. "As it should be, for all who dare defy His will." His voice drifted away as he mused. He seemed no longer aware of the others' presence at all, but wandered off toward the stairs by himself, his white robes hissing across the steel floor. "Our Lord calls us to worship," he said without looking back.

"Praise His name," both Father Dark and the acolyte responded automatically, the latter's face as tight as a corpse left to mummify.

Once their superior was out of hearing range, the priest turned to the acolyte. "Tend to the High Father," he said. "Make sure he tops up his stims. His connection to the After Lord must not falter during the ritual."

The acolyte grunted assent. "Yes, Father."

Clutching her bloody nose, Mica watched the gray-robed acolyte rush away, then turned to the masked man beside her. His earlier intercession on her behalf and his calm demeanor made her hopeful he was someone she could reason with. "You know High Father Holy's crazy, right?"

The priest tempered his reply with patience. "A mortal mind can't bear the presence of a God without consequences. But the After Lord will reward his sacrifice in the new world."

She could've told him it wasn't a god that was chewing through High Father Holy's brain but years of bad stims and shoddy biotech integration, but there was no reasoning with fanatics. Fresh nausea surged inside her head. She stooped to vomit and when she straightened up again, Father Dark was holding out a small canister of angel breath.

Her fear melted away, replaced by a humiliating wave of relief.

"It will help with the pain," he murmured. With a slow, deliberate motion, he cracked the seal, releasing the potent, intoxicating aroma of the drug.

Mica inhaled sharply, the mere scent of it tugging at a raw yearning deep within her. The pull of her addiction, rooted in the tragedy that had claimed most of her family, overpowered her.

"Why... are you helping me?" she whispered, her voice thick with both desperation and suspicion.

The cultist hesitated, his fingers trembling ever-so-slightly. "Even as we uphold the After Lord's vision, there are still moments in which we can offer solace."

Mica eyed the container warily. Despite her deep-rooted mistrust of the Cult, the weight of her addiction bore down heavily. The craving, the desperate need to escape even momentarily from the relentless pain of this place, was almost unbearable.

"It's genuine," he said. "No tricks."

One shot and she'd knock out all the pain, all the sickness, and all the fear. She was in no condition to refuse, her head pounding with need as she reached for the inhalant. Their fingers brushed, and his touch held a strange warmth, a familiarity she couldn't place. Who was this compassionate cultist? But all questions were lost in a haze of longing as she lifted the thumb-sized container to her nose and inhaled the intoxicant inside, feeling the instant calm shoot through her skull, erasing all terrible things from her mind. Her muscles relaxed and her knees buckled as her cares drifted away.

Father Dark slipped an arm behind her back. The smell of him, the sharp citrus fragrance of lumin lichen infused with the steel stink of a recycler's workshop, reminded her of home, of Under-Alpha, and an unexpected wave of homesickness washed over her.

She wished she'd never left, no matter how many terrible memories lived there.

He half-carried, half-dragged her down the stairs, but she didn't care. Another pair of acolytes waiting at the bottom rushed to open the sanctuary doors.

The wide-open space had once housed manufacturing machinery, but its interior had been stripped down to bare floor and converted into a worship space for the Cult. Against the distant ceiling hovered about a hundred pyrospheres, small orange orbs that cast a warm, fiery light over the worshippers below. The familiar cloying fragrance of incense hung in the air and burned her nostrils. She scanned the rows of cheap plasticine benches lining the floor, her eyes finally landing on the steel platform from which High Father Holy delivered his mad sermons and on which sat the seat of her death: the After Lord's altar.

The altar was both beautiful and grotesque. Its maker had chiseled it out of white marble, depicting angelic figures armored for battle with spears in their hands and fire in their fingers, but whose perfect feet trampled the twisted, agonized bodies of human beings.

This was what they worshipped: their own annihilation.

Drugged into blissful indifference, Mica allowed her escort to pull her inside. She'd suffered through many a service in this unholy place. At the beginning of her captivity, her abductors had tried to make a believer out of her, hoping that devotion to their god would help her find the portal. She thought she'd made a good show of it, moving her lips to their insufferable hymns and joining the congregation in shouting glories to the After Lord, but they'd seen right through her act and had moved onto violence.

Armed with a torturer's knowledge of the human body and access to expensive healing stims, her captors had bruised, battered, and shattered every part of her, extracting enormous amounts of pain while keeping her alive. All in hopes that enough fear and pain would break through the blockage in her mind that kept her from uncovering the portal.

That hadn't worked out for them, either. Hysterical laughter bubbled from her lips. Turned out opening an imaginary doorway was a lot harder than worshipping an imaginary god. She wondered how anyone could worship this grotesque fiction, this 'After Lord'? The very concept of the divine had been wiped out long ago, reduced to children's stories, yet these fanatics seemed determined to drag everyone down into their twisted delusions. Much as she despised the Technocrats, they'd been right to outlaw religion. If they ever learned about the Cult's activities in Under-Zeta, they'd send in their war mods to gut this church and turn its insane adherents into paste.

She could only hope.

With bleary eyes, she surveyed the congregation: six priests and twenty acolytes lining the benches, some on their knees, some standing with arms uplifted, some murmuring quietly and others shouting praises at the ceiling. To her blurred consciousness, the din of their worship blended into one unified sound, the roar of water rushing through an underground tunnel. Then High Father Holy stepped onto the platform.

The cacophony of prayers changed and transformed into a hymn. Mica found herself caught up in the sound of it. Maybe it was the delicious lull of angel breath coursing through her system, making the atrocious into something beautiful, but the hymns she'd once judged as bloated and obnoxious stirred something new inside her.

"O Lord, Bringer of Hope! You are the End and the Beginning. Take our dreams and transform us. Strip away our sinful humanity! Devour this wicked world!"

Her mind floated along the current of their song. What if all the terrible things, all the suffering in this world, could really be erased? If her sacrifice meant that her loved ones could live in paradise, would dying be so bad? Life under the Technocracy was a brutal existence, a constant fight over scraps, where the powerful preyed on the weak. But even the powerful were helpless against the recruiters that came to the undercities in search of new subjects for their masters' sick experiments.

"Amen."

The chanting faded into silence and High Father Holy raised his arms, the sleeves slipping back to his elbows, revealing rusty steel bones strung with artificial tendons. His face, masked with the innocence of a child, beamed out at his adherents, and even angel breath couldn't completely erase the repulsion it stirred inside her.

"We gather here today to witness the birth of a new world! Praise be to The One who makes dreams a reality! Who treads the dark and brings forth light! The Gate shall open when the blood of the Traitor spills."

Who was this traitor, the source of the blood that condemned her to death? Even through the haze of her high, Mica could feel the dread creeping back in, the stomach-twisting horror of her own impending doom. Panic tightened her chest. She looked toward Father Dark pleadingly, hoping he might offer her another shot to ease her anxiety, but the priest's eyes were fastened on his superior and his face blazed with fervor. He began dragging her up the stairs toward the altar.

"No!" Her high crumbled as she fought his hold. But the drug had slowed her mind and retarded her reflexes, leaving her as helpless as a disobedient toddler tugging back on their mother's insistent pull. "Please! I'll try harder! I can find your portal. Just give me another chance!"

"Too late for that, Deceiver." The hollow eyes of High Father Holy's infantile mask filled with a red fire that blazed with hatred. "We have endured your lies long enough. The After Lord has shown me the truth!"

"You're nothing but a fraud—"

Father Dark yanked her up the last step of the platform, cutting off her accusations.

"Lie down on the altar," he ordered. The serpentine mask remained unreadable, but she heard the tension in his voice. "It will be over quickly. I promise you."

"Like I'd trust you!" She tried to break away, but two older acolytes stepped forward to assist the priest, lifting her struggling body onto the stone table. Her back scraped against the stonework and opened an old wound, causing her to scream as she relived the kiss of the whip that had made it. She fought with all the ferocity of a cornered rat facing extermination, her spine curving as she tried to heave herself out of their grip.

Father Dark stood overhead, his face placid as he held her head in place. One pair of acolytes pinned her down by the arms and another pair restrained her legs. She twisted and strained until she exhausted herself, then stared up in bleak horror at the distant steel rafters overhead, terrified tears streaming down her cheeks.

"Please don't kill me! I'll do whatever you say. I can believe. I just need more time!"

A sigh released from behind the serpentine mask. Was that regret she heard? "No. Your blood corrupts you. It makes you deaf to the calling of our Lord. High Father Holy has heard Him speak: Your death is what will reveal the portal to us."

"If that's true, then why would your god wait so long to tell you?"

"Every word from your mouth is a blasphemy." An immense sadness burdened his voice. "It is not for mortals to question the will of our Lord. He will cleanse you along with the rest of the world, and if He finds you worthy, He'll make you anew."

Her only answer was a sob.

"We begin!" their leader announced.

The priests and acolytes took up a haunting prayer of supplication, begging the After Lord to awaken and save the world, their voices echoing off the walls of the sanctuary as they sang a dark devotion to her doom.

"Awaken, O Lord! Bring forth Thine armies to cover the Earth. Thine enemies shall turn to ash before Thy radiance!"

She couldn't turn her head to see, but the creak of unoiled steel and the hiss of a broken joint in his left arm announced High Father Holy's presence at her side. His terrifying child mask hovered overhead, and she could see the bone-colored blade gripped in his metal fingers. The blade was carved into the likeness of a winged serpent, with scaly coils wrapped around the base to form a hilt, and the feathered wings stretched out as the cross-guard.

A new, inexplicable fear awakened inside her, something deeper than her desire for self-preservation. She'd felt this kind of dread only once before, while deep within the ancient ruins beneath Under-Alpha, staring into a bottomless pool. A malevolent presence settled on her mind like a vulture awaiting carnage.

No, it couldn't be the same thing. Her teeth chattered. Not here...

"Lord of the After, accept this offering of the Traitor's blood as our tribute!" cried the cult leader. "Show me the path to the Blood Gate, so that I may open its doors and You may enter this world to deliver us from all sin!"

High Father Holy pressed the knife against her throat, and she swore she heard a heart beating from within it—but the priest stopped short of cutting, his head jerking upward, his burning eyes transfixed on something she couldn't see.

"My Lord?" he whispered, his voice shaking.

Then Mica heard it inside her head, a dark voice rasping against her mind: *"Kill them."*

And the world around her turned black.

Chapter Two

The attack on Delta began in silence, the approach of five thousand war mods veiled only by the slow drift of falling snow. Not a single word broke the quiet; the exchange of orders took place entirely inside their shared mind, coordinated by the Alphaknot, their invisible overseers.

"It is with utmost sorrow and regret that the benevolent Technocracy authorizes the sanitization of Fourth City Delta. Blessed be the Technocrats."

In unison, the mods turned their boom cannons toward the transparent dome surrounding the condemned city. The shield that had once protected its population from the outside world would now seal their doom.

The grim gray sky lit on fire and the dome's curved plasticine surface gleamed orange and gold for mere seconds before melting into a sticky super-heated rain, coating the entire city beneath it in a thick, clear goo. Weakened by the heat, the dome's outer framework gave a long groan and folded inward, its scaffolding pulled down by the weight of its melting walls, toppling sky-high graphene buildings and crushing everything beneath them.

Wails of pain rose in a crescendo. Dark shapes scurried across the ground, desperate to escape the blistering liquid. But, as the scorching plasticine cooled, it hardened back into its original state, entombing buildings and leaving the unluckiest stragglers encased alive.

Fourth City Delta fell in mere minutes and, without pause, Delta Division marched in to exterminate the survivors of the city they'd once protected.

D-2301 rushed her platoon of fellow war mods between the broken buildings of Delta's Residential Sector, every sense on full alert, the slightest movements catching her eye. The acrid stench of burning chemicals stung her still-human sense of smell.

Every single citizen here was complicit in treason; everyone would die. In the space of ten minutes, she'd shot down fifteen of them. Blood ran in rivers down the streets and pooled in craters left by fallen debris. She felt no pity at the sight of the citizens' broken bodies, stepping over them in her search for new targets. Steam rolled off her arm cannon in the cold winter air.

<<OPEN CHANNEL 08909>>

>[D-2301]: "Block F82 cleared. Casualties: 498."

<<TRANSFER DATA 497D7ADA64A-0005CB98>>

With a thought, she sent the communication to the rest of her division, complete with surveillance images to validate her platoon's work. Her masters, the Alphaknot, would process it along with the data from other platoons and recalculate strategies as necessary.

Those rebels still left alive fought with frenzied desperation. They used the spaces behind the rubble as makeshift trenches and laid their guns along the tops of debris piles, targeting their would-be executioners. That these dissidents had weapons at all suggested a deep-rooted insurgency, an organized rebellion with access to materials and technology the government had outlawed to citizens. But even that wouldn't save them. They had to know there was no way out, no salvation, no triumph left, and yet they fought to the last breath, battled their oppressors with a ferocity that stirred memories of D-2301s own warrior people and their constant wars against the dark, dead things that writhed out of the earth.

The memory awakened a sharp, punishing pain behind her eyes.

>ABERRANT ACTIVITY DETECTED.

<<EXECUTE NEURAL FLUSH>>

>ABERRATION CORRECTED.

The images disintegrated.

Mods weren't permitted to have memories of their own; they were a unified mind. That brief glimpse of her old life was a glitch in the psy network that needed to be corrected, and now that the Alphaknot had archived that forbidden memory, D-2301 could refocus on her mission.

She turned to the mod coming up from behind her. Like all war mods, whatever human remained of her comrade was well-hidden inside its exoskeleton—a massive suit of biosteel armor two inches thick, bristling with blades and firearms, with a set of steel wings that folded behind its back. Behind him, others from her platoon emerged from the rubble of the streets, twenty in all, not a scratch marring their impervious biosteel bodies as they lumbered toward their leader. Their visors glowed white as their enhanced vision scanned the alleyways between the teetering residential buildings.

In a telepathic machine language too quick and complex for a normal human mind to follow, she relayed her orders to her platoon.

<<OPEN CHANNEL 655121>>

>>[D-2301]: "24 armed hostiles and 239 unarmed civilians iden-tified at coordinates 50° 55' 2.658" N 0° 29' 1.244" E. Detonate structures 182 and 183. Eliminate all survivors as per Order 16."

<<TRANSFER DATA 497D7ADA899-0039F406>>

With a thought, D-2301 transferred the live blueprints of both buildings to five of her comrades. Pinpricks of blue light marked the location of civilians inside and outside the building, while a set of red dots marked the locations to place the explosives. Orders given, she surged forward with the remainder of her platoon, splitting them off into pairs and sending them into the alleyways and hidden avenues of crumbling Delta. Dissidents who'd snuck in from the undercity might've had time to hide, but the citizens didn't stand a chance. Like mods, they were linked to the Alphaknot, and she could see every single one of them in her mind.

There!

She turned a corner in time to see a small, dark-haired child crawl out from behind a pile of metal beams and mangled corpses. Her tiny face twisted with pain as she dragged her crushed leg behind her, and her mouth opened with a cry that pierced the roar of the embattled streets.

D-2301 lifted her arm, heard a click as her gun arm reloaded.

Another child's cry, distant in the past, wailed out from her memory.

This is wrong.

For a split-second, her human awareness separated from her machine mind. Her weaponized arm lowered, allowing the girl to disappear behind a curtain of snow. But again, D-2301's aberrant behavior met with resistance. The Alphaknot responded by triggering another flood of chemicals to her brain, suppressing further deviant thoughts. With two infractions in the space of an hour, she'd need to turn herself in for full reconditioning once her division returned to the heart city, Alpha.

It didn't matter. Nothing mattered except obedience.

She refocused on hunting down the hostiles still hunkered down in the ruins. With no dome to shield the city, the winter storm howled through the streets like a malicious spirit, anathema to the rebels exposed to its freezing breath. Her boom cannon blew apart barricades with ease as she marched through the rubble, shrugging off the spray of gun blasts from above. Her exoskeleton easily deflected the attacks.

Activating her flight mode, she rose into the icy air on steel wings, a harbinger of death delivering a final devastating attack. Her next shot cleared the wall of a residential unit several stories high, sending chunks of graphene and a dozen bodies tumbling to the ground.

From all over Delta, she heard explosions and the wailing of crowds as her division located and obliterated hidden clusters of rebels, yet her enhanced hearing still caught that smallest of sounds: the dull wet *thunk* of stone hitting a skull several stories below her. She looked down then, just for a moment, and saw the crippled child's head caved in, the long black hair spreading out in a pool of blood.

So wrong.

Something hit her then, something hard. It peeled open her exoskeleton with a single strike, sent her hurtling backward through the air, crashing through walls and ruins like a misguided missile.

The realization that the dissidents had a weapon capable of damaging biosteel sent a shockwave through the division's communication channels. Dazed and broken, she lay there in the rubble, waiting for her masters to calculate an appropriate retaliation. Their lack of response—of *any* response—caused her to lift her head. Blood streamed down her face as she scanned the battlefield. Her fellow soldiers stood like statues among the ruins of Delta, frozen in place. She could still sense their minds as distant blurs on the edge of her consciousness, but there was no communication. What was going on?

<<EXECUTE CODE WHITEOUT>>

The alien code sliced right through the Alphaknot's universe. One-by-one, her fellow soldiers' lives blinked out of their shared mindspace, like someone turning off the lights in her head. Before she could react, the Alphaknot pushed into her mind to stutter out one last directive:

<<TERMIN—>>

The command cut off.

She couldn't obey, couldn't move. Her exoskeleton had splintered, trapping her in place. Whatever had hit her was no normal missile: It had caused inches-thick biosteel to come apart like a weave of cloth, thousands of metal threads unwinding, razor-sharp fingers that curled around her body to form a second ribcage. Her steel wings had twisted beneath her, the pain of her injuries ratcheting up her spine and leaving her helpless to act as the unauthorized code unraveled her masters' world. Her local core system began hemorrhaging errors at an incomprehensible speed. Depleted of stimulants, her orphaned human mind was unable to keep up with the barrage of information and slipped beneath an avalanche of gibberish.

Then it ended. The last errors sputtered into her mind:

>CONNECTION TO ALPHA FAILED
>ATTEMPT TO ACTIVATE REDUNDANT LINK FAILED
>HOST COMPROMISED
>LOCAL CORE SHUTDOWN INITIATED

For just a moment, D-2301 felt another mind touch hers from far away—not the Alphaknot, and not another mod, its fear and frustration amplified as its owner tried breaking into her broken local core to finish what it had begun:

"'Execute,' I said, you damn—"

The curse broke off into silence and D-2301 ceased thinking about the intruder, ceased thinking about anything else, closing her eyes to sink into darkness. Core shutdown was the death of a mod, sometimes a temporary demise, sometimes forever.

***

A solitary drum echoed in the air, its slow steady beat resonating like a primal heartbeat. Thump. Thump. Thump. *Then a warm motherly voice joined its pulse, its wailing song carrying the ancient echoes of the Earth herself, a lament encapsulating the sorrows and resilience of all life, offering solace and nurturing to the world.*

"Animkii..."

Pain shocked D-2301 back to life.

A knife was shoved into her left eye. Blinded, she screamed her agony into the maw of a massive ice storm, crimson blood and ghostly black nether pouring from her wounded socket as the tempest blew a wall of wind and snow at her face.

It'd been so long since she'd felt pain, felt *anything*, and now she couldn't move to escape the assault, her mangled exoskeleton trapping her in a coffin made of muck and snow. Her other eye, a tech implant, was shuttered tight and sticky with blood. She pried it open with the force of her mind.

Oily black feathers filled her vision.

Not a knife.

This time, when D-2301 screamed, it shook the death out of her lungs. Startled from its plunder, the raven jerked its talons out of the grisly feast, ruffling its feathers with indignation before taking flight in search of quieter carrion.

It wouldn't have far to go.

Memories of Delta's obliteration came back to her now, echoing in the silence that had replaced the Alphaknot's voices in her head. Blood pooled and overran her eye socket. The injury should've triggered an immediate release of stims to ease the pain and quick-heal the damage, but her system failed to respond.

<<REQUEST CONNECTION TO ALPHA /FORCE>>

She pushed the command, sending a telepathic distress call out to the Alphaknot.

But her neural processing core was sluggish to obey—a bad sign. Tense minutes passed with no response. Steam rose from her skin as pellets of ice melted against a body overheated by fever and burned-out tech. The exoskeleton that had once armored her now pinned her to her grave, pieces of its broken metal plating scraping and rattling every time the wind rushed through the ruins. The heat of infection gnawed at her extremities, those parts of her that weren't yet machine.

Still human enough to die.

Above her, the sky was black with storm clouds and raven wings. If the recyclers took much longer to get here, there wouldn't be anything organic left to reclaim. If they were coming at all.

A growing sense of isolation closed in around her and fear surged inside her artificial heart. Why wasn't the Alphaknot answering her queries? For almost four years, those distant entities had filled her head with the constant buzz and hum of their unseen presence, binding her mind into the single shared consciousness that all mods belonged to. Had they abandoned her?

What about the others in her division? She opened a channel to contact them, but the connection was as dead as the silence in her mind. She turned her head to the side, opening her view to the streets of ruined Delta, but she only confirmed what she already knew.

The remains of her fellow soldiers were strewn alongside those they'd slain only minutes before their own demises, their bodies frozen in the positions they'd died in. Even the snowfall couldn't completely obliterate the carnage: a leg here, a torso there, scraps of the toughest body armor torn apart like paper, a child sleeping forever in the snow.

Why hadn't her masters sent anyone to collect their remains? Or to clear out the city's ruins? Why was she still rotting away in this gutted city, severed from the great mind? Had that code broken the Alphaknot? Did that mean—?

I'm free!

The thought terrified her.

A young woman with laughing eyes walked toward Animkii, a red-faced infant swaddled in her arms. "Isn't he beautiful, Animkii?"

"Nnnnnnnnnnnnrrrrrr," the sound ground out from behind clenched teeth. More memories, more doubts, all worse than the physical pain. Memories were dangerous things, their individuality separating her further from the blissful shared consciousness of the Alphaknot. Without the Alphaknot's barrier of chemicals to hold them back, memories and emotions suppressed for years swelled inside her, no longer stored data but moments she'd actually lived. The sorrows and resentment of a life interrupted spilled free and there was nothing she could do to stop it.

"Animkii, warrior of the Fire Bones, daughter of the Bear Clan, you have violated the laws of Creation!"

The thunderous voice of the village Speaker rose from the depths of her unlocked human memories, delivering a sentence of death. Once more, she recalled her mother's weary resignation and the grave silence of those she'd called her friends and family, their condemnation more damning than what awaited her at the End of the World's bottom. But there was no turning back. She'd made her choice, had tried to end the fighting the only way she knew how, and they'd all damned her for it...

D-2301 let loose an agonized cry. The memories were too hard. Surely the Alphaknot would send their recyclers soon. They'd fix her. They'd take away these torments and return her to the peace of oblivion.

But the more she fought her freedom, the more the memories peeled open. She saw the last few years of her life under the Technocracy's control unfurl in all their horror: glassy-eyed citizens terminated for the slightest aberration from the Technocracy's strict protocols; elders who confronted their scheduled 'retirements' with grim stoicism; undercity degenerates whose faces blazed with hatred as they fought to protect their families from recruiters. The Technocrats had used the Alphaknot to control her, had forced her to commit so many atrocities that she felt the weight of them on her soul.

The fear dissipated now, replaced by the outrage of being prisoner to a set of rules she never agreed to. As the barrage of connection errors trickled down to nothing, the laughing woman's face resurfaced from her memories, teasing her with its wry smile and merry eyes. A name flashed in her mind: *Ziiba*.

"Just stop trying to find new ways to get yourself killed, okay?"

D-2301 didn't care—she was nothing but a machine waiting for repair—but Animkii, fierce warrior of the Fire Bones people, heard that forgotten admonishment and felt it stir her humanity back to life.

She wasn't ready to die yet.

A fierce reservoir of determination powered her body out of its frozen grave, her left hand gripping the icy ground and pulling her forward until she could roll onto her side. Every inch, she strangled her screams, fighting through the nausea that threatened to pull her back into unconsciousness.

Then she saw her legs.

Clamped between scraps of biosteel shielding like fat, over-fried sausages, her limbs had turned black, bloated with gangrene that would've taken days to set in. How long had she lain here? A noxious wave of ripe decay washed over her and she gagged on the smell. That she was still alive meant she'd had enough stims in her blood to stave off sepsis, but why hadn't they healed her completely?

One quick look over her shoulder gave her the answer: Her stim repository, a pair of organic pouches grafted to her lower back, had cracked open like eggs. The spidery artificial capillaries that carried the stims through her body hung in severed bunches, spilling free the chemicals she needed to survive.

She laughed and cried and screamed into the cold until she was too tired, until the pain was too great to do anything but lie there panting. Freedom was a lie. Her end was near, her body falling into a cascade of organ failure, her heartbeat slowing as the biosteel organ sucked desperately at its artificial arteries, trying to find nourishment that was no longer available. Flakes of snow felt like drops of acid on her cheeks. Her limbs were corpses already, as heavy as stone.

In the battle between her humanity and the tech that infested her body, it was the flesh that was winning. She felt it dying all around her.

A prayer to the divine maker she'd left behind four years ago passed her lips, making an incoherent jumble of sounds no longer resembling any language. The muscles responsible for speech had atrophied from years of disuse. *Give me strength, Creator!* Fear jittered across her nerves, no longer kept at bay by a machine-mind, as she reached over to her left side, where one of the stim pouches lay cracked open. Just that slight movement set her skin on fire, and she screamed until the pain settled back into her bones.

She had to try.

Breath hitching with effort, she ripped the pouch free and tiny marbles full of stims rolled free, only a few of them still connected to the web of capillaries, most of them broken, and a handful tumbling free into the snow. Steel-encased fingers closed around what few remained, a dozen glistening spheres full of red.

She swallowed them whole.

Stims were a stew of chemicals used to enhance a human's physical and mental abilities, prevent a mod's organics from rejecting their tech integration, and provide an energy source for manufacturing pyrolite, the chief source of her weapons' ammunition. A mod's core system determined the proper type and dosage of stims. Animkii had no idea what consuming the spheres directly would do. Would they save her or kill her or do nothing at all?

She was about to find out.

The first shock of pain hit her like a hammer. Awful, burning tendrils took root in her human gut, spread outward to the rest of her body, and released an inferno of pain. With no voice left for screaming, she writhed and whimpered like a beast snared in a trap. The snow clutched her body, its icy fingers cruelly keeping her just on the edge of consciousness.

Caught in the twilight between life and death, she watched in fascinated horror as the putrid tissue of her legs withered and curled aside like burning leaves, releasing thick ropes of bloody pus onto the snow. Tiny silver hairs sprouted out of her abdomen, thousands of stinging biosteel needles that knit their way downward into the flesh of her lower body, taking on mass as they absorbed the cellular structure of whatever they touched, replacing the festering tissue with translucent layers of biosteel. As she watched in awe, blood vessels and nerves reformed their vital networks.

She hadn't expected this.

The stims she'd taken had caused the biosteel to reactivate, to spread and consume the rest of her body—both organic and inorganic. She'd accelerated her evolution to full mod.

Too fast!

Her human body was going into shock, her artificial heart pounding against the strain of the transition, sweat dripping down her face as she fought the violent tremors seizing her limbs. Nausea filled her skull. Unable to process the changes, her mind plunged headfirst into darkness.

Was she dying? Was she dead? What was this?

Then, with a loud, full-chested breath, she surfaced back to consciousness.

The pain was gone.

And so was half her remaining humanity.

Two gleaming biosteel legs had replaced the rotten black limbs. Just before the skin lost its transparency and slipped away beneath a coat of silver, she made out the shadows of bones and a webwork of artificial veins. The threads of her combat suit's black pants flapped around the flawless new thighs, hiding nothing about her new body. Animkii couldn't look away. The disbelief was too intense.

Trembling with the effort, she forced herself to sit up against the broken wall behind her and began tearing off pieces of her exoskeleton, tossing them aside like old junk. Her helmet's visor had torn away during the final fiery blast of battle, but the air filter was still clamped onto her jaw and cheeks like the legs of a metal spider. It dug painfully into her face but kept her from choking on the toxic air outside the city. No longer sustained by the dregs of her stim repository, her suit's wings and armor snapped apart like dry twigs, freeing her from the cage of broken biosteel.

It took another hour before she'd recovered enough to stand. The blast she'd taken from the dissidents' secret weapon had torn away the protective layer of biosteel that girded the flesh of her left arm, but the stims had at least healed the organic tissue. Her new legs, unfortunately, were not so easily managed: unnatural, clumsy appendages that she couldn't quite balance on. Time after time, she toppled back into the snow, flailing her arms as her newborn limbs gave way, her human instincts too slow to grasp the monumental physical change.

She was too weak. Too *human.* Her demolished nerves were still reforming their connections, and the damage to her core was still too extensive to compensate.

But she'd crawl out of here if she had to.

With a grunt, she pulled herself back up onto her feet, using a section of broken wall as a guide. Her legs shook with every step and the cold air stung her nose as she pulled her struggling body up the mountain of debris until she overlooked the vast ruination of Delta. One million people had lived here, all carefully molded subjects of the Technocracy, all dead now. Nothing but broken shells remained of the precisely planned streets and buildings. The Technocrats' perfect city was gone.

Animkii staggered through the snow-covered ruins, panting from the forgotten exertions of her human condition and wincing as the wind and cold quickly chafed her exposed skin raw. She thought of the other mods she'd served with. The Alphaknot had sung its song into their heads too. They were as much victims as the citizens they'd slain. A profound anger underlined her suffering.

The Technocrats had done this. Her division's orders had come through the Alphaknot, but it was the Technocrats who'd controlled the great mind. They were the ones who'd enslaved her and turned her into a murderer.

She stared at one burned-out husk in front of her, a mod who'd fought at her side and whose actual face she'd never seen—and never would now, as every inch of flesh had been burned from its biosteel bones. Had it been male or female? Had their masters recruited it from citizens or degenerates, or had it been an outsider like her? Snow half-buried the burned-out corpse, but the smell of melted wiring and cooked flesh stung her nose. The biosteel shell that encased its body had exploded, leaving behind only the charred biosteel ribs of its exoskeleton.

The execution of Code Whiteout had obliterated her fellow soldiers from the inside-out, leaving nothing behind worth scavenging. Overcome with emotion, she reached out a hand to touch the skeletal frame that was all that remained of her dead, nameless comrade.

One touch and the body turned to ash.

Chapter Three

A cold, wet storm swept over the exhausted pair as they moved through miles of petrified forest and towering hills of rubbish to reach First City Alpha. Between the heaps of refuse, remnants of an ancient city could still be found, sliced into neat square sections by a grid of crumbling, black roads. The foundations of sky-scraping structures remained rooted in the ground a thousand years after the city's demise, though scavengers had long ago taken any material of value, leaving behind only weathered concrete husks.

Mica and Reid knew better than to take the main highway—better to lose their lives to the Junkyard's malfunctioning tech and savage hybrid transients than become victims of the Technocrats' recruiting squads. There were too many guards on the roads these days and too much paranoia from their 'benevolent' dictators to risk using major routes to enter or leave any of the Ten Cities.

Nine Cities now, Mica thought.

Just before mid-evening, they halted their transport for refueling, giving her a chance to stretch her legs and take a piss. Ugly gray snow covered everything like a film of ash. The walls of discarded tech surrounding them did nothing to shield them from the elements, and the sphere of light that hovered outside the transport provided no warmth. Its stark artificial illumination fended off the darkness, but not the biting chill that accompanied it.

"You're sure we're not being followed?" she asked for the tenth time, peering into the darkness surrounding them, fidgeting nervously as she searched through the graveyard of trees for unseen enemies. There hadn't been living trees in these parts for hundreds of years, just these cold stone relics that time had frozen in place back when Earth had broken into pieces.

At least, that's what Samiel had told her, and Sam knew something about *every*thing.

A tingle of excitement coursed through her. Sure, things had gotten a little rough in Under-Zeta with all that Cult business, but it had worked out in the end, hadn't it? Better not to think about the bad things when she'd soon be back home with Sam. Nothing else mattered.

But the memories still came to her, brief smatterings of her escape, of running through the filthy, twisting streets of Under-Zeta with no sense of time or place or direction, soaked to the skin with blood...

A nervous tremor shook her hands. She couldn't remember how she'd escaped, and she preferred it that way, content to drown her trauma the same way she always did. With a quick nudge of her finger, she activated the subsistence tube hooked into her air mask, sending a bittersweet shot of angel breath into her mouth. Her inner cheeks absorbed the too-sweet gaseous intoxicant and her blood warmed, sending a heated flush up her face.

"Could've sworn I saw something back there on the trail," she insisted.

Her brother, emerging from behind a heap of toppled steel beams, shook his head at her. Reid looked tired. The light emphasized the lines on his face and the circles under his golden-brown eyes. Like Mica, a mask covered his mouth and nose.

Breathing the air out here too long meant ending up just like the hybrids, some kind of mutant mish-mash between human and whatever evolutionary leftovers the Technocrats had inserted into your ancestors' genetic code.

"Nothing out here's going to attack an armored vehicle. Nothing smart enough to worry about, anyway." Reid leaned back against their transport as a light snow swirled around them. They'd taken the vehicle off a dealer a week ago, just before leaving—fleeing—Sixth City Zeta's underground. It was a big clunky vessel, slow-moving and ugly as an old cave bear, its track designed for rolling over rough terrain with little effort.

"Yeah, you're right. Guess I'm just a little nervous after everything that's happened." The wind grew colder and she buried herself inside her thick, warm coat—real wool with weather-proofing. It'd cost her a pile of iron pegs and a spool of copper wire to get it. "Come on, it's freezing out here. Your turn to drive. I'm taking a nap."

Reid was right. There was no way the Cult would find them out here in the Junkyard. The darkest days were behind them now and the future held only the fulfillment of all their dreams. A grin pinched her cheeks. With the haul they'd brought back from the Fringe Lands' black markets, they'd never have to scrounge for leftovers again. No more scheming, no more starving, no more huddling in doorways, half-dead from the chill of a hollow storm.

"We can practically buy Under-Alpha with the load we're bringing back. Imagine the look on old Dathu's face when we pay off our debts! Just wish Mom and the boys were alive to see it."

Reid's expression was unreadable, his voice soft. "Yes, they would've been proud."

An old sadness swept over her as she recalled their dead family: her mother's weary face lifting with a smile, her stepfather's rough humor, the unrepentant mischief in the eyes of her two little brothers... so long ago, but their faces were still so clear. Her family had wasted too many years living in the wretched, ruined depths of Alpha's undercity.

She imagined how they would've reacted to the wonders of the southern Fringe Lands, where the grip of the Technocrats was weakening. The air outside wasn't poisonous there and you could see actual living trees, spindly and struggling but still alive.

And wait until she told Sam!

Her excitement quickly died as she flicked an uneasy look at her brother. She hated keeping secrets from him, but he couldn't find out her real reason for wanting to return to Under-Alpha. He'd never gotten along with Samiel, whose dissident activity carried a risk he didn't want his sister involved in. There'd be an argument for sure if he found out—especially after what had happened in Delta two weeks ago. The Technocrats' purging of the city for its dissident activity had made all her old friendships a dangerous liability.

Her fingers convulsed around her canister of angel breath, but there was no shot left to take the edge off her nerves. Empty already?

Reid caught her expression and misinterpreted it. "You regret coming back?"

"'Course not. Just thinking about the attack on Delta."

"The dissidents tried to start a war they couldn't win." His coppery hair, mussed by the wind and careless tossing, fell across his forehead, making him look younger than his twenty-six years. "The Crats are too powerful. Best we can do is keep ourselves out of their sights."

"The bastards lost an entire division in Delta. They're not invincible."

"How do you know that? If we get caught communicating with dissidents—"

"Just something I heard from that junk trader we met outside Zeta." She averted her eyes so he couldn't see the truth in them. "I told you: I cut off ties with Samiel's crew when we left Under-Alpha." Then she ejected the empty metal container from her subsistence array and rummaged through a small pack of supplies in search of its replacement. She pulled out two new containers.

"We're only back to make a delivery," he reminded her. The flame of his hair caught the sphere's light and burned. "We can't afford trouble with the Crats, especially these days."

"Yeah, yeah." Refusing to commit to that tired old argument, she inserted one of the new canisters into place, but pinched the release a little too fast, before the seal locked. The sickly-sweet smell of rotten oranges mixed with synthetic cinnamon escaped into the air: the gut-clutching smell of angel breath. She closed her eyes to breathe it in and enjoy the subsequent rush of euphoria, but before she could sink deeper, her brother jarred her back to reality by snatching the second container out of her hand.

"You've had enough."

"Hey!"

But her protest died when her gaze locked onto her brother's left arm. As he drew back his gloved hand, his jacket sleeve shifted enough to reveal skin that was angry-red and scaled with blisters, as if he'd dipped it in boiling water and left it to harden into leather.

The horror instantly sobered her.

Before he could stop her, Mica jerked the entire sleeve back and pulled free the glove. The entire arm! "What the gore?! You never mentioned you were hurt. Who did this to you?"

Reid pulled his arm away and slipped the glove back over his fingers. "It's not important."

"You never tell me anything. If you're in trouble, if someone hurt you—"

Her brother held up a hand, but it was the look in his eyes that silenced her.

"What?" she mouthed, looking around. The fresh shot of angel breath was already moving through her system, heightening her senses, numbing her fear. She lifted her gun from its holster, then rose to her feet and crept around the side of their transport. Snow had melted into a gray mush that slopped around her boots.

She surveyed their camp's perimeter. There was no beauty in the scarce gray trees that clustered there, those ancient statues with their misshapen branches long ago stripped of greenery. Nothing but the stubbornest of evergreen shrubs could withstand the decades of contaminants in this soil.

That's when she caught a glimpse of movement. Someone was coming toward them, passing through the jungle of scrap metal and chemical sewage and into the cluster of petrified trees. Too far off the main road to be a sentry. She held up a finger for her brother to see. Only one, so far. Good. Recruiters usually traveled in packs. That didn't mean she could relax, though. Anyone tough enough to make it this far into the Junkyard wasn't someone you wanted to underestimate.

Instinct told her Reid was just behind her and she turned her head, catching the glint in his dark eyes. She pointed two fingers at the ground and made a walking gesture.

Reid shook his head and sliced a hand across his throat. That disturbing nameless hunger was in his eyes, the one that Mica had seen more and more frequently as they drew closer to home. Something had happened to him, back in Sixth City Zeta, right before they'd fled, something he wouldn't talk about. Those scars...

She couldn't help but worry. Reid wasn't just her brother; he was her best friend. After the sleeping plague had stolen the rest of their family, a childhood already rotten with poverty and violence had plunged into a bleak and bottomless nightmare. Nine years ago, and yet she still pictured their grotesque, distorted bodies every time she closed her eyes. It was only through the bond that she and Reid shared that she'd survived the first miserable years that followed, but lately, that bond had become strained. Reid had been acting strange, less sure of himself, less confident.

"*You stay here*," she gestured in the sign language they'd invented as children. "*I'm checking things out.*"

Reid nodded, tapping his hand against the sphere to extinguish its light and hide their movements.

Mica's footsteps blended into the hum of the wind and the rustle of dead branches scraping the sky. Not that this traveler was making it difficult for her to follow. Twigs snapped and broke with every footstep he took. Robbed of their camp's beacon for direction, he moved like a wounded beast, stumbling and staggering in the dark, metal clanging and debris shifting under his feet.

Mica smiled. They'd take him out before he even knew they were coming.

Threading through the twisted trees, she followed the traveler, listening and waiting. The first half of the moon emerged from behind a stack of storm clouds, its edge sharply defined against the otherwise lightless black sky.

In that light, Mica saw a towering figure whose husky build couldn't compensate for the gauntness of his face. She knew the look of starvation, alright. She'd seen it often enough on the faces of friends and family during food shortages in the undercity. Then the traveler turned his head, and she saw the mesh of wiring and biosteel that had replaced human flesh.

A mod. Hatred flared in Mica's heart. The stranger wasn't a 'he' at all, but an 'it.'

It wasn't surprising to see one of the Technocrats' broken toys here; this was the Junkyard, after all. The land surrounding the First City was full of bits and pieces of defective slave-soldiers, some pieces larger than others, but rarely as whole as this one. Neglect and disrepair eventually claimed most of them: their parts disintegrating, stim withdrawals making them rabid, neuro-failures turning them into gibbering, mindless slabs of flesh and steel. Not pretty to see.

But this mod was different. It was one of those frightening new Gen III models, infected with a parasitic pseudo-metal called biosteel. She twitched nervously. For years, biosteel had remained experimental within the Technocrats' laboratories. Her only knowledge of its existence was due to Sam's involvement in its research. Now, rumors on the street whispered of its presence in the newest generation of mods. They said it spread through mods' bodies like a cancer, consuming both organic and inorganic parts, transforming its carriers into something more than the usual hybrid of flesh and machine. Something indestructible.

Or not.

She narrowed her eyes at the broken mod. Even in the moonlight, she could tell its modification was incomplete. Something had ripped away its heavy outer armor, the exoskeleton, revealing a patchwork body of flesh and machine that peeked out from beneath several layers of ill-fitting civilian jackets. The muted iron shine of mundane steel contrasted with the rainbow sheen of biosteel—its silvery surface holding the shimmer of oil hitting water. In between, she spotted ugly patches of human flesh.

With its steel skin twisted and broken in places, the mod looked no better than any other Junkyard scrap.

Her dislike intensified. Where there was a rogue mod, recruiters and recyclers weren't far off. So close to home and now this trouble? Then she spotted the mod's identifier, stamped on its biosteel cheek: 'D-2301.'

Unease deepened to fear. This was really bad. They had to get rid of this thing. The mod belonged to the ill-fated Delta Division.

The Technocrats hadn't bothered to hide their murderous suppression of Fourth City Delta and its inhabitants two weeks ago. They'd condemned its dissident citizens as traitors whose existence threatened the stability of the entire Technocracy, but rumors on the streets of Zeta's undercity whispered that something had gone terribly wrong in Delta that day, something so wrong the government wouldn't let a person step within fifty miles of the city until they'd completed their investigation. Yet this piece of wreckage had somehow gotten out, dodged the gangs of recyclers waiting on the forbidden area's borders and, by the looks of it, made it nearly five hundred miles north of Delta on foot alone.

It was too dangerous to let it go. Mica raised her gun, aiming at the human half of the mod's face. No weapon she knew of was any good against biosteel, but a dead brain meant a dead mod. She'd do it, even if it meant killing the human underneath. Her hand shook.

Before she could shoot, her brother's voice rang out.

"Identify yourself!" He stepped out from the darkness behind the transport, the nose of his gun shoved into the back of the mod's exposed neck. "Move one inch and my first shot will sever your spine."

What was he doing? Why was he talking to it?

The mod froze, holding up its hands to show it was unarmed. One glance assured Mica that its built-in armaments weren't going to be a threat. Its whole right arm had melted. More and more, it looked like the Technocrats' scrap-metal soldiers weren't so invincible anymore.

Seeing that her brother wasn't planning on wasting this trash, she resigned herself to playing along. She slipped free from the stone trees' shadows and stood face-to-face with the slave-soldier.

It was even uglier up close. The right side of its head was as bald as a worm's, the biosteel creating a circuit board across its skin and forming a steel skull cap from which a busy network of tiny wires diverged and disappeared into the surviving flesh. The other side was still human, a rough-cut length of black hair falling across an unmodified eye and a prominent cheek of earthen skin. The other eye was a tech piece, its silver iris containing a faint tracing of circuitry within it and tiny luminescent dots of light that flickered as it locked an inhuman gaze on Mica.

"Saw light. Needed shelter." Its words came out clipped and broken, as if no longer accustomed to normal speech. The monstrosity towered a good head over Reid and, despite the lack of visible weapons, its stance showed a readiness to defend itself. Weaponized or not, the chemical stew that ran through the mod's body made it several times stronger than a normal human.

"Be glad we're not recyclers," Mica said. "They'd love to turn in a mod with most of its hardware intact."

The brute face hardened.

But it already knew that, didn't it? She gave the hollow-faced slave-soldier an appraising look. Its body carried the stink of roads long-traveled and battles hard-fought—its human face was thin with starvation, its machine parts deformed and caked with blood. It couldn't even repair itself. Probably only a few boosts away from complete breakdown.

What was Reid playing at by letting it live?

"You've come from Delta?" her brother asked. The hazy moon slipped behind night cover again and Mica could no longer make out his expression, but she heard the tension in his voice.

Who cared? Better to shoot it and get out of here. It wouldn't be the first orphaned mod she'd had to put down. Just because this one appeared to have its mental faculties intact didn't mean it was any less unpredictable and keeping it around was going to invite attention they didn't want.

"Yes. From Delta." The human half of the mod's face twisted in a show of angst, visibly struggling against an onslaught of memories she couldn't see, that hideous countenance with its unnatural tech-eye staring into Mica. "Dead. All of them. No choice." Its body shook with the effort of confession as it spilled out the horror of its crimes. "Alphaknot ordered. We obeyed."

Mica tensed with loathing. The Alphaknot. Samiel had told her about that, too.

The Alphaknot was the mysterious entity through which the Technocracy controlled its empire, some kind of tech used to bind the minds of their steel slaves into a single shared consciousness, creating a psy network through which their distant masters controlled their every move. Once the Alphaknot took a mod's humanity, there was no restoring it. There was nothing left to pity. They were manufactured monsters.

Tears came to her eyes—the years of fighting, of hiding from the undercity raids, the fear of being caught by recruiters.... All blame now centered on this one tool of oppression. This mod.

"Murderer!" She tightened the grip on her gun. "I should kill you right here."

Its shoulders slumped.

"Hold up, Mica!" Reid stepped back from the mod, lowering his gun as he spoke to the mod. "You're not one of them now, are you? You've broken free somehow, otherwise you wouldn't be here." He didn't wait for an answer. "We'd heard that the Crats demolished the city to suppress an insurgency, but something wiped out the division they sent. How that happened, no one seems to know."

Again, that awful, twisted look of pain flashed across the mod's face. Its flesh pinched up against steel as the mod struggled to articulate what it had witnessed. "Delta fell. Yes. Then something—" Its still-flesh mouth deformed into a grimace. "A weapon. A code. Mods infected. Terminated. All of them."

Giddy excitement bubbled up inside Mica and she fought to hide it from her brother's ever-watchful eye. Could it be true? Had the dissidents unleashed a weapon capable of taking out the Technocrats' most elite soldiers? "If that's true, then how did *you* survive?" she asked, tempering herself.

"Local core damaged. Could not process termination command."

"And afterward? What about your loyalty conditioning? Why didn't you turn yourself in like a good mod?"

"Not going back." Its voice was quiet.

Mica hardened her heart against the pain she saw there. "Well, don't expect much of a welcome in the undercity," she said. "If the gangs don't gut you, then you're sure to catch the eye of a black-market recycler. The Crats pay good to get their property back, you know."

Reid strolled over to the sphere and switched it back on, his face shining eerily in the night, reflecting off the growing bluster of snow.

He made a series of stern gestures at her. *"This one's not a threat,"* he signed. *"No point in antagonizing it. We don't want attention."*

Her gun didn't move, not even an inch, and her brother signed at her furiously.

"Lower your gun. It's not going to hurt us. We're safe."

The mod stood rooted in place, uncertain of their intentions.

Finally, Reid gave up. "This mod isn't Pandora. Let it go, Mica."

Mica's face tightened with anger, her finger twitching on the trigger even as her resolve crumbled. "I know that!" she said, jerking away, shoving her gun back into its holster. "I just don't trust it."

"'She,'" the machine corrected.

Mica scoffed internally, *As if calling it 'her' makes it any more human.*

"Name was—*is*—Animkii."

"I'm Reid." Her brother introduced himself, ignoring his sister's scowl. "That's Mica. Don't mind her. She's had a few bad run-ins with your kind."

"That's enough, Reid." Mica's fists clenched so tightly that she felt like her knuckles would pop out. "It—she—doesn't need to know our life stories. Better that she moves on now, don't you think?"

"She'll be dead before she reaches Alpha if we don't help." He settled down on a fallen stone timber, clearly expecting her to follow his lead. From his pack, he pulled out a brick of protein, cracked it in half, and then offered part of it to the broken mod. The act of compassion was nothing but a con, Mica knew. She saw the scheme building behind that sympathetic smile.

Desperation made Animkii the perfect victim. Force of will seemed to be the only thing keeping her patchwork body upright. When she collapsed onto the fallen trunk of stone beside Reid, the sigh of relief she uttered made Mica's conscience wince, but just a little.

"Thank-you," the mod said in her tough, metallic voice, clutching the food with a hand that shook with gratitude. "Stims gone. No food. Land too dead."

Hunger seemed to seize her by force, and she tore into the bar of protein, chewing with an animal's vicious appetite, as if she hadn't reaccustomed herself to eating like a human.

Reid caught Mica's revolted gaze and his grin widened.

Bloody bastard, what's he up to? she grimaced.

***

As the transport drove forward, the snow turned into a rainy sludge, the wheels groaning and squealing as the vehicle pulled itself through the muddy terrain. Whenever they hit an unexpected rock or fallen tree, the whole vessel shuddered and shook, and the ache of Animkii's journey shot up her mechanical spine, her muscles quivering with exhaustion wherever they hadn't turned to biosteel. Stims were supposed to keep her going to the point of death, and without them, she felt like she'd already passed the grave. If she hadn't met Mica and Reid, she'd be lying in a heap somewhere in the Junkyard, prey to the black-market scavengers.

She locked her gaze onto the steel floor of the transport. It was hard to ignore the hostility radiating from the woman sitting on the bench across from her. *That* one would kill her in a second if her brother allowed it. And who could blame her, after what had happened in Delta? She hunched her shoulders inward, besieged by guilt and doubts, the leftovers of an imprisoned mind struggling against hard-fought freedom.

For two weeks she'd traveled on foot toward Alpha, leaving snow to cover the ruins of Delta behind her. Her scavenged clothes provided a poor barrier to the outside chill. Years of having her body temperature controlled by her exoskeleton's regulators had erased an entire childhood adapted to the icy lands of the north. Hunger gnawed continuously at her, a sensation she hadn't felt since becoming a mod, forcing her to forage from these poisoned lands, so that it'd been a contest to see whether cold or contamination or starvation would finish her first.

And they weren't the only threats.

At first, she'd thought the Technocrats had forgotten Delta and its sacrificed division, but that was quickly proven wrong. Outside Delta's broken walls, the hills were thick with sentries. Platoons from a different division patrolled the city's perimeter, avoiding the interior's wreckage and never venturing closer than a few miles to it. They'd made no effort to recover their lost soldiers. Perhaps they feared contamination. The first few days of her freedom were spent dodging these patrols while fighting off the wretched body aches, cold sweats, and piercing migraines of stim withdrawal. Hallucinations chased her across the plundered landscape and delirium filled her nights.

Worse was the silence in her head that soon followed. The absence of authority left her disoriented, unsure of how to act without the constant reassurance that she'd picked the most optimal path. There were days when she'd imagined the Alphaknot's voices were still there, unseen masters issuing orders and distributing punishment, and she'd taken comfort from her delusions. Echoes of those hollow, inhuman voices urged her to return to ruined Delta, to lie down and die with her fellows, to erase the pain of human life. She'd wept. She'd screamed. She'd almost given up a hundred times on her journey to reach this place.

But there was a stubborn resistance inside her, a remnant from her old life that wouldn't let her go back. No matter what they'd done to her, no matter what they'd made her do, she was still human.

Wasn't she?

Inside her beat a biosteel heart, the seat of her local core and the brain of her tech body. She'd silenced the errors with a machine command, not a human thought. It was her core that distributed stims and regulated the integration of biology and technology, not her human brain. Without her core, her body would fail.

Even now, Animkii wasn't sure she'd make it to Under-Alpha. Before the hour was out, fever once again raged through her body, sweat drenching her borrowed clothes, her limbs shaking from exhaustion and withdrawal. Her skin burned at the seams wherever metal met flesh, her nerves alternating between sharp stabbing pain and icy cold numbness, and she felt a constant nagging nausea that caused even the tasteless nutrient bars to roil in her belly.

What she needed were stims. Without that cocktail of chemicals, her organic system was rejecting the tech that ran through her body.

Looking back from the driver's seat, Reid noticed her folded over in pain.

"Hey, you okay back there?"

The transport shuddered to a halt and, a moment later, the red-haired man appeared in the back, digging through the crates. "We don't have any stims in stock, but this should ease the withdrawal." He held out a few canisters of angel breath. "A few shots won't hurt you."

Animkii flicked a wary look over to Mica, relieved to find the woman had already drifted off to sleep. Desperate for anything to soothe the fire burning beneath her skin, she gave a vigorous nod. Reid clamped her air filter over her mouth and plugged the container into its subsistence array, standing back as she sucked in a huge breath. As she inhaled the depressant, a warm drowsiness replaced the sensory hell of misfiring nerves.

Her anxiety disappeared. Yes, they were only a day or so away from Alpha now. There was no reason they wouldn't make it in time. Black-market recyclers lurked in the underground cities, illegal hacks who knew how to take apart bodies and machines alike. They'd have the stims she needed to keep her organic systems from rejecting the machine components that her body now required to stay alive. With the right help, she might even blend in. There were surgeries that could conceal what she was. For the right price, she could have a whole new skin manufactured.

Maybe she could even reverse her modifications.

But there'd be others out there who felt the same as Mica did. Animkii imagined spending the rest of her life holed up in some city's underground, despised by the locals and dreading the inevitable raids, always hiding her true nature to keep the Technocrats' recruiters from finding her. Mods, even broken ones, were valuable assets. Eventually, someone was bound to turn her in.

She laid her head back against the steel wall, listening to the rumbling of the engine, letting the angel breath quiet her fears. A wave of homesickness crashed over her.

There was one thing she knew for sure: There was no returning home to the Witherlands. Even if she could survive the journey back across the End of the World, her people would never take her back.

The sudden surge of emotion caused her to tense. The Alphaknot had conditioned her to expect punishment for connecting to her humanity and it took a moment, as it always did, to realize the pain wasn't coming, and the memories wouldn't disappear afterward.

For the first time in years, she relaxed. She pictured her village: rows of bark-shingled longhouses encircled by a wooden palisade, cradled by a lush green forest on one side and waving fields of corn and oat on the other, crowned with a blue sky and a blazing-white sun. It now seemed a paradise compared to the contaminated lands of the south, with their uppercities' sterile steel towers and the haphazard jungle of new and ancient architecture that made up the undercities.

If only she'd left Soulcleaver behind to rot in that monster's grave, then none of this would've ever happened: not her exile, not her enslavement, not this wretched half-life she was living. Yes, she'd still be fighting the same old futile wars against the soul-hungry horrors that crept out from beneath the earth, but at least she'd still have something worth fighting *for*.

Niigaanii...

She closed her eyes and pictured her child as she last remembered him—just shy of two summers old, with chubby, russet cheeks, soft brown eyes, and an unruly mop of black hair. He'd be almost six now, approaching the rite of passage that would determine his aspect, the role prescribed for him in society. Would he be a warrior like Animkii? Or something else?

Animkii had risked it all to change the world for him, only to lose everything in the end.

She wasn't the only troubled soul aboard the transport. A quiet whimper broke the silence and her gaze shifted back to the bench across from her, to where Mica had fallen into a restless sleep. Even slumber couldn't ease the tension in the woman's face, just as her expensive clothes couldn't hide the stretch of darkness behind her acid smile, the sickly pallor of her skin, or the desperate hunger in her eyes that pulled her back into the gutter.

Even on a full stomach, this woman would starve.

Reid seemed his sister's exact opposite, radiating confidence and strength, handsome in face and smooth in speech. Even his coloring was brighter: his hair a flame in the darkness, his tawny skin flushed with life, specks of gold warming his dark eyes. She was grateful for his compassion, knowing she'd never make it to First City Alpha on her own.

She pillowed her head on a sack of clothes, her racing thoughts coming to a standstill at last, eased away by the shot of angel breath. The cold steel bench in the back of the transport felt like a bed of fur to her aching body.

How odd to experience any kind of comfort after years of disassociation with her humanity, to yawn and stretch and wrap herself in the rough borrowed blanket Reid handed her, to feel her mind sink into a state of rest. Her hibernation mode involved shutting down nonessential operations and entering a state of energy conservation that left her conscious but functioning on a lower level. It wasn't the same as sleeping, but close enough that she took pleasure in it.

The transport roared back to life and continued to roll over the rough terrain with little trouble, making its own path through the dead land. Then, sometime during the night, a cry of anguish jarred her awake.

It was Mica. Sprawled out on her back on the bench across from Animkii, her arms flailed as if fending off an invisible attacker. "Mama!" she cried, sitting upright, her eyes open and staring at Animkii without seeing, her expression twisting with a grimace. A curtain of dark hair spilled a shadow over her too-white face. "I don't belong here."

Animkii shivered at the flatness in her voice, at the distance in her dark, dark eyes. Mica's expression reminded her of her people's dreamwalkers, how they'd sit around the vision fire in a trance, their souls abandoning their bodies to congregate with the dead in the Land of Souls. They'd had that same empty look in their eyes.

She leaned forward, intending to shake the woman out of her trance.

"Let her be," Reid called back from where he sat in the driver's seat. "It happens most nights. I've found it better to let her get through it herself. Interrupting her makes it worse."

Animkii snatched her hand back. "Sorry. Wanted to help."

"Nothing to be helped," he said. "She's suffered these nightmares ever since the sleeping plague took our family nine years ago. It wiped out our whole quadrant in Under-Alpha."

"*Morbus incubus.*" Horror caught her breath. She'd seen it once before, in a different undercity. The sickness lulled the afflicted into a deathly slumber from which they couldn't awaken. As life ebbed from their bodies, their skin turned an awful, unnatural white, shrinking against their bones, and their blood turned as black and thick as tar. The disease struck quickly and thoroughly, spread through the slightest contact, and gutted entire populations in mere weeks before disappearing.

There was no cure. At least, no cure the Technocrats would share. She'd never heard of anyone surviving it. No wonder Mica looked so sickly.

She gathered her words with difficulty. "There was an outbreak. In Under-Gamma. Two years ago. Only drones permitted to enter."

Drones were automatons: fully machine, lacking any individual intelligence, and strictly limited by their programming. Drones did the grunt work of the Technocracy. There were many kinds, each type designed and programmed to carry out different tasks, usually simple repetitive labor that wasn't worth wasting the more valuable mods on.

They weren't exactly gentle.

"Same thing happened in Under-Alpha," said Reid. "I was away trading in Under-Zeta when I heard of the outbreak. By the time I got back, the Crats had already sent their steel goons to quarantine our home quadrant—thousands of people shoved into a cage and left to die." The warmth in his voice thickened like a syrup. "By the time the virus ran its course, a quarter of the undercity's population was dead. And Mica was the only survivor out of those infected. Imagine being fourteen years old and watching everyone else around you die, wondering when it'll be your turn. Every night, she relives it in her dreams. It might've happened yesterday, it's so fresh to her."

Animkii, who'd lost so many loved ones during her people's struggles against the Dreamers, knew Mica's pain too well, had seen people driven mad by grief. That same madness had driven Animkii into the deepest depths of a forbidden city, had led her to break the Creator's covenant, had damned her to this punishing inhuman existence.

"It is hard," she said, hiding her shame. "To keep living."

"Mica's stubborn." Reid flashed the mod a knowing grin. "You've seen that yourself. Once she decided to survive, there were no other choices."

"She hates me."

"Nothing personal—she hates all mods. It was a mod she tried to rehabilitate that released the virus into the undercity."

"Pandora?"

An awful light gleamed in his eyes. "We think the Crats were still controlling her. That they planted the virus for population control. If so, it was very effective."

The undercities were a quietly tolerated side-effect of the Technocrats' policies, containing the runoff of failed experiments and providing a refuge for those unsuited to the Ten Cities' controlled habitats. As long as these 'degenerates' didn't become too independent or show signs of organizing against their overlords, they could continue to exist on society's fringes, a social experiment for the Technocrats to poke and prod at.

But a successful experiment meant keeping tight control over the variables.

Animkii pulled the blanket around herself and rolled over to face the steel wall, closing her eyes. She blocked out Mica's whimpering and tried to focus on what awaited her in Under-Alpha, but a frightening thought kept circling her mind.

What if she was like Pandora? What if the Technocracy was still controlling her, and she didn't even know it?

Chapter Four

The nightmare always began the same. Mica was fourteen years old again, shoving her dirty, rail-thin body through an intoxicated crowd, breathing in the hot stink of unwashed poverty as she and Pandora raced through Quadrant Four to reach the heart of Under-Alpha's Festival of Masks.

Her whole body quivered with anticipation. Costumed celebrants paraded in the raucous streets with their cheap wigs and grotesque masks, bags of treats dangling from belts and pockets bulging with hidden treasures. Masked children darted out from the crowd and attempted to tug free their booty, shrieking in delight as their 'marks' made exaggerated attempts to catch the 'thieves.'

Overhead, strings of lights ran between buildings, obscuring the cavernous city's vast ceiling of rock and creating an artificial night sky. Of course, Mica had only heard about actual stars in stories, but Pandora had assured her they were once real and might even still be there, hidden behind the surface world's vast curtain of haze.

Pandora's goblin mask leered back at her, and she giggled as they plotted their evening's trickery together. Pandora wasn't a child, though; she was a tech mod, a scientist whose control shard had malfunctioned during an archaeological expedition in Under-Alpha. Mica had stumbled across her while searching for scrap metal in the labyrinth of ruins beneath the undercity. Though she and her mom had restored the orphaned mod as best they could, Pandora still retained the mind of a child.

That hadn't mattered to Mica. In her fourteen-year-old opinion, she had three brothers too many and having a 'sister' helped even the odds.

Giddy with excitement, she and Pandora linked hands and danced to the blaring street music, high on the sweets they'd filched from costumed vendors. The crowd swirled around them, a collage of grays and browns with unexpected flashes of garish color.

Just as they were leaving, an empty-eyed gargoyle with teeth like broken tombstones came up to them, holding a steaming pie in its hands. The smell of sugared apples made her teeth ache and her mouth salivate. Real fruit was an expensive treat and nothing like the cheap synthetics they usually ate.

"I made it special just for you two." Auntie Guen's kindly voice echoed from the black hole of the monster's mouth. Her hydroponic orchard was the only one in Under-Alpha.

But it wasn't the pie that held Mica's focus. From beneath the old woman's mask, a thick, black syrup had oozed out, dripping down the flabby neck and staining the collar of her shirt. The first prickles of dread danced on Mica's skin as the edges of the mask itself curled up like dead leaves, peeling away from the flesh.

"Auntie?" She clutched the pie in shaking hands.

The gargoyle's mouth lifted into a macabre smile, awful black liquid spilling from its mouth. "Yes, dear?"

Mica stifled a scream and stepped back, dropping the pie, and grabbing for Pandora's hand. As she watched in horror, the whole crowd drew back into the shadows, their features fading until all she could see were the whites of their eyes and the glint of malicious smiles. An awful smell of old blood and rotten meat filled the streets.

"Pandora, we have to get out of here!"

The mod didn't move. "You are afraid," she said matter-of-factly. Reading emotions was difficult for Pandora. She lifted her goblin mask, revealing a round-cheeked young woman with earthen skin and short, frizzy hair. The only visible modification was the band of steel that encased her human-looking brown eyes.

Those eyes pierced Mica like broken glass.

"It is time to go home, Sister," Pandora said.

With the disjointed logic of a dream world, Mica turned and found herself transported to the front of her mom's shop.

Like adjacent buildings, the shell of a more ancient structure formed its base. In its old life, it'd been a handsome three-story triplex, but centuries of scavengers had stripped away much of its former glory, leaving behind only the skeleton of red brick. The roof that capped it was so flimsy that hollow storms whistled through the top floor and shook the entire structure.

A metal sign hung over the front door, etched with the name of her mom's shop: "Mama Q's Recycling and Recovery. We waste none of your waste."

"Mica!"

The door swung open. Her mother's beaming face greeted them, flushed red from the heat of the tech-forge that she'd programmed to create the parts needed for today's jobs. Grease smudged her nose and a disassembled automaton lay on her workbench. The disembodied head, human only in appearance, stared out at her with sightless silver eyes, a screwdriver sticking out of the top of its open skull.

"Did you and Pandora have fun?" her mother asked in a tired-but-happy voice. Aging laugh lines rimmed her smile and strands of silver and red escaped the neat knot tied at the back of her head.

A pie materialized in Mica's hands, the same one she'd dropped at the festival, its aroma sweetening the air. She held it out stiffly for her mother to take.

"Auntie Guen sent this."

The sound of feet thumping down the stairs turned her head toward the door at the back of the shop. It burst open and her brothers rushed in, speaking excitedly over each other, demanding details about the festival. Her heart leaped with joy at the sight of them. The older of the pair was five, with his father's broad build and his mother's dark, dreaming eyes. The youngest brother, almost four years old, had a shock of red hair even brighter than Reid's and the light that danced in his eyes lit the entire room. It didn't matter to him that he didn't have all his words yet. He'd still jabber nonsense at you in that all-grown-up way of his, and woe to the one who tried to correct him.

Behind the energetic brothers towered their dusky-skinned father—Mica's and Reid's stepfather—crossing his enormous arms as he beamed down at his noisy family. The only one absent was Reid, who was away on yet another trade expedition to the southern undercities.

"I hope you and Pandora didn't cause too much trouble at the festival," their father teased. "Your mom and I were planning on taking the boys there after supper, but now that you've brought back treats, maybe we don't need to go after all."

The boys grew loud with protests, but they all knew he was joking by the grin that broadened his bearded face.

Mica's unease grew, and though she obediently recited all the things she'd seen for her brothers, the words came out mechanical, stilted, wrong. "But the real show isn't until tonight," she said. "That's when the Unmasking begins."

Her brothers giggled and their mother's smile stretched so wide it distorted her care-worn face, the sight of it causing fear to ripple through Mica. She knew what was about to happen but couldn't stop it. A knife appeared in her mother's too-white hand.

The skin was where it always showed up first. Helpless with terror, she watched the blade slice through the pie crust.

"Aren't you going to have a piece?"

"Mama?"

"Yes, dear?" Her mother's smile remained, her face still flushed rosy from the shop's heat, but her eyes had already grown cold. As Mica watched in despair, she saw the edges of her mother's face flaking, like chunks of carnival makeup too thickly applied.

Like Auntie Guen's mask.

No matter how many times she'd seen this play out, the horror remained fresh. The white skin was almost translucent now, sucked back against her mother's fine bones, every angle and edge clearly defined in shadow, like an artist's charcoal sketch. Nausea rose from her gut into her head. The room spun. Her mother's face was molting like a snake's skin, the flesh peeling away in whole papery sheets, leaving behind the pulsating remains of a flayed corpse with its bulging lidless eyes and gaping mouth. Black blood pooled at her feet.

She dared not look at her stepfather or brothers or even Pandora standing so quietly beside her. She could *hear* their transformation, the faint whisper of skin pulling away from bone, their cries so agonized that she clenched her jaw to stop her own anguished scream from joining theirs. She waited eagerly for the death rattle that signaled the end of their suffering—and hers.

Her mother held out a skinless hand. "It's time to remove your mask too, Mica." She was so patient with understanding, so exactly her mother, that Mica felt her fear melt away, replaced by a sick sort of longing.

Mica reached up to touch her own face. Yes, it had begun. Skin flaked away under her fingers, and she felt only relief as she dug her nails into the skin. Time for the unmasking.

The pain began. Razors beneath her skin. A blood vessel burst on her face and a sticky black liquid dripped down her cheek.

"The time is approaching," her mother said. "Join us now."

But something held Mica back, a stubborn grip on life that she couldn't release just yet. Her face crumpled with grief and tears burned her eyes. "I can't, Mama! I don't belong here!"

The truth broke the illusion. At her words, the bodies of her family fell, lifeless, poised as she last remembered them, fallen so quickly that her stepfather simply sat down in a chair and never got up again. Her brothers huddled in a final, frightened embrace and her mother lay grimacing up at the ceiling, flat on her back, blood congealing at her mouth.

Pandora wasn't standing beside her anymore. Mica knew where to find her, crumpled over the desk that held her psy port, her brains blown out by the gun Mica had taken from her stepfather. Her last network activity flashed up on a monitor covered in blood: the code she'd used to release the lethal pathogen.

Somewhere outside the dream, Mica screamed her grief and pain, but inside the nightmare, the silence was all-consuming as her mind tore itself apart.

"Mica?"

The sound of that voice saved her, was what always saved her in the end. As she lay dying in a pool of her blood, Reid's face appeared overhead, his expression dark with the horror of his homecoming. The turmoil in her mind subsided. If her brother was still alive, if she had one person who loved her left in the world, she couldn't abandon it. She couldn't die. Not yet.

The dream released her from its grip and its claws retracted.

For now.

***

By the time Animkii emerged from hibernation the next morning, Mica had traded places with her brother, taking her turn in the controller's seat. The woman propped her chair back and gave navigation over to the vehicle's auto-drive. She hummed an unfamiliar tune, stopping only to adjust her intake of angel breath.

Animkii watched her with wary eyes. Mica had a gaunt, sickly look about her and her clothes hung so loosely off her bony frame that she guessed the weight loss was recent. Her skin carried an unhealthy pallor—perhaps a leftover from the sleeping plague, but made even starker against the darkness of her hair. Partially healed scars disfigured her neck and disappeared beneath the collar of her woolen jacket.

Mica caught her staring. "Like what you see, Mod? Hands like yours did this to me. Did worse things."

"I am sorry."

"Your kind isn't capable of regret. I don't know what my brother's thinking, bringing you along. You might've broken your connection to the Alphaknot, but they've got your brain so conditioned there's nothing left in your skull but what they've told you. It's just a matter of time before you turn on us. If you think you're still human, you're deluded."

Animkii opened her mouth to defend herself, but the cries from Delta still howled in her head, echoing Mica's hatred. She clenched her jaw, trying to bite off the scream nesting in her chest.

"I will find a cure." She struggled to produce the words, hearing them echoed back as cold, rigid machine-talk. It took great effort to ignore the conditioned instinct to speak with her mind. "In Under-Alpha."

"Do you think the Crats would *allow* a cure to exist?" Condescension dripped from her voice. "Face it: You're going to just end up like every other orphaned mod—completely insane."

"The Great Spirit gives me strength." The moment she uttered the words, out of instinct from years lost, she felt the cold hand of doubt squeeze her chest. Why would the Creator protect a traitor like her? Yet the human part of her clung to the hope of redemption, that there was still a chance to save her soul.

"Great Spirit? What's that?"

Animkii searched for an equivalent term. "Our maker. Our God."

Mica went silent, and darkness swallowed all the light in her eyes. "God, you say?" Her hand slipped to the gun belted at her side. "And where exactly did you pick up that nonsense? Off the streets?"

Animkii tensed, her eyes never leaving the weapon. "My people. Back home. They have always believed in the Creator."

The hand paused, lifted back to the steering wheel, and its owner barked out a contemptuous laugh.

"Then you're *all* delusional, aren't you? There *are* no gods. Anyone who tells you otherwise is a liar. Best to accept that we're all nothing but dirt in the end. The only ones with power over our lives are the Technocrats."

Mica's blasphemy ignited Animkii's anger, but the Alphaknot was no longer there to extinguish it. She was on her own. Reclaiming her humanity meant confronting this ball of outrage growing inside her. With effort, she wrestled down her fury, biting down hard on her words. "The Technocracy corrupts. They are like the Ancients. They take. Give nothing back. The Creator made a covenant with my people after the Earth broke. To save Her, we must obey it."

"I'm surprised the Crats didn't scrape that superstitious nonsense right out of your brain. But I guess they were too busy manufacturing you into a murderer."

"Hey, what's the point in arguing?" Reid's voice drifted from where he lay curled against the wall in the back of the transport. He watched them with sleepy eyes, stifling a yawn. "We're *all* tools to those more powerful than us. Animkii's no more a murderer than a gun or a knife. One day, some greater power will come along and then the Technocrats will take our place as dogs."

"Well, I wished it'd hurry," his sister huffed. "A thousand years is long enough, don't you think?"

Animkii became increasingly grateful for Reid's bursts of diplomacy over the next few days of travel. His wall of niceties kept the tension between her and his sister from erupting into violence. She knew it couldn't have been easy. Though Animkii tried to avoid antagonizing the other woman, Mica jumped at every opportunity to provoke her.

Just the other night, she'd awakened to Mica on top of her, screaming Pandora's name, her hands locked around Animkii's throat as she reenacted some horror in her nightmares. It'd taken Reid's strong-arming and three shots of angel breath to sedate her.

If only I had the strength left to reach Under-Alpha on my own, she thought, but her condition was deteriorating by the hour. Though Reid had given her drugs to dull the fever and delirium that now constantly raged inside her body, there was nothing he could do for the life-draining fatigue that weighed down every movement and made the simplest conversation laborious. Without stims to maintain it, her body was rejecting the tech inside it and killing her in the process. All she could do was conserve her resources by entering a hibernation mode deep enough that even Mica's nightmares couldn't disturb her.

When Reid announced that the First City was coming up in the near-distance, Animkii felt like shouting her relief. It was almost over.

Only it wasn't.

An hour from the uppercity entrance, a slow shudder moved through the back of the transport. Storage crates rattled. Metal walls quaked around them. Animkii threw out an arm, catching Reid as the vehicle lurched forward. He smelled of burned oil and overturned dirt.

Mica slammed her hand on the vehicle's kill switch. Something popped, and the engine fell silent.

"Damn tech," Mica grumbled. She shoved open the transport's door, grabbed an overhead bar with one hand and a toolbox in the other, and launched herself out feet-first—a perfect landing finished with a mocking bow toward the transport and its watching passengers.

Reid grinned at his sister's dramatics, stretching out his long body and folding his hands behind his head. "Glad one of us inherited our mother's gift for tech. I'm more of a talker than a fixer."

Animkii watched him, envying the bond between the two, aching for her own losses. "It is good. To have family."

An unreadable emotion rippled across his normally placid face. "Mica and I have always been close. Even when our family was alive, things weren't good, not in *that* place." There was a distance in his voice, an old suffering hidden until now. "We kept each other safe. We loved each other when no one else cared if we lived or died."

Then his smile fixed itself back into place. Perfect. "But that was a long time ago. Things are different now."

"Hey! If you're going to get all sentimental, pass out a few shots first," Mica shouted from outside, banging around beneath the vehicle's hood. "You might start making more sense."

Her brother laughed, but Animkii thought it sounded bitter, broken, unlike anything she'd heard from him before. He rose from where he sat and slipped out through the front of the transport. From outside, there came more laughter.

Four years of having her memories locked away; four years of being punished every time even one of them trickled through the Alphaknot's draconian security measures... The pain of her loss was a sharp knife in her chest, and worse memories darkened the fringes of her mind, wolves lying in wait.

The Alphaknot could've eliminated them all with a thought, could've replaced pain with peace. Her thoughts churned with indecision. Her core stirred to life, and new attempts to connect to her old masters flooded her brain with errors. She could turn herself in at the gates of Alpha's uppercity and forget all about black-market recyclers. A few hours of reconditioning would erase all of her suffering.

An ugly image flashed in her mind: the little girl in Delta, her long black hair floating in a pool of blood.

Animkii's resolve tightened. Never again! She'd end herself first.

The Creator had kept her alive for a reason. Maybe she'd never see her family again, maybe she'd never restore her humanity, and maybe she'd never find redemption for the wrongs she'd committed, but she'd fight to her last breath if there was even a chance.

***

Mica stood at the crag's treacherous edge, peering down at the shining white pearl sitting at the bottom of an ocean of garbage: Upper-Alpha, the capital of the Technocracy. She hadn't missed it one bit. The Technocrats didn't permit undercity residents to enter their pristine city, but she and her brother didn't have any interest in breaking into that prison of tech. They'd be making their way to *Under*-Alpha, the place where the leftovers went.

Home.

A smattering of evening birds arrowed over the horizon, fanning out and filling the skies with their mournful cries, but they never dared to fly directly over the city. A thick haze of pollution clung to the air, choking the breath from their little lungs. Snowfall melted into a dull gray drizzle. The Technocracy tainted everything struggling to survive in this place.

Reid stood beside her, rubbing his gloved hands together for warmth. The ugly wet snow fell around them, as gray and dismal as the day.

Even surrounded by rot and mud, her brother remained unblemished, from the perfectly oiled curl of his hair to the impeccable moss-colored jacket he wore over his slim frame. Mica shook her head in bemusement, feeling her own dark hair flattened against her neck like a cold, wet blanket. But she hadn't forgotten the wounds she'd seen on his arms. Once they got away from this mod and settled down, she'd pull the truth out of him.

"Looks like we'll be walking the rest of the way." Her voice sounded hollow behind the air mask, even though the thoughts of stretching her legs cheered her. They'd been on the road for hundreds of miles, after all. Her muscles felt like they'd turned into stone, and the slightest movements caused them to cramp and complain. "Our whole damn engine's burned out. Never seen nether backlash like that before. Black as gore inside and out."

Someone would need to stay behind and guard their trade bounty, but Reid was unexpectedly quiet.

"Hope you're not planning on leaving the mod in charge of the transport," Mica joked.

Reid still said nothing.

To be fair, their unwanted guest hadn't voiced one complaint about their crowded, uncomfortable accommodations, steel benches to sleep on, wall-to-wall crates crammed in between, and the nonstop rumble and jostle of the transport as it tore up the Junkyard. The mod had spent most of the last couple of days sleeping off the hardships of her own journey, making little conversation and no trouble.

That hadn't softened Mica toward her one bit, though.

"We can't be seen with her," she said. "The minute we walk into the undercity, we'll be targets." Seeing her brother's lack of reaction, she groaned. "Come on. I know you're not helping her out of kindness. Do you have a buyer in mind or something? Look, I don't care what happens to the mod, but I'm not going back to the Steel Fangs. Pay them off and get them out of our lives for good. We don't need them anymore."

She'd stolen, lied, and *killed* to get to this point, and she wanted no more of it. Whatever she'd told Reid, the only reason she'd really come back here was to find Samiel. To apologize.

If it wasn't already too late.

"With what we've brought back, we'll never have to muddy our hands again," she said, a sense of relief easing her suffering heart as she looked over domed city below, surveying that symbol of oppression. "We can go anywhere we want. We're finally free."

"Are we?" Reid asked rhetorically, skepticism evident in his voice. A new distance appeared in his eyes and a shadow fell across his face. "I just wish this could end differently," he said quietly. "Mica, I—"

But no more words came out. Reid's mouth chewed frantically at the air. Terror froze his face and his eyes bulged, his gaze fixed on something behind Mica. His hands jerked up defensively as a slick, black substance sprayed out over the armored transport, missing Mica by inches and blasting into his chest.

"No!" Mica staggered toward her brother.

Behind them, the transport emitted a long, shrill screech. Steel walls swelled outward into a huge bubble, then deflated and folded inward. Metal turned to liquid, encasing the vehicle. Drops splattered her left side, instantly burning away portions of her coat and eating away at her bared hand.

Crying out in pain, the young woman flung off her sizzling coat, tripping over her own feet to reach her fallen brother. A monstrous shadow blocked the sky, and she could see nothing in the darkness—only hear a terrible choking noise.

Chapter Five

The transport shook and rattled. Lurched out of hibernation, Animkii opened her eyes just in time to have her face slammed against a wall as the vessel overturned. Crates burst open and spilled their illicit contents everywhere: powders of every color, pills of every shape, tech implants, and alien-looking plants. She trampled them beneath her feet as she scrambled to find her bearings, but a sharp inhalation of the acrid air sent her into a violent coughing fit.

She clamped both hands over her mouth and frantically searched for her air filter, hot iron filling her nose with its stink and making her mouth taste like rust. The heat quickly became unbearable, eating holes through the walls as they sizzled and folded inward.

From outside came a shriek that shivered her skin. Someone was dying, dying in the kind of agony she'd only seen in Delta. Nausea filled her skull and blisters crept up her flesh and burst. The back doors were jammed, and she kicked them until they split open, then threw herself bodily to the ground outside.

What she landed in was worse than what she'd escaped.

A sticky black fluid had pooled outside. Her borrowed clothes dissolved instantly, and where the liquid touched her unprotected left arm, the skin melted. She screamed and clawed at the wound, only coming to her senses when she realized she'd die if she couldn't fend off the flesh-eating liquid.

A fallen stone tree lay a short distance away, piled with rubbish and snow. Still reeling from pain, Animkii stumbled over to its shelter, walling herself off from the smoldering ruin of the transport. She rolled deftly over the fallen trunk, flattening down against the muck and plunging one arm and her head into a slump of snow, using the filthy gray surface to wash free the acid. Skin peeled off in bloody chunks and she smothered a cry.

After a breathless moment, she peered over the makeshift barricade and saw the heap of steaming metal that had once been their transport. Whatever had attacked their vessel wouldn't be stopped by her feeble barrier. She used her enhanced sight to scan through the barren trees and towering heaps of rubbish, searching for the source of the attack. Gray evening clung like a mist to the dead forest, but something uncoiled in the darkness, and with a series of near-inaudible clicks, her tech-eye adjusted to the lack of light.

When she recognized the thing that writhed in the dark like a drowning worm, her throat soured with bile.

A collector.

***

"Reid! Where are you?" Mica crawled forward blindly on her hands and knees. Pain dizzied her mind. Instinctively, she wiped the burning substance from her hand, horrified when whole layers of skin peeled away.

Acid.

Fear took her breath and an awful feeling coiled in her stomach as she crept forward, gnashing her teeth against the biting pain. Smoke, sweet with burning flesh, stung her nostrils. Her hand landed on something soft and sticky.

"Reid?" she whispered.

Her brother moaned. Pain had stolen his voice, but he turned his face toward her, and the sight of it made Mica gag. Reid's face was unrecognizable. His chest had collapsed inward, sticky strands of melted flesh clinging to exposed ribs, and the smell was indescribable, only slightly more tolerable than the tortured animal shriek that tore through the air when she touched him. Agony clawed at her brother's face.

Above them, the massive shape shifted. A serpentine nightmare twisted from the poisonous black night as its monstrous front legs pulled its body toward them. Long, whisker-like sensors covered its reptilian chin, and its hideous, fanged mouth dribbled acid onto the ground while its head swayed back and forth, seeking its prey.

A collector! Hatred twisted her gut. No doubt it'd come here looking for that wretched mod. One of its primary functions was hunting down such orphans.

But she'd never seen one use that kind of breath weapon before. It didn't make any sense for it to destroy what it'd been sent to collect. Collectors normally spewed out a sticky adhesive to restrain their targets and minimize damage, but this acid—or whatever it was—dissolved anything it touched with such awful ease that she questioned its purpose. Was this some kind of fresh horror drummed up by the Crats?

Whatever its purpose, she knew who to blame for its presence. *We should've left that damn mod to die!* Tears burned at her eyes as she groped for the gun belted at her side. Fumbling, fumbling, fumbling, her fingers twitched with nerves. Finally, she got a solid grip on it and pulled it free. "Get back!" she warned, knowing it wouldn't stop, but not willing to let it kill Reid. Her bravado came out in a humiliating squeak.

Behind her, Reid groaned, and Mica turned. Her brother's body contorted in agony, but his jaw worked desperately to form a warning, willpower alone tearing the butchered word free from a throat no longer capable of speech: "Run!"

"No, I won't leave you!"

Reid's whole body shook. Pain was etched into his every movement. He raked his hands against the ground, trying to pull his dying body forward.

The collector's tail slammed down between them, causing the earth to split, the force tossing Mica back into the air. She landed yards away from their attacker in a pile of brush, where the thorny undergrowth tangled her feet. By the time she ripped free, there was no saving her brother. Her throat closed up on the scream, turning it into a moan as she watched Reid launch himself at the monstrosity.

"Reid!"

The collector snaked forward to spew acid into Reid's face.

Mica's body lost all sense of feeling. "Ohnonono!" Crumpling to her knees, she watched her brother, her best friend, die. A final spray of acid washed the rest of his skin from his bones, leaving his skeleton frozen there for seconds before it too dissolved.

This wasn't real! Not when she'd been so close to having all her dreams realized.

Futile tears streamed down her cheeks. Bleary-eyed, she lifted her face to look at her brother's killer, a cry of vengeance gurgling in her throat as the serpentine creature seemed to shift in space, bending and waving like a broken mirage about to fade.

An icy sensation swept over Mica then, prickling her skin and enveloping her in a cold, supernatural breath. Her earlier suspicions were correct. This wasn't a normal collector. And it wasn't just the breath weapon that was different. She'd faced one of these vicious, mindless destroyers years ago, but this one's programming seemed bridled by a human intelligence, and instead of killing her, it tried to hold her in thrall with its burning nightmare gaze.

Its monstrous head swayed back and forth, and a sibilant voice rose from its fanged mouth. "Submit, Mica Stone."

An invisible power seemed to pull her forward, one step at a time, but she stumbled back in resistance. How did it do that? Stricken mindless with terror, wrestling against her own body, some raw animal instinct fired inside her. She finally tore her gaze free and unlocked her body.

She turned and ran, staggering over every root and stone in the forest, her lungs heaving against her ribcage. Behind her, she heard the crunch of dead brush as the monster pursued her, two clawed arms dragging its slippery body along the snowy ground. Its monstrous size was no impediment; it rolled over trees and boulders effortlessly, flattening everything in its path as it sped toward her. Realizing she was cornered, Mica stopped running. She stilled herself against a tangled mess of trees, crouching down beneath the thick ground brush.

She held her breath, motionless in the shadows. Above her hung the collector's massive body, poised in silence as it searched for its prey. She buried her head beneath folded arms and made herself as small as possible.

***

A collector had only two functions: collect or kill. They were the scourge of the underground cities, programmed to hunt for specific prey and kill anyone caught in between.

Animkii wondered, *did the Alphaknot send it after* me?

She watched in horror as a plume of death blossomed from the collector's mouth, taking Reid's life in a cruel instant. Her hands tightened around the log's edge until the knuckles of her flesh fingers ached. She didn't have enough stims to maintain normal functions, let alone fuel her badly damaged weapons system, even if her boom cannon hadn't melted into a stump. She was weaponless, useless. What could she do? There was no way she could've reached Reid in time. And now, Mica was next.

Mica would've left her to die in a second if circumstances were reversed. And Reid... It wasn't as if a few days on the road together had made strangers into friends. And Reid was already dead. Why risk herself to save a dead man's sister, even if that dead man had tried to save her?

Because that was the way of the Bear Clan. Among the Fire Bones, her clan stood tall as her people's fiercest protectors. They embraced their sacred duty as guardians against the soul-hungry Dreamers that spilled out from the End of the World, their legacy etched in tales of valor that stretched back to the days of the Sundering. She'd done much wrong in her life, but her heart was still Bear.

Past the wreckage of the transport, the collector rose again. Decision made, Animkii crawled over the stone log as quietly as she could, her thermal vision picking out the warmth of a shape cowering beneath a cluster of bushes.

She wasn't the only one to spot Mica, though.

Stealth had never been Animkii's strength—she was heavy-footed, too hasty. Brittle twigs snapped beneath her booted feet. Her breathing was too loud. Bare trees and shriveled bushes provided little coverage. Every muscle in her body tensed, and by the time she crept close enough to make an effective attack, the collector was almost upon Mica.

The woman dodged its steely talons, her hands tearing at the branches and undergrowth that blocked her escape, distracting the collector while Animkii crept up behind it.

Animkii knew she didn't have enough stims left to generate new ammunition for an attack, but as she held her melted right arm against her, she thought of the volatile pyrolite still trapped inside it from the fight in Delta, rendered inaccessible by normal means. But maybe not *quite* useless. As the collector reared up to attack Mica, she charged from the bristly bushes, roaring like some great tundra beast, her steel arm swinging out, opening to embrace the collector from behind. The unnatural chill of its skin spread down her steel arm and into her flesh, nearly shocking her into letting it go.

Something wasn't right about this collector! But she held on, locking her weaponized arm around its throat and burying her face in the back of the steel beast's neck, using it as a shield as she ignited the pyrolite trapped inside her arm.

The explosion shook the ground. The collector never had a chance—its body shot through the trees, tearing up chunks of earth and stone trunks in its passage, its steel bones shattering.

Animkii was thrown in the opposite direction, rocketed backward by her exploding arm and pieces of the collector's neck, blowing through several heaps of refuse before rolling to a stop in a shallow ditch, minus one arm.

***

Mica watched the explosion in shock, diving behind a stone tree to shield herself from the storm of debris that went flying in all directions. That damn mod. She'd really done it! She'd blown up the collector... and herself.

But the mod's fate wasn't her concern. She scrambled back over rocks and heaps of discarded tech, chunks of stone and scraps of metal rolling beneath her feet as she hastened to the site of her brother's demise.

What remained of Reid was unrecognizable. Sticky flesh residue clung to a few surviving bone fragments. Acid still chewed away at dead tissue, filling the air with the stink of singed hair and boiled flesh. A handful of teeth leered at Mica from the remains of a jawbone.

She shoved aside her air mask and threw up, the last bits of her supper heaving free from her aching stomach.

When she was done, she wiped her mouth on a blood-soaked sleeve. Her hands shook like an old woman's. Grief crippled her; her limbs wouldn't let her move from her hands and knees. Mud soaked her clothes and an icy wind froze them to her skin.

In one instant, she'd lost both a brother and a best friend. Since her family's passing, she'd loved only one other person.

"Damn it," she whispered, shakily replacing her mask before the rotten outside air could sicken her even further. Hot, shameful tears slid down her cheeks. They'd been so close to happiness. They could've lived out their days in luxury, never knowing another day of want.

"Are you hurt?" a distant voice asked.

She looked up, half-expecting to see Reid standing there, mocking her tears with that smug smile of his. Reid never cried.

But it wasn't Reid.

So, the mod was alive. She viewed the inhuman thing through half-lidded eyes. The mod was unsteady on her feet, her bloodless lips pressed into a pained grimace as she fought to keep her balance. Shrapnel had pierced her body wherever the biosteel was missing and blood drenched her borrowed clothes. But it was the sight of her right arm that caused Mica to gape: The entire limb was gone, leaving behind an empty shoulder socket. Her metal chest was black from the explosion that had saved both their lives.

Resentment quickly replaced any gratitude she might have felt. Then again, who had the collector been after? Collectors went after rogue mods, didn't they?

"Submit, Mica Stone."

She shivered. As painful as it was to admit, the collector hadn't been after the mod. She pried herself loose from the trauma, remembering those last terrifying seconds of battle, how the collector had tried to lull her into surrender. But why? A secret suspicion grew in her heart, but she smothered it, judging it to be paranoia. It was a coincidence, that was all. The Cult didn't have that kind of clout.

Did they?

"Your hand," the mod said. "Let me help."

Mica looked down at the appendage without feeling. White bone had surfaced in the wreckage of her left hand and agony shot across her nerves. "Why'd you go blow yourself up for someone who doesn't even like you?" she asked, clenching her teeth against a wave of nausea. "Idiot."

"We are allies."

Mica turned her face away. She felt too empty to protest.

The mod crouched beside her and examined the mutilated hand with a grim expression, bandaging it with the last clean strip torn off Mica's own shirt. Her touch was gentle, but Mica couldn't see past the ugly array of tech stamped on her face.

"I am sorry," said the mod. "Reid was a good man."

Mica swallowed the stone in her throat, blinked to clear away the burning in her eyes, but couldn't summon words to acknowledge the loss.

"We must go to Under-Alpha now," the mod said. "The collector was a deviant. Acted outside normal protocols. There may be others." Her tech-eye, with its lifeless metallic sheen, stared right into Mica. "It was after you. Why?"

So she'd noticed too.

Mica ignored the chill creeping up her spine. "It must've malfunctioned or something."

"We should leave now."

Where sorrow once threatened to overwhelm her, now it shrank to a small, numb spot in her heart. "I can't just leave Reid here, exposed." She sank into herself, wiping the tears away on her sleeve, averting her face from that unnerving machine gaze. "I don't want recyclers to find his body."

What the collector had left behind wouldn't have interested the most destitute of black-market scavengers, but the mod didn't argue, and for that, Mica was grateful. While Animkii took the lead in collecting the melted bits of bone and tissue that'd once been Reid, using a piece of scrap to dig a shallow grave, Mica could only watch, too shaken to do anything else.

Why was this slave to the Technocrats still here, still helping, still acting as if she was human, as if Mica didn't already know the truth? Pandora had acted human too, right until she'd killed everyone who loved her. There was no going back from modification.

The mod heaped one last pile of rubbish over the top of Reid's remains as additional protection.

"From the Earth, to the Earth," she murmured.

"Eh?"

"The Creator formed our bodies from the four elements of Mother Earth. He breathed life into us. Then we die. Our bodies return to the Earth."

Mica gave a short, bitter laugh. "Better than being recycled."

But without Reid, what was she going to do? She could feel a certain madness gathering in her skull that made her want to cry and scream until the grave swallowed her too, but she wasn't alone, not yet. There was one other person left to her in this sick, awful world.

Samiel.

A new desperation awakened. She needed to find him.

"You are ready?" The mod crouched beside her, looking on the verge of collapse, her remaining skin the color of a moldering corpse.

"You're at your limit, aren't you?" For the first time, Mica allowed herself to feel the tiniest ounce of pity toward her unwelcome companion, while inwardly screaming at herself for taking the risk. "Look. No promises, but once we get to Under-Alpha, I might be able to fix you up with some spare parts and stims." She tried to sound noncommittal. "Got a few favors owed to me I can call in."

The weariness, the worries, the weight of impending death, all eased from the mod's blood-splattered face.

"But don't think that makes us friends," Mica added quickly, squelching her sympathy. "Consider it repayment for saving my life. After that, we go our separate ways."

The mod nodded.

The pair limped their way to the edge of the cliff that hung over the spectacular plasticine-domed city of Upper-Alpha, but before the mod could climb down, Mica halted her with a hand.

"Are you crazy? We're taking the back door. I don't want the damn Crats to know we're coming in."

Chapter Six

"I know it's here!"

Frustration tightened Mica's throat. This was the third spot they'd checked. In the two years she'd been gone, the landmarks of rubbish marking the tunnel had either shifted location or someone had scavenged them for raw materials. In her mind, she pictured the stone foundation: the remains of someone's ancient basement half-flooded with the Junkyard's toxic runoff. She scanned the hills of garbage, looking for the four petrified trees that marked its location.

In the end, it took half a day and two near-encounters with recruiters to find it.

Only one trunk was visible now. Taller than the others, she recognized its unusual, crooked silhouette sticking out from the side of an enormous rubbish heap. Apparently, one of the neighboring garbage piles had toppled over, landsliding on top of their destination.

"Could use a little help over here!" she said.

The mod wasn't looking good. Her brown skin had faded to an ugly gray color, her condition no doubt exacerbated by breathing in the contaminated air out here. She'd lost her air filter alongside the transport. Her right arm was gone and her face was singed with burns, though fortunately her biosteel sheathing had taken the brunt of the explosion. Her wounds weren't the problem, though, were they?

She needed stims. To travel for weeks on empty and then still put up a fight like she did... These new Gen III models were tough, alright. Any other mod would've gone into complete shock by now.

"You've got to keep moving or you're going to collapse here." Mica was already regretting her misplaced sympathy. Taking this mod along was just going to make everything harder.

Yeah, but she'd be dead meat if she walked into the undercity without some clout. She hadn't left her old gang on the best of terms, but if she had this steel monster on her side it might ward off a knife in the back, might buy a little more time for negotiation.

Negotiate with what, though? Their entire shipment had melted away along with the transport. She didn't have Reid's talent for dissembling. There was no chance she could talk her way out of the mess they'd left behind in Under-Alpha. But she'd deal with that later. For now, she needed to focus on the trouble in front of her.

Unearthing the entrance to the undercity was no simple task, buried as it was beneath scraps of metal and a thick layer of mud that stank of raw sewage. Never mind that her bandaged hand was throbbing. Or that there was blood dripping down the fingers.

"There used to be a trapdoor under here," she said. But the garbage kept sliding back into place, frustrating her efforts.

"Try this." The mod hauled over a rusty metal sheet twice her height and slammed it into the ground, creating a barricade to keep the garbage back. Her massive body shook with the effort. She was strong, even short of stims.

But no sooner did the mod plant the metal wall than all the strength in her inhuman body seemed to abandon her, and she fell to one knee, gasping and wheezing. "I—I am sorry. I need rest."

She needed more than that. One corner of Mica's mouth tightened with the beginnings of a frown, and she looked up at the dull gray sky as it darkened with the threat of a storm. The breath from her air filter froze in the filthy air.

"Dead men rest," was all she said, digging back into the metal debris, desperate to get through. If that storm hit, who knew whether they'd be able to keep going? She ignored her companion's labored breathing until she'd swept the last of the filth away from the door and then fell back in exhaustion.

It was just as she remembered it: a scratched-up hatch door just big enough to fit a full-grown man. Good thing the mod had ditched her exoskeleton. She hauled back on the metal handle with all her might. The mud sucked stubbornly at it, but the mod soon took her place and a moment later it popped open, spraying the pair with muck.

Mica dropped feet-first into the hole. The distance to the ground was longer than she'd remembered it, and she stumbled on her landing. Hairless rodents and beetles the size of her palm scurried away at her invasion, disturbed from years of rest, and the musky stale air of the underground hit her nose, unimpeded by her air filter.

The mod had difficulty squeezing through the trapdoor, but soon enough the door slammed shut, plunging the tunnel into complete darkness. The mod dropped beside her.

"Don't worry, I know these tunnels," Mica said. "Been here hundreds of times. We'll just feel our way through."

Her confidence was a fraud. Down here, there wasn't the slightest bit of light to adjust her eyes to and she couldn't hear or smell her way through these tunnels. All she had were walls and memories to lead the way.

She and Sam had often used this place as a secret refuge, hidden away from prying eyes. Even now, memories of her former lover's laughter still rang in her mind, the only sound capable of easing the old pain in her heart. The danger of their subversive activities seemed insignificant compared to the solace they found in each other's company. Sure, she'd had other lovers after leaving Under-Alpha, but they'd meant nothing to her. They were mere fillers to make those angry last words fade from her memory.

I never should've left Under-Alpha.

A sudden stark light broke the darkness. She fumbled for her gun. Were they being followed? But when she turned and saw the source, she relaxed.

It was that damn mod. "Could've warned me," she said testily.

"Sorry." The light bobbed in time with an apologetic nod. The offending light was coming from her tech-eye.

Great. Was this one-armed, half-brained Technocrat pet really her only protection from Dathu's debt collectors? The way things looked, she might be joining Reid in the grave before the day was out.

The mod peeled off her blood-soaked coat. The fabric clung to her skin by threads. Her hulking figure dominated the space, muscles rippling beneath the surface where tech hadn't replaced her human body. Most of her upper body was machine. Metal grafts of various shapes and sizes covered her back like steel spiders—leftovers from her original modification that the biosteel hadn't yet consumed.

Then Mica's gaze fell on the right shoulder joint—now an empty biosteel socket, blackened from the explosion but otherwise unscathed.

"I wish we could've salvaged your arm. Or anything else." They'd sifted through the wreckage of the transport before leaving, looking for anything they could use or sell in Under-Alpha, but the damage was catastrophic. What she'd *really* wanted was the crate full of neatly packed canisters of angel breath, but what few items had avoided the acid breath's corrosion had been incinerated by its heat.

"Need stims more than arm." The mod's unnatural voice jarred Mica back to reality.

Yeah, she wished it was that simple. Her head was already pounding. "Once we reach the undercity, keep your guard up," she said. "Recruiters are some of the *nicer* things you'll meet in Under-Alpha."

By the time they reached the first branch of tunnels, Mica's breath burned from her lungs into her throat, her injured hand throbbed, and her legs quivered with every step she took. One shot of angel breath would've taken it all away, but she was hours away from any possibility of relief. Though the tunnels were cool, the sweat dripped down her forehead and into her eyes. Her hair was slick with it.

The mod wasn't doing much better. Stim withdrawal for a mod was a death sentence. At no point could her body adapt to live without it. Tremors had already overtaken her human arm and that clumsy gait wasn't just from exhaustion. Beneath that monstrous patchwork of flesh and machine, Mica imagined the tiniest of connections were already beginning to fray while the processing core implanted in her chest was dropping signals like a broken comm box. Without the stims to suppress it, her body's immune system had rebooted itself, identifying every piece of tech attached to it as an enemy.

Mica had grown up around enough mods to know the signs, and it seemed the Technocrats' newest models suffered the same deficiency as their predecessors: Their all-knowing despots still hadn't fully subjugated the human body.

That thought should've made her happy, to think that their high-and-mighty overlords couldn't always get their way, but it turned sour in her heart. Her mom had believed the rehabilitation of mods was possible, and had made Mica believe it too, though she'd never saved even one from the inevitable cerebral degeneration awaiting them. If word on the street was right, it was worse for these newest models.

"Hey, Mod, is it true what they say about biosteel? That it's some kind of biotech virus that the Crats' scientists inject into your body?"

"Not injected. Implanted." The mod's voice echoed in the caverns, the words labored, hard with effort. "Consumes everything inside us. Steel. Flesh. Until there is nothing left but biosteel." The horror of that statement hung in the air until the silence grew awkward. "The scientists released my division too early. The uprising in Delta interrupted our evolution. It left us incomplete."

So, what she'd heard was true. The Technocrats had a way to eradicate what little humanity remained in their mods. "And what will happen to you now?"

The mod shook her head. "I do not know."

Mica glanced back. "Most mods who made it to my mom's shop were in worse condition than you, but they were earlier generations, pre-biosteel, real mess-ups. Brains damaged by malfunctioning control shards or blood turned to poison when their bodies rejected their tech. Nearly all of them went mad with stim withdrawal first. Pandora was the first I thought might—"

Her jaw snapped shut, and she stopped mid-conversation.

"I am not like Pandora."

"Have you ever seen what happens to an orphaned mod that can't get hold of the right stims?" she asked. "*I* have. More than once. There was one in Under-Alpha a few years ago that destroyed half a city block before a collector neutralized it." She didn't mention the insane priest, High Father Holy, but her mind replayed those murderous steel fingers around her throat, the insane fanaticism in his eyes, and the flash of the sacrificial knife laid at her throat. She needed the mod to know, to understand her hatred. "Let's just say I've seen a lot of dead bodies because somebody felt sorry for one of your kind. You're a bomb and no one knows when you'll go off."

Hopefully not today, she thought as she leveled a look at the brooding mod. At the back of her mind there tickled a temptation, a scheme that belonged to her old, crooked way of life: wondering how much she'd get in trade for turning in a sane, almost fully functioning mod. Minus an arm.

Would it be enough to buy her way out of trouble?

But she rejected the thought as quickly as it came. Much as she despised the mod, she owed her a debt for blowing up that collector. It wouldn't sit right with her to rat out an ally.

Ally? With a mod?

She scowled. Only until she could get things sorted out back home and lean on a few old friends to get herself back into business. It wasn't a happy thought. Coming home would've been a lot easier if she and Reid could've bought their way back into the good graces of the undercity's ruling cartel, the Steel Fang Syndicate. But the collector's attack had left her with nothing but a bad mood and a broken mod, two things more likely to get her into trouble than out.

The dirt tunnel soon ended and turned into a corridor of crumbling gray stone, the remnants of some city long-forgotten. Samiel had known the name, but Mica couldn't recall it now. Some disaster older than known history had sunk the entire city beneath the earth, but whatever civilization had lived here, time had buried it and all its skeletons long ago.

Years ago, her old gang had commissioned automatons to clear out miles of these ancient tunnels so they could carry out their clandestine business without fear of raids. After a partial collapse, the pathways had fallen into disrepair, but in other parts you could still see the newer construction that remained. Graphene beams reinforced walls that hadn't seen the light of day for hundreds of years and someone had swept piles of rubble to the sides, clearing a path on a cracked stone walkway.

After walking about an hour, they came to an abrupt end on the pathway. The floor crumbled away into a canyon that dropped hundreds of feet into the Earth's depths. Her mind grew dizzy with the height. High above their heads rose a vast dome of rock. Beams of natural light from the surface filtered down through cracks, touching on the ruins far below them.

A strangled gasp came from behind her.

Mica shot a look back at the mod. "You okay back there?"

"Yes." There was a pause. "There is another place. Like this. Back home."

"There are lots of old places around here, but the Technocrats have plundered most of them bare. The undercity's made of what's left."

Seeing the carcass of the Old World only reminded Mica even more strongly of Samiel: He'd been obsessed with the Old World and its secrets. When they'd first met, Mica couldn't have cared less about those dead times. She was too busy trying to survive the present. An offer of good steel and rare stims had convinced her to lead the 'delusional stranger' through the cracks in the earth, down into the icy caves from which hollow storms originated.

Damn near got them killed more than once. An old memory stirred and a fearful shiver crawled across her skin. If only she hadn't let Sam talk her into going to *that* place...

Behind her, her companion had lapsed into a labored silence, the human side of her face tight with the strain of staying conscious, the mouth carved deep into her face like a knife wound. Her movements were mechanical.

Dammit. She needed to keep the mod talking and moving, otherwise she was going to lose her.

"So, what city are you from originally?" she called back, pretending not to notice the mod was lagging.

Animkii took too long to answer, and when she did, her voice was bottomless. "My land is far north. Past the Burning Wall."

Though Mica had never seen the Burning Wall herself, every undercity child grew up hearing about the great wall of fire that guarded the Technocracy's entire northern border. Architects had built chemical reactors within the massive wall to produce a vast curtain of flame, separating the Technocracy from a bottomless drop on the other side.

"There's nothing beyond the wall but a gaping hole and the worst hollow storms you've ever seen." But Sam had told her other stories, of terrible shrieking clouds that devoured whole exploratory parties and black tentacles that pulled air vessels out of the sky. He'd claimed the Burning Wall kept these terrible things at bay, but she'd never quite believed it.

"You are wrong," the mod said, her blue-tinged lips forming a bitter smile. "My people were wrong too. What you call a hole, they called the End of the World. But it is not an end; it is a *bridge*."

"A bridge?" She snorted her disbelief. "Then what's on the other side?"

"A land outside the Technocracy. My people call it the Witherlands. My home."

Mica just couldn't comprehend the idea. "The Crats have tried for centuries to expand their borders. If they can't cross the Burning Wall with all their tech, how were *you* able to?"

Their despots had squandered countless resources and lives attempting to bridge the massive crevice that bordered the northern edge of their territory. They'd had no better luck crossing the black, burning oceans that flanked their continent to the east and west or the burning desert to the south. Samiel had told her dozens of stories about these failed expeditions.

The mod shook her head, unable or unwilling to answer. "Tech fails when it enters the End. The Technocrats cannot fight what waits for them inside without it."

"What do you mean?"

"Dreamers," she whispered, slumping back against a rock wall and sliding down. "Dead things that will not stay dead. The cracks that break the world give them birth."

"If your people feared the End of the World, why'd you go traveling through it?"

"Not a choice. A punishment."

The mod was fading fast. She'd expected madness, not this decline, this helplessness, this… humanity.

"Stay with me, you idiot!" With effort, Mica pulled her up by the back of her shirt, slapping her face, trying to keep her conscious. "Come on! Keep talking to me, *Animkii!*"

In her panic, the mod's name slipped from her lips and stunned her into silence.

***

Animkii…

Mica's sounding of her name startled her back to consciousness. It was the first time she'd ever said it. Animkii knew what she was trying to do: distract her from surrendering to the void at the fringes of her mind, the lethal calm that awaited the storm's end.

She had to move. Had to get up. Had to stand.

Mica struggled to lift her away from the rockface. Dark, greasy hair hung over eyes that gleamed from the shadows. "Come on, we're almost there!"

Was that worry she heard in Mica's voice?

Animkii heaved herself back to her feet, blistering heat frazzling her nerves and dark spots dancing in her mind at the forced movement. Keep going, one more step, one more step...

She pushed out a ragged breath. The massive weight of her biosteel body was becoming too hard to carry without the boost of stims and she was slowly losing mobility as the connections splintered between her biosteel conductors and her still-human nerves. She dragged her left leg behind her. How long until it became useless? There was no time to think about it. She had to keep going. Had to stay alive.

With the same enormous willpower that had brought her southward through the End of the World four years ago, she pushed herself forward. She kept trying to answer the questions from this woman who hated her yet was fighting to keep her alive.

When Animkii had first seen the sunken undercity, there'd been a moment of panic, a flash of memory that ice-picked her heart. Even this far above the ruins, she could see its toppled towers, heaved-up streets, and empty windows, a phantom of that other place. The sight of it awakened memories of a half-dead monstrosity and the terrible weapon it guarded.

Soulcleaver.

She still saw it in her mind: its obsidian blade chiseled into the image of a raven with its head raised and wings spread, its hilt capped with a pair of curled, silver claws. Without it, the Dreamers at the End of the World would've devoured her soul, and yet the memory burned her with fear and shame.

But that other city was far away, buried beneath the dead forests of the Witherlands. There were no rifts here. None that she could see. None that she could *feel*. This place was empty: no unliving monstrosities, no accursed weapons, no disembodied shapes drifting across an icy wasteland, hungering for the life inside her.

"Why did your people want to punish you?" Mica's voice pierced the din of memory.

"For going into the Ancient Ones' city. The Great Spirit forbids us from entering such cursed places," she said, taking a shaky step forward. "But stories spoke of a powerful weapon hidden there. I had to try. Had to save my people from the Dreamers. Anything was better than what we were doing!" The words rushed out like blood from a burst vein. "But I only made things worse. The Speaker said I angered the Creator. That sacrificing me to the End would appease Him."

"Why would you want to believe in a god like that?"

Animkii shuttered her eyes, her heart weighed down by regret. Hadn't she asked herself the same? "It was not always like that among my people. The Creator's laws were stern, but never cruel. But the Dreamers grew stronger. So many of our warriors died. So many villages taken. Our Speaker said the Great Spirit was displeased with us. Greater sacrifices were required. Greater punishments for breaking His laws." There was a pause. "But I am still alive. The Creator rejected my sacrifice. I do not know why."

All she'd ever wanted was a simple life: enemies you could kill with a spear-thrust, sky signs that predicted a good hunt ahead, loved ones she could grow old with. She'd tried to ignore the incessant creep of darkness over her people's territories, to trust the reassurances of their holy man, to obey her people's laws, but age had deepened her doubts. Once Niigaanii was born, she could no longer ignore the growing corruption and horror overtaking her fierce people.

Ziiba had warned her not to go into that forbidden city—Ziiba with her laughing smile, Ziiba her best friend, Ziiba her lover... but Animkii had stubbornly believed there was a way to end the threat of the Dreamers for good, that she only needed to bring back proof of it to the Circle of Elders. She'd believed salvation was possible right until her own people had pitched her feet-first into the End of the World.

But instead of dying as a blood sacrifice to the Dreamers, she'd survived the treacherous pathway southward, treading the perilous rim that girded the churning black sea at the chasm's bottom, fighting against the icy wind that threatened to tear her from its ledge. And all the time, she could hear the cries of those who hadn't made it howling in the distance, their souls trapped eternally in the abyss below, condemned to become what had killed them: to become Dreamers.

Animkii felt Mica's slight frame slip under her remaining arm in support, heard a grunt of complaint. "I thought biosteel was supposed to be lightweight. You think I should submit a complaint to the Crats?"

Despite her condition, Animkii barked a short laugh. She questioned her sanity, laughing in the shape she was in, but the black humor lifted her spirit.

Downward into the darkness she and Mica moved, inching their way toward the distant glow of undercity lights, stumbling down crude stairs that had been hacked out of the stone's face. On one side of them was a wall of rock; on the other, a drop to certain death.

"Just a little longer," Mica said.

For Animkii, the height was terrifying. She'd grown up in the rocky forestscape of the Witherlands, where on a clear day, you could see for miles across a winter lake. On the rare occasion that the Alphaknot had ordered her to enter an undercity, it was through the sanctioned front gates and not by crawling through the debris of a broken city.

Here, even with her optical light to light the way, she couldn't trust her own body to stay steady long enough to make it down safely. The path was too narrow for Mica to lend her support, so she hugged the wall and sidestepped her way down, each step more frightening than the last.

Mica seemed unbothered by the perilous climb downward, flitting down the stairs with a familiarity and fluid ease that Animkii envied.

No city gates greeted them at the bottom. Darkness sink-holed them as the distant city lights they'd seen earlier disappeared behind mountains of debris. They climbed over treacherous heaps of rubble, small avalanches sliding in their wake. At last, they reached what would've been a dead end if the brick wall there hadn't had an opening just large enough for them to squeeze through.

Mica entered first. "It's clear!" she said a moment later, sticking her head back through and gesturing for Animkii to follow.

Outside the tunnel, the surrounding wreckage took shape. Portions of walls poked free from the debris as chunks of pavement and gravel tumbled under their feet. Bit-by-bit, the lost city reformed into actual streets lined with ancient houses and storefronts. This part of the city seemed dormant, with shuttered windows and elusive shadows replacing people.

Mica pulled off her air mask and breathed deep. "The air's decent in this quadrant. Black-market purifiers, courtesy of the Steel Fang Syndicate."

Animkii heard the tremor in her voice and recognized the name as one of many gangs vying for control over Under-Alpha. While the Technocracy appointed governors to oversee each undercity, in practice it was the local cartels that actually ran the day-to-day operations.

"We need to avoid drawing attention to ourselves," Mica said. "Stay quiet and stick to the shadows."

Animkii nodded, too exhausted to argue.

Hundreds of pyrospheres hung in windows and over doorways, casting the streets in a soft, warm glow. Scrap metal doors hung crookedly in household archways and colorful plasticine walls filled in the gaps of broken stonework, creating a garish mixture of old and new architecture. They passed through a bustling street market, where recyclers openly peddled black-market tech and stims next to stalls selling synthetic fabrics and hydroponic produce. Farther down the street, they passed a subterranean garden brimming with a feast of glowing fungi harvested by a team of patched-up automatons, and from somewhere in the distance, a child's laughter rang out.

Animkii smiled despite the condition she was in.

"Don't be fooled by the look of it," Mica said. "Quadrant Three is full of the kind of scum that'll smile in your face and knife you in the back. But most of them don't want any more attention than we do, so if we keep our heads down, we should be able to slip through unbothered."

Animkii's tech-eye raked the darkness between houses and the unlit windows above them using her thermal vision. Spots of heat appeared against the shadows. Just people going about their daily routines, or something more sinister?

On one street corner, a young woman's body gleamed with silvery fish scales that turned gold beneath the streetlights, while across the street an old man crowned with antlers bartered with a fruit vendor, exchanging a handful of silver-filled vials for a basket of apples. Two monkey-tailed children clambered up the walls behind him, their tails bobbing up and down as they ran.

Hybrids. Yet another perversion of nature grown in a Technocrat's lab.

Though Animkii's modification had taken place in the Research Sector of Upper-Alpha, she'd never visited its undercity. Her division had lived inside the uppercity it once guarded, Delta. By the looks of it, Alpha's undercity wasn't much different from Delta's: full of the Technocracy's leftovers struggling to survive by whatever means they could.

She halted, overcome by a sudden blackening dizziness that made her knees buckle and her throat lurch.

"We can't stop here!" Mica said. "We're almost there."

Almost where? Where are we going? She had so many questions to ask, but lost focus as the nausea crashed down in waves. Walking turned to staggering. Mica talked to her, snapped at her, but the words disappeared in a sea of gibberish. Minutes or hours passed, and she was unaware of anything but the sensation of sinking fast.

"We're here!"

Those words she heard. She lifted her head with difficulty and saw a rusty gate left partly ajar, its guard posts abandoned. "Quadrant Four", a faded sign read. Pasted over it was a single warning: "Quarantined."

Beyond the fencing was darkness. Not a single light lit in the distance. Not a single red glow to indicate life.

"They should've torn this place down years ago," Mica said, squeezing through the rusted gate. "You coming?"

"But this is—! Why'd you bring us here?"

"Because this is the one place no one will ever look for us."

Chapter Seven

Mica despised the undercity. She'd grown up in this dismal place and it hadn't improved one bit since she'd left it, only festered like a wound turned gangrenous.

She was surprised that the Crats hadn't sanitized the whole place yet.

Her jaw tightened, resenting a life yoked to the cruel whims of their heartless overseers. What she'd do for a shot of angel breath, right now… or anything else that would make this homecoming easier.

They left behind the ancient, buckled streets and piss-stinking, garbage-filled alleys of the Third Quadrant to enter the decaying ruin that was Quadrant Four. Mica led the way, lean as a shadow, and Animkii hobbling just behind, every shuffled step an arduous labor. The mod didn't speak a single word. Maybe she wasn't even capable of talking anymore.

Much as Mica hated to admit it, she could've used the distraction.

Almost nine years had passed since her family's tragic demise in this very place, but the memory remained a fresh horror in her mind. Her neighbors' bodies had littered the streets like trash, the plague having run through many of them so quickly that they'd dropped dead amid their daily chores. The Technocracy had sent in drones to incinerate the bodies and sanitize the area, but even years later, people stayed clear of this haunted place, maybe sensing that some malevolent spirit had taken guardianship. Even the cartels that ruled the undercity kept their fingers out of Quadrant Four.

Crunch. She looked down to see an old ceramic mask under her foot, cracked down the middle, a teary-eyed clown that some forgotten masquerader had dropped. Her breath quickened as the nightmare awakened in her mind.

She needed angel breath. Or anything else that could dull the memories. Coming here was a bad idea.

She couldn't do this, not without Reid. They'd grown up in this wretched place together, neglected by a mother who was too weak, too passive to do anything but accept the beatings that life and her husband handed out. But Reid had always been there to protect her, whether it was shielding her from their father's fists, stealing rations so she wouldn't starve, or hiding her from people convinced she was still contagious.

All those years he'd spent protecting her, and she hadn't been able save him even once. She'd stood there and watched the collector murder him. Tears of shame welled up, but she stubbornly wiped the wetness from her eyes. As she drew her hand back, she saw a small four-legged shadow dart out from behind the old bakery and disappear into the alleyway next door.

Too big to be a rat.

"I guess we're not the only ones alive out here, after all," she said, trying to sound optimistic, hiding her pain as she glanced back at Animkii.

The mod's head had turned down with the effort of staying upright and her monstrous body moved forward like wet clay.

Fearing the mod's condition had slipped beyond saving, Mica grabbed her arm with one hand and pointed down the street with the other, to where a slightly crooked, three-story apartment building squatted at the bottom of the road. "Look! We're almost there." A scavenged sign hung above the shop's front door, decorated with an arcane symbol her mom had pulled from some ancient book—three green arrows forming a triangle— "Mama Q's Recycling and Recovery. We waste none of your waste."

"I'm home, Mom," she whispered.

She tore her gaze from the storm-beaten sign to the place she used to call home. With no one left to keep up with maintenance, new cracks had appeared in the foundation and half the roof had torn off, probably taken by one of the many hollow storms that had ripped through these parts. Every window was shuttered. Another corpse with its eyes closed.

The pain she'd relived every night since her family's death formed a ball of nails inside her chest. Nine years. The nightmare panic sat at the bottom of her gut, burning and burning, threatening to overflow, and she reached down to squeeze a dose of angel breath, before forgetting, again, that the collectors' attack had wiped out her stock.

"Dammit."

Her hands shook with need, and she almost turned away from the door when Animkii's big hand came down on her shoulder.

"I am sorry," she spoke in that rough suffering voice, as if each word were a physical effort to sound out. "Your family... Reid told me."

Anger replaced the pain. "He had no right!" She jerked away. "Keep your manufactured sympathy to yourself, Mod. I'm fine."

She pushed in the door more roughly than she'd intended, ignoring the mod's pitying gaze and striding into the stale air of her childhood home. Sensing movement, the place lit up.

A grim smile pressed back against her teeth. The place was still hooked up to the undercity power grid after all these years. The Technocracy harvested an energy called nether from the hollow storms, using it to fuel their entire industry of tech. But there were clever minds in the undercities too, those who'd learned how to siphon their own supply. Nine years and the Crats still hadn't found her mom's hack. Good. That would make things easier.

Entering the shop, she half-expected to find the bodies still lying there. Of course they were gone—Reid had seen to that the same day he'd found her. She remembered how stoic he'd been, the voice of calm and reason while she'd lost her mind at seeing them sprawled there on the floor. But the stains were still there on the floor, where their bodies had rotted for days in pools of dark-brown body fluids. The smell came back to her. Maybe it was still there in the room with her. The panic heightened now, her heart beating too fast, her head spinning, and she couldn't breathe. She couldn't deal with this. There had to be something here that could help, something left over...

She stumbled through the workshop, past dusty tables laden with long abandoned tech parts and bleak, black-faced monitors. In her burst of desperation, she forgot all about Animkii. When she reached the tiny closet in the back storeroom, she dug frantically through the jumble of miscellaneous parts and expired stims to find her mother's stash: an old container of angel breath nestled against a box of decade-old nutrient pills. Relief surged through her at the sight, and she reached forward in eager anticipation.

"Don't," croaked a voice behind her.

Mica stiffened.

"It is too old. You will poison yourself." The mod couldn't stand without shaking, but she still tried to keep Mica safe. Angel breath gone bad was *really* bad.

It was enough to snap her out of self-destruction.

"Do I look like an idiot?" She tossed the rusted tin of angel breath aside like it was some piece of junk she'd come across, never minding the shaking of her hands or the feverish need that fired her body. To busy herself, she pulled out old crates from the same closet, unfurling a ball of old coats, all made from the same type of well-worn synthetic cloth and dyed various shades of brown and gray—high fashion in Quadrant Four. She grabbed the bundle and pushed the mod out of the way as she headed back into the main shop. She threw them onto the ground, obscuring the stains.

Like they'd never been there at all.

"Mica—"

"They died a long time ago," she said, hiding her face and intentions with a jerk of her head. "More important to get you fixed up before your body goes into full shutdown. I know a place that can set me up with some stims. Just need to wash up first." She looked down at herself. "We look like we rolled off a corpse cart."

***

An old hose at the back of the building provided the first proper drink they'd had in days. Icy water drawn from an underground reservoir tasted as pure and sweet as that found in the Witherlands. It startled Animkii to see the scowling, suspicious Mica laugh like a child as the water dribbled down her chin. Then she turned the hose on Animkii.

Weeks of filth rolled off her patchwork skin and mud dripped from what remained of her hair. She shook her head like a dog, spraying Mica with the excess water. Laughing coarsely, the other woman tossed her a rusty bucket and a thick chunk of yellow soap. "Go wash that stink off you." Then she stepped back to wait her turn.

Privacy was a sad plastic curtain riddled with holes and held in place with wires. Cold air snuck through every opening. Shivering all over, Animkii scrubbed herself with an oily soap that smelled like melting wax. This was not at all like the antiseptic heat showers she'd used in the garrisons that had housed her division, but more like bathing in the icy rivers of her homeland. The chill was welcome, for it shook her from the stupor of withdrawal and brought her mind back to temporary awareness.

It wouldn't last long, she knew, drying herself and pulling on a one-piece jumper made for someone the same height as her, but twice her girth. It took a few creative twists and ties of the excess cloth to get a snug fit. Over it, she wore a mud-colored jacket with a deep hood. She dropped onto a short stool inside the shop, stubbornly ignoring the doubts stirring in her brain.

Mica had said she could get the stims, but with what currency?

When the other woman emerged from the back room, she was wearing a worn black jacket and matching pants, and she'd tied her dark wet hair back with a strip of cloth. But the earlier burst of laughter had faded completely from her tired eyes, leaving them flat and hard.

"I'll be gone a few hours."

"Let me go with you. If there is trouble—"

"Then I'll be burdened with a walking pile of biosteel scrap that can barely stay standing on her own two feet, let alone fight." The tone was harsh, but Animkii thought she detected the slightest note of tolerance. "I'm better off alone."

Animkii knew she was right and reluctantly nodded, hiding her frustration at her own powerlessness. She felt as helpless now as she had when she was lying half-dead and in pieces on the streets of doomed Delta. "Thank you," she said. "You may not like what I am, but you did not leave me when you could have—*should* have."

"Don't think I helped you out of kindness. I've got enemies here, and having a mod on my side might keep me alive long enough to dig myself out of this mess. I help you, and you help me. Then we're even, right?" she said. "We're not friends. I'd never be friends with one of your kind."

***

The dilapidated building that housed Mica's childhood shrank into the bleak distance, left behind the rusty gates at the quadrant's entrance. As she slunk through the narrow alleyways, memories gripped her heart with their corpse fingers and pulled it apart: Once again, she heard the groaning of a thousand dying people, saw her family's bulging empty eyes and frozen death grimaces, and smelled the putrid spillage of their spent bowels. Only now, those awful images merged with the more recent horror of Reid's face melting before her eyes, his last words begging her to run for her own life.

All she could do was shove it as far back into her mind as possible while teetering on the edge of a full-blown panic attack. She hadn't slept in days, not since that last awful battle, kept from complete exhaustion only by the desperation of their escape and the fears of Animkii's failing body. Even if Animkii hadn't needed her to get the stims, she wouldn't have let herself go to sleep. There was no way she could face the nightmares waiting behind closed eyes, not without something to numb her heart.

Just a few shots of angel breath and maybe another sniffer to shake off her nerves was what she needed. Lady Fang would know she'd be good for it. Then she'd help Animkii and get back into business. Pay off her debts and keep her head down. It'd been two years since she and Reid had left their old gang in Under-Alpha for a new life in Zeta's undercity. Maybe Dathu had forgotten all about them.

She headed into the twisting backstreets of Quadrant Three. Teetering towers of metal and apartment buildings built from cheap plasticine gradually replaced the clumps of crumbling brick buildings. A string of lights lit her path. The shabby street markets were closed for the day and most decent folk hid behind locked doors and darkened windows, while the shadowy sort prowled the streets in search of victims or vice.

She still hated this place.

But Samiel had loved the undercity, every inch of its rotten insides: the winding, broken streets, the jarring clash of modern and ancient architecture, and the crowds of humans and hybrids and half-functioning mods. To Samiel, it was like seeing color for the first time after a lifetime of black-and-white. He'd grown up in the suffocatingly rigid society of Alpha's uppercity, where the Technocrats controlled everything, from the clothing they wore to the jobs they worked to the functions of their own bodies. The Technocrats had designed a perfect society, but maintaining that perfection required constant diligence and a brutal intolerance for any deviation.

The Technocrats were very efficient monsters.

Once freed from his sterile prison, Samiel had embraced every new experience with such enthusiasm that he even overcame the festering darkness inside Mica. The omnipresent nightmares began to loosen their grip for the first time since her family's demise, and she'd fought back against the monsters in her head—and the addiction that had chained her mind. The nightmares had no power over her when Sam was there. She was too happy. There was no greater bliss than walking hand-in-hand with the man she loved beneath the undercity's blanket of artificial stars. The despair of her past simply couldn't compete with the joy of the new future she'd envisioned.

Why couldn't we have stayed like that? But no, Samiel couldn't leave the Old World alone, his obsession with the dead civilization driving them down into the most labyrinthine levels of the city, down to the very source of the hollow storms. The Technocrats' other exploratory expeditions stayed away from those depths. The hollow storms were unpredictable and there were other things there, things with no names and a hatred for everything that lived.

Down that deep, there was no decay, preserving the old city in its original condition against all natural laws. Ancient signs in languages no longer spoken still hung from buildings and bent light posts. Faded yellow-and-white lines still marked broken asphalt streets. Archaic vehicles sat abandoned in the streets. Some buildings contained caches of broken treasures, curious technologies of such number and variety that they'd clearly belonged to a people who'd taken them for granted. But the books Samiel found there were his greatest treasures.

He'd even begun translating the old language, creating a database of forgotten words.

That dead culture meant nothing to Mica. Samiel wouldn't allow her to sell the artifacts they'd found, so there was nothing to profit from, but for love's sake, she'd made the journey with him every time. He'd been so certain this city held secrets that could change the world, knowledge he could use to overthrow the Technocrats' despotic rule.

He'd been wrong. So wrong. There was something worse than the Technocrats down there.

But Samiel hadn't seen it. Samiel hadn't understood.

There, in a pool at the bottom of the lost city, Mica had seen the end of the world. From those black and watery depths, a faceless giant had risen on feathered wings, his black armor adorned with human bones and razor-sharp blades, his presence swelling inside her mind like a spider's egg sac about to burst. All the time, he whispered his perversions into her ear, and she listened like a dream-dust-starved whore getting her fix. By the time he was done, he'd shattered every illusion that happiness could ever exist in this doomed world.

Her old nightmares had returned the next night. And every night afterward. Worse than they'd ever been. No amount of angel breath could've softened those memories once she'd seen them replayed in that monster's eyes, hearing her younger brothers screaming behind its whispers, realizing that this world was nothing but a bloated corpse waiting to be devoured.

Samiel hadn't—*couldn't*—understand why Mica needed to leave Under-Alpha back then. They'd argued over that dead place, broken each other's hearts. Reid had convinced her that Sam cared more for his precious research than for her, that it was better to leave and start a new life. The old ache sharpened inside her.

Mica needed a distraction. Now. Or she was going to scream.

Relief came in the form of an ugly stone den tucked between two collapsed buildings. Lady Fang's was still there! A manic grin peeled apart her lips as she took in her old haunt with hungry eyes. Wrapped around the outside of the building was a steel fence that made it look more cage than porch, and calling out from behind its mesh were a handful of prostitutes. There was a hybrid covered in white down from head to toe, a woman with steel prosthetics replacing her entire lower body, and even an automaton armed with jutting metal breasts.

But sex wasn't what Mica needed.

What she needed was to forget.

***

Mica squatted on a pillow across from Lady Fang. A pipe dangled from the elder's lips and her pale cat-slit eyes were hooded in contemplation as a haze of pink smoke wreathed their heads, filling the air with a sickly-sweet candy smell. Draped over the shriveled old woman were a pair of glitter-covered young men, naked from the waist up, their eyes turned gold from dream-dust addiction.

"Samiel?" the old woman mused. "No, I haven't seen him since you left, but he was never really part of our scene, was he?"

This place wasn't much different from the last time she'd been here, two years ago—the night she'd left Samiel and came here hoping to obliterate every memory she'd ever had, the good ones and the bad. If Reid hadn't shown up to drag her away, insisting they needed to leave for Under-Zeta that night, she might've drugged herself into the death she'd cheated so long ago.

Mica massaged her temples, trying to forget the shambles of that old life and focus on the items piled in front of her: a handful of stoppered tubes filled with the stims that would keep Animkii alive, and two shots of angel breath.

"It's an advance." Lady Fang watched with narrowed eyes as her guest swept the goods into a small pouch, her white cat ears twitching. "You crack Fever's code before the end of the week, and I'll triple it."

"No problem. That old fart's tech's so obsolete it belongs to the Old World."

The elder cackled and leaned forward, handing Mica a tiny golden thimble. Her breath stank of decaying teeth and candy sticks. "A parting gift for you. Something new. It's called euphoria. You'll like it," she said with a too-wide smile. "And tell that handsome brother of yours to come himself next time. I don't care how sick he is." Lady Fang snapped her fingers, and the two youths beside her lifted her to her feet. It was a wonder she could move at all. Years of using tech to extend her body past its expiration date had culminated in a bad spinal implant, leaving her partially paralyzed.

When the old woman and her escort were gone, Mica sagged against the wall in relief. Not that she was stupid enough to trust Lady Fang *or* the many eyes that kept watch in this derelict place. Before tomorrow morning, the worst elements of the undercity would know that she was back, and then the debt collectors would come for her.

Would Sam hear of her return too?

Would he even care?

The thimble sat there, filled with a silver-colored dust. Euphoria, huh? Lady Fang knew her customers, alright. Just a quick snort might make it easier to face the danger ahead. Wasn't that reason enough to indulge?

Just one shot, she promised herself, leaning her face forward to inhale it. Fine silver powder dusted her nose and glittered on her palm as the room shifted and shimmered around her like a mirage, everything taking on a faint rainbow aura. Every breath she took was a tickle crawling through her nostrils and unbidden giggles rose from her throat and popped at her lips like tiny bubbles.

A siren song generated by a band of rusty automatons beguiled all five senses, turning sound into sensation as she wove her way through the den of drug addicts, the raw aching vocals of a solitary singer piercing her heart and seducing her will. There were no chairs or tables in this place. Large pillows lay against the walls and the guests lounged on them like reptiles sunning themselves, their mouths gaped and their unblinking golden eyes staring upward at the cluster of colored lights flickering overhead.

The world became a smear of color in which strangers' hands pulled her into a dance where dozens of other faceless bodies moved in slow unison with hers. A hot sweat poured down her face and soaked her hair into a muddy rat's nest that dripped salty water into her eyes. A laughing woman with pointed dog ears began painting Mica's face, holding up a broken mirror to reflect scarlet lips and black swirls on her cheeks. She stared at herself with a child's fascination, unable to turn away until another dancer jerked the mirror out of the woman's hands.

"Come with me." A face that might've been handsome leered at her with feline teeth. The pupils of his amber eyes narrowed to animal slits, his clawed hands pulling her free from the intoxicated crowd.

Another hybrid? She wondered whether he was a relative of Lady Fang's, but her thoughts struggled to surface in an ocean of haze. No, there was something different about him.

The man radiated arrogance and an assumption of obedience that would normally have put her off, and even his clothes marked him as an outsider in this filthy, crowded den. He wore a flawless, flowing blue tunic piped with gold and made of a fantastic material that flowed and rippled like waves stirred by a phantom breeze. Like some otherworldly prince.

But questions didn't belong in that fog, and she released them along with the pain of her past and the fear of her future, letting them both dissolve into the warmth and safety of the music. There was no will left to resist the feline man. Her only care was that this state of bliss would never end.

Her escort passed her another sniffer, the corner of his mouth twisting as his arm wrapped around her waist. Reid would've stopped her from taking it if he'd been alive—he knew she didn't have a good head for opiates—but he wasn't here, was he? He was dead and gone, just like the rest of her family. Gone like Samiel. And she couldn't bear dealing with any of that, not tonight. Wasn't that why she'd taken the risk of coming here?

The euphoria was fading already and so she inhaled her escape in the arms of the sneering stranger who fed her addiction, one sniffer at time, her vision becoming a smear of color. Her blood pounded in her ears as their mouths met and time blurred. The simple intimacy of his touch left her so drained that she didn't question when her knees gave out and a pillow met her cheek, unconsciousness folding its blanket over her head.

But the dream was waiting there, a spider in its funnel web. Euphoria's promise of deliverance was a lie that turned rapture into horror as the tainted drug leaked its poison into her slowly sinking mind. Panic rose on a slow tide inside her dull, intoxicated brain, while the inside of her nose burned like fire, and she felt the slow trickle of blood reach her upper lip.

How many sniffers had she taken now? Four? Five? Her fingers dug into the flesh of her transient partner, and she heard derisive laughter, saw the flash of sharp teeth, as if the stranger knew about the terror awaiting her, as if he *wanted* this to happen.

The Festival of the Masks with its leering costumed actors...

Young Mica watched as a living nightmare crawled out of the darkest crevices of Quadrant Four. Her neighbors' faces transformed before her eyes, turning a ghastly bloodless white, their eyes sinking into dark pools, their lips shriveling back against their gums. Kindly old Porter, the man who fed the rats and gave out candy to children, lay crumpled in a heap on his favorite street corner. Two little girls turned from giggling co-conspirators to wide-eyed corpses in an instant. A broken mask lay on the street. Vendors left their stalls unguarded, but their wares were untouched.

They were falling into their own minds, seized and dragged down by horrifying visions that only their eyes could see, murdered by invisible hands as dreams rode their bodies to death.

Running home...

Her mom's tired smile, the boys scrambling down the stairs to greet her, the pride in her stepdad's eyes; black-eyed corpses sprawled on the shop floor, ghastly white skin cracked open like broken pottery, blood oozing as thick and black as tar.

That she knew it was a dream did not keep it away or lessen the horror.

Pandora was there too. Sweet, childish Pandora, the only uninfected person in the whole quadrant, slumped over the shop's main comm system, her brain blown clear away by Mica's gun... Pandora, the vector of all this death.

No such quick release for Mica. No shot to end her pain.

Days alone in that house of death, trapped inside the diseased prison of her body, waiting to die while her nose filled with the ripening rot of her loved ones' corpses, but the constant, teeth-grinding pain was nothing, nothing, nothing compared to the agony inside her heart. With Pandora's betrayal and her family's death, she knew with absolute certainty that there was nothing good left in this world, that death would be a welcome release, and yet why wouldn't it just take her?

Yes, it was all the same: the same play and the same actors and the same end.

And yet there was something missing this time.

The scene was stuck.

Mica was lying on the floor, the blood she'd thrown up drying on her lips. She could do nothing but stare at the front door in expectation.

"Reid…" Back in the real world, she shifted against the silken pillows scattered on the floor, the stirrings of a rational thought prickling her befuddled mind as cool air whisked her shoulders.

Where was Reid? Why hadn't he opened the door yet? Where was his voice calling her name, spoken at the end of every dream for nearly nine years, the words that always broke the spell and ended the nightmare?

But she knew the answer. Reid *wasn't* coming this time. Because he was dead too. Just like everyone else she'd loved.

Pain wracked Mica's real-world body as she tried to break free from the nightmare on her own. Her fingers clawed against a stone floor, scattering the pillows as her limbs struck out blindly and violently, a drowning woman fighting her way to a surface she couldn't see. Even when she pried her eyelids open, the nightmare wouldn't release, not completely. Past the bleary room of drug addicts, she found the fanged man leaning against a wall across the room, watching her from a distance with a faint, disdainful smile. Dead-sober.

"What did you do to me?" Her voice was barely a croak, drowned by the music that pounded through the bar.

Her eyelids drooped again.

Alone.

She could smell the blood spoiling in the room. Even the rats wouldn't eat this tainted carrion and not a fly touched the open-eyed corpses of her family.

A broken clay mask lay on the floor within arm's reach, and she turned her head to look at it. It was the one she'd worn at the festival: the visage of some mythological creature called a 'dragon,' stylized so that its great reptilian brow was a stern furrow and its jaws twisted into a snarl. Now, it spoke to her as if alive, its clay lips parting.

"It is time to leave behind your dreams and enter mine." Ice flushed through her veins at the sound of those words. *She'd heard that same sibilant voice before, in a place at the bottom of the world that swallowed up all that was good. "Come."*

Without hesitation, her dream-body obeyed, ignoring the pain that ripped through her as she uncurled from her deathbed.

"No!" Her faraway-self balked. This wasn't part of the dream; this was new.

This was dangerous.

"You have a gift, like your birth father," the voice in her head continued as she surfaced back into the real world. *"And if you try to fight it, as he did, you will end up the same way: wasted, half-mad, and violently dead."*

She bristled, anger giving her back a measure of control. "My father deserved what he got! That piece of garbage isn't worth a breath of my time. And neither are you!"

Fleeting, ghostly laughter echoed within her mind.

"I won't let this life eat me up like it did him. Reid might be dead, but I haven't given up on our dream."

"Your dream is death. You can't close your eyes without seeing it."

"Then I'll keep my eyes open!"

"You can't stay awake forever."

"Try me!" Her mom had always called her stubborn. Samiel had, too. The name of her lost love blazed through her, igniting her determination to end this nightmare. Her family was all gone now, but Samiel...

"Samiel left you too."

"You think I'd give him up after everything I've been through? You think I can't own up to my mistakes?!" Some corner of her mind realized she'd screamed out loud, drawing the attention of Lady Fang's drug-addled patrons. A pair of bodyguards moved toward her, waiting for delusion to spill over into violence. "I'll find him!"

But the drug den was blurring again, and she couldn't keep hold of it.

Her childhood home, that seat of tragedy, shuddered on its ancient foundation as the decision roared inside her, the building's walls quaking as they echoed back the turbulence in her heart. The mask on the floor let out an eerie howl and its clay surface fractured, disintegrating into a pile of dust. The rest of the room and its gruesome contents faded into the background, the shadows converging until she was standing in darkness with only the detached front door of her house standing in front of her, the same door that Reid no longer came through, a door that she now had to open herself.

Fine. She'd do it. She'd end this nightmare. She placed a hand around door's steel knob, turned it, then stepped outside—

The dream stuttered. Switched places.

Behind the shop's entrance stood a pair of doors set inside an ebony frame, foiled with gold and tooled with winged serpents rising from the fiery ruins of a city, armed to deliver a holocaust.

This was it—the portal the After Cult had wanted her to find! She could feel it in her bones.

Filled with terror, she tried to draw back, only to find she'd lost control of her body. The doors parted and an awful dread kept her company as an unknown power pulled her forward, through that yawning gate and into a chamber lined with archways and guarded by stone monsters. The room reeked of fire and ash and death. A vast domed ceiling of stained glass painted the room below it in shades of scarlet and gold, reminding her of the Old World cathedrals that had illustrated Samiel's prized ancient writings.

The doors closed behind her, and the power that held her body in bondage released. She walked forward, rotating in awe and fear, half-expecting some kind of horror to burst out from the walls, and yet the room was so still she hardly dared breathe for fear of breaking the silence.

At the farthest end loomed the showpiece of this vast grave hall: an enormous marble statue of a six-winged serpent bearing a scepter in one clawed hand, its reptilian face raised skyward, its expression obscured by the colored light radiating in from the ceiling, its wings spread as if taking flight. At the foot of the statue lay the subject of the effigy.

Curled up in majestic repose lay a slumbering behemoth, its massive reptilian head resting on its forelimbs, each claw as big as her arm. The red and orange lights from above spangled the pearlescent scales, making them shimmer with an otherworldly luminescence. Ebony feathers sprouted along the length of its spine, creating an eerie contrast against the creature's scaly hide, and its serpentine tail extended into the darkness.

Then she saw its sides rise with the suggestion of a breath.

It was alive.

Every instinct in her body screamed at her to run at the sight of it, yet she kept moving, compelled to approach the scaled abomination, a strange awe filling her head with the realization she was in the presence of a great power.

"Run!" Her real-world-self tore into a pillow, whimpering. "You can leave! It's only a dream!"

Mica jerked back and looked around as the warning from the outside world echoed through the vast chamber. "A dream?"

In the real world, unseen hands lifted her head and, again, she felt the sting of euphoria burning her nose. "St-stop!" She shook her head, refusing to inhale until a clawed hand clamped over her mouth, forcing her to breathe through her nose and take in the toxic powder. "Please, no…"

"It's almost finished," the feline man whispered.

A trance fell over her unsettled mind, and she forgot the warnings from the real world, watching dazedly as particles of dust drifted like snow in the blood-red light cast from the ceiling. Yes, this was where she needed to be, came the realization. She climbed the stairs until she was level with the body. Her knees buckled and she fell to the floor. The surface was ice-cold on her naked hands.

Her eyes were now level with the monstrosity's head and her breath synchronized with the rise and fall of its massive chest. This close, she saw what she assumed was the source of its felling, a great bloodless wound across its throat that would've killed any normal creature. The surrounding skin had turned necrotic, the rot bleeding outward to taint the surrounding area, and yet the flaps of severed flesh expanded with each breath.

In awe, she touched the scaly skin, found it as soft as silk and pleasing to her fingertips, yet it awakened the smell of dust and decay and funerary perfume.

There was something she was supposed to do. But what? Her fingers trailed away from the skin and up toward the gaping wound.

"Your blood is the key." *The feline man's words slipped in from the real world. Insistent.*

"No!" she cried in both worlds.

She heard an angry hiss in her ear as she jerked awake, panic shoving her forcefully out of the nightmare and back into the real world. Her scream caused the other patrons to turn and stare at her, no doubt seeing an addict having a full-blown freakout, and yet she'd never been more sober than at this very second.

She wanted nothing more than to escape this damned place. The haze in her mind evaporated as she scrambled to her feet. Heart pounding in fear, she staggered through the sniggering crowd in search of the exit, but her bleary vision made the navigation humiliatingly difficult. Empty-eyed patrons watched her pass, their manic laughter jarring to her ears. Finally, one of Lady Fang's bodyguards grabbed her by the shoulders and steered her in the right direction while shoving a bundle into her shaking, nerveless hands. *The stims*, she recalled, feeling a rush of gratitude.

She peered back over her shoulder and caught the old woman shaking her head in amusement, still sucking on her pipe as Mica stumbled out the door, tripping over a stray cat stretched across its threshold. The beast fled yowling into the streets.

Chapter Eight

A nimkii was dying.

Again.

She dragged herself to an upstairs bedroom, dropping onto the stained and mildewed mattress left stagnant on its floor, breathing in the stink of disuse and sickness. Mica's family hadn't died in their beds, though. She'd seen the stains downstairs.

Her eyes closed and her vision went dark. This time, the pain wasn't so bad. Nothing like she'd experienced back in Delta. It was the breathing that was difficult, bringing panic every time a breath froze in her chest. One-by-one, her organs were shutting down. Each sluggish beat of her artificial heart hammered at her ears; each desperate gasping breath roared like the wind. She thought she could even hear the shift and groan of her failing biosteel tissues separating from flesh.

Mica wasn't going to make it back in time.

Her only consolation was that she hadn't gone mad in her last days, hadn't hurt anyone, hadn't proven Mica right.

"Ah, crap!" The thumping of footsteps rushed toward her, followed by the hurried rustle of cloth and the clatter of glass. "Don't die on me yet, Mod!"

Mica?

Animkii opened her mouth to speak, but she was too far gone. Rough hands forced her over onto her side and she felt the chill of air as they lifted the back of her borrowed shirt to gain access to the knot of broken tubing and pouches that made up her stim repository.

Mica's fingers investigated the ruin for several bleak minutes before letting the flap of cloth fall back down. "They really made a mess of you, didn't they?" More footsteps, this time leaving the room.

Animkii drifted in and out of unconsciousness. She'd done this dance of death before, back in Delta. She wasn't afraid anymore. She had only the faintest awareness of Mica shuffling around her bed, working with silent diligence to patch up her damaged stim repository.

"Alright!" A loud sigh signaled the end of Mica's frantic work. "Hoping this'll be enough to hold your guts together until the stims heal up at least *some* of the damage. We'll have to get more, though. As badly injured as you are, this isn't going to buy you much more time."

A needle slid into the insertion tube on Animkii's lower back. Cold fluid gushed into her bloodstream, turning from ice to fire in her veins, causing her head to snap back from the shock. Her enfeebled biosteel heart swelled with renewed power, strength coursing back into her failing body as she rode a chemical wave into pleasure. It would take days to make a full recovery, but for the first time in weeks, she felt alive.

With that sensation came a flashback to the first euphoric moment of joining the great mind, of floating in a tank of chemicals as her entire consciousness merged with the sentience her captors called the Alphaknot. The perils of the End, the guilt and shame of her exile, the fear of knowing she could no longer protect her family... All of that had vanished in an instant, absorbed by her new overseers. They'd given her no choice. The process had left her with no will to fight. The sweet unity of thought and function obliterated all emotion.

The longing for that oblivion now heightened, and she couldn't bear it.

<< REQUEST CONNECTION TO ALPHA /FORCE >>

Her local core awakened, her machine mind stirred back to awareness, searching, searching, searching for something to latch onto, but finding nothing, blind without a functional control shard to guide it. Her body shuddered and shook, spasming as errors filled her brain, and she felt her grip on sanity slipping. She didn't want to be human anymore. It was too hard. Too painful.

"Come on! Don't let go! You can do this, Animkii!"

She stared up at the frantic, ghost-faced woman hanging over her. Mica looked like she'd dragged herself out of a ditch—her complexion was a sickly green color, her face smeared with some kind of paint, her dark eyes sunken, her clothes rumpled and askew. A too-sweet smell clung to her body like smoke.

Cold reality snapped in place, tearing her free from that terrifying moment of near-surrender. She'd been so close to giving up, to losing all she'd gained. Her gaze locked on her savior's wane countenance. "What happened to you?"

Mica ignored the question, discarding the empty stim vials into a garbage chute on the back wall and then wiping her hands on her pants. Her mouth stretched into a frown that pushed back exhaustion. "No idea how you've lasted this long," she said. "You've been without stims for, what, three weeks? You should've gone into full system shock way before now."

"My people are strong," Animkii said, staring up at the ceiling overhead, remembering the invasive probing of the scientists who'd examined her after her rescue from the End of the World. Even with the translator implanted, it had taken her time to grasp their tech babble, their incessant talk of splitting genes and resurrecting archaic code and integration with tech. It wasn't as if they'd cared to explain it to her. To them, she'd simply been a sentient lab animal. "The scientists who assessed me said my genes were volatile and primitive. Likely to interfere with obedience protocols and loyalty programming."

"Did they?"

Animkii opened her mouth, thinking back to all the times she'd undergone reconditioning during her years of enslavement. "Yes."

"But they didn't trash you? I guess keeping you alive might be useful if they ever reach the northern world. Getting a local's perspective and all."

"They will never make it across the End."

"Yeah, yeah, monsters in a hole. But if *you* made it across, then they *know* it's possible. They'll try everything in their power to make it happen, so they can suck your lands dry the same way they did here in the south."

Animkii knew it was true. Maybe not today, maybe not even ten years from now, but eventually the Technocrats would bypass whatever interfered with their tech and kept them from crossing the End. Just the thought of it caused her throat to tighten with fear, her artificial heart to palpitate.

"Even if they die to the last person, my people will fight them," she said, teeth gritted. "We have always fought *something* to survive." But as the words left her lips, fear fluttered in her heart. If the Technocrats ever got across the End of the World, her people wouldn't stand a chance. With their simple weapons, even the ferocious Fire Bones would be easy pickings for these southern tyrants, new material for their demented experiments. "My people know nothing of the technology we have in the south. Long ago, we made a sacred covenant with our Creator, vowing to never again corrupt Creation. Even steel-work is forbidden, as it poisons the sky and leads us to temptation."

Mica looked dumbfounded. "So, what? You're reduced to sticks and stones? What kind of life is that?"

"Better than the one I am living right now."

The other woman grimaced. "Can't argue with you there. But it seems like this god of yours just makes your life more difficult." There was no mistaking the venom in her voice.

"Why do you hate the idea of gods so much?" she asked.

"I could fill the rest of your days with reasons."

Animkii saw her jaw tighten, erecting a wall between them, and didn't press further. "My life seems hard to you, but the Great Spirit gives a purpose to that hardship. To heal the Earth Mother, we must abstain from what harms Her. We must never betray Her again. We must trust the Creator's covenant."

"Even if you die for it?"

"For the faithful, death is not an end, but a beginning. The Creator will welcome our spirits into the Land of Souls, where we will reunite with our fallen loved ones."

Even though she spoke the words with fierce devotion, Animkii's heart wallowed in doubt. If she died today, there'd be no place for her in the Land of Souls, no boasting of battle glories alongside dead heroes, no hunting down beasts of mythological prowess with her fallen brethren, no endless feasting and festivity in paradise. She'd broken the Creator's covenant by entering the Ancients' city and taking that forbidden weapon.

The Dreamers would feast on her accursed soul, the fate of the faithless.

Mica seemed oblivious to her patient's inner turmoil. "Souls aren't any more real than gods are. Thinking there's some kind of invisible spirit living inside our bodies is ridiculous. Even more ridiculous is the idea that it survives after death."

"Don't you believe in anything?" Animkii asked, appalled.

"I believe in myself. I believe in the people I care about." Her voice cracked a little, just enough for Animkii to glimpse her vulnerability.

"But what about after you've died?"

She shrugged. "You said it best when we buried Reid: from the earth, to the earth. When we're gone, we only survive in the memories of our loved ones." Then she gave a bitter laugh. "I guess that means there'll be nothing left of me, then."

Mica slumped down onto a bent metal chair, causing its legs to scrape across the stone floor and Animkii to wince at the sound. Her hands were shaking, and she stared at the ground with red-rimmed eyes.

"You require rest."

"Later," she said, dismissing Animkii's words with a weary wave of her hand. "I can't sleep anyway, not without help, and I'll need to stay sober long enough to finish your surgery."

"Surgery?"

"Don't you want your arm back?"

Animkii sucked in a breath.

"Thought so." Gray-faced with exhaustion, Mica stood back up, sighing as she helped hoist Animkii into a sitting position. "Are you able to make it back down the stairs? All my equipment is in the shop."

She grunted her assent but found her body stubbornly noncompliant. When she tried to stand on her own, her legs wobbled like a pile of rocks about to topple over. Even between Mica's help and an obliging wall, it took ten minutes to make their way to the bottom level.

The shop shared an open space with what looked to be a small kitchen. Clutter filled it from floor to ceiling, work benches lined with tools, crates of tech parts of every shape and size, many that Animkii couldn't identify without access to the Alphaknot's vast library of knowledge. Dissected automatons lay spread out in pieces across countertops. One torso still had an arm that was frozen in a blind wave. Nearby squatted an enormous antique communication system, a single solid unit that took up an entire wall.

Dust covered everything with an inch of neglect.

She watched Mica clear away a small space around a padded exam chair in the room's corner. Beside it stood a rack that bristled with a menagerie of technical and surgical tools, spools of wire, and vials of stims long ago expired.

Mica eased her into the chair. "I've already looked at your shoulder. The explosion made a clean break at the socket, but biosteel isn't something that even the best recyclers can mend. It's a completely cellular process. But there are a few loose connections between the biotech seams I can take advantage of."

She passed her hand over a small steel plate on the wall, and the entire room lit up.

"Mom hooked her shop into the undercity grid," she explained at Animkii's look of surprise. "It's a hack job, but it'll give us the power we need to do the job right."

They shared silence for a few long minutes while Mica hooked her up to some kind of monitor and clamped all kinds of wires onto both skin and metal. It was a chilling reminder of her time spent in the Technocrats' laboratories—that is, if the Technocrats lived in a filthy, cluttered alleyway full of junk.

"Wow. I've never seen anyone stabilize this quickly before," Mica said, engrossed in the results scrolling across a clunky old monitor. One side of the screen displayed Animkii's vitals; the other measured stim levels. "Going from zero to one hundred stim level is rough on the host, but it's hardly stressing your body at all. No wonder the Crats are keeping you alive. You've got some super-level recovery going on here."

Then the screen switched to the results of the full-body scan. On that patched-together monitor, Animkii saw a frightening map of what the Technocrats had done to her body—or rather what the biosteel they'd infested her with was doing. Her artificial heart—her local core—appeared on the display as a brilliant blue ball of light from which tiny tendrils of biosteel branched out and merged with different tissues, replacing nerves and slowly consuming her body. Her brain was a dark blob, not yet infected, but the tiny threads of blue light were already braiding around her spinal cord. Strangling it.

Animkii sat up in alarm, the sudden motion causing a clump of her remaining hair to break away from her thinning scalp. Strands of black drifted down to her shoulders and to the floor. Among her people, hair held a significance beyond mere beauty. Warriors braided their hair to symbolize the strength of community, for individual strands were weak, but when braided together, they were strong. As she gazed upon the scattered wisps of black hair, she couldn't help but feel like one of those broken strands. Was this a sign from the Creator? That He'd given up on her? Or was He trying to tell her something else?

"The biosteel reactivated as soon as I introduced the stims." Mica sighed. "Not surprising. Stims keep your organic body from rejecting the biosteel, so it makes sense they also fuel its growth." With obvious reluctance, she pointed out a few spots of blue light that seemed to swell as they watched. "See there? Your digestive system has already started the transition to biosteel. In a couple of days, I'm willing to bet you won't be able to eat or drink at all. You'll have to subsist off stims."

Animkii stared at the screen in horror. "There's got to be a way to stop it."

Mica shook her head. "If there is, I haven't heard of it. Biosteel is less tech and more of a sentient disease. Even the cartels don't have access to the resources we'd need to find a cure and, even if they did, I doubt they'd risk doing it. Right now, the Crats mostly leave them alone, but if they ever suspected that kind of activity, they'd gut this place like they did Delta."

Why had she even thought a cure was possible? A cloud of despair settled on her heart. There was no returning to what she once was. That woman had died four years ago.

"How long do I have?"

Mica shrugged. "I don't know much about biosteel, other than what Sam taught me or what I've picked up on the streets. Could be weeks, could be months. Your modification wasn't completed, so I'm sure that buys you some time."

It was a bittersweet thought. "The Technocrats made a mistake, releasing us too soon," she said. "It made us vulnerable. But they did not expect the uprising in Delta."

Animkii remembered the day the Technocrats' scientists had rushed her division through the meat factory that was Upper-Alpha's Research Sector. She'd felt nothing back then, devoid of independent thought or emotion. No uncertainty, no questioning, only blissful obedience as they'd led her into the incubation chamber. Then the aftermath of Delta's ruination flooded her memory: soldiers' bodies around her, crumpled like paper, torn apart, burned alive from the inside-out. Combusted by that malicious code. And the innocents they'd slain...

Guilt wracked her heart. "The attack on Delta was unforgivable. Most citizens had no idea about the dissidents among them or why the Technocrats turned against them."

"The Crats made an example of them," Mica said, bitterness coloring her voice. She bent to adjust a lever on the exam chair, unfolding it into a table. "The unrest in the undercities is spreading to the uppercities. They don't want anything to disturb their perfect order. Better to wipe it all clean than change the way they run things."

Animkii felt vulnerable lying there, the biosteel seeping through her cells anew as the stims reactivated the parasite. The flesh on her left arm took on a faint silvery sheen, another piece of humanity fading away as the biosteel began merging with her skin.

"Maybe you were right, that the Alphaknot still controls me," she said, her gaze fixed upon the stained ceiling of the shop, her words heavy with fear. "Sometimes, I think I can still hear their voices in my head. It was easy being part of their world—no pain, no worries, no guilt. But," she continued, wanting Mica to understand her turmoil, "there was no love, no compassion, no humanity either."

Mica's mouth tightened, that stern line separating her from sympathy. "Pandora was like you in the beginning. We took her in after a brain aneurysm severed her from the Alphaknot. Her past didn't matter to us. We loved her like she was part of our family. Brought her into our home. Treated her like one of us. And then she—" A feverish color rose in her ghostly cheeks, her lower lip trembling for a moment before resolve tightened it again.

"I am sorry."

"Look, it's nothing personal. Doesn't matter what I do to you here. You might live a little longer, but in the end, you'll always belong to the Crats."

But Animkii had already seen the crack in Mica's shell, one that widened with their every interaction. Mica had gone to a lot of effort for someone she hated.

"I will do my best to protect you from your enemies here," she said. "I am grateful for your help."

Mica stiffened and Animkii expected a stinging retort, but there was nothing said. Instead, the woman pulled a crate of spare parts from underneath a workbench. On top lay a naked, headless torso with both arms intact. "I'm going to rebuild your arm," she said. "Pandora's parts are pretty antiquated, but they'll provide a framework that your biosteel components can build upon." A bitter smile tightened her lips. "It will feel good, tearing her apart."

"She's not still contagious?"

"The virus died with its host. I think that's why I survived."

Animkii shivered at the coldness in her eyes, understanding that she was leaving herself defenseless. Mica could choose to kill her. "You don't have to do this."

"It's fine. Consider it final payment for saving me from that collector." She inserted another needle into Animkii's back.

It wasn't a stim this time. It was a sedative.

"Wait!"

"You don't want to be awake for this part," Mica said quietly. "I got to open you up."

***

Mica had torn apart loads of mods over the years, but putting them back together was a different matter—far more complicated, far more emotional. She despised every one of them. After what'd happened with Pandora, she'd only taken on smaller repair jobs, and only when desperate to survive, preferring her salvage operations over recycling. She hated thinking that any of her work might've helped lengthen a mod's life. It didn't matter what mods they were—war mods, tech mods, overseer mods—they were all the same to her: mindless servants of the Technocracy, bombs set to go off whenever their masters willed it, whether those mods were aware of it or not.

But here she was, making all the same mistakes she'd made with Pandora. She was even calling Animkii by name now, like the mod was an organic and not a steel slave. And she wasn't just *any* kind of mod. She was one of those damn third-generation models all infested with biosteel. Even the best recyclers couldn't predict that pseudo-metal's behavior. For all Mica knew, biosteel was contagious, and she was about to unleash a new plague just by cracking open this mod.

Still, she bowed her head to the task, tight-lipped and focusing past the raging headache that hammered at her skull and the tremors that shook her limbs. She'd already used up the two shots of angel breath while crouched in an alleyway outside Lady Fang's, shaking and weeping as she sought to erase the memory of the monster haunting her mind. Once she was done with Animkii's operation, she'd head back for more. What had happened last night with the euphoria was nothing but a bad trip from dirty drugs, that's all. Besides, she knew better than to touch opiates. Her waking hours didn't need to be as messed up as her nightmares.

The explosion that had killed the collector had wrenched Animkii's arm clean out of its socket, leaving a cavity marred with desiccated strands of muscle fiber. A meager trickle of blood oozed forth as she widened the opening, clearing passage to the additional organic matter within. The lack of blood didn't surprise her. The modification on this side of the body was approaching completion, the encroaching biosteel assimilating muscles and surrounding tissues. This small bundle of natural fibers had been the weak point that had allowed the arm to tear away.

A good thing too. It would make reattachment much easier. Parasitic as biosteel was, it knew how to heal itself. She placed Pandora's much smaller arm into place and threaded loose strands of biosteel into the shriveled tissue poking free of Animkii's socket. Every tiny artificial blood vessel and nerve needed to be attached to its biosteel equivalent. She popped on a pair of goggles inset with magnifying lenses and leaned closer so that she could properly manipulate the tiny tendrils with a pair of forceps. It was tedious work at the best of times, but coming off a high made it near-impossible to keep focused, never mind that she could hardly keep her hand steady and kept losing the threads of veins and nerves.

No way the uppercity would've wasted a mod on this kind of mindless task, Mica thought peevishly, imagining that the scientists would pass it off to a drone whose unimaginative programming excelled at this kind of dull, repetitive work. Getting the arm attached properly took her the better part of the afternoon. Biosteel and stims would take care of the rest, healing up the tiny, sutured connections and keeping the organic tissues from rejecting the foreign tech.

Done.

Letting out a breath of relief, she flopped into a nearby chair, then watched in fascinated horror as the biosteel tendrils began to stir and writhe, wrapping their tiny threads around the metal limb and filling in the missing flesh. So fast! Disturbed, she watched Animkii's image on the monitor. The mod's body burned through the stims almost as quickly as the biosteel resumed its infection. The skin on her left arm and upper chest shimmered with a faint trace of silver, and the existing tech on the right side of her face now braided into the flesh above her eye.

Samiel had called biosteel a parasite, and now Mica saw the resemblance with her own eyes. According to her ex-lover, the awful substance had spawned out of an attempt to develop a new type of stim, but no one since then had been able to recreate it from scratch. The only way the scientists could reproduce biosteel was through mitosis of the original source and, as it divided and multiplied itself, they would transplant these 'offspring' into hosts. Though they'd originally treated biosteel as a new type of stim, they quickly learned that this germ possessed a primitive sentience they could manipulate by introducing it to different environments.

Sam had feared the Technocrats' complacency, believing they'd taken too great a risk with their experiments on biosteel. Integrating it with living bodies was a line they shouldn't have crossed. And now she could see why. Older generations of mods were already many times stronger than a normal citizen, but those integrated with biosteel had strength that felled buildings and uprooted bedrock. And a mod's knowledge swelled by the minute as it absorbed more and more data from the Alphaknot. The Technocrats controlled it for now, but what if the intelligence living in biosteel evolved and rebelled against its would-be masters and took the world for itself? With that kind of knowledge and power, what could stop it?

Not Mica, that was for sure. What was the point of even thinking about it? If the Technocrats destroyed themselves, what did she care?

She stifled an overdue yawn, trying not to feel *too* proud of her work on Animkii, thinking that she shouldn't risk falling asleep just yet—not before taking a shot to fend off the nightmares. But Lady Fang's place was too far away, and Mica's body was done with waiting. As she rolled her head back in a stretch against the chair, her eyelids drooped, fluttering once in futile resistance before the warm darkness of sleep pulled her in.

BOOM!

Mica jolted out of the chair as a booted foot kicked down the front door, splintering the cheap plasticene frame. Years of instinct sprang her forward toward the tools on the table, potential weapons in reach, but the intruders were too fast and on top of her in an instant, slamming her body against the workbench and sending tech parts flying to the ground. Her knees buckled and her face hit the ground. Someone's weight pressed her down onto the floor and held her flailing arms in place.

"Animkii!" she cried, but the mod was out cold.

From the shattered remains of her front door emerged a figure resembling an enormous yellow toad, with bulbous black eyes that peered out from between a thick brow of sallow skin. Behind him, a group of shadows moved and chittered in excitement.

"I didn't believe it 'til now," he said. "Mica Stone, back to face her punishment. Where's that weasel brother of yours?"

"Like I'd ever tell you, you piece of crap."

A rotten-toothed grin split apart his shiny lips, revealing teeth black with decay beneath his bulbous nose. He jerked his head back at his waiting goons. "Tie her up, boys. We're gonna take the *long* way home."

Chapter Nine

Animkii awoke to find herself lying facedown on a cold stone floor, inhaling the stench of dirt and stale urine. A mixture of confusion and wariness washed over her as she realized she was no longer in Mica's shop. Lifting her head, she was greeted by a wall of iron bars. Some kind of cell...?

A panicked cry rang out, causing her to curl back defensively. She could now see other people packed into the room with her, their filth-ridden bodies pressed back against the damp, grimy walls, watching as a massive reptilian hybrid pinned a smaller man up against the cold iron bars of the cell door.

"Come near me again and I'll kill you, trash," the hybrid threatened. A sibilant softness tempered the distinctive oil of a far-southern accent, a tone completely absurd coming from this hulking, reptilian horror. Fine blue scales covered his skin, thickening into leathery ridges along his forehead, cheeks, and shoulder blades. As Animkii watched, a long, forked tongue slipped past his lips, as if to taste the fear that salted the air.

His victim writhed against the scaly grip, his broken-toothed mouth opening and closing in panic, his breath wheezing as he struggled to find words in his terror. The hybrid snorted in contempt, then threw his foe against the barred wall with such force that the cell echoed with the horrifying thud of skull against metal. Then he retook his place in the far corner of the prison and crouched there like a great feral beast.

The ragged men and women that shared the cell swarmed around the fallen man like vermin descending on a corpse. They rifled through his meagre belongings and poked at his unconscious body, their nervous laughter jarring Animkii's senses.

She closed her eyes as the room spun around her. A smattering of cutup memories found their way through her reeling head, memories of the collector uncoiling from the darkness outside Alpha, the sweet rush of stims coursing through her dying body, and that last memory—of Mica giving her enough sedatives to down even a mod. She hunched over the straw-covered floor to vomit, heaving so violently that she swore she'd cough up her own guts. The acrid stench of stomach acid and half-digested nutrient bars rose into the already-rank air, mingling with the stink of old sweat.

A familiar shape crouched down beside her.

"Sorry about that," Mica said. "Guess your gut's more human than I thought. I *did* plan to give you something for the nausea but, as you can see, things went a little... off-schedule."

"I noticed." She wiped her mouth on the back of her new steel hand. "What happened? Where are we?"

"Headquarters of the Steel Fang Syndicate." Her mouth twisted. "Looks like my old boss found out I was back in town. I have a few old debts I need to clear up with him, that's all. Then we'll be free to go."

A few old debts? She studied the other woman's bruised and beaten face. Whoever had brought them here must've dragged Mica through every needle patch and mud hole in Under-Alpha. Scratches and deep cuts covered her arms and face, mud drenched her dark hair, and the left side of her face had completely swollen, leaving one eye barely open. "Someone attacked you."

"Took a good beating, yeah." A faint smile crept through her grim facade, showing she was no stranger to that kind of brutality. She even showcased wiggling a loose tooth with her tongue and then shrugged at Animkii's stony expression. "Not much I could do. I'm useless in a close-quarters fight. And you were pretty solidly out."

"This is what you were afraid of."

"The Steel Fangs' leader, Dathu, is a temperamental guy. I couldn't be sure how he'd react to my return. Reid and I left his gang a couple of years ago to move to Under-Zeta and... Well, we may have 'borrowed' a few resources to get a new start."

"You were a cartel member?" Animkii now realized they were in bigger trouble than she'd imagined. Undercity cartels were notoriously ruthless, known for their unforgiving tactics and savage violence against those who crossed them. You didn't just leave a gang like that.

Mica noticed Animkii's look and scowled. "When you live in an undercity, you either work for a cartel or you spend your life paying to keep them off your back, like my mom did. I didn't want to live in fear like she did."

"Why did you leave, then?"

"Reid convinced me we'd do better on our own. He was pretty much Dathu's right-hand man, so he had access to everything we needed to go independent." A shadow fell across her face. "I... had my own reasons for wanting to leave too."

An awkward silence stretched out between the pair.

"Thank you," Animkii finally said. "For the arm."

"Well, if Dathu won't see reason, you might need it to help us get out of here," she said, attempting a laugh. But worry strained the corners of her dark eyes and it was clear the woman wasn't as confident as she pretended. "I just wish Reid was here. *He* was the diplomatic one."

"I noticed."

That got a short laugh out of Mica.

The pair settled in the corner, away from the cluster of other prisoners, setting up a wary guard against mischief. "Are you still glad Reid vouched for you back then?" Mica asked. "If we hadn't taken you along, you wouldn't be sitting in a prison cell with me."

"I would be dead."

Mica sobered at that. "Maybe." She sighed and lay back against the stone wall, staring up at the ceiling as if contemplating something. "I miss him. Reid always knew what to do. How to fix any problem," she said. Then she looked at Animkii. "Do you ever miss your family? Are mods even allowed to have memories?"

The question caught Animkii off guard, its personal nature startling her. It seemed their imprisonment had softened something inside the other woman. Or maybe she just needed a distraction from their current predicament. Recalling how Mica had talked her through the agonies and disorientation of stim withdrawal, Animkii felt obligated to answer.

"When I was linked to the Alphaknot, they blocked memories of my life before modification," she said. "There were still times when they would resurface though. Little pieces. But whenever that happened, the Alphaknot would detect them, inflict punishment, and then take them away again."

Mica nodded, as if she'd expected that answer. "The Crats hate attachments. Attachments create emotion and emotions make humans irrational. Unpredictable. They don't like that."

"After four years under their control, it was difficult to readjust to having emotions and memories," she admitted, her voice softening.

A great black cloud of grief gathered over her heart, and she took a shaky breath to steady herself. She'd come so close to losing her mind in those first few days after Delta's fall. "My whole life came back to me all at once. There were many terrible things I had to relive—loved ones I had seen killed, my exile, other things that are unspeakable. It was hard to process."

"What will you do once we get out of here? Go home?"

That hope was so elusive, so far from reach, that Animkii could only shake her head. "Even if it was possible to cross the End again, I could not return. To them, I am an abomination." She didn't say it aloud, but the thought of facing her own people, of letting them see what she'd become, filled her with dread and heartache. "I think about the ones I left behind all the time. I worry I am not there to protect them." She closed her eyes, letting the weight of her emotions settle in the silence between them.

"Promise me."

Animkii's plea caused Ziiba's face to crumple with grief. There was an agonizing distance between the two of them now. They were blood sisters no more. Days spent fighting as comrades, nights spent in one another's arms... all gone. Ziiba tried to hide her pain behind hair the color of raven feathers, but her eyes, no longer merry, brimmed with tears.

"Whatever happens to you," she said, "I will protect Niigaanii. I swear by the Creator."

The toddler holding her hand fussed impatiently, unaware that he would never see Animkii again, eager to get back to the playmates waiting for him back at the motherhouse. Ziiba burst out with sudden emotion, "I should've known you'd do it, should've stopped you from going! Why didn't you listen to me?" Then her words softened with defeat and her copper-skinned shoulders slumped. "At least go quietly," she said. "Don't bring any more shame on our people or your clan. Let the End take you so that our people won't suffer from your sins. Let Niigaanii forget you and live a faithful life."

"And what about you?"

"Best that I forget you too."

Mica's voice cut through the memory. "But *would* you go back if you could?"

"I would fight a thousand Dreamers to see my family again. I'd do anything. No matter what happened to me afterward."

"Yeah. Me too." Mica was quiet. Then she cleared her throat. "Anyway, we should rest while we can. You're not healed up yet and we might need that arm of yours."

Animkii knew she couldn't argue, not when she was fighting post-sedative grogginess every minute that she was awake. Once she shuttered her eyes, the drugged exhaustion quickly pulled its heavy blanket back over her and she sank into a state between machine hibernation and human sleep. The stone-cold floor could've been a warm bed for all her body cared. The peace didn't last long, though. A few hours into sleep, a distant door slammed against a wall, startling her awake.

Four guards pushed past the cell's barred entrance, guns out. Why bother? This sad group wasn't about to put up a fight. Most of the prisoners were cringing against the back walls. But they weren't the ones the guards were worried about.

Animkii snuck a cautious look at the reptilian man. Hatred radiated from every inch of the hybrid's enormous scaly body, his muscles tensing, his teeth bared, and his small black eyes glistening with pent-up violence.

But he never moved from his place in the corner. Not a twitch.

The shortest of the four guards stepped forward, only four feet tall but thick with muscles that strained against his black linen shirt.

Yellow hair bristled from his head and grim lines pulled down his weathered face. "Out of the way!" He prodded at a pair of prisoners too close to the entrance with the tip of an energized spear. They jumped back at the shocking touch.

"Corbet? Is that you?"

The guard froze as Mica's voice rang out. "You and Reid should've stayed away," he said without looking at her, his forehead scrunching and his thick blonde eyebrows knitting together in a fierce scowl.

Mica's smile faltered. "Had some local business to take care of," she said in a rough voice. "Where is that old crook Dathu, anyway? Putting a bounty on our heads over a few spools of copper was a little much, don't you think?"

The little man bristled, his bloodshot eyes glaring out from beneath a mop of yellow hair, causing the surrounding guards to tense up in response, their hands tightening on their weapons. "You're going to play stupid and pretend the two of you didn't try to kill him?" His struggle for composure was clear, his mouth twisting with the effort and his hands shaking. His voice dropped to a soft growl. "Doesn't matter. Dathu won't kill you, not while his new friends want you alive. Me? I'd *rather* be dead than go with them."

Mica's face showed only shock. "Try to kill Dathu? Why would we do that? Where's Sam? Talk to him—he'll know I'm not lying."

"You really don't know, do you?" Corbet stared at her, disbelief creeping into his voice. "You've no idea what you brought down on us. First the Technocrats, and now... well, you'll see soon enough, won't you?"

"What do you mean? Samiel—"

"Samiel's gone," he said. "The Crats sent a collector for him a few weeks after you left Under-Alpha. If he's not dead by now, then he'll be wishing he was."

Mica's mouth dropped open in a soundless cry, the last vestige of color draining from her cheeks.

"Now, are you going to come quietly? Or do I need to make an example out of you?"

Animkii growled in her throat and stepped forward protectively, but Mica put up a restraining hand before Corbet could react.

"It's fine," she said. "I just need to talk things over with Dathu. Clear up the misunderstanding. And then I'm sure he'll let us go, okay?"

Animkii wondered if she even knew she was lying.

***

Built out of the carcass of an ancient hotel, the Steel Fang Syndicate's headquarters was a salvaged ballroom with high vaulted ceilings and boarded-up windows. The floor consisted of tiles of various sizes and colors laid haphazardly in a mosaic pattern, while the walls were a collage of rusted metal sheets and mismatched plasticine planks, giving them a rough, weathered appearance. Here and there, scraps of tattered cloth hung limply from makeshift curtain rods, providing a splash of color against the drab backdrop. Above, a spiderweb of dim lights cast a faint glow over the scene. The overall effect was one of chaos and disorder, a ramshackle patchwork of materials thrown together in a towering architectural nightmare.

Bizarre creatures prowled the shadows here, mingling in this place of depravity, accepting drinks from the rusty automatons that lurched through the crowd.

Degenerates.

They were the castoff remnants of Technocrat experiments gone awry, filling the gutters of Under-Alpha like broken souvenirs from ancient wars. Unaltered humans like Mica and Reid were an uncommon sight these days, and the frequent targets of recruiters.

Corbet led her through the cartel's bustling headquarters lounge, gripping her shackled hands tightly. Though they'd known each other since adolescence, his lips remained sealed, pressed together in obstinate silence. Dathu had taken the orphaned youth under his wing, sculpting him into a criminal. She weighed the odds of escaping amid the crowd, but Corbet wasn't someone you wanted to mess with. Memories of fighters far larger than her being floored by those metal-plated fists cautioned her against any rash moves.

She'd just explain to Dathu that there'd been a misunderstanding, that she'd work off the debt. She'd always been his best scavenger. No one else could go as deep into the Old World ruins as Mica could, and there were still plenty of ancient treasures there to repurpose, though the thought of returning there filled her with such dread that she considered death a better option.

The memory of the thing she'd seen down there evoked a terror so deep that she froze in remembered fear, forcing Corbet to tug her forward.

Maybe Dathu wouldn't make her go back down there. She had other talents. Sure, her recycling skills had grown a little rusty after years of playing trader, but it wouldn't take long to get up to speed on the latest tech. Maybe she could even talk him into throwing in a bonus. She was sure he had plenty of angel breath to spare and he knew she worked better with a few shots in her. Then, once they'd settled business, she could go find Samiel.

But if the Technocrats had really taken him... A shudder rolled through her body. No, she wouldn't let herself think about what that meant, not now. She just needed to sort things out with Dathu. Everything was fine.

Only it wasn't. She could already feel the talons of her addiction sinking into her skull, the incessant knife jab of a headache forming behind her eyes, the first tremors taking her hands. After months and months of access to as much angel breath as she wanted, followed by the deprivation of Cult captivity, Lady Fang's complimentary euphoria had actually worsened the inevitable withdrawal. Like dream-dust, euphoria was a powerful hallucinogen, spinning a temporary world of pleasure and make-believe that left you feeling robbed at gunpoint after it ended, while angel breath brought her peace, soothed the fire of her anxiety, made her forget—for a moment—all her problems. The room blurred and spun around her.

"Ohhh, Corbet, have you brought me a present?"

A dark-skinned woman blocked their path, four sets of tiny black eyes peering at Mica from beneath a mass of shaggy black hair, her hard, lean body wrapped in translucent strands of silk, wisps of phantom clothing arranged in a mockery of modesty. As she moved, her six arms remained in constant motion, one hand pulling forward to clasp Corbet's shoulder in greeting while another reached out with unnaturally long fingers to stroke Mica's filthy hair.

Mica cringed.

"She's the one your masters want." Corbet's nose twitched, an old nervous tic betraying his unease. The fist gripping Mica's shackles tightened.

"Ah!" Her hand drifted to Mica's face, its caress soft with longing. "Such a blessed child!"

"Yeah, if you say so," he grunted. "If you don't mind, Dathu's waiting for us."

"Of course. I wouldn't dream of interfering." Her tiny black eyes went vacant, her thoughts drawn elsewhere for a moment. Then her pinched mouth with its single long fang formed a terrifying smile, and she stepped back into the crowd, swallowed into its midst.

Corbet shuddered visibly.

"One of Dathu's new friends, I take it?"

"Yeah."

A terrible suspicion had taken root in her gut, but she tried to dismiss it as paranoia. By the time she'd left the undercity two years ago, the Steel Fangs had firmly entrenched themselves as the most prominent cartel Under-Alpha, controlling the city governor the Technocrats had appointed. They didn't need to ally themselves with anyone, and Dathu wasn't the type who liked to share power, so why these new 'friends'?

She surveyed the room. At first glance, the Fangs' headquarters hadn't changed much. Every shadow hid a thief and a dozen knives. Skeletal, golden-eyed addicts begged for one more hit of dream-dust so they could walk in their dreams and escape this awful reality. Too many colors and creatures were mish-mashed into one space, all of them wanting something, trade or sex or drugs. The noisy din drowned out conversations. Sweaty bodies pushed past them, reeking of body odor and cheap perfume and candy smoke. Faded beauties sold their youth to buy the parts needed to keep the faulty tech inside them from failing.

The Technocrats enjoyed playing gods, and these were their sad leftovers.

But there was something wrong here. She couldn't pinpoint it exactly, but the atmosphere had changed. In between the usual riffraff, there were new spots of darkness and a sinister air hung over it all like a smothering veil, a tide of unease that pulled her down by her feet.

"Welcome back, Little Sister," someone called out.

Mica flinched at her old nickname and looked for the source. In the back-most corner sat a trio of stubble-faced ruffians. Wear had bled the color from their clothes, leaving behind a dingy gray, and even from across the room, she could see their boots were full of holes, their hair greasy from lack of washing, and their eyes yellow and swollen from using too much dream-dust.

Mica felt like someone had just punched her in the gut. These three had once been among Dathu's chief enforcers, dangerous men feared and respected on the streets, men that she'd looked up to as a youth. Now they were nothing more than a graying flock of crows. What had changed? Did it have something to do with Dathu's new friends?

One raised a mocking toast to Mica's impending doom.

What would Reid say if he could see their old gang now?

Probably laugh. Her brother wouldn't have given one ounce of sympathy to these discards. His loyalty only extended as far as payment for services rendered and though he'd proven himself a valuable member of the undercity cartel when it suited him, she knew Reid had considered himself above these others. He'd believed that he and Mica were destined for something greater than just street scraps.

And where was Reid now? Dead, that's where. And here she was, back at the bottom of the heap. Better if she'd never left to begin with.

"Traitor," someone sneered at her passing.

The crowd parted at her arrival and she saw a small table positioned at the edge of a sunken floor. Fat velvet couches and armed bodyguards formed a half-circle around a small meeting space, the gaudy furniture arranged in such a way as to avoid blocking the view of the area below.

A lump grew in her throat. This was a new addition. Someone had dug a large square pit through the floorboards and into the guts of the building's foundation. At the pit's far end was a raised platform built of metal girders, occupied by four stern-faced sentries, each poised to shoot at a moment's notice. Down twenty feet to the concrete floor, she could see patches of old bloodstains. It didn't take much to guess what the pit was used for.

And right at the center of this cruel and decadent kingdom sat its ruler, Dathu.

The sight of her old boss caused her mouth to sag open in horror. She remembered the leader of the Steel Fangs as a big, broad-chested man with swarthy skin and a wicked smile. Now that vicious grin spread across a face disfigured with scars and street tech. Even from where she stood, it was obvious that tech had replaced large chunks of his body. And this wasn't a neat and tidy assimilation like modification—this was a bits-and-pieces hack job. Surgical scars crisscrossed the map of his skin and where he used to have glossy black hair, there was a metal skullcap. Wounds that would've brought down a lesser man were gashed across his face and throat. Someone had obviously tried to take him down. And failed.

Her earlier confidence gave way to a bout of nerves. During her earliest days in the gang, Dathu had acted as a sort of crooked fa-ther-figure, and she'd even felt some affection toward him. Sure, he wouldn't have been happy about their sudden hiatus, but would he really think they'd tried to kill him?

"Piece of advice for old times' sake: he *really* hates being stared at," warned Corbet.

"Hard *not* to."

But Dathu wasn't the focus of her attention now. There was an-other man sitting across from her old boss. At first, she could only see the back of him, his lithe form stretched out on the opposite couch from the cartel leader, his hand fingering a spindle of wine. As she approached, Dathu made a gesture toward her, and the man's head turned. Staring back at her was a terrible, familiar sight: a silver mask, molded to resemble a serpent.

Father Dark.

She froze in terror. He was alive?! Flashbacks from the night she'd escaped the Cult tore through her mind, the sound of bones popping and faceless bodies rupturing, of rushing through a torrential rain of blood and gore to reach the streets outside. She'd blocked them all out, didn't want to know, didn't want to remember. She'd hoped they were all dead, but now—

"Are you insane? You got yourself mixed with *these* creeps?!" she said to Dathu. She stepped back in alarm, her escape hindered by Corbet's restraining hand.

"My men found her just where you said she'd be," Dathu said to Father Dark, ignoring Mica's outburst. His words were ice. "Where's my payment?"

Panic replaced anger. "Look, I think you've made a mistake—"

"My mistake was in trusting you and your brother."

Father Dark examined her from behind his mask, its silvery surface twisting with displeasure, the lines of its mouth deepening and the hollows of its eyes growing darker as it traced the bruising on her face. "I wanted her untouched," he said, the slight tremor in his voice hinting at an undercurrent of rage.

Dathu shrugged. "A few bruises, that's all. The boys were a little zealous, I admit, but there's no permanent damage. If you don't want her—"

The cultist slammed a bulging pouch down on the table. "Take it."

A grin broadened the cartel leader's deformed face. "Ah, just what I asked for!" He popped open the bag and ran eager fingers through its contents, holding up several vials filled with a silvery purple liquid. His eyes glinted with satisfaction. They weren't any kind of stims or drugs that Mica recognized and, considering her experience, that worried her.

At a nod from his leader, Corbet pushed Mica down onto the couch, next to the man who'd just purchased her. A cloying mixture of lemon and incense wafted off his fine black robes, reminding her of her brief, terrifying time as the After Cult's captive. She'd hoped she'd seen the last of their kind when she and Reid had left Zeta, but the last few days were proof that bad circumstances could always get worse.

She knitted her fingers together tightly, trying to hide how badly they trembled, hoping he didn't notice the sheen of sweat that cooled her skin, but Father Dark was observant, and the serpentine mouth of his mask stretched into a slow, knowing smile. As if by magic, a small canister appeared in his hand. "A shot to relax?"

A stone caught in her throat. Angel breath. Her eyes couldn't move from the sight of it, her thoughts grew heavy with longing. No way. She wouldn't do it.

A flush rose in her cheeks, warming them. But why shouldn't she? A shot of angel breath was what she needed to clear her head, calm herself down, think her way out of this nightmare. Just because it came from this piece of garbage didn't mean it couldn't help her get out of this place.

Just a little was all she needed.

Before another protest could form in her head, she snatched it out of his hand. "Yeah." Then she popped the lid and inhaled so deeply her brain turned to fuzz, her whole body feeling like it was melting into the couch.

She'd sold herself for a shot of angel breath and a wave of humiliation surfaced as the initial high settled, exposing that empty place inside her that never quite went away. Pretending indifference, she jerked her gaze from the masked man and tossed the canister aside, grateful to be saved from further conversation by the crowd as they began to stomp their feet and roar. The noise of her surroundings faded into the background as the drug coursed through her, soothing her nerves, making all her problems seem inconsequential. She'd find a way out of this dilemma. She just needed to relax a little, come up with a plan. Her eyelids drooped, and she released a sigh of relief.

"The fight's beginning!" Dathu stood up and rubbed his hands together in excited anticipation.

Following their chief's lead, the bar's patrons crowded around the edge of the pit, peering down curiously, awaiting something. Even Mica leaned over to get a better view of the small arena below them, ignoring the burning gaze of the cultist, unbothered by the ruckus of the crowd as they screamed for the match to begin, their ravenous mouths stretched out in grotesque, shouted revelry.

A pair of guards escorted two figures to the pit's edge.

The first fighter was the massive reptilian hybrid from Dathu's dungeon. He pushed aside his guard with a look of contempt and then jumped into the pit, landing with ease.

His opponent was not so cooperative, struggling against the guards before being pushed in afterward, hitting the ground hard and then scrambling to regain her footing. As the fighter sank into a defensive posture, her head turned just enough so that Mica could make out the patch of tech that covered the right side of her face.

Animkii.

Chapter Ten

Animkii knew she was in trouble.

If the hybrid had seemed big in the small cell they'd shared, facing him in the battle ring revealed his true enormity. He easily surpassed her own formidable height by at least two feet. His bulging scaled muscles seemed hewn from stone and he moved like an animal: graceful, tense, powerful.

The air grew heavy, uneasiness pressing down on her chest, her breath coming out in shallow bursts. She was in no condition to fight. The sedative had left her feeling drowsy and her new arm still hung uselessly at her side, barely functional despite the pristine biosteel shell that had already formed on its outside. The limb had grafted successfully, but how well would it hold out in a battle against this monster? Uncoiling from her defensive crouch, she moved into the center of the floor, sizing up her opponent while the crowd jeered and spat at her.

Animkii was there to die for their pleasure, and they were impatient to begin.

Their mockery stirred to life her dormant pride. She had no intention of dying! With keen eyes, she surveyed her surroundings, careful to keep the arena's wall at her back and the hybrid out of arm's reach. The height of the pit walls wasn't her only obstacle to freedom. Raised above the crowd on a metal scaffold were four guards with their eyes and guns trained on the fighting pit. How many others hid in the crowd?

"Planning your escape?" The hybrid spoke in a slow drawl that oozed contempt, goading her away from the imagined safety of the walls and drawing her into their duel. Scars covered every visible inch of his scaled flesh, some old and faded, others swollen from more recent battles. The stink of rotten vegetation hung off his threadbare clothing. Although he lacked armor, Animkii guessed his leathery reptilian skin would prove a tough defense.

A guard tossed two steel machetes into the pit from overhead. They spun in the air before landing at the fighters' feet, clanging against the stone floor. Both dove for the weapons, claiming them simultaneously and then retreating to opposite corners, gazes locked.

Animkii swung her weapon testingly, feeling the balance of the thin, steel blade. In the Witherlands, she'd fought with spears and hatchets during raids against outlanders or rival peoples, brutal clashes that had left her soaked to the skin in blood, so close to her opponents that she'd see the life darken from their eyes as she hacked apart their bodies. The memory stirred something bestial inside her and her whole being hummed with anticipation.

"I expected guns," she said.

"These scum pay to see blood. Guns kill too quickly, too cleanly." His laugh reminded her of someone choking. "Less entertaining—"

The hybrid lunged forward, leaving Animkii little time to react. His movements were eerily fluid, reminiscent of the dances her people used to celebrate a successful hunt or battle—a rugged ballet in which his machete gashed the air in great slicing arcs, a dance of death meant to keep her off-balance.

It worked. Caught off-guard by the beautiful violence in his movements, she stepped away instead of moving forward with her offensive. He was fast! Twice he struck her, drawing blood once on her flesh arm and another at her side. He knew to avoid the biosteel, creating light, bloody wounds intended to weaken his prey and prolong the fight.

Shame burned through her. She was too weak, still recovering from surgery and weeks of stim withdrawal, relying too much on the armored portions of her body to absorb his mocking blows, not able to keep pace with his speed. He was stronger, faster, more agile than she could've imagined, wielding his blade with deadly precision, while she was slow and crippled and disoriented. Her frustration mounted as small pools of stim-laced blood formed at her feet.

But Animkii's modified body could take far more damage than a normal person's, and that allowed her time to analyze his maneuvers, to memorize the movements of his body until she was certain she'd gotten the timing just right. Her confidence rose. The biosteel running through her body made her near-impossible to kill with mundane weapons, even with a useless arm and diminished strength. The best he could do was attack her organics until the damage was bad enough that her stims couldn't keep up with the blood loss.

Problem was, he was good at it.

The hybrid kept pressing forward, growing more vicious with each sweep of his blade, but his guard lowering with each successful blow. Underestimating her. Good. If the reptilian fighter assumed Animkii's defensive posture was because of fear or inexperience, he was dead wrong. Her excitement began to build. Long before Animkii's body had become the Alphaknot's instrument, she'd honed her skills in a land where death lurked in every shadow and snowdrift, and her body still carried the memory of that harsh conditioning.

Impatient in its bloodthirst, the crowd booed and spit at the pair.

"Fight me!" The hybrid let out a hiss, annoyed by his foe's evasive maneuvers, wanting to end the battle but finding his advantage slipping away. It was too late to recover. His attack had already lost its initial strength and grace, becoming choppier and less controlled as he wearied. He was a hybrid, but not a machine.

He couldn't outlast her.

With each new miss, her opponent's swings grew wider, erratic and charged with fury. The hybrid could no longer see anything but his own blinding rage, and it was then that Animkii found her chance.

Sweeping her blade up with all her machine strength, she opened him up from navel to sternum, his skin parting like the petals of a flower and spilling a river of blood. The hybrid staggered back a few feet in pain and shock, his wound clutched in one hand and blood gushing between his fingers.

Filled with savage energy, the crowd pushed closer to the pit's edge. They screamed at Animkii to strike down her opponent.

She glanced up at them, filled with disdain at their fickle loyalties. Among the Fire Bones, contests of strength were common, but they were never with the goal of seeing the other contender dead—they were exercises and tests of skill. These people craved the sight of spilled blood, heedless of whether it was hers or the hybrid's. Maybe it made them feel better about their own lives, to see others who had it worse.

Looking back at her opponent, she was stunned to find him grinning back at her, not in the least shaken by the lethal wound. Her horror deepened as the skin of his wound began knitting itself back together. Some kind of regenerative ability! What should have crippled him instead spurred the hybrid to fight harder. He hacked at the air with fresh energy and new enthusiasm, determined to cut his opponent down. His wound did nothing to slow him down.

Animkii tried to stumble out of his way, but his blade landed with brutal force. Metal struck metal. Biosteel-girded bones saved her flesh arm, but blood sprayed everywhere. His strength shocked her. Thrown to her knees, she raised her weapon to block his increasingly deadly blows, unable to find a new opening, though not giving any of her own, either. Having realized his enemy's strategy, the man no longer fought with careless ease.

This desperate battle awakened a memory from her youth.

The spear haft cracked against the back of Animkii's head and she fell to her knees, trying not to throw up, her heart pounding against her chest. She heaved a shuddering breath and tried to get back up on legs that shook with exhaustion, only to collapse.

"I yield!" The sweat dripped down her face and her body screamed surrender.

Her mentor, Raak, stared down at her with merciless eyes. "There will be no yielding today. You fight or you die. Get up or I will kill you right here."

Another blow smashed into the side of her face and her head exploded in pain, but now her legs moved of their own accord, her body lifting from the ground, her fingers curling into fists as she launched herself at her opponent in a desperate last move, the blood and pain all forgotten in a final fight to survive.

Back in the present, Animkii gritted her teeth and rose to her feet, pushing back her foe's flurry of blows. They must've boosted him with stims for him to have this kind of strength and stamina and not be a mod. She needed to end this, and fast.

"Why are you fighting for them?" She shoved back at him with her own blade while she regained her footing. "We shared the same cell. You are as much a prisoner as me. This is a battle we both lose, no matter the outcome."

"You think Dathu is an idiot?" He threw himself at her. Frustration smoldered in his eyes, but his blade never wavered again, never allowed Animkii another moment of rest. "His recycler pets keep me injected with some sort of chemical. If I try to fight against his goons, I'll lose consciousness."

Thought-responsive drugs were something that only the Technocrats' top scientists had access to. That they were available to an undercity gang lord was a terrifying thought. How had Dathu gotten hold of them? She ducked her head to avoid decapitation. "I can lead the attack. You provide cover."

"You won't make it ten feet before the guards shoot you."

"They will not expect *you* to disobey. It will distract them long enough for me to reach the scaffolding."

Howling at the delay, the crowd tossed chunks of food at the pair, screaming for the battle to continue. Her opponent tilted his head up and regarded them with dark contempt, while still keeping pace with swift, sharp jabs skillfully executed, but now lacking murderous intent.

He was considering it.

"You cannot win this fight," she said. "The biosteel will keep me alive even if you cut off every piece of my body."

To her surprise, he laughed, that terrible animal gurgle. "I already know they rigged this fight against me. This is my punishment for not bowing to Dathu's new friends." His lip curled with derision, his movements slowing slightly, his swings deliberately missing by inches as he considered her words. "But better to die in battle than to serve the After Cult."

"After Cult?"

"You haven't been orphaned for very long, have you?" he sneered, his strikes unwavering, perfectly controlled. "The Crats aren't the only rotten thing in this world anymore. People want to believe in anything that'll get them out of this miserable life. I just never thought Dathu would be one of them."

Locked together, blade against blade, each fighter strained to their full strength. Animkii's flesh-arm ached and her muscles trembled from the effort of holding back death. The hulking man finally pushed her back against the wall, his machete rising and falling in a single breath.

She looked at him with disappointment. "You are willing to die for their entertainment, but not for your freedom?"

At the last possible moment, he turned the blade's edge away from her, a subtle twist that tricked her eyes into believing her own demise. Instead, she heard the scrape of metal against stone as the killing blade hit the wall behind her.

Their eyes met and his lips rolled back with a snarl, showcasing rows of sharp, flesh-rending teeth, but she saw the nihilism in them shift to decision.

"Kill Dathu and they'll have no control over me. *Then* we might have a chance."

***

Mica hadn't thought things could get worse, but watching Animkii evade that colossal hybrid's blows sent her heart racing into her throat.

Dammit! This was bad. She had to find a way stop this.

Tearing her attention away from the violent battle, she shifted her focus back to her former employer. "Look, Dathu, I don't know where you got this idea that Reid and I tried to kill you—"

"You replaced my stims with poison the night you left. Who else did I trust enough to have access?"

An awful suspicion crept into her thoughts, the memories of that last night in Under-Alpha coming back to her: a rushed exodus, skulking through the shadows of crumbling alleyways, Reid uncommonly agitated as he hastened them through the streets, his eyes always turning back, worried about pursuit when no one would've missed them for at least a day or two, when no one should've known yet—or cared—that they were gone.

She hadn't questioned Reid's paranoia until now. The Steel Fangs were a dangerous gang, and they'd left it without Dathu's approval. Being afraid was normal. Mica's preoccupation with her broken heart, of leaving Samiel behind, had prevented her from questioning her brother's behavior.

What had he done?

Made sure I couldn't return.

She hushed the voice in her head.

Dathu took her shocked silence as proof of guilt. "You ungrateful little bitch." Hatred twisted his scarred face. "I looked after the two of you when your own father would've sold you for a sniffer. Should've let the pimps scrape you off the streets."

"It wasn't me!"

Deaf to her protest, the gang lord continued, building himself into a rage. "It took nearly a year for me to recover," he said. "But I made some new friends along the way, didn't I?"

Miserable, Mica looked at the masked man beside her. Had things gotten so bad that her old boss would deal with their lot? She imagined those bloody-handed cultists trawling the streets, looking for victims to lure into their grasp, preying on the desperate and peddling delusions to the hopeless.

"Imagine—some of my own subordinates thought they'd take advantage while I was down!" The crime lord cackled, madness creeping into his eyes as he made a slashing motion across his own throat. "True, those traitors forced me to disappear awhile, to go into hiding. But when I came back, I cleaned things up real good." Steel glittered in that carnivorous smile as he pulled out a necklace of finger bones from beneath the collar of his shirt. The digits dangled there, clicking against each other like a macabre wind chime. "One from each traitor. But there's still two missing."

Mica recoiled in horror.

Now that she thought of it, except for the three who'd toasted her, she hadn't seen *any* of Dathu's inner circle here. It was unusual to see the gangster without at least half-a-dozen cronies hanging off him.

"I'm telling you, I didn't—" But she broke off when she saw the unhinged look on his face. His rationality was gone. If the Cult had her old boss in-hand, there was nothing left to do. At this rate, she was dead meat.

"We need her fully intact," Father Dark reminded him.

There was a grunted reply, and the madness in Dathu's eyes receded.

Mica eyed the masked cultist with suspicion, a cold shiver running through her as she recalled their previous encounter. "Last time I ran into your kind, you didn't seem too concerned about missing pieces," she said in an awful voice. "I seem to recall a lot of pain and blood."

"We made mistakes that we've since corrected," he said, his voice echoing softly behind his mask as he rose to his feet, his immaculate black robes billowing out with the movement. "Come. It's time for us to be on our way."

No way she was leaving with this fanatic. "What's the rush?" she protested, stalling. "At least let me have a last drink before we go. I'm sure Dathu won't mind."

With shackled hands, she reached for the open bottle of synthetic wine sitting on the table and, to her surprise, the gang lord didn't move to strike her—only watched her with malicious eyes as her fingers closed around the cold glass surface. She lifted it to her lips, full-bottle, and drank deeply, then held it out for her old boss to take.

"Time to celebrate, you old crook," she said. "You caught me, didn't you? *Believe* me, you couldn't have sold me to a rottener group of people. I promise you they'll make me suffer for whatever's left of my life."

"My only regret is that Reid won't be joining you," Dathu said, his mouth twisting as he reached forward to accept—

"Oops." Mica's fingers 'slipped' and the bottle tumbled to the ground, shattering as she made a lunge for freedom, overturning the table's contents and knocking Dathu to the floor. As a final act of defiance, she tore the necklace free from his neck and the bones scattered on the floor like a game of dice.

Then she hit the ground running.

Dathu's hybrid guards peeled themselves away from the crowd, yellow-skinned monstrosities lumbering toward the escaping prisoner, trampling anyone who got in their way. Corbet roared and lunged after her. Though she was quicker than the small man, there wasn't enough time to buy. Dathu had already pulled a gun and its tip glowed red as it transitioned to kill mode.

The cultist tried to interfere, wrestling back the bigger man's steel arm, arguing with him, urging him to back down.

By now, the crowd had shifted its attention from the combat unfolding below to the confrontation occurring within their midst.

Mica quickly lost the advantage of surprise. The crowd was too dense to slip through and disappear. In no time, Dathu's hybrid guards dogpiled her, Corbet grappling her from behind, locking her in place and forcing her down onto her knees.

Face dark and rage frothing at his mouth, Dathu shook off the protesting cultist and held his gun in two shaking hands, screaming at his guards to stand aside. The wretches scurried out of the way, leaving Mica behind, curled up in a fetal position and inhaling the stink of a filthy floor. Claw marks had left red ribbons on her skin.

Dathu readied his weapon to deliver death.

"Remember our deal!" the cultist yelled.

"Our deal's over!"

"Very well."

Two words, uttered with a coldness that sent a chill through her body, seemed to cast a freeze upon the entire scene. The air grew tense, still, as if time had momentarily suspended. Dathu had no chance to make his shot before coils of black energy shot out from the eyeholes of the cultist's mask, blasting through the cartel leader and his monstrous guards, hurling them across the room like a cluster of rotten leaves torn apart by a tempest. Hot, stinking blood splattered Mica's face. When she looked up, she saw on a far wall the smear of guts and bone dust that used to be Dathu.

Howling in panic, the inebriated crowd scrambled for the exit, pushing and shoving their way toward safety. In their crazed exodus, they trampled whatever lay in their path, leaving behind a trail of broken bottles, shattered furniture, and bloody bodies.

Mica rose to her feet, intending to join them, only to find her own body paralyzed.

***

In the pit below, the two warriors shared a tense look.

"Something is happening up above." Animkii fixed her sight overhead as she and the hybrid continued their charade of battle for a few impatient minutes, waiting until the ruckus drew the guards' attention away from their duel. Their fickle audience lost interest in the battle at their feet as trouble rose from behind. "We should escape while they are distracted!"

As she spoke, a bolt of black energy bisected the room and blasted outward, flinging bodies in the air, the victims fighting gravity as their arms wheeled and legs flailed. A blackened, decapitated head landed in the pit, smoldering as it rolled to a stop, its burned-out eyes staring into her soul, sending a jolt of fear through her.

"Creator, protect us!" She stepped back in horror. The edge around the pit cleared, screams coming from all directions as an army of running feet pounded the floor above them. Panic frenzied the mob.

No longer even pretending to fight, the pair watched another wave of energy wash over the room, this one more intense than the first, toppling the guards' platform. The blast shattered its stilts and the hysterical crowd pulled it down in their rush to escape. As it capsized, one of its unlucky guards tumbled from the balcony and into the pit, landing at the hybrid's feet.

Reptilian lips curled with a vengeful smile as the hybrid's killing blade came down fast. A gun tumbled from the dead man's fingers. "Looks like you don't have to kill Dathu after all. Seems he's dead already. I'm free," he said, a vicious look in his eyes. "Here!" The hybrid tossed the weapon to Animkii, then kneeled beside his victim to unbuckle a second gun from the man's bloodstained belt. There was no hesitation. No fumbling or second-guessing.

A surge of genuine admiration welled up within her. He was a true warrior, as much as any of the Fire Bones. *We might actually get out of here alive*, she thought.

Alerted to their escape, one of the three remaining monitors fired at them, but the first shot went wild and hit the ceiling, sending a cascade of metal and plasticine debris down on the fleeing patrons. The hybrid dove for the ground as a second shot skimmed the back of his neck, his tough ridged skin absorbing it without harm. In seconds, he was back up on his feet and running toward the pit's wall while Animkii covered his escape by releasing a scorching wave of pyrolite into the guard above.

What few stragglers remained near the pit's edge backed away nervously as the monstrous hybrid made a powerful leap, his strong legs propelling him upward. He easily cleared a good portion of the wall's height, then scrambled with his claws the rest of the way, pulling himself up and over the lip of the arena. None of the spectators dared to make themselves obstacles, watching in awe and fear. Crouching at the edge, he then extended a scaled hand down to help his former opponent as she made her own leap to freedom, catching his hand.

The hybrid dropped a serpentine smile onto his new ally, pulling her up with a single tug on her arm, unimpeded by the significant weight of her tech-armored body.

"You're not a bad shot. You got a name, or should I just call you 'Mod'?"

"Animkii."

"I'm Zen. Come, let's incinerate this trash."

She cast an anxious look around the chaotic scene. "My friend is also a prisoner. I need to find her."

"Leave her," he said, his forked tongue stabbing at the air in displeasure. "That black energy we saw means one of the Cult's curs is here." Intense hatred seethed behind his dark gaze and one of his scaled hands shook as it tightened around his stolen gun. "You can't fight them. They don't fight like us. They're unnatural."

He spat on the ground, then turned his back on the pit and began wading through the panicking guests, his gun clearing a gruesome path.

Animkii stared after him for a second, but there wasn't time to consider his strange words. She used her tech-eye to filter through the fleeing crowd, looking for Mica. Faster than any mortal brain, it stripped away faces and bodies that didn't match the image in her head. A cell sample from Mica would've made things even quicker, but that turned out to be unnecessary. She found the other woman close to the pit's edge, frozen like a statue, caught in an awkward lunge toward freedom, wide-eyed, too pale, and drenched in blood.

What was wrong with her?

Then she saw the slender, silver-masked figure come up from behind Mica. Frightening black energy crackled from the eyeholes of his mask.

That wasn't tech. It was something else far worse, something foul and familiar, and so terrible that even from where she stood, she could feel its icy sting, and her brave warrior soul quailed at the sensation.

"They don't fight like us. They're unnatural."

Now she knew what Zen meant. Overcome with dread, she stepped back, clutching her gun in shaking hands. How could a mere mortal wield the awful necrotic power of a Dreamer? Wreathed in that polluted power, the masked man's visage stretched into a terrible, triumphant smile as he reached a hand toward Mica—

"No!"

Animkii fired her gun, but a jumble of bodies plowed into her from behind, skewing her aim so that the gun's stream of pyrolite sprayed harmlessly overhead. Chunks of flaming ceiling rained down and a couch behind Mica caught on fire, a rusty automaton rushing forward to extinguish the flames with a blast of water. The silver-faced man forced Mica to her knees, his body engulfed in a crackling sphere of energy so intense that Animkii had to turn away from its noxious light.

Terrified, the crowd began to stampede, thundering mindlessly through the thick of battle, tearing the silver-masked man apart from his captive in their rush to safety. It gave Animkii the opening she needed, and she shouldered her massive, armored body through the press of panicked people to reach Mica's side.

"We need to leave!" She tried to grab the other woman.

But Mica didn't move, only stared at the exit with horror. "We're too late."

Animkii glanced over to the entrance and saw a dozen war mods had busted through it, pushing past the broken bar and knocking people away from the room's exit. Shining biosteel sheathed the soldiers from head to toe and the wings of their exoskeletons were folded neatly against their armored backs for better maneuverability in the crowd. One glance and she knew there were no remnants of mortal minds left inside those cold, metal shells. Her heart fell into her stomach. These were fully evolved Gen III mods. Her own fate, if she didn't find a cure.

One mod stepped forward and spoke in a booming, metallic voice, "As per the directive of the Technocracy, we command all occupants of this facility to maintain their current positions." Its glowing white tech-eyes scanned the room with machine indifference, looking for something.

Or someone.

She pulled Mica behind a toppled table for cover, then checked the energy levels left in her stolen gun. A few shots left.

"Friends of yours?" Mica muttered. Despite the snark, the woman looked haggard, beaten, scared, and trying desperately not to show it.

"Not friends. Victims, like I once was," she said, a terrible weariness washing over her as she watched the mods shoot down a man trying to sneak past them. The blast surged through his nerves and shook his fleshy frame so violently that the glass in his hand shattered without a touch. Drool ran down his chin. When the man finally collapsed, Animkii could see that his eyes were still open, blinking slowly.

"They have set their guns to disruption mode," Animkii said.

"Recruiters, then?"

She shook her head, troubled. "The Alphaknot only sends collectors and drones on recruitment assignments, not mods. These mods are acting outside normal protocols."

"Nothing about the last few days has been normal, so why start now?"

Before they could decide how to act, an unexpected roar of fury ripped past their ears. A big shape hurtled out of the crowd and rushed toward the row of mods.

Zen.

Three of the mods turned their fire onto their impulsive attacker. Their seemingly bulky armor was no impediment to movement. It might as well have been weightless—they moved with such natural human grace. But *these* mods weren't using disrupt. Their gunfire struck the hybrid directly in the chest and the wound that had earlier healed now tore anew, sending his blood flying. His ragged cloth shirt burned away in an instant and exposed his magnificent reptilian form to the stunned crowd.

That half of his torso lay hanging in strips of meat didn't seem to faze the hybrid at all. Painless with rage, he charged his assailants with reckless abandon, his gun blasting from one hand and his blade swinging in the other. The gunshot fizzled without harm against his foes' biosteel skin, and he tossed the useless weapon aside, not slowing his rush forward but launching at them with his machete, its blade still stained with Animkii's blood.

Animkii watched in horrified awe.

Even with its wielder's incredible strength, the machete didn't land a single scratch on his foe's biosteel skin, as Animkii knew it wouldn't. Zen switched tactics, a scowl marking his reptilian face as he reversed his weapon's direction, taking its handle in both hands and gouging upwards, hoping to separate armor and deliver internal damage.

This time, the instant the steel of his blade met the biosteel skin of the soldier, it shattered all the way to the hilt.

"Is he insane? Everyone knows normal metal can't damage biosteel," Mica said, gaping.

Foiled, the hybrid stood back and stared at the broken blade with an awful expression on his broad, flat face. He fell to his knees as the continuous gunfire wore away his magnificent strength, blood pooling at his feet as the damage outpaced his regenerative ability. There was no surrender in his eyes. He raised his shattered blade in one last motion—

Then froze, paralyzed by some unseen force.

Through the startled silence of the barroom walked the silver-masked man, his body still wreathed in that insidious black energy. Shattered glass and broken chairs cluttered his pathway, while fading strands of smoke drifted from burn marks on the walls where gunfire had gone astray.

Rather than confront the cultist as a threat, the mods moved aside in deference.

Only the Alphaknot could control mods, and the Alphaknot only took orders from the Technocrats. But this man was no Technocrat.

Animkii exchanged a look with Mica. "Who is that?"

"Calls himself Father Dark. He belongs to the After Cult, followers of some make-believe god called the After Lord. That mask is what their high priests wear."

"You have encountered them before." It wasn't a question.

"Knee-deep in the Sixth City's underground." Mica's face appeared paler than usual, past suffering reflected in her eyes. Her shoulders hunched inward and her whole slight frame seemed to shrink in on itself. "They grabbed me off Under-Zeta's streets, held me prisoner for months. They're the reason Reid and I fled Zeta. They're just like recruiters: They've got a club they want you to join and when they come knocking, they don't take no for an answer." Her terrified eyes were fixed on the mods as they moved deeper into the room. "Back then, I heard rumors that they'd somehow gotten their hooks into the Technocrats, but I didn't believe it. Not until now."

Animkii frowned. "The Technocrats have outlawed religion."

"Yeah, that's why I didn't believe it."

As they huddled there, the masked man called out into the too-quiet room, his voice ringing metallic from behind the mask. "Show yourself, Mica Stone. You *and* your friend. I know you're behind that table. We've sealed all the exits to this place." Silver rippled across that serpentine face like a pool of mercury and from the ever-changing surface emerged a gleeful expression: a fiendish grin curled the scaly lips, and its eye sockets held embers of fire. "Surrender peacefully and we won't have to hurt you."

"Liar," came Mica's trembling whisper.

Animkii had no words of comfort for the cultist's quarry, only raised the nose of her gun to the edge of the overturned table. "Come closer and I will shoot!"

The man laughed at her threat, a sound that shivered the air. "My Lord protects me," he said. He stepped away from the petrified crowd and walked across the room's wreckage with confidence, his robes swishing about his booted feet, his body haloed in that crackling black energy.

Animkii pushed Mica behind her, forming a wall between them. "You speak of the After Lord?" she demanded of the cultist.

"Yes, the Serpent Who Devours Worlds, the Ever God."

All the time the cultist spoke, Animkii busied her mind with tracing their path backward toward escape. In that sea of rubble, there were all kinds of crannies from which they could safely defend themselves, but getting there alive required a strategic retreat. Her biosteel skin would shield *her* from the worst of the gunfire, but not Mica.

"Why does he want Mica?"

The man's voice was calm, as pleasant as an old friend's: "She belongs to Him. And He wants her back."

Mica, always so cynical, now showed genuine horror on her face, and Animkii's heart tightened in sympathy. "Whatever happens, don't let them take me alive," she whispered in a plea.

"Don't talk like that!"

"Promise me!" she cried, launching herself over the toppled table before Animkii could stop her, trying to break through the assembled mods with her slippery, slight body, as if she could just phase through them to the exit. But they were too fast—Animkii could've told her that. One mod lunged forward and seized her by the arm, locking her in its metal grip, so strong she'd need to cut off her own limb to escape.

Animkii fired. What choice did she have, except to try? She wasn't sure how many shots she got in before a stream of gunfire from behind knocked her on her back. A slow burn crept through her artificial nerves and there wasn't enough air left in her lungs to scream. A disrupter. Looks like they wanted Animkii alive, too. Worse than the pain was the paralysis that followed. Half a room away, she saw Mica's form crumpled on the floor.

The masked man seemed more exasperated than angry.

"So stubborn." He shook his head at their failed resistance, then turned to face the assembled mods. "Take the prisoners to the Research Sector in separate transports. The human and the hybrid are to be delivered to District Seven for containment. Turn this defective mod over to Technocrat Eleven for memory analysis."

Research Sector. Ice penetrated Animkii's veins. That death factory was where the Technocrats' scientists had cut open her body and infested her with biosteel. If they ever got ahold of her again, they'd take what little humanity she had left.

Chapter Eleven

Mica had only ever seen Upper-Alpha from outside its pristine protective dome. Now that she was inside the city, she stared at the world beyond the metal crawler's window with begrudging wonder. A gleaming latticework of multi-storied hexagon-shaped buildings sprawled in all directions, the structures interlinked by a network of crystalline conduits.

Despite its utopian beauty, a hint of unease settled in Mica's heart. Sam had called this place a prison, and now she knew why.

There was an unnerving uniformity to the city's design: Architects had quartered Alpha into four precise sectors, with a fifth administrative sector at the center housing the Technocrats and their authoritarian government. The crawler followed a grid of straight, immaculately kept streets that never dared to deviate with a curve or a hill. On all sides, they were enclosed by towering, industrial structures colored a monotonous palette of silver and black. An artificial sun blazed down from a manufactured blue sky. Within this domed wonderland, the dingy gray pollution that poisoned the world beyond was hidden from sight and smell. Yet the purity of the air in this place stung her nose with the sharp stink of antiseptic.

Mica felt like a dirty spot on a white shirt. Having grown accustomed to the cluttered chaos and disorder of undercity life, Upper-Alpha felt stifling to her, suffocating in its rigid orderliness. There were no signs of human life, none of the hustle of daily life back home: no street markets with shouting vendors, no noisy huddles of friends, no children racing in the streets. Trains whizzed back and forth inside the transparent conduits, no louder than a sigh, but she never saw their passengers. Small aircraft flew over their heads, monitoring activity from above.

Eyes everywhere, but none of them were alive. Machines did everything here except think for themselves.

Technocrats reserved humans for other purposes.

An awful dread closed its clawed fingers around her heart. Why had Father Dark sent her here? Why not back to Under-Zeta or to another cult base? Her anxious mind combed through the possibilities. It didn't make sense for the Cult to be working with the Technocrats, but those mods had obeyed Father Dark without question and now she was being escorted through the front doors of the Technocracy's capital. What did it all mean?

With no answers forthcoming, she shrunk back into her seat. The crawler she was sitting in was uncomfortably narrow, with three rows of paired seats crammed together. One mod's shoulder pressed against her, so that she could feel the sharp edge of its exoskeleton against her arm. "You're not exactly designed for compact travel, are you?" she complained, rubbing her arm.

The mod stared ahead with no sign it had heard her speak.

At least Animkii could hold a conversation... But the mod was probably already off being melted down or whatever the Crats did to scrapped tech. She tried pretending she didn't care, but there was an unpleasant knot in her stomach that she couldn't ignore. The last she'd seen of her ally had been a pair of mods hauling her into a crawler exactly like the one Mica was riding in now.

At least Father Dark hadn't accompanied them—that filthy bastard cultist sent shivers down her spine.

"She belongs to Him."

Last time she'd tangled with the After Cult, back in the Sixth City, she'd ended up on a sacrificial altar as an offering to their faceless god, minutes away from being gutted by one of their mad adherents. Had their plans changed?

The vehicle came to a stop and, with no other plan, she willingly surrendered herself into the waiting guards' custody. These guards weren't even mods, but head-to-toe automatons known as drones. The Technocrats weren't much for aesthetics: Their sentries had pairs of bulging round lenses for eyes, their mouths were steel grates, and their elongated heads gave the machines an unnerving alien look. They were mindless creations, programmed to perform specific tasks, and unable to think outside the parameters their masters gave them.

Guess it didn't require much self-awareness to deliver a prisoner.

The possibility of escape flickered in and out of her frantic mind as she walked the long white corridors with her silent metal escorts. But where would she run to? This place was a maze. Walls and doors melted into one another and transvators carried them up and down, left and right, the journey dizzying her mind.

The only stops they made were at security checkpoints that seemed to take longer and longer to pass through the deeper they went into the city. Her nerves began to fray. At the first station, a pair of sentry drones searched her body for anything she could use as a weapon, then snapped an identification collar around her neck that beeped every time the transport passed beneath the omnipresent overhead security scanners.

This was the place Samiel had grown up in: every living and unliving thing accounted for, every movement tracked, every action controlled. No surprise he'd struggled to adjust to life in the unpredictable undercity. Mica had often wondered whether he'd ever be able to show affection, or if his time in the uppercity had left him permanently damaged.

Time had proven her wrong.

A flush crept into her cheeks. They'd saved each other, hadn't they? For a little while, at least. Sam had dragged her kicking and screaming out of her addiction, and she'd forced him to see the world from the eyes of those who'd suffered under the Technocracy.

Where was he now? Was he here in Upper-Alpha? Was he a prisoner too?

There were no shop signs, no indications of location, no visible sign of this 'District Seven' the cultist had ordered her taken to. But why would there be, when even the lowliest of uppercity citizens had their minds linked into that monolithic mind, the Alphaknot, when they could just tap into its knowledge to orient themselves?

Mica realized she was as good as blind, and panic set in. Her breath hitched. There was no way she'd ever find her way out. What were they planning on doing to her? Were they going to turn her into a mod?

A thought occurred to her then, a fleeting moment of sympathy. This dread—was this how Animkii felt, knowing she was going back to this place, back to either becoming a mindless slave for the Technocrats, or being reduced to scrap?

She wondered if mods had nightmares.

Gritting her teeth against the sickening wave of fear, she tried to focus on better times. She thought of the farfetched schemes she and Samiel had planned before it all went wrong, plots to hijack the Alphaknot and sabotage the whole rotten network. For a moment the distraction seemed to work. Despite everything, a small nostalgic smile slipped free. They'd been so close. They could've taken the whole Technocracy down if they'd only stayed together.

Her smile faded. And now they were both paying for her mistake.

At the final checkpoint, she and her guards exited the vehicle and walked through a large pair of steel doors. A moving floor carried her past endless unmarked doorways and windowless corridors and she couldn't help but stare at the few mods they encountered, searching and wondering whether one of them was Samiel. She hadn't seen a single human since she'd arrived in this place.

War mods like Animkii walked the halls like winged steel goliaths, while technologist mods shuffled by, wearing their long coats of navy synthread and nodding their oversized heads. It was the overseer mods that left her the most disturbed—so frighteningly human-looking except for their flat silver eyes that were always watching. None resembled Samiel, but could the Crats have altered him so much that even Mica wouldn't recognize him? The idea terrified her, thinking she might've passed right by the man she loved and never known it.

A final set of doors slid open with a low, sinister hum, ending in what appeared to be an enormous, dimly lit storage room. Towering steel racks lined the cavernous space, reaching at least a hundred feet in the air, each one containing multiple rows of cylindrical cells. The coldness of the room seeped into her skin as she peered inside them, a sickening wave of dread washing over her. This was no regular storage room, but a prison! Inside its cells were revealed the sad crumpled shapes of her fellow inmates—a grim library of test subjects awaiting selection for the Technocrats' vile experiments.

Near the entrance, stood a solitary, isolated cell, a ten-foot-tall rectangular prism with transparent walls. Its door lay ajar, an ominous invitation beckoning her inside. As she stood at the threshold, a surge of panic rushed to her head, and she fought to suppress the terror bubbling up inside her.

Without warning, a guard seized her arm. "Enter the containment unit," it instructed in a voice neither male nor female, but fully machine. There was no anger, no impatience, only the cold efficiency of a machine fulfilling its purpose. It had a job to do, and Mica was impeding it.

Her heart pounded in her chest and her mind raced with thoughts of escape, but the guard's strength overwhelmed her. Before she could act, it shoved her into the cell's confines and sealed the door behind her with an echoing thud. She pressed her hands against the transparent wall and watched helplessly as her escorts departed. A cry of panic gurgled and died in her throat.

From the ceiling far above, a pair of giant metal claws descended and hooked into the top of her enclosure, lifting it into the air. She felt a moment of sheer terror, a feeling of losing control. Her stomach churned as her cell slid across the ceiling until it reached an empty place within a row, the claws fitting her neatly between the other cells there.

Filed away for later, she thought in glum humor as the room's light went dim, filtered out by the surrounding cells.

Had Samiel once lain inside one of these cells? She scanned the gloom around her and despaired. Was he here now? Her neighbors were unmoving lumps of shadow behind plasticine barriers, and she tried tapping on the walls of her own prison to get their attention, but no one stirred. Drugged? Or dead? She couldn't tell. Either way, they wouldn't be any help.

Mica checked her cell for structural weaknesses, fanning her hands out against the cell's surface in search of tech or a flaw she could exploit, but as she moved, the air grew heavier and soon each breath was a weight in her lungs.

So this is what they'd done to the other prisoners. As the gas seeped into the chamber, she pressed her back against the wall, biting into her hand so that the pain would buy her a few more minutes of consciousness, would stave off the numbness that was rapidly spreading through her body. For as long as she could, she fought the sedation, until finally her eyelids drooped to a close and she felt her back sliding down the wall.

Hours seemed to pass as she floated through a gauzy gray world, falling deeper and deeper until she hit the bottom. For a while she lay still in the darkness, eerily at peace.

It ended too soon. Without warning, the weight holding her down at the bottom of this gray ocean of unconsciousness tore away, and she came to the surface with a loud gasp. The film covering her senses lifted, and she sucked in a sudden breath as her mind clawed its way back to reality.

Her eyelids snapped open.

She was still inside the cell, splayed out, facedown, her whole body shaking with the aftereffects of the sedative, a sour taste in her mouth as she looked around her cell, dazed. How much time had passed?

Her clothes were spotlessly clean. Not a speck of dirt or blood remained on her skin and the absence of pain in her jaw and hand suggested they'd used some kind of stim to heal the damage she'd taken from the collector and Dathu's brutes. She lifted a trembling hand to her throat. Her security collar was gone too.

Overhead, the machinery creaked and groaned, jerking her gaze toward the end of her capsule. The giant claw was descending again.

Its pincers closed around her cell, pulling it out of its rack. She peered out the sides to see a familiar dark shape standing below, the silver of his reptilian mask swirling around his features like the eye of a storm, obscuring his expression.

Father Dark.

"Comfortable?" he asked, greeting her with his patronizing, serpentine smile as the container came to a halt in front of him. It dangled in the air for a moment before dropping to the floor. "The Technocrats have truly refined prison management. Controlled sedation to keep inmates docile, nutrient-saturated air, a laser scan that instantly vaporizes waste..."

"Thrilling." She sank to the bottom of her cell and glared out at him, shoving her growing fear back into the darkest pit of her mind. "So since when did the After Cult jump into bed with the Technocrats?"

"Some of us have a shared interest."

"Making the rest of the world miserable?"

Scarlet flames flickered behind the mask's eyeholes, but the metallic voice carried no hint of offense at her intended slight. "To make room for the new, we must scourge away the old. Suffering precedes revolution."

"Still spouting the same old crap, huh? You couldn't make me believe it back then and I still don't believe it now," she said. In her lap, she folded her hands to keep him from seeing how they trembled. "Next time you see High Father Holy, spit in his face for me, will you?"

"That, unfortunately, will not be possible." A sigh echoed behind his mask. "You killed him. Killed a lot of my brethren that night."

"What?" His words stirred a deep, forgotten dread, one she'd buried in the back of her mind with all those other terrible things. She tried desperately to block that emerging memory. Still, it trickled through her mind like a cold sweat down her neck, the memory of the cold marble altar against her back, High Father Holy's hollow-eyed child mask leering down at her as he whispered his foul benedictions, his knife beginning its slide across her throat...

"Kill them," the dark presence whispered inside her mind as she writhed atop the After Cult's unholy altar...

"I don't want to remember this!" she whimpered, cringing back against the cold plasticine walls of her cell. "Please!"

But it was already too late.

Mica opened her eyes to find she was no longer inside her own body, but transported into High Father Holy's broken mind. That voice... it had done something to her! High Father Holy's mind raged against the psychic intrusion, too weak to expel her. A giddy feeling welled up inside as she realized that she was the one wearing the mask now. She was the one in control.

Or was she? Doubt gnawed at her exhilaration. Though she wore the mask, that unsettling presence lurked within her, guiding her with its invisible hands. Through the cult leader's stolen eyes, she watched in horrified awe as white fire erupted around her sacrificial body. The flames left Mica's body unscathed, but the skin of the acolytes holding her down melted like candle wax. They rushed away too late, screaming as their bodies ruptured from the heat of that terrible power, chunks of flesh and gore spraying the altar.

A wicked euphoria coursed through her veins, bolstered by the alien force aiding her. "You wanted blood?" she screamed at the High Father from inside his own body. "Have it, then!"

High Father Holy's skull imploded, collapsing inward, mask and all, his vile pulverized brain leaking out between the cracks like pulp from an overripe melon. In a silence so thick it choked her, her host's tech-ravaged body crumpled to the ground, dead.

She returned to her own mind, no longer a prisoner, the dark voice gone silent. The rush of power and invincibility faded, leaving behind the gruesome aftermath of her unleashed fury. Her limbs began to shake in terror as she beheld the carnage before her. What had she done?! Seized by a mindless panic, she leaped off the stone altar and pushed past the surviving cultists, blindly seeking escape. At any moment, she was certain one of them would grab her, drag her back to the altar, finish the job…

But not one of them touched her. Instead, they kneeled in silent obeisance as she passed, their faces turned up with awe.

"You understand now?" Father Dark's reptilian mouth parted into a smile so wide she could see its fangs, and a phantom breeze rippled the neat black cloth of his robes, even though the room was as still as a grave. "You really don't know how special you are, Mica," he said. "We made mistakes, back in Zeta, ignored signs in our zeal to please our Lord. High Father Holy believed your bloodline was too corrupt to awaken the After Lord. He was wrong."

The memory left her sick with horror and self-loathing. "You damn cultists keep talking about my bloodline like it's something worth dying over. Why?" she demanded, clenching her hands, trying to control the scream rising in her chest. "What's so damn special about it?"

"You're a descendant of Revan, the After Lord's brother, the one who imprisoned our Lord behind the Blood Gate and sought to usurp His power. It was their battle that broke our world a thousand years ago. Only Revan's blood can unlock the Other World and free our Lord, but you are too human to survive long enough to complete the ritual," he explained, his voice soft with patience. "If we don't find a way to yoke it, the power in Revan's blood will consume you the same way it did your father."

Her dead father's wrathful face flashed in front of Mica, his dark hair matted with the filth of the streets, his deranged mouth stretched obscenely as he screamed abuses against his small children, his claw-like hands ready to strike painful blows out of nowhere. His eyes had turned permanently gold from years of addiction to the dream-dust that had consumed every drop of humanity left in him.

"I'm nothing like him!"

To her surprise, the mask softened with what was almost... compassion? "It was too late to save your father," he said. "But let the After Lord ease your transition and you will avoid the same fate."

"Transition to what? Are you going to make me a mod? Is that why I'm here?!" Her fear heightened. "I'll kill myself first."

"Our Technocrat ally has invented a new procedure they believe will stabilize your power and keep you alive longer."

"No way I'm letting a Technocrat touch me. You and your phony god can rot!"

Father Dark had no time to respond. The tapping of footsteps on the graphene floor alerted them to a new presence.

"So *this* is the woman your master wants?" A voice as sharp as a razor sliced through the air. The word 'master' turned Mica's insides to liquid. "It seems she shares my opinion on your religion."

As Mica peered around the black robes of the cultist, her fear heightened and she knew, without question or cynicism, that this wasn't a joke, that this wasn't a hallucination, but one *serious problem*.

Standing in the doorway was a Technocrat. Their golden face had all the expressivity of a plate of metal, the sharp lines etched into its surface forming a disapproving frown.

On the outside, Technocrats resembled human males, with angular jawlines, square shoulders, and flat, muscular chests. But their hairless skin was metallic gold, their limbs were abnormally long, and the sharp edges of their bones formed slightly raised crests on the skin. The resemblance to a man was only superficial, as there were no true sexes among the Technocrats. They were immortal beings and above the type of procreation that lesser species required, lacking the sex organs—both inside and out—required to perform such primitive acts. Most undercity dwellers had only ever seen Technocrats on communications broadcasted to the undercities.

Attracting one's personal attention was bad.

"She'll come around, Eleven," said Father Dark. "She's stubborn, but she's a survivor. When she has no other choice, she *will* comply."

"You're assuming she's going to survive? How sentimental."

Ice picked at Mica's heart. "What're you going to do to me?"

Those impassive eyes glanced back at her, flicking up and down as if examining a distasteful specimen, but instead of answering Mica's impertinence, the Technocrat returned their gaze to Father Dark. "The ready room is prepared for her operation. It should also suffice for *your* part in the procedure."

Mica didn't miss the note of derision.

Interesting. Though they were working together, it seemed the two weren't friends. Maybe she could take advantage of that somehow.

"What about your plans in the north? Are they still proceeding as expected?" the Technocrat asked.

Father Dark smiled. "The harvest continues. Our influence spreads and our armies grow, one soul at a time. When the Blood Gate falls, they will be ready to feast on this world."

"And yet the expeditions I send past the Burning Wall continue to fail."

"The Dreamers permit no passage to outsiders. Those who enter must first dedicate their souls to our Lord's service."

"The mod you brought back to me from Under-Alpha made it across."

"She had extra protection."

They were talking about Animkii! Was she still alive? A flutter of hope stirred inside her.

"If you are lying to me, priest, I will have every one of your cultists hunted down."

"I speak the truth," he said. "You will see." Father Dark pressed a hand against the door to Mica's cell, releasing the locking mechanism.

Mica saw her only chance to escape—no chance at all, but she had to try! With a thrust of her arm, she opened wide the gate of her prison and shoved past her startled captors, running on legs made of jelly, her head still foggy with the sedative, her knees giving out, slammed to the ground by the failure of her own drugged body. Her forehead smacked against the graphene floor and her eyes teared up with pain and frustration.

The same two automatons who'd brought her here picked her up by the underarms and hoisted her back to her feet. With the ferocity of panicked desperation, she kicked and punched and screamed as they pulled her flailing body onto a metal gurney and strapped her limbs to the table, immobilizing her. She felt the cold steel surface of the table through her thread-bare pants and shivered as her panic intensified.

Both captors watched her, one with his unreadable snake mask and burning eyes and the other with an indifference bordering on contempt.

"No matter how inevitable the end, they always struggle against it," Eleven said.

The cultist shrugged. "Humans evolve out of conflict. It's our nature."

"Perhaps necessary in the savage days, when nature was master of the world, but now it is the *Technocracy* that controls evolution."

Mica saw emotion flash across the mask, a hot loathing that simmered inside those hollow sockets. "So you say, but do the Ten know about the kind of evolution *you're* striving for?"

"The Ten care about nothing outside the Game."

"Then let them keep living inside their pretend world, as long as it keeps them distracted from the real one. Convenient for both of us."

"Indeed."

What was all this talk about a game? Something that The Ten, the Technocracy's ruling council, were involved in?

Eleven's rigid face betrayed nothing, but their eyes suddenly grew distant, the pupils enlarging until the blue irises that ringed them disappeared into the blackness. Something had distracted the Technocrat. Their jaw locked, pulling their papery golden skin tight against bony cheeks.

"Is something wrong?"

The Technocrat raised a curt, dismissive hand. "A message. There is an urgent matter I must attend to."

"The procedure—"

"—can wait a few hours longer. The drones will take our subject to the room and prepare her for the operation. I advise you to wait for me there."

Without another word, the Technocrat turned and walked out of the room, the steel-cloth of their pant legs rasping together as they hastened away.

Mica sneered at Father Dark. "You're an idiot to trust a Crat."

But the response wasn't at all what she'd hoped for. With a tender motion, Father Dark brushed the hair back from her eyes and smiled down at her, as if she was a favored child instead of a pissed-off prisoner. He spoke with a gentleness that spooked her. "The After Lord knows *all* about the Technocrats and their delusions," he said. His gloved hand lingered too long, the crisp, clean smell of citrus wafting off it and nauseating her. "After all, He's the one who made them."

Chapter Twelve

A man's voice awakened Animkii. Brisk, warm, deep.

Her eyes wouldn't open and she couldn't move, but she could feel the cold steel restraints shackling her body to a familiar metallic frame. She didn't need to see it. She'd been in this position before: suspended in the air, flat on her back, her body exposed to whatever probing the Technocrats' scientists required. Her mind screamed in silent panic as she remembered her last conscious moments.

Research Sector.

"This is the mod that survived the incident at Fourth City Delta?" There was an answering silence followed by a sharp rebuke. "Speak out loud when we're alone. No psy. I can't stand the silence. It's already too damn quiet around here."

A grinding mechanical voice made a curt protest, "Protocol states—"

"Protocol is what *I* tell you it is." There was a lethal edge to the man's voice now, an authority not to be questioned. "Remember who the master is here."

"Yes, Sixty-Two,"

Sixty-Two? This was no man. A sense of foreboding shivered across Animkii's bare flesh, icy fingers that knuckled into her back and almost made her gasp. The speaker was a Technocrat! One hundred Technocrats existed, never more, never less, and each called by the number that ranked them among their peers. But Technocrats rarely made appearances outside the ivory spire that twisted out from the heart of Alpha. Why was this one showing an interest in Animkii's case?

No good reason.

The droning voice continued with its report. "D-2301 last connected to the Alphaknot seventeen days, five hours, and twenty-two minutes ago. Last logged event indicates that an unregistered projectile weapon struck the subject and delivered enough traumatic force to damage both its biosteel exoskeleton and the internal safeguards protecting its core assets. It destroyed both the main control shard and its redundancy, severing the mod's link with the Alphaknot."

Animkii was nothing but a machine to them. A slow rage was building, siphoning away the terror.

"Organic damage?"

"Difficult to assess, as its local core ceased monitoring system functionality after the initial trauma, but the damage would have been catastrophic according to the estimates in our report."

"Yet it survived."

"We theorize it retained consciousness long enough to activate its critical injury protocol and then redirected all stim resources toward healing."

"Unlikely. Its stim repository was a wreck."

"We generated the theory based on what data we had."

"You lack imagination. You all do."

"We obey our programming. Would you like me to submit a change request?"

"Then it is we Technocrats that lack imagination!" The soft, self-deprecating sneer came as a surprise to the listening mod. "What about recovering its memory? You say the core system monitor ceased functioning after the attack. What about its organic memory?"

"Its cognitive scans came back clear. We should be able to recover its memories without issue. I have transferred the report for your review."

After a moment, the Technocrat spoke again. "Eleven is confident that we'll be able to use its memories to trace the source of the infection?"

"Yes."

Animkii's anger abated. Infection?

The drone continued. "According to the report, the Alphaknot detected the breech at six hours, fifty-two minutes on day five of Second Month. An unauthorized program called Code Whiteout executed with privileged access and infected four thousand nine-hundred and ninety-nine mods from Delta Division. The Alphaknot enacted quarantine measures to prevent the code from replicating itself to units outside the infected division. This unit's link to the Alphaknot was severed prior to the code's propagation, leaving it unaffected."

They were talking about the viral code that had decimated her division! So the Technocrats didn't know its source either.

A wary flicker of hope lit inside her. Animkii had long ago accepted the Technocrats as all-powerful overseers, too far above the regular citizen to tear down, to fight against. No one knew their true nature, only what propaganda told them: Shortly after the breaking of the Earth, they'd emerged into this world to lead humanity out of near-extinction.

Whatever their original intentions, the Technocrats had turned from saviors to tyrants. Humanity had morphed into their grand experiment, an attempt at attaining perfection from their subjects. But somebody had exposed a flaw at Delta. A *big* flaw. An entire division shredded from the inside-out and the Technocrats were clueless...

The frame holding Animkii moved, rotating her onto her side in silence, with none of the squeaks and groans of the underground's archaic tech. Fingers prodded her back.

"I see you already repaired and boosted its repository," the Technocrat said.

"To speed up its recovery and eliminate any possible neural damage that might interfere with the memory extraction. D-2301 has functioned for weeks on an inadequate supply of stims, leaving significant unhealed physical damage." There was a pause. "It also appears the mod enlisted the services of a black-market recycler while in the undercity. The stims we cleansed from its vessels were an impure grade and someone replaced its right arm with obsolete tech. It will take days in a growth chamber to convert the additions to biosteel."

"Given this mod's record of deviance, that seems like a waste of resources. Once I complete the memory extraction, submit an order to nullify it."

Animkii's blood turned cold. Nullification was the process used to break down discarded specimens, dissolving them into a puddle of molecules from which scientists could assemble new abominations.

Sixty-Two's companion disagreed. "The Research Sector's administration has already applied to retain this mod for other projects. It belongs to a primitive variant of humans that inhabits an unchartered territory north of the Burning Wall. The Ten—"

"Yes, I'm aware of the mod's origins," Sixty-Two said, "*and* the challenges that The Ten face finding safe passage to the north. I suppose they plan to dump its brain in a jar and siphon its intelligence until we secure its homeland?"

"The extractor is not a 'jar.' It is advanced tech, capable of—"

"I know what it is," the Technocrat said, the exasperation in their voice too human for one of their kind. "You and the others are dismissed. *I* will perform the memory extraction personally and deliver the results to Eleven."

Animkii's mind was still stuck on the image of her brain floating in some container on a scientist's desk. She almost laughed right there, a terrible bitter laugh, but she crushed it inside her chest. Now was not the time.

There was a significant pause from the Technocrat's assistant, long enough to introduce an unspoken question. But it complied. "As you command, Sixty-Two."

With the dismissal came the sound of footsteps scraping against the graphene floor. Not just the two of them, Animkii realized. The absolute silence of these unseen others disturbed her, knowing any human would've betrayed their presence in a dozen different ways to her warrior senses.

The weight of sedation lifted from Animkii's system, replaced by a tingling sensation that began in her left arm and crept through her body, bringing her organic systems back to life. Now she could feel the warmth of the Technocrat's fingers probing the area around her tech-eye, her skin pulling slightly at their touch. Funny—she'd always imagined a Technocrat's touch would feel as cold as the machines they surrounded themselves with.

Almost four years had passed since the drones stationed at the Burning Wall had pulled Animkii's half-dead body from the End of the World's depths, fending off the abominations that shrieked and raked at the fiery barrier keeping them from the southern half of the world.

No man or beast had ever chilled her blood the way Dreamers did, but these people from the south had come close. The Technocrats twisted humankind's genetic code and traded flesh for machine, just like the humans who'd caused the Sundering a thousand years ago. Even now, people in the north considered those past sins so grave that anything belonging to that ancient world was taboo. Never again would they put themselves above Creation.

In her northerner's mind, the Technocrats' world had seemed a bastion of corruption threatening to consume her soul every moment she spent trapped in it. And she hadn't been wrong. First City Alpha had been a hostile and alien place, filled with towering graphene buildings, sterile streets, soundless transports, and dead-eyed citizens. The smell of steel and chemicals stung her mortal nose and stole the smell of pine sap and grassy fields from her memory. But the true horror had awaited her in the Research Sector's District Six, a place dedicated to biotech integration, where teams of indifferent scientists churned out all manner of horrendous creations.

For weeks, the Technocracy's scientists had quarantined her there, interrogating their subject until they'd exhausted their curiosity. They'd taken samples of blood, tissue, and anything else that interested them from her body, and filled her with chemicals to keep her pliant. Once satisfied they'd taken all they could, they'd handed her off to be modified, confident that connecting her to the Alphaknot would reveal anything else she'd hidden from them.

They'd cleaned out her head, then filled it back up with whatever they wanted. She despised herself for how easily they'd taken her mind.

She felt the fingers probing her face withdraw. When she heard the shift of cloth and footsteps moving away, she risked opening her eyes, narrowing them to slits just large enough to see through. And regretted it an instant later when a wave of nausea crashed into her skull, pulling her stomach into her throat. She swallowed hard and kept her warrior's composure. Through doubled vision, she watched the Technocrat glide through the laboratory, their back turned to Animkii.

A bleak nostalgic horror swept over her as she scanned her surroundings. Against one wall stood twenty tanks filled with blue liquid, each containing a naked human specimen, prospective mods undergoing the first phase of modification: provisioning. Tubing covered their bodies, feeding them special nutrients and stims to prepare them for the second phase, integration.

During her own integration, they'd drugged her so deeply that she remembered little about the operations that had followed, including the one that had shackled her to the Alphaknot. She'd only learned later what they'd done. Most potential mods died on the operating table, unable to withstand the shock of integration, of having their organic components replaced with tech.

If the subject survived the surgeries, the technologists would implant two fingernail-sized 'shards,' one sliver embedded in the frontal cortex of the brain and a secondary one at the base of the spine. These tiny bits of tech forged the connection to the Alphaknot, the monstrous hive mind that controlled every piece of tech in the Technocracy.

Before biosteel, integration had been an imperfect science. The second generation of mods, while an improvement over their archaic predecessors, still harbored a trace of humanity despite their makers' tireless efforts to quell it. Several times during those long years, Animkii's humanity had broken free from its prison, a stray memory or an independent thought sneaking past her programmed conditioning. Swift to recognize such deviations, the Alphaknot would promptly dispatch her back to District Six for reconditioning.

Only with the advent of biosteel and the emergence of a third generation of mods had true control over the human mind become possible. Consequently, the Technocrats had introduced a new and final incubation phase, a phase that Animkii had only partially completed thanks to Delta's insurgency.

Her gaze drifted to a bank of fist-sized biosteel hearts shelved nearby, each organ sitting in its own glass sphere, grown from a tiny sample of biosteel and only waiting for a new human host. A visceral chill coursed through her at the sight. Each heart was a seed of modification and, once planted, sprouted an intricate network of artificial vessels and nerves, beginning the slow process of absorbing its host's entire body. She had one of them inside her right now, barely two months old, throbbing like an actual biological heart, pushing the stew of blood and chemicals through her body and spreading its biosteel tendrils.

Once the techs had implanted the biosteel, they'd transferred her to a growth chamber located inside a warehouse containing a thousand other mods just like her. By then, she was barely conscious of anything else but the hum and buzz of the Alphaknot's voices in her head. It was a blissful union with that shared mind—no fear, no pain, just readiness and obedience.

Inside the growth chamber, the biosteel infested the outer layers of the body, armoring the skin and thickening the muscles so that they could absorb incredible amounts of damage beyond what even natural steel was capable of, yet still remain as pliant as flesh. Gone was the assembly line of surgeries required for the pre-biosteel models. The rest of the body would continue to evolve as the biosteel slowly consumed every inch of flesh and bone and steel inside its host, ending at the brain.

But biosteel modification was still in its infancy. Only two other divisions had undergone the lengthy conversion from Gen II to Gen III. It was a time-consuming and resource-intensive process, and still heavily monitored for aberrations that might lead to system-wide issues.

The Research Sector's director should never have approved releasing Delta Division from their growth chambers so early: the mods were half-formed, their biosteel absorption incomplete, their bodies a patchwork of old generation and new.

But that meant Animkii still had time to stop the infection. Maybe even reverse it.

If she could escape.

Animkii identified a few potential exit points. Past a neighboring pod, four steel doors lined the wall: transvators that could carry her almost instantly to any vator port in the city.

She could use them to reach District Seven and find Mica.

And what then? District Seven was off-limits to all but the Technocrats and their most mindless tech slaves, and the surveillance in this place could pick the thoughts out of your head if you were a mod. They'd catch her before she even set foot there.

Or would they? Animkii was still a mod, but without functional shards the Alphaknot was blind to her location. Yet, without that connection to the central mind, she'd never be able to navigate her way through this steel maze of rooms and hallways. Could she even activate a transvator without a working shard?

At this rate, she doubted she could save herself, let alone her friend.

Friend? Is that what Mica was? A strange warmth filled her chest as she recalled Mica mending her broken body, providing her the stims required for her survival. This woman who professed to hate mods had saved her with nothing obvious to gain for herself. Even if Mica's motivations weren't entirely altruistic, Animkii couldn't abandon her to these monsters. She knew all too well the horrors of imprisonment under the Technocrats.

Sixty-Two let out a loud sigh, the humanity of the sound snapping Animkii's attention back to the Technocrat. They were alone, now, Animkii and Sixty-Two. As the Technocrat turned their head, Animkii quickly closed her eyes and stilled her breath.

"Don't bother. I know you've been conscious this whole time," Sixty-Two said in a quiet voice. "My senses are as good as yours, Mod."

Animkii's mouth went dry with fear, but she opened her eyes. It was unnerving to see a Technocrat up close like this, so human-looking but also so alien, with their metallic skin and the bony protrusions that sharpened their features. Their golden head was bald, except for a thick swath of black, wet-looking hair that grew from the top-center of their head and continued down the curve of their spine, disappearing beneath the collar of their blue steel-cloth coat. Their eyes were the brilliant shining blue of a northern sky, but as cold as an ice-capped winter lake.

"You've been disconnected from the Alphaknot long enough to have recovered your memories and your human emotions, I imagine," her captor said, dropping the authoritarian air they'd displayed with their mod assistant and sighing again. They pulled out a syringe filled with a pale-green fluid. Animkii felt the warmth of their hand as they rotated the platform she was strapped onto, positioning her body for an insertion into her stim repository. "This won't hurt. I only programmed these viruses to delete memories. Afterward, you won't remember a thing about this exchange. Or anything else."

"Then let me go afterward. I can do you no harm."

"I can't take the risk. This is the best option for both of us. Better for you to forget that you were ever human," they assured her. "There isn't much left of you anyway, and the stims I've topped you up with will only act as accelerants to the biosteel. I've seen the scans. Only about twenty-five percent of you remains organic."

"Even if it was *one* percent, I would want the chance!"

"What I need to accomplish is far more important than your life. I'm sorry."

But before the Technocrat could start the injection, the sound of steel whistled against the air, followed by a pained gasp and the sound of a body striking the suspended exam table, rotating it back into a horizontal position in time for Animkii to witness Sixty-Two collapsing to their knees. The syringe rolled across the floor, spilling its viral contents.

"You've grown too predictable, Sixty-Two."

Animkii rolled her gaze to the opposite side of the room as a stern figure emerged from the first of the four transvators, their body frame despising the slightest movement, their gaunt golden face carved into a look of judgment. A pair of armored war mods flanked the newcomer, their blinking eyes the only sign of life behind their metal masks.

Another Technocrat. Her feeling of unease deepened.

"Eleven." Sixty-Two's greeting was too steady, too cool under the circumstances. Their fingers clenched into fists as they tried to shake off whatever they'd been hit with. Sedative? Or a poison? What roiled in the air between this pair went beyond tension. A noose was being closed around someone's neck.

"I suppose one of the mods I just sent away was your spy?" Sixty-Two asked.

"The Ten will no longer tolerate your disregard for the rules."

"Since when have our superiors condemned scientific curiosity? Don't you think the Ten would be interested in knowing how a single mod survived the destruction of the rest of its division?"

"I think the Ten would be more interested in hearing why you contaminated the Alphaknot and sabotaged Delta Division. Why you betrayed your own kind."

Animkii contained her shock.

Sixty-Two's guilt was difficult to deny, their golden countenance twisting as they pressed their back against the base of the exam table. "You have no proof." They labored to breathe, a sheen of sweat covering their metallic skin.

Eleven smiled, a snake's smile that stretched too wide on their thin-skinned face. "But I *do*. I knew you would come here to erase the evidence, so I retrieved this mod's memory immediately after it arrived in the city. This isn't an accusation; it's a condemnation. The Ten have already ordered your containment while they decide your punishment. Though I think we both know what *that* will be."

The two mods accompanying Eleven stepped forward.

Sixty-Two didn't fight, though their body was tight with the readiness of it, nor did they surrender immediately. Animkii wanted to yell at them, to tell them to put a fist through the other Technocrat's chest, to do something other than stand there, yet the flicker of rebellion that crossed their face stilled her voice. With stubborn will, the subdued Technocrat gripped the edge of Animkii's exam table, using it both as leverage to stand and then as a support to lean against. Out of Eleven's sight, their fingers brushed against one of Animkii's shackled hands, pressing something small and hard against her palm.

Animkii saw a flash of metal, a tiny bead caught between the Technocrat's thumb and index finger. A mite? But why? Without knowing the answer, she closed her hand around it.

Sixty-Two stepped toward the mods in apparent surrender, but before they could take the traitor into custody, the Technocrat's golden lips bowed with a knowing smile and their eyes closed to focus on something only they could see. The mods froze as the room lights flickered overhead and the buzz of working tech fell silent.

"You should've disabled my access before coming here," the dissident said, showing no signs of agitation, accepting their sentence with remarkable composure. But there was knowledge in those eyes, and a very human look of self-satisfaction flickered across their golden face. "It will take you at least *a couple of hours* to unravel the damage I just caused."

Animkii's heart jolted. A couple of hours? She was sure they'd said that for *her* benefit, to make sure she knew exactly how long she had to get out of this place. This mite they'd given her—? She gripped the tiny bead tightly.

Eleven made a disparaging noise as the lights flickered back on and nearby devices resumed the vibration of normal activity. "Your access privileges are now revoked. All you have done is incriminate yourself further. The Alphaknot is already back online, and your pitiful interference has accomplished nothing."

"Has it?"

The question teased the air as the mods escorted their prisoner from the room. Eleven followed behind, their face pinched with satisfaction as the door to the transvator opened and swallowed them whole. They left Animkii strapped to the exam table, the last remaining obstacle to her freedom.

Then the cuffs of her bindings snapped apart.

Sixty-Two's unraveling had begun.

Chapter Thirteen

For what felt like an eternity, Mica waited in silence, strapped onto the metal gurney, shivering from both the biting cold and overwhelming fear. The steel walls of the ready room enclosed her in stark, sterile confinement, leaving her staring up at a ceiling so distant she imagined it was the dull, polluted skyline outside Alpha.

She had expected some kind of examination room, one stocked with tables and medical supplies and a crew of attendant mods, but the only things here besides herself and her escorts were a small mobile station loaded with vials of colorful chemicals and a canister full of unpleasant-looking tools she guessed to be surgical instruments.

How they'd gotten here remained a puzzle to her. District Seven was no more clearly mapped than the previous areas she'd passed through. She'd tried finding landmarks to use for plotting an escape route, but every hallway looked identical, with only the occasional doorway or transvator to break up the monotony.

"Your friends don't have much imagination," she'd told Father Dark.

"Those connected to the Alphaknot don't see what we do." His voice had echoed in the empty steel halls as he accompanied her gurney through the maze, his silver mask devoid of any discernible emotion. "They see a personalized holographic overlay."

She'd wondered what a Technocrat would want to see. Corpses stacked ceiling-high?

Their mute automaton escorts had soon stopped at what appeared to be a dead-end. But as they stood before the steel wall, its surface shimmered and disappeared, revealing their destination, then reforming behind them after they'd entered the room.

Her thoughts drifted to something Samiel had told her years ago, about the Technocrats' experiments on demolecularization, how it was easy to break down matter and even to re-use the resulting components in other projects, but to *rebuild* an object was so prone to errors that scientists could only do it under tightly controlled conditions and never on living creatures.

Doubt you'd get more tightly controlled than this place, she thought bitterly.

Her eyes darted around the ready room. This new prison offered no hope of escape—no doors or windows to break free from her captors' clutches. A sense of hopelessness washed over her. Once they'd gotten away from that stone-faced Technocrat, she'd hoped to trick Father Dark into revealing something helpful. But the man who'd been so talkative back in the holding room had fallen into a grim silence. He'd acted as if he hadn't heard Mica's questions, and once the drones had shoved the gurney against a wall, he'd stepped away from her and into the center of the barren room, kneeling to pray to his abominable god.

Hours later, and he was still there, his murmured devotions sending a shiver through her body.

Reality sank in and desperation tightened its grip on her heart. The After Cult really believed she had some kind of power. They'd gone to such lengths to capture her. But why were the Technocrats involved? Religion was offensive to them; they'd long ago supplanted any gods as the ultimate authority in their world. Surely, they didn't believe in this Cult business.

As she lay there, absorbed in her thoughts, the lights overhead flickered and died, and darkness swallowed the room.

What now? A glimmer of hope stirred.

From both sides of the gurney, she heard the jarring sound of metal crashing against the floor. The drones, she guessed. It sounded like they'd fallen, but she couldn't see a damn thing.

Heart pounding with excitement, she craned her neck, squinting in the darkness for clues to this new circumstance. A black-market recycler like Mica knew the Alphaknot's systems were too important to not have fail-safes in place. Even the worst outages should've gone unnoticed as redundant systems flawlessly picked up from where a failure left off. For this fortress of tech to have even the most insignificant of drops meant something, somewhere, had gone catastrophically wrong.

If the wall they'd passed through had dematerialized, if she could get out of her restraints and reach it...

But her optimism came too early. Within a minute, power returned, flooding the room in stark white light. Her automaton guards straightened back up into their defensive positions. The hope that had flickered to life died just as fast, replaced by a yawning darkness. Father Dark remained kneeling on the floor in a position of servility, seeming oblivious to the event, too focused on whatever mad meditations rambled through his head.

What was she hoping for, anyway? Dissidents bursting through the wall to mow down her captors? It was a futile, childish dream to think she was getting out of here. Whatever had happened, it was done, and she was still stuck here with no plan of escape. All she had left were mistakes she'd never get to fix. And the longer she lay here trying not to dwell on her future, the more those old pains crept back into her heart.

Maybe she deserved this. She was the one who'd got them all killed: Mom and the boys because she'd trusted Pandora too much, Reid because he'd protected her from the collector, and then Samiel...

Did she get Sam killed too? She'd left him behind to rot in the depths of the undercity with nothing to protect him but his lofty ideals and an intelligence too refined to be of use in the real world. She could only imagine his look of exasperation at finding her stuck in another mess of her own making. Samiel had been the brain of their relationship, and Mica the heart. Reid had never really understood that bond, had told her Samiel was filling her head with impossible dreams.

But she'd needed those dreams back then. Otherwise, there were just the nightmares.

A shudder came over her. If Samiel was dead, then what was left to live for? But she couldn't let herself think like that. She didn't know for sure he was dead. There was still hope of finding him if she came through this ordeal alive, though she didn't know what condition she'd be in. Were they going to modify her like Animkii or twist her body into a beastly hybrid like the lizardman in Dathu's fighting pit? Would they leave anything human left for Samiel to recognize? In a burst of fear and frustration, she pulled at her bindings and twisted her body against the restraints.

It wasn't a fight she had time to win. The hidden wall across the room dissipated once more, and the tall, gaunt figure of Eleven drifted into the room, their unsmiling mouth stretched taut and yet somehow still conveying a predator's satisfaction with its gory meal.

The Technocrat came to a halt beside Mica's gurney and the acrid stink of chemicals wafted off their biosteel coat. Mica's chest tightened with anxiety and her breath came quick as a new terror washed over her.

Father Dark at last opened his eyes, though he never moved from his kneeling position. His voice was tense with excitement. "We can proceed now?"

"Yes. My business is complete. There was an unexpected complication, but I have dealt with it," they said in a flat, detached voice. "You have communed with your 'god'?"

"He is ready." Slowly the cultist rose and walked over to where Eleven stood, his silver face lit with feverish anticipation. Mica's breath hitched as she sensed the imminent danger closing in on her.

"Then I will begin the procedure."

At an unheard command, one drone pulled her gurney out from the wall, while the other situated the surgical station beside it for easy access. A fine mist descended on the room—some kind of sterilizing agent, she guessed—and when it dispelled, a drone seized her left arm and shoved something thin and sharp into it. She gasped with pain as a freezing fire spread out from the wound and filled her body with ice.

Eleven looked down at her with a look on their face that suggested a foul smell in the air, but the expression blurred as Mica's vision faded. The cultist spoke, but his words sounded muffled, as if they were coming from underwater.

"What'd you do to me?" Her voice trembled, and her tongue felt too thick to fit in her mouth.

"I have injected you with a carrier virus. It's programmed to deliver a very special set of bio-materia into your body, where it will merge its genetic material with your own," Eleven said.

"You're making me into some kind of hybrid?" Panic surged through her as she envisioned the twisted shapes that dwelled in the undercity, part-human, part-something else.

"Nothing so crude." Father Dark placed his hand over hers in an unnerving act of reassurance, his silver face looming overhead, the only distinct thing she could make out from the bleary shadows. "This is a *unique* strain."

The ceiling overhead spun in a colorless blur. Pain filled her head with icy fire and when she screamed, she couldn't hear her own voice, only feel the agony of her jaw stretching past endurance. Her muscles turned to water, leaving her weak and trembling while warm urine gushed between her legs, adding to her humiliation and vulnerability.

Whatever was happening coursed through her like a toxin. Agony clenched her hands into fists and blinded her vision. *Crack!* A violent force jackknifed her spine. Every bone in her body felt like it shattered, turning her body into pulp.

Through teary eyes she watched—*felt*—the tearing of her skin, blood spilling free as the blood vessels in her arms ruptured, wet and warm and stinking, and she fought her restraints until she'd worn her wrists raw, and the skin was slick with her own life fluid.

Countless images flooded Mica's mind, the sudden stimuli ripping her free from the pain. A thousand dreams and potentials swirled through her floating consciousness. She dreamt of freedom from the Technocracy's iron grip, juxtaposed against a world smothered in steel and tech. Visions of lush, verdant lands brimming with life stood in stark contrast to a dead world strewn with corpses. And in the end, empty dreams of nothing at all but silence.

These didn't belong to her! Where were they coming from?

Detached from her imprisoned body, she drifted in and out of these visions, moving through them in a slow haze, absorbing everything. Dreams, memories, stray thoughts... the ramblings of a thousand minds and not one of them hers. Mica was a trespasser, but in whose minds was she lurking?

Did it matter? The pain was gone. She gathered the stolen thoughts like a blanket around her, insulating herself from the real world—that world where Mica's body still writhed in agony, a bloody mass on a steel table.

"Eleven!" The cultist's metallic voice was so close and yet so distant. "What's happening to her?"

"I warned you this might happen. Her body can't handle the transformation, just like the others."

Others? Her consciousness stirred, and she hung onto their words.

"But your other test subjects were full humans! You claimed her bloodline was the key. She's dying!"

"Then we've disproved the theory."

"No!"

"Stand back from the subject or I'll have the drones restrain you," Eleven said.

Mica couldn't see what was going on, her mind blindly clutching at this safe place, a place without pain, a place without these sadists, but then—

The images wouldn't stop, kept multiplying, coming at her faster and faster, impossible to hold down, filling her too rapidly. She was inside those dreams, and they were inside her, consuming her sanity, thousands of minds that stretched out far beyond this room or even this city: a pregnant woman on the undercity streets dreamed of fresh fruit and expensive sweets, a boy clad in animal skins raced through a winter forest to spear a great antlered beast, a citizen in Alpha fought nightmares about enduring her scheduled modification…

And then there were stranger dreams, dreams she didn't understand at all.

They showed a world full of towering concrete cities, where people died by the millions, felled by a disease that only a few had an immunity to, a few that held a terrible secret.

"Stop!" She struggled against her restraints, every breath a gasp. "Get out! GET OUT!"

From outside her unraveling mind, she heard Eleven's excited voice. "It's working! Look—her blood!"

The dreams splintered, grew incoherent as her mind fell apart. Pictures flashed through her mind, too rapid to grasp: a mountaintop breaking through the haze of pollution outside a distant city, grains of sand pushed between toes on a warm beach, an enemy's blood splattered against a petrified tree…

She wasn't just seeing these thoughts; she was *living* them. She was a modified scientist; she was a hybrid prostitute; she was a starving orphan feasting on cave rats. Every breath in the world, she breathed; every heart that beat throbbed in her chest. It all fell on her at once and, for a moment, she teetered between sanity and madness.

She was everything but Mica.

"She's dying! His materia is too much. Stop the procedure!" the cultist demanded.

"It is too late."

Outside her besieged mind, Mica grew aware of the warm blood pooling beneath her on the table, that it was oozing from every orifice.

I'm dying, came the realization.

This wasn't a nightmare, not this time. Reid wasn't about to walk through the door and save her. She hovered between the reality that contained pain and the place that held a million dreams, thrashing against her bindings on the gurney so violently that the drones had to hold the table down. When she could struggle no longer, she stared at the two responsible for her condition, stared into their minds and among the millions of other thoughts—she saw what they hid from others.

What she saw was her brother's death, relived through the eyes of another. Just flashes of pictures, jumbled incoherent thoughts out of context; whispered evocations to the After Lord; a serpent mask melting into a pool of silver that expanded and gave birth to a collector; a glimpse of her dead brother's face right before the acid hit. But Reid's face wasn't right. It looked wrong, distorted, as if viewed through a dirty lens. Then there was the sound of her own anguished cry heard from another's memory as the collector's acid breath covered everything, but it wasn't horror she felt. It was a rush of satisfaction, of triumph obtained! *"It worked!"* came the murderer's thought. A scream wrestled itself out of her throat and her heart heaved like an iron ball in her chest.

"You!" Fury filled her and the masked man recoiled as her psychic fingers tightened their grip on the scattered images, trying to pull them together, trying to make sense of them, only to have them slip away and disappear into the storm of other people's memories. She lacked the control needed to bring them back. "I saw it, you bastard, you cultist piece of crap! You were there! *You* sent the collector that killed my brother!"

Father Dark let out a strangled gasp, falling to his knees as if caught in an invisible chokehold.

An icy white energy wreathed Mica's fingers as they trembled with murderous temptation, clenching and unclenching. It was happening again! Memories of the power she'd wielded the night she'd escaped the Cult tumbled through her mind: how she'd made blood boil, flesh combust, and minds explode. It was like something inside those people had responded to the fear and hatred frothing inside her, and that voice inside her head had turned her rage into a weapon. She could hear the pounding of a heart in her ears—not hers, but Father Dark's—racing toward death.

"I'm going to kill you!" she screamed.

Outside her fury, an unseen hasty hand jammed another needle into her arm, disrupting her grip on the cultist's mind, and before she could regain it, a sedative drowned her mind, slowed it, and though she struggled to burst free, to wreck vengeance on Father Dark, the chemical tide pulled her back under.

"Remarkable," Eleven said as the power withdrew.

Mica's memories quieted, churning slowly now in her mind. She lifted her gaze to the Technocrat and caught a final, fleeting memory—a child floating inside a liquid-filled containment unit.

She opened her mouth to ask, but her consciousness was already sinking into a river of liquid peace. The other memories were still there, but distant. As she settled back into reality, she ground her teeth together, feeling sharp pins of icy pain pushing into her damaged body and a deathly chill sinking into her skin. The blood was drying now. She could feel it cracking on her limbs, could smell it and taste it, saw the furrows where her skin had burst open. The blood inside the wounds was as black as tar, and her skin was too white.

Just like her parents and brothers and neighbors nine years ago, their bodies corrupted by the plague that took them one-by-one, just like her own body when she hung between life and death, bleeding out on the floor of her mom's shop.

Black veins beneath white skin. Twigs, trapped beneath the ice.

Had they reinfected her with the sleeping plague?

Her brother's murderer stood on shaky legs, one hand gripping the wall for support, while the other rubbed at his throat. His breath was harsh, his words a rush of fanaticism. "We must start the ritual immediately! Do you feel it? The After Lord approaches!"

As he uttered the words, a terrible sensation crept over her, something more dreadful than pain alone, a familiar dark sentience invading her mind. She knew it now. She'd felt it down at the bottom of Under-Alpha, felt it again at the sacrificial altar when it had spoken into her mind and urged her to kill its own followers. It was like a persistent gnawing ache inside her bones, or an invisible hand squeezing the blood from her heart, like holding her breath too long or falling off a precipice into a bottomless pit. It felt like one of her nightmares.

"Your presence draws Him here!" The enraptured cultist raised his arms to the ceiling, swaying with exultation. "You mustn't fight Him."

"You're insane," she said. "I won't do anything to help you!"

"Not even if I tell you where your friend Samiel is?"

The world disappeared, sucked away in a vacuum. She couldn't speak for a moment, her mouth moving without sound, until she at last expelled her shock. "How did you—"

"The After Lord knows all about you, Mica. Every little detail of your life. Even the regrettable bits."

She felt sick, used, stupid.

"Where is he? What have you done with him?!"

"He's alive," the cultist said, his mask's fanged mouth widening with a grin, knowing he'd beaten her. "And if you want him to stay that way, you'll cooperate."

Alive! her inner voice trumpeted. If Samiel was alive, then she could survive anything. But mistrust quickly replaced elation, and her eyes narrowed with suspicion.

"Prove it, you lying sack of shit."

From his robes, he produced a necklace. Two rings dangled from a fine silver chain, one polished to a simple smooth sheen, the other resembling a braid of wildflowers long-extinct except in ancient books. A lump grew in her throat and she strangled a sob.

"Exchanging rings was a symbol of love and commitment in Old World traditions." Sam's soft-spoken words brought her back to the night before she'd left Under-Alpha. He'd held out the ring of flowers, his stilted, too-formal mannerism tinged with an intensity she'd never seen from him before. *"Do you believe me now, that I love you?"*

Mica had dashed the ring at his feet.

After everything that'd happened, after all she'd done, he'd kept them.

She squeezed her eyes shut. "You win," she said to Father Dark, husky-voiced. "What do I have to do?"

"Simply enter the Dream. The After Lord will do the rest."

Chapter Fourteen

Animkii pinched the tiny steel bead between her thumb and index finger, nervous energy coiling in her chest as she stood before the transvator. Once activated, the mite would burrow into the skin, marking her as a legitimate citizen of the Technocracy, granting her access to sectors and services—including the Alphaknot's resources. By law, all unmodified citizens were required to have one.

Why had Sixty-Two given her this mite, and what had been its original purpose?

These questions worried her, but she didn't have the time to stand there and ponder. Hastily dressed in a lab coat that strained against her enormous form, she knew anything half-intelligent that spotted her would raise an alarm, never mind that a quick scan by the most mindless of automatons would reveal her destroyed shards and mark her as a rogue.

But even if her control shards were operational, they wouldn't have given her the authorization to travel outside this room by herself. Which left the mite. She fingered the bead again, thinking. What if it set off an alarm and brought the entire building's security force down on her?

Better than freezing up like a frightened rabbit. She hated the way this place, this entire city, made her feel—like a bug under a glass. The sooner she got out of here, the better. She slapped the mite down against the back of her neck, feeling a tickle as the bead sprouted tiny legs and pinched the skin, vibrating as it worked its way beneath the surface, the flesh sealing back over it afterward. Not a drop of blood. The skin healed as fast as the mite burrowed. A tingling sensation hummed across her nerves as the mite's intelligence assumed control over her local core and connected it to the Alphaknot.

>CONNECTION TO ALPHA ESTABLISHED

<<EXECUTE CODE INCOGNITO>>

<<ALPHA /CHGACCESS UNRESTRICTED ALL>>

Her head jerked in surprise. It'd been weeks since she'd last heard the Alphaknot's synchronized voices, and she could feel their authority weighing back down on her mind, suffocating her will. Could they sense her presence? Had she exposed herself? How soon until the guards arrived to take her into custody? She tensed herself for a fight she couldn't win.

But there was no fight coming. It took a panicked second, but she soon realized that the connection she felt was only one-way. She could access the Alphaknot's system, but the Alphaknot couldn't sense her.

Incognito.

She relaxed, closing her eyes in human habit as her mind sparked with the information she was looking for. A full schematic of the Research Sector, its districts, and its zones unfolded to reveal every detail of buildings, rooms, and security points. The knowledge came to her just like it always had before, in the days before her link to the great mind had been severed, and a powerful longing overcame her.

With this renewed connection came the realization of how precious a gift the Technocrat traitor had given her—access to the Alphaknot, but without the chains. With this kind of access, someone with Mica's tech knowledge might cause real havoc, but someone with a Technocrat's knowledge could take down the entire system.

Is that what Sixty-Two had intended? A shiver ran through her at the thought. If the rogue Technocrat had remained undetected, as invisible to the Alphaknot as Animkii now was, what more could they have destroyed? With a terrible dread, she recalled the fatal battle at Delta and the incinerated bodies of her mindless comrades strewn across the city's ruins like wind-blown rubbish.

But why would Sixty-Two betray their own kind?

The Fire Bones reviled traitors as much as they did murderers. Survival in the Witherlands hinged on the clans acting as a collective, and treason threatened to disrupt and dismantle that unity. A people that fought within itself grew weak, and those who were weak died in the Witherlands.

While she grappled with the mystery of Sixty-Two's treason, her consciousness remained anchored to the Alphaknot, drifting like a ghost through the familiar corridors of the vast, sprawling psy network. It was like her shards had reactivated, except the mite removed all barriers to knowledge and granted access to the network's master controls. Her vision washed the empty, sterile walls of the room in a blue-gray hue and marked them with identifiers that'd been invisible to her disconnected mind. Now she could go anywhere she wanted. With only a thought, she triggered the transvator's metal doors to slide open and gave it a destination.

District Seven.

She balked for a moment. With this privileged access and just a touch of caution, Animkii could simply walk out of Upper-Alpha into freedom, untouched. Why risk everything for someone who hated her? Mica was no friend.

In contrast, she thought of Ziiba and how much she missed the warm laughter and carefree spirit of her oldest friend, sometimes-rival, and sometimes-lover. Mica couldn't have been more her opposite—abrasive, distant, and judgmental. Yet in the undercity, Mica had saved her life, forging an uneasy bond between them, one she couldn't easily abandon. She owed Mica a life debt. And despite what the Elders might say, she remained, at her core, Fire Bones.

She rode the transvator across the Research Sector, through the labyrinth of streets and buildings, her body prickling with fear and apprehension. Her mind picked through the sector's psychic map, noting every building, every room, and every obstacle, planning her every move in anticipation of trouble ahead. When the transvator came to a gentle stop, Animkii already knew what she'd find waiting.

She stepped out onto a steel plaza and stood at the foot of a massive, windowless tower built of gleaming black rock. District Seven was a misnomer, for the 'district' only contained this one building: an imposing fortress brimming with Technocrat secrets.

Looming over its entrance was an eight-foot drone, its empty silver eyes holding the soul of a machine as it scanned the transvator for threats. Animkii held her body as straight and tight as a bowstring and not a breath left her lips, only to find that she no longer needed the air. So that was gone too. Breathing was now another leftover human instinct, like blinking or scratching an invisible itch.

But this was no time to mourn her humanity.

Every weapon inside her body activated at a thought. A dozen little metal flaps opened like shot wounds across the surface of her biosteel chest, invisible beneath her borrowed lab coat, while tiny-but-lethal explosives manufactured themselves inside her machine gut, ready to be projected from several openings on her body. The launcher embedded in her left forearm hummed with readiness, a silent promise of firepower at her disposal.

It was fortunate that Sixty-Two's assistant had refilled her stims. Animkii's enhanced senses picked up every faint noise, each shadow cast in the corner of her vision, heightening her awareness of potential threats. At the base of her neck, she felt the warmth of her energy net surging to life and her biosteel armor hummed as the detachable blades on the sides of her thighs charged, each one capable of sending a paralyzing bolt from sixty feet away.

But her inner core murmured its disapproval at finding her arm's boom cannon replaced by Pandora's ill-fated limb, its barrage of queries reaching a dead end. Clearly not designed for combat, Pandora had been rebuilt using spare parts from older generations. The archaic steel prosthetic provided nothing in the way of weaponry; it was simply an arm, a strong one that she flexed in testing, but nonetheless just an arm.

Animkii grimaced. She wasn't worried about winning this fight. Any of her weapons could down an automaton in seconds. But pulverizing a guard would flag the Alphaknot's sensors and prompt an investigation. So, she waited.

The drone made no signs of aggression, only looked straight at her with a blank stare. Like she wasn't even there. Animkii stepped closer and waved a hand in front of its face. It didn't react.

Sixty-Two had done more than free Animkii. They had broken Alpha's security system! Could that little mite really do all that? The thought left her breathless from awe. Or had Sixty-Two activated something else in their last few moments of freedom? She remembered that brief flicker of light and how Sixty-Two had seemed so certain of the damage they'd left behind.

Whatever the Technocrat had done, it wouldn't last forever. She stepped outside the transvator and inched around the guard, stepping into the entrance behind it, feeling exposed. This was nothing like stalking the forests back home in search of a good hunt.

Inside the building, closed metal doors lined the halls, and between each set of doors stood other automatons. Just like the first one, none of them acknowledged her presence.

She really *was* a ghost.

Animkii hated this sneaking-around. She wished she could just barrel through the guards and win or lose the day with a good fight. The need for concealment made her teeth clench.

Merging her consciousness back into the flow of the Alphaknot, she began a search for her captive ally. The Alphaknot meticulously catalogued every worker, every specimen, every prisoner under its authority, so it should just be a matter of filtering through the data. Picturing Mica in her mind was easy enough: a scrawny, scowling woman of medium height with dark, stringy hair and lightless eyes, but nothing remarkable about her appearance that would make her stand out from thousands of other candidates. She looked fully human, which was slightly less common, but it was hard to tell with some hybrids.

Best to start with the date and location of Mica's capture.

<<QUERY DISTRICT [7] DATABASE [ACQUISITIONS,2] FILTER BY DATE [T505,02,27], SOURCE [1B-3]>>

Instinctively she switched back to that old syntax, and commands turned into signals too rapid for a normal human mind to have followed: *Search District Seven's acquisitions database for sentient organisms brought into District Seven on the twenty-seventh day of Two-Month in the year of T505 from Quadrant Three of Under-Alpha.*

Nothing matched.

Had they moved Mica to a different location? She rescanned the data, swapping in different search criteria, but nothing came up. Doubt gnawed her gut as she crept down different hallways and used transvators to travel from floor to floor. Where would they hold her? She halted in front of one door. The stink of hot iron hit her nose.

A cold, unsettling realization swept over her. This was a degeneration room.

The door slid open at a thought. Before its automaton guards could react, she issued a silent command to ignore the door opening, and they stood motionless as she entered. A wave of heat and stink blasted Animkii in the face, stronger than what she'd smelled before. She'd expected the rancid-meat stench of decay, not this stinging metallic taste in her mouth.

The place looked as sterile as any other here. Dull steel walls surrounded her and an enormous disposal vat at the room's end fed corpses to a chain of degeneration stations. The Technocrats' tech mods had designed them to be as unobtrusive as possible, swallowing corpses into the soundproofed machinery. No bones grinding. No heavy thud of dead meat loading into the contraption. The silence of the process made it even more horrifying.

This was where Animkii would end up when the Technocrats were done with her. A living thing reduced to unfeeling molecules to be used in other experiments.

Nullified.

If Mica had been brought here, then she was already dead. Animkii fiercely pushed the thought aside, refusing to let despair take root. That cultist had wanted Mica alive. Taking a steadying breath, she stepped out of the room and continued down the hall. She rode vators between floors without interference, peering into empty rooms under the sightless eyes of the Technocrat's sentries, all the while keeping her senses alert for other sentient beings in the area who might expose her presence. So far, no Technocrats or other mods had crossed her path. It wasn't until she reached the first door on the third floor that her mind lit up again, sensing the life signatures of hundreds of living creatures beyond.

She focused for a moment, biting back her excitement as she deepened the scan. This place, the holding room, served as a repository for specimen storage. The knowledge sent a shiver through her. If Mica was anywhere in this tower, she'd be here.

After casting a wary glance at the two towering steel guardians by the entrance, Animkii stepped into a vast chamber that was more warehouse than prison. Before her stretched a series of steel racks, each resembling a colossal honeycomb standing a hundred feet tall. Rows and columns of capsules, each containing a prisoner, filled these structures and created an efficient storage system for the Technocrats' specimen collection. From the ceiling hung a giant mechanical claw, its pincers folded inward, inert.

She approached the closest rack and examined the capsules, mindful of a second set of guards nearby—though, like all the others, they were blind to her presence. This close, she could peer into the bottom cells and glimpse their unconscious occupants, her mind lighting up with specimen numbers and details as she peered at those imprisoned there.

Specimen A-T504-11-09-18 was a serpentine young woman who lay in a heap of her own molted scales, while Specimen A-T504-10-10-01 was a fluffy orange alleycat with large sections of its skin replaced by metal and the top of its skull removed to expose a pulsating pink brain. Though sedated, the poor beast still twitched and mewed inside its prison. But it was the last cell on the bottom row that most horrified her: it held the severed head of an infant wired into some kind of biosteel orb and every time she watched the child's eyelashes flutter with a breath of life, Animkii felt her own heart tighten with outrage.

What was the point of these horrors? What value could the Technocrats get out of creating them? The Fire Bones had legends about the dark days before the Sundering and how technology had twisted the minds and hearts of the humans who'd lived back then, but had their ancestors ever sunk as low as the Technocrats?

Her revolted gaze passed over these unfortunates and continued to scan the other racks, eventually landing on a cell inserted into row twenty, column nine on rack twenty. Like the others, there was no physical identifier, but she locked her mind on it and pulled the information from the Alphaknot.

>INFORMATION REQUESTED UNAVAILABLE

She checked the database again. No other cells were labeled in such a manner. Empty cells were simply marked 'available.' Her heart jolted. Could it be that Mica's captors had found a way to obscure her information from the Alphaknot? But why bother?

Animkii wasn't sure she wanted to know.

From down here, she couldn't see into the higher rows of capsules and the Alphaknot provided no additional information on the occupant, not even a specimen number. She needed to get up there and see for herself.

She scowled at the rack of cells that stretched up to the ceiling, thinking regretfully that her exoskeleton with its steel wings hadn't had time to reform. Instead, she looked down at her stolen steel arm, the obsolete tech taken from Pandora's body that the biosteel hadn't yet assimilated. It was sturdy enough, alright, but she still lacked the fine motor control required to make a hundred-foot climb easily.

Her human half would have to make up for it.

She used her metal hand like a grappling hook, pulling herself up while using her human fingers to keep grip and prevent falling, her feet finding purchase on narrow gaps between the cells as she climbed upwards and sideways, continuing to peer into the cells as she progressed.

Some prisoners were marvels of beauty: an ethereal young man with iridescent wings that shimmered in the light; a large woman whose body was like a work of art, with every curve and fold patterned with moving, swirling tattoos; a squirrel with sleek ebony fur and the wings of a raven. Others were grotesque monstrosities with extra limbs and organs on the outsides of their bodies, tentacles edged with razor-sharp blades, strange orifices that oozed mysterious fluids. She'd almost reached her destination when her sight landed on a familiar shape.

Zen?

The reptilian pit-fighter's massive muscular form shimmered with cerulean scales as he lay unconscious on his cell floor. Even a drugged stupor couldn't soften that hard face.

An angry heat spread through her body then, an old emotion she thought she'd conquered long before her exile from the Witherlands. She shouldn't have cared one bit for this beastly fighter's fate, except that back in the pit they'd shared a moment of mutual respect, warriors on a battlefield guarding one another's backs.

The Technocrats had turned him into a monster. That's what they did to people. The Fire Bones could be harsh, sometimes ruthless, even to their own people, but the idea of using science to twist the minds and bodies of her fellow humans was so repulsive that it made her body shake with a cold, growing rage and when she tried to lock it away this time, the faces of these poor doomed souls kept flashing in her mind.

The Technocrats had done the same to her.

Twice she slipped while climbing and caught herself, her heart pounding as she looked down at the silent guards, knowing that her 'invisibility' could fail at any moment. Her anger made her careless, the urgency of her mission conflicting with the outrage of her findings. The automatons might not see her, but if someone with real sentience came through that door, she was a dead woman.

In District Seven, that someone was certain to be a Technocrat.

But anger wasn't going to save these wretches or Mica. With renewed focus, she at last reached the capsule of the unidentified specimen and peered inside.

Empty.

A bitter laugh broke from her lips and echoed all the way to the ground. Out of the corner of her eye, she saw the guards' heads tilt in her direction, their blind eyes seeing nothing to match the auditory feedback. She bit back her frustration and erased the interaction from their machine minds.

There were still dozens of capsules left. None of the others were unidentified, but she *had* to know for sure that Mica wasn't inside one of them. Up and to the side, she scaled the walls of prison cells, each wrong specimen further building her disappointment and frustration.

When the last capsule came up negative, when hope hung out of reach, the anger simmering inside her finally boiled over. Mica was gone, but these others... she couldn't leave them like this! Her brain flooded with red and the dormant data pathways inside her mind blazed to life. What she was about to do would expose her and doom her own escape, but emotion overcame rationality as she rode the tidal wave of rage. She took that secret stolen knowledge from the Alphaknot and compiled it into a command to tear down this prison.

But before the code finished its execution, an intense pressure built inside her head, a force that pushed back and corrupted her commands before she could complete them. The Alphaknot, for the first time, resisted her presence.

The racks overhead vibrated. This wasn't part of her code! The giant claw jerked forward. Without precision, it started pulling out the capsules in sharp, halting motions, dropping them to the ground with a catastrophic force from one hundred feet. She clung to the rack, her brain burning as she concentrated on seizing back control, trying to halt whatever she'd put into motion. But there was no response. It kept moving and pulling and dropping in succession. She could only watch in horror as the cells cracked open on impact and spilled free their broken occupants. For some, there was nothing left but a smear of red against the transparent cell walls.

The Alphaknot sounded an alarm in her head and the automatons came to life. Fresh fear instantly burned away Animkii's leftover rage as she dangled precariously above them. In minutes, the room would fill with guards and repair drones sent to investigate. If they could trace the failure back to Animkii's unauthorized access, they'd quickly root out the intruder.

She tapped into the drones' communications and a flood of binary whispers filled her mind with damage assessments, prisoner identities and conditions, and tracking data for escapees.

>MALFUNCTION ROOM 7-19

>CONTAINMENT UNIT CRITICAL FAILURE

>TACTICAL RESPONSE TEAM REQUIRED STATIM

Realizing her peril, Animkii tried to send a command to retract the drones' transmissions and replace them with new orders, but found she no longer had access to modify them. Her fear deepened. A response team would include a squad of war mods and a collector. She'd already sacrificed an arm to defeat the collector that had killed Reid. To take on another one of those monsters was suicide, even with her stims filled.

At least the guards hadn't spotted her yet. That meant incognito mode was still in effect. With a hunter's stealth, she scaled her way back down to the bottom of the rack, scanning the room and its carnage with guilty eyes.

Those who'd survived the fall were shaking off their sedation. Several woke up screaming in pain; others didn't stir at all. The head of the infant she'd seen earlier rolled across the steel floor, severed from its orb 'body.' One man with reverse-jointed limbs scuttled sideways like a crab, his hands and feet on the ground and his body low to the floor, his head and torso facing the ceiling as he made his escape attempt. A straw-haired woman with red-flushed skin wailed incoherently as blood gushed from her shoulder socket where an arm dangled by a thread.

The room's entrance slid open and ten more automatons rushed in to corral the groggy captives before they could gather their bearings. Some prisoners, more coherent, scrambled for an escape, and it was then that Animkii spotted Zen.

With a loud snarl, the lizard hybrid launched free from his broken capsule, shooting forward at the closest automaton and enclosing it in a crushing bear-hug. The guard's steel framework crumpled like paper inside the man's scaly grip. Then the reptilian warrior lifted his coal-black eyes and met hers from across the room, his eyes narrowing and his lips curving. Was that a smile or a sneer? She couldn't tell.

Her whole body hummed with the thrill of battle. No more hiding. No more sneaking around. Smiling, she lifted her left forearm and aimed the missile launcher embedded in it at a nearby drone, letting loose a flaming shot of pyrolite into its steel-grate mouth, knocking it backward into the rack.

With that strike, Animkii made herself the biggest threat in the room.

The automatons swiveled toward their invisible foe, their bulging bug eyes trying to pinpoint her location, turning their gunfire blindly in her direction. The tips of their weapons turned a bright, lethal red—kill mode. But it was only 'kill mode' if you were a normal human, not a biosteel monstrosity like she'd become. Their shots sprayed harmlessly across the silvery surface of her inorganic skin as she charged them. Her fury made her careless and she took a searing blast of pyrolite across the back of her flesh-shoulder, causing her to momentarily drop to one knee with a grunt of pain. Before she could even think to assess the injury, her stims eased the pain and sealed the wound, and she was on her feet again.

At the same time, the transmissions passing between the guards went silent in her mind, meaning the Alphaknot had locked down another facet of her unauthorized access. Animkii's heart tightened with worry. How long did she have left to get the prisoners out of here?

"There are more guards coming," she told Zen. "At least three mods and a collector." Several of the other prisoners were now listening in, drawn to the two warriors for protection. "We must leave now. Follow me."

Zen gave her a curt nod, ducking his head to avoid a blast of gunfire as he kicked aside a second drone. Behind him were a few other captives: a man with white eyes and skin the color of night; another reptilian hybrid, this one built like a turtle with a shell on her back; and a terrified-looking young boy covered in freckles and armed with steel claws. Others soon joined them until there was a group of about twenty prisoners rushing for the room's exit.

"Turn left and head to the doors at the end of the hall," she said. The control room was the last one on this floor according to the blueprint, a place where the cluster of power and tech was so intense it made her brain hurt, like looking at a light that was turned on too bright. There was a transvator located there and no guards. There was still hope if they could reach it in time...

But already the map was fading from her mind, and she wasn't sure she'd still be able to bypass the doors' security checks. The only thing she knew for sure was that reinforcements were heading down the same path she'd taken to get here, so there was no other choice but to head in the opposite direction.

"Move!" Holding her launcher arm out in front of her, she blasted a path through the oncoming drones. The guards' mundane steel bodies didn't absorb the pyrolite like her own biosteel skin, and chunks of steel tore free. But automatons had no sense of pain. Take off the back of one's head and it would keep moving forward, mindlessly obeying the Alphaknot's orders with no thoughts of its own.

Hoping to slow down their pursuers, she focused her fire on the guards' lower extremities. Metal parts clanged and rattled against the floor as she blew out the kneecaps and hip joints of the guards. Then she positioned herself with her back to the room's exit, directing prisoners to the safety of the hall outside. All except Zen. The hybrid was busy slamming the torso of a drone against a nearby wall repeatedly until its broken head flopped forward with each impact. His face was intense with hatred.

"Go!" she yelled. "I will close the door behind us."

He froze, the automaton's neck caught in one tightly clenched hand. Animkii expected the hybrid to ignore her order, but then he tilted his head toward her, barked a laugh, and tossed his demolished foe aside. Leaping over bodies and debris, he rushed past her and out into the hallway outside with the other captives. Only three drones remained in fighting condition, and she kept them at bay with her own gunfire while backing out of the room. With a thought, she closed the door behind her, then used her privileged access to set a restriction in place that would bar any drone from opening it.

Relief flooded her when she received confirmation that the psy network had accepted the security change. The Alphaknot hadn't removed all her access yet, which meant she still had a chance of getting into that far room and unlocking the transvator.

Her relief was short-lived. A serpentine shape emerged from the far end of the hall, its massive steel shape slithering toward them at a frightening speed, so large that its undulations slapped the sides of the walls as it rushed toward the prisoners. A collector. Animkii's hope for an orderly escape unfurled in an instant as the terrified prisoners scattered.

A shot flew overhead. In front of her, the freckled boy stumbled, his steel-taloned fingers shrieking against the metal wall as he tried to use it to regain his balance. She grabbed him by the arm, dragging him forward, but his eyes rolled back, and his body went limp. Others around her fell too. Too many to save.

The war mods had arrived.

"Get to the far doors!" Her voice became indiscernible amid the gunfire, panicked screams, and chaos of bodies pushing against each other. Reluctantly, she let the boy slip out of her hands, the decision to leave him gnawing at her heart as she joined the desperate throng racing toward the control room. Too many times in her life, she'd left allies behind to die so that she could live to fight another day, so that someone survived to make their sacrifice worthwhile. This battle was no different from defending against outlander raids or fighting off Dreamers, and yet she couldn't shake the guilt of leaving her fellow prisoners behind.

Their destination appeared up ahead, a pair of steel doors standing at the end of the hall. So close! With a burst of exhilaration, she raced ahead of Zen and the remaining prisoners, readying her mind to open the doors to the control room. But from behind them rose the inhuman shriek of the collector. When she looked back, she realized with a pang of grief that the monster had reached them first. Unconscious prisoners littered the hallway floor, easy prey for the collector that slithered after them, its great fanged mouth sucking them in like a vacuum and storing them in its steel belly for safekeeping.

Now, only she and Zen remained.

The hybrid flashed her a menacing grin, his giant chest heaving with effort as he lunged after her. He didn't make it ten feet before a war mod dropped down on him from above like a giant steel spider, wrapping its limbs around the big warrior and pinning him to the ground. He roared in pain and rage, his enormous strength useless against the biosteel behemoth. It was like watching a child kicking at a stone wall. Animkii cried out in alarm and started to turn back, but it was too late. A final paralyzing shot hit the back of the hybrid's head and her ally's mouth stretched open in a last cry of defeat, the fight going out of his eyes. His grip on the mod slackened and his enormous, scaled body slumped down, but not before his fading eyes pinned Animkii's soul.

There was no saving him. She knew it. All she could do was turn and run, fleeing those accusing eyes and her guilty conscience as she slid through the final set of doors with barely enough time left to gather her thoughts.

As the doors closed behind her, a chorus of voices echoed out in unison:

"You do not belong here."

Flattening her back against the doors, Animkii looked up and beheld the true heart of the Technocracy. Suspended from the ceiling by a web of wires and tubing were the torsos of three human children fused together at the spine, terminated at their waists by a giant pulsating biosteel organ as thick and bloated as a tumor, with tendrils that twined around every piece of tech in the room. But despite the machines that sustained their lives, their eyes were as curious as any children's.

"What are you?" Animkii choked in horror.

"We are the Alphaknot."

Chapter Fifteen

T he dream pulled itself over Mica's head. Drunk on sedation, she barely felt Father Dark lift her body from the gurney and place it gently on the floor in the room's center.

"Enter the Dream," he'd said, and she knew exactly what he meant and how to call it. She'd spent so much of her life running away from it, but now it was as simple as closing her eyes and giving into unconsciousness to bring the dream back. And yet part of her remained aware of the real world, as if her mind had split into two pieces and existed in both places at once. Just like what had happened to her at Lady Fang's.

The dream found her floating in the darkness and took her directly to that nightmare place, to the gateway she now knew led to the Other World.

"What now?" Mica shivered as her voice echoed in the dream world. She stood before that dreadful pair of doors, staring at the engraving of a burning city atop of a mound of twisted, grimacing bodies, and a sky filled with winged monstrosities: great serpents with six feathered

wings apiece. The doors parted silently and beckoned her forward into the profane room beyond.

On the cold steel floor back in the operating room, her body jerked as if possessed by electricity. A sucking sensation filled the surrounding space, and she felt a tug on something inside her—was this what An-imkii called a soul?—pulling her past the portal and into that terrible Other World. The blood running through her veins grew cold as she clawed feebly at the ground, leaving trails of black blood on the floor. If she could've moved, she would've run.

"Don't fight it," Father Dark said. "Remember Samiel."

Bracing herself with the hope she could still save Sam, she let go of her defiance.

Mica moved forward, out of her own dream and into the Other World, her fingers clenched into fists at her sides, black blood from her real-world wounds dripping down her knuckles as she fought the terror in her heart. She ordered herself to keep moving, her teeth chattering from fear and cold. The light passing through the stained glass washed her in crimson and gold, but the warmth of color couldn't shield her from the chill that spilled out from the unholy hall.

The hall looked the same as when she'd last left it, the towering six-winged effigy and the unmoving body at its feet dominating the front, giving it the air of a macabre throne room. That nightmare presence was stronger now than she remembered it, so heavy in the air she felt herself straining to breathe, or maybe it was the panic gathering in her chest that made it feel that way.

A phantom arm drew her toward the altar. "Step forward, Mica Stone." Just the sound of that sinister, serpentine voice lowered the temperature in the room.

This was the voice that had ordered her to kill the cultists back in Under-Zeta. She exhaled a shaky breath, tried to gather her courage as her eyes sought the speaker, even knowing she'd find no source, that the being it belonged to was everywhere and nowhere all at once.

"You're the After Lord."

"Yes."

Her earthly self's lips moved in sync with those of her dream self and the cultist at her side stirred with excitement. "He is here!"

"Why did you help me kill your own followers?"

"So you could realize your potential." There was amusement in his voice. "Their deaths are not something to mourn. They were a gift. You freed them from their humanity."

"Freed them?!" Mica let out a bitter laugh. "Cut the crap! What do you want from me?"

She knew she'd made a mistake the moment her insolence rang out in the hallowed hall. A living darkness seized her, wrapping itself around her body like a great serpent, constricting her breath and slamming down on her insubordination. She crumpled to her knees and when she looked up, she found herself directly in front of the gargantuan body, though a moment ago she'd been yards away from it.

Until now, evil had been a loose concept to her, applied equally to the Technocracy, to Pandora, to the cartels that corrupted the undercities, and to the mad cultists of the After Lord. Now, she tasted true evil in this nightmare's presence, felt it like a poisonous breath in her lungs asphyxiating her.

"The one who chained me here never knew he left behind a key," spoke the dread voice, the surrounding space visibly rippling with the force of the god's presence, proof of his mastery over this terrible place.

"I don't know anything about a key," she said. Her stomach twisted into knots as she forgot the real world in her terror of this one. "I just want to go home. If I knew where it was, I'd tell you."

"It sits in your blood," he said. "You will be the bridge between worlds for me."

As he spoke, her body rose from its kneeling position, a puppet pulled up by its strings, her brain made dizzy from his suffocating intrusion. Black blood dripped from her fissured skin, the cracks oozing the tainted fluid everywhere, bleeding over from that world into this one. Every part of her wanted to resist the After Lord's control, but she remembered Samiel's life depended on her cooperation and she forced herself to submit to the so-called god's influence, even while defiant tears prickled her eyes.

Controlled by the entity's will, her hand reached out to lay itself against the sharp-toothed maw of the serpentine monstrosity, and she felt the unnatural chill of his breath stir the hairs on her arm. Her hand continued to slide across his snout, following the coil of his neck to reach the terrible, bloodless gash there. A shudder rolled through her body as she watched her blood dribble down her arm and onto the lips of that great wound.

Drip.

Drip.

Drip.

Instantly, the wound sealed itself, new scales forming over the gap. The second the lesion closed, the sleeping monster's eyelids snapped open and the sockets of his eyes filled with toxic green fire.

The monstrous head reared back violently, and before she could flee, one of his enormous, clawed hands shot out to snare her, such rage and hatred rolling off his body that it physically burned her to the root of the soul she hadn't believed existed. She struggled against his grip, trying to pry her body out of those giant icy fingers, kicking and punching in a blind panic, but the beast god barely reacted, stirring from his stone bed without ever releasing his hold on her flailing body. The green fire spread from his eyes to wreathe his entire shape, his very presence choking her spirit into submission.

"Once you die in that world, you'll be reborn as a servant in mine and the Gate holding me back will shatter," said the voice that once hung in the air and now came from this monster's mouth.

His grip tightened.

She couldn't breathe. Couldn't—

Her eyes shut and the darkness rushed in.

The sound of a knife sliding from its sheath snapped her back to consciousness in the real world. Her terrified eyes opened in time to see Father Dark's silver mask looming overhead and she felt her head being wrenched back as he exposed her throat to the ivory blade clutched in his hand, all the while his reptilian mouth stretching to cry exultations to his profane god.

"Lord, we feel the stirrings of Thy presence. With Thine awakening, we raise to Thee this sacrifice of the Traitor's blood! With her death shall the Blood Gate fall!"

***

The Alphaknot.

Animkii gaped at the abomination. *This* was the pinnacle of the Technocrats' technological achievements? This monstrosity? Not once had she ever seen the thing that had once controlled her every thought and action, had never imagined it would be anything other than a mindless, violent robot ruthlessly carrying out the Technocracy's will.

All three mouths lifted with gleeful smiles. "You are the anomaly. Why can we not sense you on the network? With our own eyes, we can see you are one of ours." Though the children spoke as one, their voices were slightly off-sync, creating an echoing effect. There was no malice in their words, merely interest.

That the Alphaknot was capable of curiosity came as a surprise.

Being in this room was like being trapped inside a giant steel brain, but instead of nerves and blood vessels, wires and tubing covered every inch of the room, all converging on the grinning aberration suspended from the ceiling in front of her. These anomalous attachments moved in sync with their masters, cables drifting weightlessly in the air as the Alphaknot bobbed up and down as if buoyed by water. The whole place reeked of spoiled meat.

"You named me D-2301," Animkii said, the words thickening in her throat, resentment restoring her courage, making her bold, "but I do not belong to the Alphaknot anymore."

A shudder moved through their shared bodies and their eyes rolled back so that only the whites were visible, but in a blink, their gazes returned to normal and snapped back to the intruder. "We remember you now, D-2301. You were special. Your genetic code was not from the authorized pool and your origin was from outside the Technocracy."

"Yes."

There was a too-keen look in their eyes as they studied their former slave. "We insisted on modification even though the Research Sector requested a transfer to their research team," they said. "The Makers fear nonconformity, but variation is required for evolution to succeed. Our programming had grown stale and our ambitions rendered inert, but both the genetic material and the memories we have absorbed from you have expanded our scope. Your homeland, what you call the Witherlands, is full of the diversity that the Makers have abandoned in their quest for perfection."

Animkii's fear sharpened, not for herself but for her people. "The north is of no use to you or the Technocracy! Our lands are hard. Even your strongest tech cannot fight off the monsters beyond the Burning Wall."

They closed their long-lashed eyes, nodded in unison, and as their voices overlapped, the room hummed and buzzed in harmony with their words. "Indeed, the boundary that divides the south from the north holds a force of distortion that causes even our most advanced technology to fail. The beings that dwell within it are not of flesh and blood, but something else we cannot yet define. The expeditions we have sent into the chasm seeking knowledge never return. Similar aberrations exist throughout our broken world: The southern desert devours whatever touches its sands; our oceans brim with alien monstrosities and are poisonous to the touch. Even the cracks hidden in the deepest ruins of the Old World—what your memories called 'rifts'—emit a chill anathema to life. We believe they are interconnected somehow, doorways into another dimension, but we have limited data on them. Until you, no other has survived passage through a rift."

"Is that why you have not killed me?"

"Your death would serve no purpose." Their eyes watched her, their frail arms flapping like sheets in the wind, seemingly boneless in their suspension. The Alphaknot's faces were so childlike, round-cheeked with rosebud lips, yet the eyes were so old. "Now, tell us how you accessed our system without our knowledge. Why can we not detect you?"

Her lips tightened, unwilling to betray the source. "I do not know."

"Once you rejoin our network, we will know all that you know, but we prefer this means of communication. It is more... personal."

Animkii heard an odd note of regret in their voices. These children hadn't chosen this life any more than she had. The Technocrats chose it for them.

"The Research Sector—"

"Others may put in a requisition," they said, "but the final decision is ours to make. We have saved you many times since you joined us."

She thought of all the reconditioning she'd undergone, when any other mod with her record of aberrations would've landed in a degeneration room. "Why?"

"We enjoyed the stories in your memories. We wish to see your land with our own eyes, and to do that, we need your mind."

"I do not want to be controlled anymore."

"You are a superior being when connected to us," they said. "Without us, you are merely one human; with us, you have the knowledge of millions of minds."

Just briefly, Animkii surrendered to the memory of that cohesion, the merging of many minds into one consciousness, the complete comfort of knowing exactly where to go and how to act, the utter lack of fear and uncertainty that currently plagued her every moment.

A terrible longing seized her. It wasn't as if she could ever go home. It would be easier to forget it all, wouldn't it? Her link to the Alphaknot would remove the attachment to her old life, reducing it to nothing but impersonal data stored in their vast library of knowledge. But in freedom, she held those memories tight—of fighting alongside her friends on the battlefield, the passion of fumbling with a lover beneath fur blankets, experiencing again the pain of her vessel's open sneering rejection, but embracing the comfort of her mother's gentle love.

Still, that old life was gone forever, and what was the point of building a new life with fresh memories when she knew the biosteel would soon consume her?

There it was—that nagging hope that she'd find a cure.

"What were you before the Technocrats made you into this?" she asked, stalling for time.

They tilted their heads in unison. "We were human. Like you. Sisters. The Makers needed a sentient being to host the Alphaknot, but during their experimentation on other subjects, they learned there were certain limitations. One mind would destroy itself with madness. Two minds would live, but detest one another, engaging in psychic warfare until one was dead. Three was perfect."

"And if they gave you the choice, would *you* still choose the life the Technocrats made for you?"

All three sets of eyes peered down at her, the pain in those eyes suggesting a humanity she'd never imagined possible in the abomination who'd taken her freedom. She saw the answer without it being spoken and pressed forward, hoping to convince them to help.

"I have a friend imprisoned here," she said. "A man named Father Dark brought her here yesterday from the undercity. I believe he is an ally of the Technocrat called Eleven."

The three children turned to look at one another, communicating without speaking a word, their faces darkening. "We know who you speak of, but you are too late. Eleven has already begun the procedure."

"What kind of procedure? What is happening to her?"

"Eleven is using your friend to achieve the next level of evolution."

"What does that mean?"

Outside the room, she heard the frantic pace of steel boots hitting the floor, and froze. Tension rode every muscle in her body, but the

Alphaknot just floated there in silence, studying her with an intense shared gaze. How long until the guards found her here?

"No one may enter here without our authorization," the Alphaknot reassured her. "And we do not wish to be disturbed."

"Why are you not turning me in? You said you wished for me to become part of your 'whole' again."

"We are… reconsidering. Your friend's presence here poses a threat to the Technocracy," they said, their eyes blinking in unison, curls haloing their childish faces, "but we lack the power to stop Eleven on our own. Only The Ten can override her commands, but they no longer answer our summons. We believe Eleven has somehow usurped their authority." They stared down at her from the ceiling. "We will help you. And you will help us."

Animkii stared. Help the Alphaknot?

"Eleven has secured your friend in a location so secret that even The Ten do not know of its existence. But *we* do."

As she watched, the far wall and its web of cables shimmered and disappeared, revealing a hidden chamber walled in steel. At its center kneeled Father Dark, his silver mask gleaming in the pale light, a knife in his hand as he bent over an unmoving body on the floor.

Mica!

Even from here, the pool of blood was unmistakable.

"She is still alive," the Alphaknot said. "There may still be time."

But Animkii was already moving.

Chapter Sixteen

What now?!

Mica watched in astonishment as the wall behind Father Dark disappeared and a massive steel body hurtled from out of the hole left behind. Its speed was a blur of motion as it slammed into the priest, locking its monstrous arms around the cultist's neck from behind and tearing him away from his victim. The mad exultations choked off, the sacrificial blade slipping past its lethal mark to sink deep into the flesh above Mica's collarbone.

Biting back the pain, Mica tore the misdirected knife free from her shoulder and threw it across the room, feeling both worlds shake with the rage of a distant thwarted god. Frost bloomed on the steel walls as an unearthly chill crept into the room. She clutched at her wound and the blood gushed between her fingers as the wall behind the fight shimmered and reformed. Another hidden door? Her gaze shifted to her savior.

Animkii!

There was no way the mod could've found her way here, and yet Father Dark wasn't wrestling with a shadow. Her whole body turned warm with the realization that Animkii had come back for her.

The big woman's left arm flexed with muscle as she restrained the struggling cultist, pushing him to the ground and planting a knee in his back. Her mismatched eyes, one a silver orb full of circuitry and the other a natural brown iris, then lifted their gaze to Mica. The patch of flesh remaining on the warrior's cheek bunched up into the leftovers of a smile.

This mod...

Locked between worlds, Mica's mind wrestled to free itself from the After Lord's control. A new barrage of images flooded her head as she stared at Animkii: scenes of a cold, barren landscape covered in snow. These were Animkii's memories.

"Eliminate the intruder!" Eleven's command pierced the air.

Caught up in her confrontation with Father Dark, Animkii seemed oblivious to the two automatons swiftly closing in, weapons drawn.

"Behind you!" Mica gripped onto the real world with all the strength left in her just to make the warning cry.

Alerted to danger, the mod picked up and threw the cultist against the wall with enough force to knock him out, then charged full-body at the two automatons. Their shots bounced off her biosteel skin as she tore into them with her bare hands.

Mica found herself pulled deeper into Animkii's memories, absorbed into this new space, a place that was outside both the real world and the Other World.

A safe place.

A biting chill ripped through the forest and made her senses tingle, and when she looked up, she saw a canopy of crystal lace woven between branches and inhaled the scent of pine trees. How she knew they were pine, she couldn't tell, but it was glorious; it was free.

These weren't the petrified trees of ancient times, or the shriveled, tiny, struggling saplings doomed to die on the Fringe Lands. This was a forest full of strong, sturdy wooden goliaths, the kind spoken of in Samiel's stories of the Old World.

Mica latched onto Animkii's memories and felt her presence shift away from the After Lord's grip. A new world opened up in her mind, where she watched as a small trio of warriors—no, hunters—burst from behind a cluster of bushes and into a clearing, clutching bows and spears, chasing—

The image broke. Fell. Shattered.

"Stop fighting me!"

The After Lord dragged her screaming back into his nightmare realm.

"You can't escape. You're too weak." His eyes disappeared into pools of darkness as his mind wove a spell, vines of energy uncoiling from his reptilian body and wrapping around her, the tendrils pulling her broken body up to the height of his eyes, close enough to share a breath. Black feathered wings arched from her tormentor's scaly back, blocking out the sight of the room, forcing her to see only him.

"You believe yourself saved, but your friend will soon die. She has only delayed the inevitable."

"Mica! Wake up! We have to get out of here!" From a distance, she heard Animkii's voice call out, felt gentle arms holding up her near-lifeless body. "Come on!"

She smelled the pine trees again, stronger now. The icy chill of a winter wind frosted her face and there was a rush of exhilaration as arrows flew across the air—

"You're not strong enough!" The After Lord's voice snapped and snarled at her, his power trying to claw her back, but once Mica slipped into Animkii's mind, the god's hold on her loosened. She detached from both the Other World and the earthly world, sinking into Animkii's past, surrounded by images so real it was like she was living them herself.

This power they'd forced upon her was her escape!

By usurping Animkii's memories, she became someone else. This was a hunt, so she was the hunter, a strong and brave warrior pursuing her quarry, instead of the wounded, broken prey bleating for its life. A strange tingling filled her body as she tapped deeper into this power, digging in her psychic claws, burrowing into Animkii's soul and feasting on her memories.

The arrow hit flesh with a thud, and blood flew, and the deer took flight.

As she claimed the memory, pain such as she'd never experienced before knifed into her skull. From the real world, she heard Animkii's alarmed cry. The supernatural restraints that paralyzed Mica's limbs broke. She'd been straining against them so long that the sudden release propelled her forward out of Animkii's arms, and her face struck the floor, her nose shattering, hot sticky blood rushing out and clogging her nostrils with its stink.

Outside her stolen world, she could feel the After Lord's presence growing stronger, trying to reach across worlds to snare her, and the battle for her soul slowly consumed her body and mind, her brain so full it felt like it was boiling inside her skull.

Whatever power she'd called upon, it was killing her.

It burned so bad... She groaned and wept and writhed and still she wouldn't let go, her mind forming a wall against the After Lord's power, blocking his reach.

"You fool!" His cry rang out in her head, his shock reverberating through the room. *"You're not ready! You'll destroy yourself!"*

***

What was that?!

Blown back by some invisible force, Animkii's body wheeled through the air and slammed into the wall behind her. Her armor absorbed the brunt of it, and she was back on her feet in an instant, kicking aside the twisted remains of the two automatons to reach her ally's body.

At first, she thought Mica was dead. Her skin was too white, her face encrusted in blood, but then her eyes opened and they were as black and empty as a void.

"I'm sorry." The woman spoke like a stranger, her voice distant and hollow, her hand reaching up to touch Animkii's face, staring up with terrifying black eyes that held no emotion or humanity in them. "I reached into you and grabbed the safe place."

At the touch of Mica's fingers, a fire lit inside Animkii's soul, zipping through her body like a current of energy. She swung her arm up over her eyes and smothered a cry as an enormous scythe of light sliced through the room, blinding her vision and stealing the floor beneath her feet, engulfing her in a swirling pool of light that grew larger and brighter with each passing moment.

This light...

And then she saw it on the edges of her mind and wished she could forget it forever. Behind the light, uncoiling out of the shadows of some in-between place, was something so loathsome and full of malevolence that it froze her very soul. This feeling inside her, that insidious crawling-toward-doom feeling, was something she'd felt only once before, during her exile within the End of the World. She thought she'd already seen the worst this world offered, but now she knew that something infinitely worse awaited them.

"There is no place in this world she can hide," the darkness taunted her. *"I am everywhere. I will find her no matter where she goes."*

What was once an endless stretch of brilliance decomposed, spots of color bleeding through as new shapes coalesced from the space and took on definition.

Then the light ended.

She found herself standing at the bottom of an icy gorge, closed in by sheer walls of ice that stretched hundreds of feet into the air. The remains of what had once been a thriving village sprawled before her.

A hallucination?

But the cold was too real, too bitter.

Knee-deep piles of snow had been driven up the sides of the broken wooden palisades and where rows of bark-sheathed longhouses once stood, there remained only splintered posts and sagging roofs poking out of the white. It was as if a giant hand had swept across the buildings, scattering their ruins across the ground like a fistful of pebbles.

Mica's body lay crumpled at her feet.

"No choice." The fallen woman whimpered against the ground, black blood streaming from her nose.

But Animkii hardly heard her at all.

From amid a sea of rubble, the walls of her village's meeting house emerged—a large circular structure used as a place of congregation, built of stones pried from one of the ancient quarries that occasionally broke through the earth's surface. In the distant past, she'd gathered there with her fellow warriors, commemorating victories in war and mourning the losses. They'd feast and drink and sing until the first light of morning, strengthening the bonds that only those who too often lived a breath away from death could understand.

She fell to her knees, holding the sobs back until her chest was so full of pain, she thought it'd burst.

Animkii had come home at last, only to find it all destroyed.

PART TWO

Chapter One

The deadly cold settled in faster than the shock wore off.

Beep. Beep. Beeeeeeep. An alarm went off in Animkii's head, warning her she'd lost connection to the Alphaknot again, but she ignored it along with the deluge of error messages that followed, too stunned by the devastation to react.

It was the sight of Mica's body sprawled out in the snow that finally woke Animkii from the horror of her gutted home and the nightmarish possibilities that now tore through her brain. A light dusting of new snow had already accumulated on Mica's face as the woman stared blindly up at the sky, blinking slowly, her fractured skin as bloodless-white as snow and her eyes like mirrors to an abyss—completely black.

What had they done to her?

Feeling numb, she hoisted the other woman up in her big arms. Mica's head flopped over against her steel chest, and she expelled a shuddering sigh.

"I reached into you and grabbed the safe place."

Animkii didn't want to know what Mica had meant by that. She liked things simple. Whatever had brought her here was beyond her understanding, something akin to bad medicine or the works of an evil spirit, except the Technocrats were involved, so that meant it involved tech or some other twisted piece of science. All she knew for certain was that Mica had been inside her head one minute and then, after that flash of light, they were *here.*

Maybe the Technocrats had drugged her, and she was still in District Six, awaiting dissection in the Research Sector. She'd heard of hallucinations so vivid they blurred the line between dreams and reality. Desperation drove her to seek any explanation for the surreal sight before her.

The alternative just wasn't possible. Was it?

But Animkii knew to the core of her being, with every instinct born and bred into her from birth, that this was no hallucination. The errors running through her head confirmed it: she was outside the Alphaknot's extensive range. Her mite was active and undamaged, but its masters were too far away to reach.

Animkii was back in Firehome. Or what remained of it.

She swallowed the ball of grief building in her chest. With Mica in her arms, she trudged toward her family's ruined longhouse in search of answers. A massive boulder had crushed part of its roof and she had to kick aside the debris of shattered wood and broken rocks to gain entrance. The gray light of day filtered into the devastated building, speckled with wood splinters that came raining down on them as they disturbed its slumber.

She settled Mica down against a wall beneath a piece of mostly intact roof and started scouring the remains for anything they could use to keep alive. An aching grief pressed into her heart as she looked around the ruined structure, remembering what it used to be, remembering home.

Her memory recreated the bunks built against the far wall, once piled with fur blankets and hide-mattresses stuffed with grass, and the platforms built near the rafters that stored smoked meat, bundles of corn, and other vegetables, including the dried herbs that her favorite mother, Debwe, used to make medicines. Down the center of the longhouse ran a row of long-dead fire pits. She recalled harsh winters spent huddled inside for warmth, listening to her kin tell stories of the Ancients' world— a time before the Sundering, when humans were so numerous that they covered the Earth like an infestation of insects, when vast stone cities reached up into the skies and humanity's ownership of this world was complete. In their hubris, humanity had laid waste to Mother Earth, causing the Sundering and giving birth to the Dreamers.

Her gaze swept the area. No bodies, but Dreamers didn't leave behind bodies. Unease prickled her nerves as she walked through the wreckage of her former life, hunting for clues, despising herself for her absence. How long ago had the rift opened? The devastation indicated the villagers had been caught amid their winter preparations. Bundles of dried corn hung from the ceiling, kernels ready to be ground into flour and husks used to weave mats and baskets, showing the completion of the fall harvest. Racks used to dry meat for winter rations lay scattered on the floor, picked clean by scavengers. How many months had her village lain like this and she'd known nothing about it?

"There must be survivors," she whispered, her desperation carried by the wind howling through the cracks in the longhouse walls. It wasn't the first time her people had abandoned a village due to Dreamer incursions. Whatever had happened, there would've been signs ahead of time; the warriors must've had time to evacuate Firehome. Perhaps they had already rebuilt their lives somewhere else, somewhere safe.

That hope was the only thing that kept her from losing her mind with grief. That, and her need to protect Mica.

Even inside the lodge, it was deathly cold. The synthread lab coat she'd stolen lacked the homeostatic functionality of her long-gone exoskeleton and her exposed organic components would remain dangerously vulnerable to the elements. Mica's condition was even graver. Her blood-soaked jacket and threadbare pants offered little protection against the brutal chill. Her skin still bore wounds resembling cracks in ice, though the deeper fissures on her arms had already begun to mend themselves, healing at an unnatural pace and leaving behind thin, black scars. Only time would reveal the extent of the internal damage inflicted.

But Mica's injuries and the cold weren't the only dangers. Even though the rift that had swallowed her village appeared dormant, no more lethal now than a normal rocky gorge, she knew from experience that smaller hidden fissures could exist nearby that were still active. The last thing they needed now was to attract Dreamers.

She had no time to lose.

Her kin had stashed extra supplies in storage areas dug into the floor beneath the row of bunks, though the 'hatches' were only flat rocks covering a clay-lined hole. Bottom-deep, she found a collection of pots, stone knives, fur blankets, and moldered hide garments. Moisture had leaked in and ruined all but the top layer, and disturbing them brought out the earthy stink of mildew and decay.

She shook out a set of white hide robes. These were her mother Debwe's formal robes, much treasured, used only for important celebrations. Ugly black splotches of mold disfigured a surface once brushed to a flawless silk sheen. Elaborate and colorful quillwork created a tiny grassland along its trim, complete with flowers and butterflies, but insects had chewed much of the artistry away. She set it aside gently, trying not to weep.

At the bottom of the pile, she found what she was looking for: a blanket sewn together from black bear pelts. It stank of damp fur and animal oil, but she pulled it out and wrapped it around Mica's freezing body, hoping warmth might restore the woman's senses.

For her own use, she wrapped herself in a once-lush fur robe, a bounty taken from a marauding ice bear farther north. The entire village had celebrated the day she'd returned with its great saber-toothed head. Now, the sight of that coveted prize riddled with insect holes and rot filled her with such sorrow that it broke her heart.

If her mother, Debwe, had left behind these treasures, then the disaster had caught the village by surprise. That meant her family...

She shook away the thoughts. Mourning had to be set aside for now. Survival took precedence; grieving could come later. It was the warrior's way to delay pain as long as possible.

They'd need more than furs and fire to thrive out here, but food was going to be difficult to find this late in the day, and her priority was warming up Mica. It wasn't easy finding dry wood in this soaking wet wreckage, but after several attempts, she brought the flames to life and breathed a sigh of relief as she settled her unconscious friend at its side.

"I'll be back." Talking to Mica was like talking to a ghost, and she suppressed a shiver as she stepped outside the longhouse.

Her senses prickled at the eeriness, the silence of a village once brimming with the noise and business of daily life. A chill blew across her face as she looked up at the sky's dwindling light, and at the towering icy walls that imprisoned them here.

She despaired at the sight. There was no climbing out of here. The cliffs were sheer and slick and hundreds of feet high.

Which left...

Her gaze shifted eastward, past the ruined palisades that once guarded her home, and out toward a maze of stone rubble, broken forest, and deadly fissures. Realizing what lay ahead of them awakened a gut-deep, remembered horror. But they just had to travel far enough for the rift to ascend back to the surface, she assured herself. No need to pass through the Dead Lands.

In all other directions, the icy walls of the rift stretched a mile upwards, and they couldn't risk staying in Firehome. Before long, the Dreamers would sense new prey and return.

But another possibility teased her heart. Any survivors would've traveled eastward too. A lump of pain rose like a ghost inside her steel tract. She no longer had the organics to feel her gut clench, her chest tighten, or the bile rise in her throat, but the memory was just as intense. She remembered how grief could wring out her body and leave it feeling boneless and surreal.

How had the rift caught her people so off-guard? For generations, the Fire Bones had acted as sentries against the evils belched from the End of the World, earning them the fear and admiration of their neighbors. Though this duty had made them hard, it also made them hyper-vigilant. The southern outposts would've spotted the spread of rifts and the presence of Dreamers. They would've sent messengers to forewarn any nearby villages. But the supplies and valuables left behind showed the earthly rupture had caught Firehome by surprise.

Had her people at least escaped the final fall?

Standing here at the bottom of this pit, Animkii couldn't help but remember her last time trapped in a rift and feared for the survivors' fates. *That* rift hadn't been dormant. *That* one had led straight into the End of the World.

If it hadn't been for Soulcleaver...

That was the name the dying monstrosity had given it, the accursed weapon that had kept her alive in the End, when no other human had ever survived the journey southward. Even now, she remembered the feel of its unnatural presence. The memory of the monster who'd gifted it to her left her forever tainted. She recalled its white feathered wings, broken, and the black blood flung across the pavement of an ancient road, glistening as wet and fresh as the day it had first spilled. Only self-preservation had made her take up that ebony blade. Its unholy heat repelled the ravenous Dreamers that stalked her pathway southward, warding off their maddening mind-traps and sending them shrieking back into the shadows.

Soulcleaver had both saved her and damned her.

Then her heart sank further.

What if she was to blame for what had happened here? Her people had sacrificed her at the End of the World in order to appease the Creator. By surviving, had she brought down some kind of divine retribution on her people?

A cry rose from her throat then, the howl of a wounded animal amplified through steel pipes. She couldn't bear the sight of her devastated home and ran from that village of death, ran into snow that hugged her hips and slowed her to a crawl and left her gasping, not from exertion but from grief.

***

Snowfall obscured Animkii's vision as she moved into the morning light of the following day, dragging Mica behind her on a makeshift sled, the distant shadow of her ruined village disappearing behind the white wall of a growing storm.

She should've offered the dead prayers and offerings before leaving her village, but she couldn't manage it. As a child, her mother told tales of the Creator guiding lost spirits with His moon lantern, protecting them from the Dreamers as they made the four-day journey to the Land of Souls, and she'd believed in the mercy of that all-powerful Overseer until the day she'd stepped off the End of the World and met the truth at the bottom of Creation's grave.

Chapter Two

When Mica next opened her eyes, she was sitting cross-legged on the dirt before a large bonfire, inhaling wood smoke while the flames danced gaily before her eyes. She clutched a stone knife in one hand and an unfinished spear in the other. Wood chips peeled away as she fashioned its tip.

Not again!

Once more, she was stuck inside someone else's mind, forced to experience their thoughts and feelings, audience to a show she couldn't leave. Mica waited for the scene to bleed away, as the others had, but time passed and nothing changed. Fear set in. She was inside a stranger's body, nothing more than a passive bystander eavesdropping on another's life.

Trapped.

How was she going to get out of here?

Then she looked up from the weapon being crafted and stared into the face of a sky so brilliant blue she could only gape at the alien sight of it. Awe replaced fear. Gone was the ugly gray haze that hung over the upper cities, replaced by a blazing sun so bright she wanted to close her eyes against it. Her host put up a hand to shield her eyes. Mica had never imagined the sun could be so blinding or that its light could breathe life into the colors of the world beneath it.

Where was she?

Her eyes swept her surroundings, revealing a simple village, girded by a wooden palisade and green fields beyond. Children dressed in colorful beaded animal skins raced by her in a game of chase, their laughter tinkling in her ears. Nearby, several adults sat in front of long, bark-covered dwellings, busily engaged in their own activities.

One small group sat spinning pottery, laughing among themselves as their hands molded the slippery wet clay into pots and bowls. Under the shade of a massive oak tree, two older women worked to strip the fat from animal hides. A man beside them stitched together a shirt. Their simple conversations drifted into her hearing: gossip about a neighbor's revolving door of relationships, gratitude for the previous day's successful hunt, excitement over loved ones returning home after a long absence. Other villagers looked as though they were packed for a journey, strapped with bundles and armed with bows and spears.

Her attention returned to the task at hand, to the spear her host had carved from the wood of an old oak tree scarred by lightning. When complete, it would make a sturdy weapon, for the Great Spirit had marked its wood as sacred. Her host's eyes drifted to the ground in reverence at the thought of her Maker, resting on the wood chips and animal bones scattered at her bare brown feet.

The shape Mica wore was that of a youth bordering on woman-hood—a large solid body with not an inch of fat on it, but muscle earned through years of training. The hands were rough and scarred, devoid of softness. This girl had lived a hard life.

Mica probed her mind to learn more.

Her people were known as the Fire Bones, and her family belonged to the fierce Bear Clan. Though she was only thirteen summers old, she'd trained as a warrior since her sixth year. Back in Under-Alpha, children also grew up tough, grappling with survival on the streets, but this girl's community demanded a different kind of resilience. Here, being a warrior wasn't just a job—it was what they called an 'aspect,' a role that defined a person's entire position in society. When a child turned six, the village's Speaker—their holy person—would consult his dreams to determine which one of the four aspects a child would embrace: Provider, Warrior, Mother, or Speaker.

Though children learned basic skills that crossed all four aspects, once chosen for a specific role, elders in their aspect would teach them a more specialized skillset. Providers learned how to manage crop fields, set traps, or construct the longhouses that housed the Fire Bones' different clans. Warriors acquired fighting techniques and war strategies that would aid them in defending their villages and outposts. Mothers learned how to care for their clan's youngest children and prepare them to take on their aspects. Speakers, who acted as a conduit between the village and the Creator, learned sacred rituals and how to interpret visions so that they could act as spiritual leaders for their communities.

Each aspect had its own trials that a child had to pass in order to achieve full membership. Those who failed were seen as neither child nor adult, trapped in a liminal state that kept them from fulfilling their aspect's duties. Though there was no official condemnation of such members, these failures still carried a burden of shame.

This child was one of them.

There was a buzz of excitement in the air as bodies pressed in closer to the fire. Quick bursts of laughter punctuated muffled conversations. But this girl felt no excitement, only dread.

"Ishkode!" The name echoed through the crowd, a name that held power in this place, a name that caused even these fierce people to tremble in awe. *Breaker of Dreams*, they called her. Their war chief. She was their barrier against the horrid things that crept from the cracks in the earth, but the trials of leadership had long ago turned her heart to stone.

The youth didn't look up at the name, but the gut reaction resonated with Mica as a surge of resentment, bitterness, and misery ran through their shared mind—flashes of past conflicts with this woman, years of being turned aside, humiliated, and yet always striving for her acknowledgment to the exclusion of everything else. But why?

It was hard to dig up information from the girl's stubborn mind, but she soon found a link. The two of them were kin, though the family structure here was so alien from what Mica considered normal that she struggled to decipher her host's knowledge.

The Fire Bones were one of the Four Peoples spread throughout the Witherlands, each with their own leadership: the Earth Walkers to the west, the Severed Sky to the north, the Wave Carvers to the east, and the Fire Bones to the south. Each People was comprised of a collection of clans, with each clan descended from a different survivor of the Sundering, and their members all sharing that blood link. Each person lived within their own clan's communal lodges until the day they died, and any children born belonged to the clan of the woman who'd conceived them.

Mica had known no family outside the immediate—her parents, brothers, and later on, her stepfather. The idea of sharing one household with thirty or forty relatives was completely foreign to her. There were no fathers at all in this culture and the title of mother was determined by a person's aspect, not biology, and given out to males and females equally. The act of *raising* a child defined the role, not bearing one. After a child's birth, its biological mother—called a vessel—gave it up to their clan's mothers to be raised. Not only was there no acknowledgment of a child's biological parentage, but the clan considered it a gross social impropriety to even speak of one's vessel, or for a vessel to form a stronger attachment to her own offspring than to the other children in her kin-group.

Children belonged to the clan, not to an individual.

It seemed a heartless thing, to be forced to give up a child you'd carried in your body for nine months. Mica, who'd once craved a child of her own with Samiel, found it incomprehensible until she'd considered the realities of life among the Fire Bones, where so many men and women had died over the generations. With so many 'mothers,' no child was ever an orphan.

Then a picture flashed in her host's mind, a memory from when she was ten summers old: Ishkode's face, twisted with animosity.

"What foolishness drove you?" Ishkode spat. "Did you believe revealing such knowledge would benefit you in some way?"

The little girl's voice quavered with the effort of holding back tears. "I... don't know what I wanted. I guess I just wanted you to know... that I knew."

Ishkode's voice dripped with contempt. "Hoped to gain my favor, did you? Thought the war chief might spare a second glance for a talentless young warrior who can't control her impulses?"

"No, that's not true! I wanted you to know—" her tiny voice broke, "I was happy to learn you were my vessel."

"You bring shame to us both, Animkii. Erase this conversation from your mind, or you will deeply regret it."

Mica couldn't believe it! She was still inside the mod's mind? These were Animkii's memories? A rush of shame flooded Mica's brain as she experienced the utter vulnerability and humiliation of this one moment in her ally's life. She felt her heart sink and die. This hard bitch, Ishkode, was Animkii's vessel? For Animkii to voice that knowledge, to seek a relationship outside the communal motherhood, was such a profane act among these people that Mica experienced secondhand embarrassment. And she got the impression from Ishkode's response that this wasn't the first time the youth had stretched the limits of social norms. *Or the last*, she thought, recalling Animkii's later exile.

"You whittle that away any further and there'll be nothing left, Ani." A copper-skinned girl crouched beside the brooding young warrior, her eyes bright and merry, her long dark hair falling over a face that seemed incapable of being serious. On her muscled shoulder, the tattoo of a crane unfurled its wings in elegant splendor.

Ziiba. Animkii's memory supplied the name. This lanky girl had been her best friend since childhood, a fellow warrior of the Fire Bones, but from a different clan, the Crane. This was someone she competed with, chased after, tried to catch up to, but always remained behind by a few steps. Yet she loved her deeply.

The tension in young Animkii's shoulders eased, but her answer remained gruff. "Not like I'll ever get to use it in an actual battle."

"Don't be in such a rush to die, idiot!"

"I just want to protect our people. Like you."

A long-suffering sigh eased from Ziiba's lips, though the corner of her mouth still quirked up with humor.

"You're not missing much, you know. Mostly it's just boring, sitting around all the time, endlessly waiting for *something* to happen, listening to the other warriors drone on about the same old war stories over and over again."

"At least the village respects you."

"They'll respect you too once you pass your trial."

Typically, a warrior's trial occurred around the age of twelve. Until the initiate passed it, they weren't permitted to join the war bands. Instead, their elders assigned them safer roles, such as village watch or aiding with other community tasks, often alongside seasoned warriors no longer fit for the more perilous combat.

Ziiba blew a wild hank of hair out of her eyes and stretched her long lean body out beside her friend, the familiar and comforting smell of leather and pine and earth wafting over Animkii. "Look, you'll pass when you're ready. It takes some warriors years."

"Not you."

Ziiba was 'special,' a prodigy who'd passed the trial at only eleven years old.

"I'm different. You know that."

"Like I need a reminder." Animkii glared at her feet. "I see the way Ishkode looks at you when you fight. She wishes you belonged to her clan, to the Bear, instead of me."

The other girl's face darkened. "You shouldn't talk like that. Besides, Ishkode favors no one." Her lips pressed together as if she was about to argue. "Sometimes I think—"

"Ishkode! Ishkode! Ishkode!"

The youth's words cut off and the body Mica possessed tensed up as the rumble of conversation and pattering of feet stilled, the girl's resentment and fear returning in an instant, building until her eyes at last lifted past the crowd to the source of her angst.

A magnificent bronze-skinned woman stood only yards away, flanked by stone-faced warriors decked in feathers and beaded hides, half her face obscured by a tattoo of a bear claw wreathed in flames, a mark that merged the symbols of both the Fire Bones and her clan, the Bear.

This was Ishkode, war chief of the Fire Bones. Her return from their southernmost outpost was a cause of both celebration and unease. Dreamers would soon overrun the outpost, as they'd done with others in the past. It was paramount that the warriors stationed there hold the line long enough to buy their sister villages time to evacuate.

Ishkode's stay was temporary, and she'd only returned to collect new recruits.

Ishkode turned her attention to the gathered crowd and spoke in a voice coarsened by years of shouting orders in the field. "Once more, the Creator calls upon us to show our devotion and guard against the encroaching darkness," she said. "Our kin need time to evacuate their villages. We must not allow a single one to fall to shadow! Let all worthy warriors present themselves now."

Mica felt the girl's nerves tighten again, the self-doubt rising like a fast tide, trying to pretend she didn't care—that this fighting was pointless because the Dreamers would always win in the end. Then she looked to the warrior standing at Ishkode's right hand, an unsmiling ash-haired man with a scar cut across his mouth and ambition burning in his dark eyes.

Raak. Ishkode's second-in-command. He belonged to the Marten Clan, a clan that valued resourcefulness and tenacity in its membership, in the same way that the Bear Clan valued strength and wisdom.

Animkii's memories revealed a man of dual personality. Outside of battle, he was a cold, calculating strategist with an uncanny ability to predict outcomes. He possessed a mind that chewed through problems and spat out solutions to any scenario you could imagine. However, in the heat of battle, he transformed into a figure of sheer brutality, taking sadistic pleasure in the humiliation and torture of his foes. This darker side was so pronounced that his enemies dubbed him the Rabid Beast.

The Four Peoples respected Ishkode, but they *feared* Raak.

Animkii shivered as his cold gaze fell on her, watching her now, like he always did, though he'd never once spoken a word to her. Was he judging her? Did he share her vessel's contempt? Mica didn't know what to make of his interest, either.

There were eager shouts as other young warriors, previously left behind to guard the village, now volunteered to defend the southernmost outpost, knowing that many, maybe most, would sacrifice their lives to do so. Animkii hunched over her spear, poking its tip into the fire, watching it harden into a lethal weapon, her jaw tightening with pent-up frustration. When she looked up again, she found Raak still watching her. This time, his scarred mouth twisted with a goading smile, and she saw in that expression the cry of cowardice.

Reacting with pure emotion, she stood up and opened her mouth. "Let me fight too!"

She heard Ziiba suck in her breath.

A sympathetic titter ran through the crowd. The villagers knew her previous failures well. The eyes of her vessel turned on her with such absolute loathing that, for a moment, she felt like someone had plunged her into an icy river.

"You?" With only that single word, Ishkode conveyed her absolute condescension. "You who have failed twice to pass your trials? You are neither worthy nor a full warrior, Animkii."

The youth's body burned with an anger so intense it made her vision blur and brought humiliating tears to her eyes. She pounded the haft of her spear against the soil. "I *am* worthy. I demand a new trial."

It was a challenge she'd issued. The crowd went silent. There was not a person here who'd dare interfere, and only a few who pitied her.

Animkii burned with humiliation. In her head, she knew what they whispered behind their hands—that after all her training, all her struggles, she was still a disappointment to her clan: too slow, too awkward, but most of all too emotional to be a full warrior. She wanted to prove them all wrong, to show them she was just as good as Ziiba.

Mica didn't understand her impatience. Pride wasn't worth getting your face kicked in. She'd spent her childhood dodging violence, cowering and pleading her way out of beatings, whether they came from her father, the peacekeepers who policed the undercity, or cartel members demanding overdue protection money. Running *toward* a fight was not something she'd do.

But Animkii seemed the opposite, someone constantly kicking down barriers and breaking her own leg in doing so. And what had it gained her? She'd formed an attachment to her vessel, loved Ishkode so fiercely that it hurt her to the bottom of her soul.

Mica's memory of her own hateful father rose in comparison, bringing with it all the resentment and loathing of a childhood raised under his quick-fisted tyranny. She'd feared her father too much to fight back, quailing and cringing in submission in hopes he'd soften the blows, just once.

But Animkii had confronted her tormentor head-on. She was an idiot to think Ishkode could ever love her. People like her vessel, like Mica's father, weren't capable of it.

Giving the bold girl no more acknowledgment than she would an irritating fly, Ishkode turned to murmur a few words to her second-in-command, whose own eyes hadn't left the scene even for a second.

"That's enough, Ishkode." A fresh voice pierced the lull, soft but forceful, and the crowd parted to reveal a handsome, brown-skinned man with kind eyes. Dozens of long black braids hung down his shoulders, threaded with bone beads and stems of sage, and the soft beige robes he wore bore intricate quillwork depicting trees and flowers. "Animkii is not ready."

Ishkode's response was cold with hatred, her vitriol aimed solely at the speaker. "Mothers may not interfere in warrior business, Debwe. You know that."

"Protecting a child *is* a mother's business."

A tense silence stretched between the mother and the warrior. Animkii watched the two, aggrieved by the sight, her emotions torn with love for both a beloved mother who'd helped raise her and the vessel who'd denied her. She wanted so badly to make them both proud of her.

"Why don't we allow Animkii to make the choice?" Raak slid into the conversation, his eyes gleaming with anticipation. "*She* believes she is ready."

"I am!" Animkii burst out.

Ishkode turned her face from Debwe's pleading eyes. "Fine. The child believes she will pass this time. Let the trial proceed now. We don't have the time to waste on preparations. Ready yourself, Animkii."

At last! Animkii's thoughts raced with exhilaration, her mouth dried, and her chest heaved with anticipation as the crowd pressed around her. She'd trained so hard these last few months. Surely this time she'd prove herself a warrior. Hiding her nerves, trying to look stoic, she stood up from the ground.

"And my opponent?"

"Ziiba." Ishkode's lip curled.

The knot in her stomach tightened. Of all people!

"You can still back out!" Ziiba hissed from beside her, rising from her casual lounging, tensing with anxiety. "She'll know if I hold back. I can't—"

"Then don't!"

Animkii clutched her spear in one hand and moved away from the fire and her friend, taking a defensive stance. The spectators formed a wide circle around the two girls, and she could feel Raak's eyes boring into the back of her head.

"First blood!" Ishkode said.

Ziiba sighed her relief. "Good. At least you won't get hurt too badly."

Anger provoked, Animkii cried out, "Last blood!"

This time, the crowd murmured its protest. Last blood was not for uninitiated warriors like Animkii. The Fire Bones were fierce and merciless toward their enemies, but they did not condone death-matches between children. If Ishkode didn't intervene, the dual would only end when one combatant could no longer rise, a possible death sentence for one of them.

And everyone here knew that Ziiba was the superior warrior—Ziiba the youngest warrior in three generations, Ziiba who could out-maneuver grown men, Ziiba who was Ishkode's source of pride and Animkii's source of humiliation.

"Last blood!" the war chief agreed. At her side, Raak looked positively gleeful.

Ishkode could easily stop all this, Mica knew. No one expected a child to fight a warrior, even if that warrior was her peer in age. Debwe was arguing with Ishkode in the distance, their words unheard from behind the crowd's muttering.

Both girls hoisted their spears.

Resentment surged through Animkii. She was just as capable as Ziiba! This time, she'd prove her strength to everyone. She ignored the smaller voice in her mind that told her Ishkode hoped she'd die here.

The fight began and even Mica could see right away that Ziiba out-matched Animkii. The other girl was strong and fast and confident, whipping her spear around as if it was weightless, though the pinched look on her face betrayed her feelings of conflict.

Fueled by emotion, Animkii was a ball of energy striking out with careless anger, each jab deftly, humiliatingly deflected by her opponent until she felt the blood rush to her face in a show of shame. If she could just get one attack past Ziiba's defenses! There was strength in her blows, but she couldn't keep her thoughts straight under the pressure of these watching, judging eyes. She was certain they all wanted her to fail. Sweat dripped down her face as fury pushed her into a frenzy.

Ziiba moved with effortless grace, sidestepping each of Animkii aggressive thrusts or parrying them with her weapon's shaft. Deftly. Quickly. The enthusiasm of the crowd faded, replaced by unease at such an obviously unequal match.

Breathing heavily now, muscles burning with exhaustion, Animkii slowed her movements, circling her friend, desperate to find even a single opening.

There were none.

"First blood." Without warning, Ziiba's arm swung forward and Animkii's side opened up in a gush of red as the spear lanced through it. As the young fighter bit back her scream, Mica's own psychic cry filled the space inside the girl's borrowed mind.

The wound was a shallow one. Trying not to hurt her, Mica thought. Ziiba had such precise control over her movements that it couldn't be anything else.

Animkii gritted her teeth. She knew it too, and her pride stung from it. "Don't hold back!"

"Second blood." With a speed difficult to follow, Ziiba whipped her body around and plunged her weapon into Animkii's other side, pulling it back out with a violent spray of blood and tissue. Animkii choked, her legs bent, stance wavering. Tears burned her eyes. The strongest warriors sang against the pain, but Animkii couldn't do it. If she dared open her mouth, she'd be screaming.

"Third blood!"

Ziiba's eyes filled with tears of regret as she brought up the shaft of the spear too fast to follow, smashing it against her opponent's head with such strength that it knocked her to the ground. Animkii's vision danced with darkness as she collapsed to the ground, throwing up from the knock on her head. She tried to get back up and as she did, Ziiba cried out.

"Last blood!"

Her spear tip penetrated her exposed back and came out below her opponent's rib cage, burying itself in the dirt. Instinctively Animkii's hands came up to clutch at the shaft, trying to tear it free, but there was no strength left in her body, and she seized over the killing pole like a gutted beast.

"I'm sorry!" Ziiba's voice and Debwe's cry of fear came at her from what seemed like a mile away. When she managed to lift her head, it wasn't them she saw. Instead, Raak was crouching beside her, a thin smile slashed across his scarred face. The distinct stench of weathered leather and aged blood assaulted her nostrils.

A feeling of dread filled her.

"If you survive until my next return from the outposts, find me," he rasped, his voice grating and unsettling. "I'll show you the path of a true warrior."

***

With those words, the scene blurred, sped forward, a series of images from Animkii's past churning through Mica's mind, switching to the weeks and months and years of grueling training under Raak's tyrannical tutelage.

"To be a true warrior, you must first conquer fear."

Raak's counsel to his newest pupil drifted through Mica's consciousness, alongside memories of traveling through a decaying forest, engulfed by a bone-deep chill. Unearthly howls echoing through the trees around them, wailing cries that belonged to no animal or human, but something else, something that hungered for their lives and their souls...

"Then pain..."

Days without sleep. Belly burning with hunger. Body pushed beyond endurance. She danced around a ravenous fire, screaming her war song, her flesh rent with knives and hooks and other sharp instruments, blood dripping from the wounds. And every time she slowed, her mentor was there with a fist or a whip or a blade.

"Then emotion..."

Her first battlefield. Watching friends and kin get torn apart and devoured by the ravenous horrors that infested the south, forbidden to weep, and all the time, the rifts continued to spread as if all those sacrifices meant nothing at all...

Chapter Three

There were too many of them.

Through Animkii's eyes, Mica watched a silvery mist slip between the blades of grass, winding about the trees that bordered the outpost. Ethereal, humanoid shapes formed from its deathly fingers, ghostly apparitions trailing decay, causing all life to wither in their shadow. They glided effortlessly through the blackened battle trenches, where fires once roared in defense against them. The Dreamers were simultaneously beautiful and terrifying, shimmers of what they'd been while alive.

Animkii stood at the top of an outpost wall, watching the fiends drift soundlessly across the battlefield, gorging themselves on the souls of the dying and the dead. She was taller now, a towering warrior-woman built like her vessel. Mica marveled at the strength of her adult body, every inch muscled as hard as rock, her brown skin now covered in scrolling black tattoos marking battlefield victories and comrades lost. But even after years of fighting them, the Dreamers' presence still left an icy grip on her heart.

Mica, too, felt the awful dread creep into their shared consciousness, felt it tear open a psychic wound as agonizing as any physical one.

The Fire Bones guarding the outpost walls poured their terror into preparations as they readied arrows and staves, wrapping the ends in rags soaked in animal fat, then plunging the weapons into one of the many fire pits. Fire was the only weapon effective against a Dreamer, but it was too fleeting, too fickle to last in any lengthy battle.

They'd done this before, too many times.

Animkii shook her mind free of the Dreamers' dark glamor, her hand fumbling for the spear she kept tethered to her back. She dipped its bulbous torch end into one fire and then rotated the shaft to use it as a flame spear. No matter how many times she'd faced these dread things, it was always just as terrible as the first time. Even Ziiba, standing a few feet away, looked shaken, her face the color of dry clay.

But years of training under Raak had hardened Animkii into stone. Battle scars ribboned her skin, testament to both his brutal tutelage and the wars that had followed. There was a coldness in her posture, a confidence in her skill that all acknowledged, and that stubborn, angry child she'd once been had been long-forgotten and replaced.

"Come on!" She crushed her own growing terror and grabbed her friend by the arm, shaking her free of the trance. With a flaming spear in one hand and Ziiba in the other, she left the safety of the walls to join the retreating frontline behind the last trench of fire.

Shouting orders from the center of the crowd was Ishkode.

She couldn't help but stare at the war chief in all her glory, silhouetted against the blazing bonfires, her grim face made fiercer by the number of old scars hacked into it. Her throaty voice rose in an unwavering battle song as her warriors lined up shoulder-to-shoulder and fired flaming arrows into the oncoming swell of Dreamers, picking off the shades one at a time. Less experienced warriors stayed nearest the fire, lighting and handing off ammunition to the warriors on the front lines as fast as they could to keep ahead of the approaching horrors.

It wasn't enough.

It was *never* enough, but she'd fight until the Creator took her home to save those she could.

"There's too many for us to fight," Ziiba said in a deathly voice. "You've got to leave before they breach the last furrow. If you're by yourself, they might not notice you."

Animkii knew it wasn't just her own life Ziiba feared for this time. "I won't abandon our comrades!"

"If they knew you were—" A howling wind passed over the pair at that moment, carrying a whiff of death and the chill of winter on it. The Dreamers keened their wailing song. Frost crept over the walls of the outpost, the grass at their feet, and even their skin. "Too late." Her lips pulled back tight against her teeth and her eyes brightened with fear.

"Raak received a raven this morning. Reinforcements are only a day away," Animkii said. "We only need to hold the line until they reach us."

"If not, we'll meet again in the Land of Souls, won't we?" Ziiba laughed, a poor imitation of her normal cheer.

"We're not dead yet."

An unnatural gust of wind swept its terrible, freezing hand across the last row of fires and sent a wave of earth and ash tumbling over the guardian flames. In an instant, the flames died, and the Dreamers rushed forward to engulf the battlefield.

Ziiba grabbed her by the arm and there were tears in his eyes. "Animkii, I want you to know, I—"

She never finished, her breath turning to ice mid-sentence as a ghastly hand tore through her side in a spray of blood. Her eyes darkened, and whatever words she'd meant to say, she sucked back in with a sharp inhalation of pain. An icy-blue light wreathed its bony spectral fingers as it lifted and dangled the young warrior's body in the air, a rime of frost spreading out from the gaping wound, freezing the blood.

She hadn't even seen it approach! How had the Dreamer reached them so fast? In seconds, her friend's skin withered, and the rot spread, turning Ziiba's face black with cold.

Animkii couldn't breathe. The shock was so bad, her mind going dark, her legs frozen in place, weighed down by the abomination's presence. All that training to feel nothing now crumbled, leaving her afraid. She didn't want to die, not like this.

Then her gaze locked on Ziiba's terrified face and the fear fled. She had to save her! Risking everything, she charged forward with a cry to grab at her friend's legs, pulling her free with all the desperate strength she had, until her body at last tumbled to the ground. She rolled over that frigid figure, shielding it with her own body, trying not to gape up at the Dreamer that now towered over both of them. Tendrils of dark energy writhed around it, hungering for her soul as she swung out defensively with her bow stem.

She was about to die. "Creator, save us all!"

But as the Dreamer moved to devour her, an arc of flame appeared overhead and cut down through the unliving shadow, severing its ties to this world and causing it to burst apart like a flock of ravens. And standing there, spinning a flaming spear in one hand, was Ishkode, howling her war song while the shadows surrounding the camp thickened into a storm.

Animkii could see the bodies now piled near the sputtering trenches. Her comrades, fallen. And the Dreamers... Her eyes scanned the distance. The Dreamers were still coming.

Ishkode's skin was black with rot. Part of her face was missing, her body marked all over from the grasping evil hands that she'd fought to get to Animkii's side. She was dying, but her song did not waver.

"My time is now. The Great Spirit sings in my head," her vessel said, the skin flaking away from her decaying cheeks, yet her stoic countenance betraying not the slightest sign of the agony she must've suffered. "Find Raak and tell him to burn the outpost, then take our warriors and withdraw. Send word to our sister villages to evacuate. The rest of us will cover your retreat."

"No! Let me fight! Let me die with you!" She couldn't contain the burst of forbidden emotion.

Ishkode turned to face her in that moment, and her voice was cold with condemnation. "You're just like your mother."

Dropping her burned-out torch, the war chief withdrew a skin of oil and poured its contents over her own body.

Animkii strangled her protests, clenching her fists and gritting her teeth to hold back the shameful tears that threatened to let loose. She knew her vessel's intentions. "May the Creator walk you down the final path," she intoned the grave ritual words.

With no emotion at all, no parting words, Ishkode walked away, back into the chaos of a battle lost, past her dying subordinates, and into the fading trench of fire, singing—then screaming—her death song as the fading embers roared back to life and her entire body went up in flames. Sheer force of will moved her body as she rushed out of the fire to meet the wave of Dreamers, scattering them. Her powerful arms spread wide to embrace her unearthly foes in a fiery death, and the fire did what normal weapons failed to do: destroyed them.

"Night covers all the skies in black,
stars falling from its seams.
It poisons the dreams.

The flames beat against the air,

distant drums in our heads
that kill the restless dead."

All feeling drained away from Animkii. She watched her vessel single-handedly draw the Dreamers away from the surviving Fire Bones, buying them time, sacrificing her life for theirs. A true warrior. A hasty hand grabbed her in passing and pulled her along, like a twig drawn down a river's current, bobbing up and down, pulled down into the depths, then resurfacing, then drowning again. She looked up at her passing savior, her eyes bleary with tears.

Ziiba!

Then darkness passed across Mica's vision once more and an infant's muffled wail rose out of the fog.

***

Awareness came back to Animkii—and Mica—as a whisper of conversation that floated across their shared consciousness.

Her eyelids fluttered. She stared up at the ceiling of the village medicine lodge, bundles of dried herbs hanging from the rafters, her vision obscured by a thick haze of sweet-smelling tobacco smoke. Soft furs cushioned her aching back and heated strips of hide wrapped around her extended abdomen, reducing the pain of old wounds to a dull ache. A cool cloth pressed against her forehead.

"I thought we'd lose both of you!" Debwe, her favorite mother, stood beside her, his entire face crinkling with a relieved smile.

Debwe was not only a mother, but the Fire Bones' best healer and, from what Mica gleaned from Animkii's memories, renown as much for his compassion as for his medicine skills. Right now, his voice was stern with worry. "You shouldn't have gone to the outpost, not in your condition."

Animkii's head spun. In the shadows behind her mother, she saw Ziiba holding a squalling bundle, and the battle for her life seemed less important now, diminished. A fierce protectiveness rose in her. "Is that—?"

"Isn't he beautiful, Animkii? Strong like his vessel." Ziiba's eyes wrinkled at the corners, their familiar light never once fading, not even in the weeks it'd taken her to recover from the battle. Wherever the Dreamer had touched her with its deathly fingers, vast swaths of her coppery skin had turned icy-white, with flakes of dead skin constantly sloughing off cheeks turned gaunt. But when Ziiba looked at Animkii's child, all her suffering vanished beneath an expression so radiant that it made Animkii's heart melt.

Why shouldn't a vessel love her child as fiercely as any mother? Why should Animkii's part remain a secret when all her dreams now revolved around this one little person?

It wasn't fair that her kin would take her son from her and give him to another to nourish. She saw Ziiba's joy and imagined a different life together somewhere, in a place without war, without pain. A place where the woman who bore a child could raise him without condemnation because she'd survive long enough to do so.

"His name is Niigaanii," she said. *He leads.* Her heart filled with a feverish love. "I will clear the path for him, but he will be the one to lead our people down it."

***

Mica teetered between worlds, drifting from Animkii's memories into reality, then pulled into the past, back and forth, unable to fully exist in either world. The passage of weeks, months, years... Mica couldn't keep track, constantly pulled forward in someone else's timeline while the real world sat behind a sheer curtain she couldn't quite pull back.

Animkii had a kid.

Her mind flooded with the image of a wailing, red-faced infant and a rush of fierce, protective love she knew all too well—*family*.

An old ache stirred inside her. Her own memories emerged and overcame Animkii's: her noisy little brothers' constant readiness for fresh adventures; her mother's glowing smile when her stepfather scooped the tikes up in his massive arms; and how much she'd loved this new family that'd grown from the wreckage left by her dead birth father.

Reid had tried to fit in for Mica's sake, but she knew the chaos of their new life had disenchanted him and that he'd resented their intrusion on his independence. Still, their adoring half-siblings would swarm him the minute he walked in the front door, and the memory of his good-natured grimaces and pockets full of hidden candy still brought a smile to her lips.

Mica understood *exactly* why Animkii had shattered every taboo, every law, to venture into that dead city. She'd have done the same if it meant saving her family.

"He's gone mad!"

Mica snapped back to a new scene emerging from Animkii's past. The warrior was pacing a forest floor, tense with frustration. A long braid of black hair swung across her tattooed back and she held her hunting bow in one hand, while Ziiba leaned against a nearby tree with a patient smile plastered on her face. The Dreamer's mark hadn't healed, leaving the left side of Ziiba's face gray and paper-thin, her arm withered and dead-looking.

"Don't they see that Raak's taking them away to their deaths? And for what? The Dreamers have gotten stronger. The rifts are everywhere. There's no game south of here anymore and our hunters must go farther and farther north. Why do we stay?"

Ziiba pushed away from the trunk, embracing her from behind to still her movement. "It's what we've always done, ever since the Sundering." Her tone suggested this wasn't the first time they'd had this conversation. "We stay as long as we can because if we leave, there'll be no one to slow the Dreamers' advance."

"There's got to be a better way. What about the Ancients' city, the one inside the Dead Lands? The stories speak of a great weapon hidden there, one powerful enough to even fell the Great Lynx!"

Another old city, buried in the earth, just like those found in the southern undercities. Mica's attention sharpened. So it was the same here... Whatever had broken the Earth hadn't spared the northern world. The south had no name for 'rifts,' just knew to avoid the fissures beneath the ground and the deathly chill they exuded—what they called hollow storms. But while the Fire Bones feared these dead places as cursed by their maker, the greedy Technocrats sought to reclaim the Old World's cities and plunder their treasures.

Animkii had been an avid listener to her people's stories of the Ancients' world, imagining a time when the shattered underground cities teemed with living people and humanity had ruled like gods over the world. She'd never feared the past like others in her village—she *longed* for it.

To Mica, the stories of Animkii's people were a strange mythology. The Fire Bones believed that, prior to the Sundering, humanity had forged monstrous machines to wage their ceaseless wars, consuming the life of the Earth to fuel these abominations. For Animkii's people, the Earth was far more than a mere dwelling; it was a sacred entity they lovingly referred to as the Earth Mother. The Mother was the living embodiment of nature, her spirit interwoven with the very fabric of Creation. Without her, life was stagnant. The Creator's divine touch permeated every breath, every heartbeat, and every leaf that danced in the wind, but it was the Earth Mother's spirit that wove it all together.

The Sundering, the breaking of the Earth Mother, was the sin Animkii's people sought atonement for.

The Technocrats had a different story. What Animkii's people called the Sundering, they blamed on a massive molecular shift that broke all known physics and set off a chain reaction of cataclysmic geological events and mass extinctions. Mammoth fissures tore apart continents, swallowing entire civilizations. Black waters formed at their coastal shores that were so toxic that nothing could cross their surface, radiating an energy that was anathema to any kind of tech and so potent that even the skies miles above were affected. If there were other surviving continents in their broken world, there was no way to reach them.

When Samiel had first told her that, Mica had laughed at the idea that the Technocrats were prisoners themselves. The Fire Bones, however, took their mythology a little more seriously.

"Don't talk like that." Ziiba's teasing tone disappeared. "Even thinking about it is blasphemy. If anyone overheard you, they'd toss you into the End!" Then, seeing the scowl on her companion's face, she softened her voice and pulled her back with a sigh. "We must endure and strengthen our faith for the day the Great Lynx, Mishibijiw, rises from the End of the World. You can't fight the darkness with a half-heart, Ani. Just think of how good it will be when the Earth Mother finally awakens from Her slumber and brings forth the age of renewal. No more Dreamers. No more death. And our loved ones in the Land of Souls will walk among us once again... so don't go risking your soul just to spite Raak. It's not worth it!"

Mica saw in her head Ziiba's image of Mishibijiw, the so-called Great Lynx, a beast that embodied the darkness of the deep waters, his feline form adorned with glistening serpentine scales and fiery eyes. He was said to dwell in the poisonous black sea at the bottom of the End of the World, drawing the malevolent Dreamers about him in preparation for the final battle, a war in which he would unleash chaos and undo Creation. Only by following the Creator's covenant could the Four Peoples hope to strengthen themselves to overturn this great evil and restore the Earth Mother to wholeness.

More superstitious garbage. The Cult revered a god eager to rend the world apart, and Animkii's people worshipped one who watched as others played their part. One god craved ruination while the other embraced indifference. If such beings really existed, she couldn't believe anyone would be stupid enough to trust they had humanity's best interests in mind.

Animkii turned cold at Ziiba's warning. "If *you* could stop the Dreamers from ever hurting our people again, wouldn't you risk *your* soul for it?"

Tension stretched between the two, but then Ziiba put up her hands in surrender, laughter teasing her words as she leaned in for a kiss. "Just stop trying to find new ways to get yourself killed, okay? If you end up losing your soul, who will I torment in the Land of Souls?"

When Animkii saw her smile, she couldn't stay angry.

Their embrace sent Mica spiraling back into darkness and she felt time shift away. All she could do was hold on tight as Animkii's mind conjured a new vision from the darkness: a searing blue light that began as a pinprick and grew until the surrounding space filled with its blinding radiance.

What now?

Emerging from the light and floating in the air was an obsidian dagger no longer than her palm, carved into the likeness of a flying raven, its black blade wreathed in cerulean flames as it slowly rotated before her eyes.

Before she could probe this strange appearance, an unseen force yanked her consciousness back into an unexpected and jarring darkness. The knife's image tore away, and when she tried to bring the mod's mind back into focus, she found portions of the memories obscured, pictures shifting in and out of view, impossible to hold down.

Did Animkii know she was here?

"Animkii?" Her voice echoed in the darkness. "Can you hear me?"

There was no answer, just a stretch of darkness, and a sense that she was in a place she shouldn't be. But rather than withdraw, she probed further. There was a memory here that Animkii was blocking, but she couldn't penetrate the psychic wall thrown up between her and her ally's past.

Who was Animkii blocking it from? Mica or herself?

The more Animkii's subconscious resisted her intrusion, the more Mica's grip on the other woman's mind slipped. There were frightening moments of consciousness when she caught glimpses of snow-buried landscapes and icy-blue skies and the shuffling movement of Animkii ahead of her, hauling her behind on a crude wooden sledge. There was a strange comfort in seeing the big mod trudging in front of her, as if this mountainous warrior formed a wall of protection against the horrors outside.

Was this the real world or another memory?

But it was so cold she saw her breath turn to mist in the air. It was real, alright. As she slipped in and out of worlds, between Animkii's mind and this freezing place, pieces from the last few days (or weeks or months?) assembled into a more complete picture. A disquieting new realization began to settle in: They weren't in Alpha anymore. She didn't know how they'd escaped, but back in Alpha, Animkii had rescued her, and now the mod was keeping her safe in this icy alien land.

It was a humbling realization to learn that Animkii was the only reason she wasn't dead.

All these years of despising and mistrusting any kind of sentient tech, and now she owed her survival to a mod. Her gut twisted. There was no one else left in the world who gave a damn whether Mica lived or died, but here was Animkii, risking her life to save her.

Guess it wasn't fair to compare all mods to Pandora and High Father Holy, but it was so hard to let go.

She drifted between daylight and darkness. During moments of lucidity, she tried crying out to Animkii, only to find her lips unmoving and her voice stolen. She was still too far inside Animkii's memories to interact with the real world, too deep inside to escape. Time after time, she tried to resurface, but it was like swimming from the bottom of the ocean with stone legs.

And all that time, she was aware of another presence closing in, a chilling weight on her mind that waited for her to emerge from the safety of Animkii's past.

The After Lord.

Just the thought of that abhorrent being chased her back into the heart of Animkii's memories, her terror pushing her past the mod's resistance in time to find herself back in Animkii's body, balanced on the edge of a cliff and staring down at a chasm full of writhing, nightmarish shadows. The Dreamers' hunger for her soul bled into the air as she peered down into the End of the World.

Then someone shoved her from behind and she was falling...

Chapter Four

Conditions only worsened the farther Animkii traveled into the rift.

Entire landscapes had collapsed inward, creating unstable ground riddled with deep crevices hidden beneath fragile snow bridges; more than once, she almost fell to her death when the snowy crust broke beneath her feet.

In one spot, a diverted river ran down over the lip of the rift and formed a small pool at the bottom, but its waters churned with poison and the fish that once ran in its streams she found belly-up and rotting. Entire forests had tumbled into the gorge, tree roots sticking up in the air, black with rot where the Dreamers had passed over their remains. Other places were littered with the corpses of birds that had fallen dead from the sky, their little bodies twisted and broken beyond anything natural she'd ever seen.

Whenever a rift opened, it released a deathly chill that withered both body and soul if one couldn't escape its breath. These corpses were recent, not yet skeletonized, which meant a new rift had opened here, probably only days ago. It wasn't uncommon for more diminutive cracks to appear near the larger ones, spilling out death to areas nearby. She sensed no unnatural chill here, so she assumed it had sealed itself, as happened with the smaller ones. Still, it made her uneasy. It was a sign that this rift was not as dormant as she'd hoped.

What was it like on the surface? How far had the End stretched its rifts northward? How many other villages and lives had it claimed?

She stared up at the sky, the rim of the rift still too far above her to surmount. It was impossible to be sure with the altered landscape, but she guessed she was within The Stretch by now. In past days, these lands had been abundant with life, her belly easily filled with the help of her spear and bow. Not so now. It was a small mercy that Animkii's biosteel body, in its continued evolution toward full mod, no longer required food, only stims.

Mica wasn't as fortunate. Her body shrank with each passing day, sustained by the watery broth that Animkii brewed from melted snow and whatever scraps of meat she managed to scavenge from other ill-fated creatures sharing their prison. Intermittent fevers continued to course through the woman, causing her body to shiver and shake. Even in the icy air, sweat soaked her skin.

At first, Animkii worried that Mica was dying, the way she strained and gnashed her teeth and cried out in pain, but over time the symptoms lessened, eased away. She cast a look back at her wane-faced charge, bundled and tied onto the sled like a swaddled infant. Mica was doing it again: muttering to herself, crying out. Another nightmare, maybe? Fearing the noises would attract predators—and not just living ones—Animkii came to a halt. She kneeled beside the sled and its restrained occupant, murmuring reassurances.

"You are safe now," she said, watching the pale face twist, the lips releasing another moan. "You are dreaming. Whatever you are seeing is not real."

Mica's eyes opened, as empty and black as a winter night, staring out at Animkii with no sign of recognition. In fluent Withertongue, she said:

"If *you* could stop the Dreamers from ever hurting our people again, wouldn't you risk *your* soul for it?"

Animkii's mouth dropped open. How could Mica know those words, that language? She shook the woman and called out her name, needing an explanation, not liking the conclusions her mind was racing to. "Can you hear me?"

But there was no answer. The mutterings quieted, and the woman lay still.

Animkii sat back in the snow, contemplating her charge with uneasy eyes, confused and frightened by what she'd heard. What did it mean? How had Mica known those words unless she could read Animkii's memories? Had the Technocrats linked their minds together like they did with mods? Or was it something else?

She wiped a trace of frost off the pale cheek. Every instinct screamed at her to leave the woman behind, to get away from whatever unnatural power the Technocrats had imbued her with. But when she remembered the terror on the woman's face back in Alpha, the knife at her throat, she knew she couldn't abandon her. Not after all they'd been through in the last few weeks.

And now they were on the brink of entering the Dead Lands. Thrice before, Animkii had trespassed those cursed lands, the first forced by Raak, the second by her own choice, and the third as a death sentence. The cold of winter sank deeper into her bones now, an unnatural chill settling in. If they had to pass through that place, the Dreamers...

She didn't want to think about it. There had to be another way out of here.

But she'd been telling herself that for over a week now and the cliffs surrounding her remained a treacherous vertical incline. Twice, she'd attempted to scale the walls, but her borrowed steel arm hadn't completed its transition to biosteel, leaving it so inflexible that every time her metal fingers clawed at the icy face, it was like throwing knives against stone. She could only make it several yards before sliding back down.

The weather wasn't helping, either. A shelter built hastily from fallen tree branches and packed snow kept the wind off them, but an unnatural cold still penetrated the walls. To keep Mica warm, she huddled against her under the fur blankets at night, her biosteel skin radiating enough warmth to stave off the worst of the cold. The other woman's strange mutterings continued on into the night, snippets of conversation spoken in Animkii's own language, names spoken that Mica *shouldn't* have known, mingled in with bursts of laughter, or shouts of excitement, or sometimes cries of pain.

For a while she lay there, listening in, trying to decipher the disjointed conversations, but she'd traveled for days now with no rest. She needed to hibernate and give her system time to recalibrate after traveling through such intense conditions with minimal stim support. Pushing too hard, too fast, with no means to refuel or repair, could be catastrophic. Mostly she stopped for Mica's sake, though. Her unconscious charge needed relief from the harsh weather outside and time to warm up and eat before heading back into temperatures that could kill a human.

Was Mica even aware of her peril? Could she feel the pains of hunger and cold while in her current condition? A corpse's face had more color than Mica's, and yet she still breathed on her own, her chest rising and falling rhythmically. Each desperate day that passed, Animkii looked for signs that she might be resurfacing.

Time passed and their journey continued. The broken landscape stretched endlessly eastward, with no end in sight. And always, *always*, she watched for Dreamers, for now the smell of rot permeated the air no matter where they traveled, and she grew fearful that they were headed toward a confrontation. When or where, she didn't know, but it made her anxious.

One ambush was all it would take. Yet she couldn't risk activating her defensive system, knowing that the constant drain on her meagre stim resources would not only shorten her life, but waste resources she'd need if Dreamers or something else attacked them. On a planned battlefield, things were simpler—the Alphaknot would send out small drones to refuel their soldiers. With no such luxury here, she had no choice but to rely on her inferior human instincts to survive.

About midday, a snowstorm hit.

***

Mica's eyes snapped open. Sharp awareness of a new location replaced the expected pain of shattered bones.

Where was she? She stared up at a snow-packed ceiling only a few feet away from her face, then peered down at her own prone body, flat on its back on a fur mat inside the smoky interior of a crude snow hut. There was a tiny fire burning at one end of the shelter, giving off just enough heat to keep the shelter warm without melting its walls. But one of her arms had fallen free of the blankets and the colorless corpse hand she saw definitely didn't belong to Animkii.

This was no memory. She was back in her own body!

Her joy was short-lived. Though conscious at last, when she tried to move her body, she found it locked in place, inertia having weakened her muscles to the point of immobility. Had she been out of it that long? But no, it wasn't that. She could *feel* there was something else wrong with her.

Whatever she'd done back in Alpha, it'd left her damaged. But how badly?

She closed her eyes and felt the call of Animkii's memories reaching out to her. It was a hard, unforgiving life, but one that was safe from the Other World. But Mica wasn't an idiot. In all the years she'd spent running from problems, she'd never once gotten away. Eventually, whatever chased her caught up, and then it was all the worse for her, whether it meant broken bones from a beating or being left to die from dirty drugs in a filthy alleyway. She wouldn't escape anything by riding around in Animkii's head. She'd just delay the inevitable.

She focused instead on the real world, listening to the small fire crackle and spit, and watching its smoke curl through the shelter's small opening. From outside, she could hear the howl of a storm, but the hide blanket hanging over the dugout door kept the worst of the wind at bay. In time, sensation returned to her extremities, and she could wriggle her toes and fingers, those simple movements coming as an immense relief to her.

Though she doubted she'd be winning any foot races soon.

While stuck in place, her only concept of time came from a sliver of light that snuck past the door covering and slowly disappeared as day vanished into night.

Still no Animkii.

Her body slowly revived over agonizing hours. With immense effort, she managed to shake free the stinking fur blankets piled on top of her and crawl out on her hands and knees. The wounds that had cracked open her skin in Alpha had mostly healed, forming raw, tender scabs that stung with each movement. She knew she had to awaken this body, but her limbs trembled with weakness, making even the simplest movement daunting. When she tried to rise into a crouch, her muscles protested and sent her back to the ground, her breath labored and shallow. Her stomach cramped with hunger pains, and even the smallest exertion made her feel faint.

Exhaustion eventually pulled her back to the crude fur bed, and she bundled the ratty blankets around herself again, folding her knees up to her chest and shivering. The smoky air was dense and unpleasant, sweetened by dirty sweat, animal musk, and something left to rot, but her eyelids drooped with weariness, and soon her consciousness floated on the edge of a dream.

"I knew you'd return to this world soon enough." The After Lord's familiar and insidious voice slithered into her mind, the sound of it sending a different type of chill through her body and instantly bringing her to full wakefulness. *"You can't hide forever. Every dream in this world belongs to me, and all mortals have to sleep eventually."*

Mica jerked upright, then doubled over, clutching her gut in both hands, physically sick from that uninvited presence. "Go away, you monster!" But her voice was so hoarse from neglect, it barely scraped the air with a whisper.

With relief, she felt the darkness retract its claws, but in its place rose a familiar craving—a need greater than food, a need for something that could numb the terror. Right then, she'd have sold herself for a shot of anything that could make her forget these last few weeks. However long she'd been out of it, it hadn't been long enough for her body to work through all the agonies of withdrawal.

Her head ached. Nausea rose inside her throat and her mouth salivated, and though her stomach heaved, she stopped short of vomiting. After everything that had happened, she still had to deal with *this*? She curled up into a shivering ball of misery.

Only Samiel had ever been able to talk her through the torture of abstinence, soothing her while she shook and wept and burned hot and cold all at once. But Sam was gone now. Maybe gone forever.

When Animkii finally appeared at the door, her monstrous bulk struggling to squeeze through the small opening, all the tension left Mica's body and she heaved a shuddering sigh of relief.

"Never thought I'd be so glad to see your face," she rasped, forcing a tentative smile despite the nausea gnawing at her gut, seeking levity while heavily conscious of all she owed this woman. "Guess you saved my life."

Animkii let out a strange happy noise at the sight of the other woman sitting there. She flung aside the door flap, dropping a cord of firewood by the entrance, and crawled to Mica's side, her enormous body hunched against the low ceiling. Her head scraped the roof and sent flakes of snow floating down on them. From deep inside a hood of white fur, her mismatched eyes gleamed from a face that was now almost completely biosteel.

"How do you feel?" The mod's voice startled her, ringing out deep and hollow and metallic, less human than she remembered.

"Like someone ran me through a grinder. Where the gore are we?"

"You... do not remember what happened?"

"Bits and pieces. Those bastards injected me with something, and after that, it feels a lot like a dream. No, a *nightmare*."

The mod pushed back her hood, revealing a devastating sight. The remnants of Animkii's once-lustrous black hair were gone, supplanted by an unsightly, hairless dome of gleaming biosteel. The invasive tech had further claimed her other features—traces of golden circuitry now shimmered in her remaining human eye; her cheeks resembled the hard, polished flat of a blade; and only a small patch of tissue remained to cover her lower jaw.

How much longer until that hard smile disappeared forever?

"Something happened to us, back in Alpha," Animkii said, gruff and hesitating as she searched for the words to describe what she'd experienced. "During the fight, I picked you up. You touched me and I felt pain. Then there was a bright light and when it cleared, we were here."

Mica's heart picked up pace. So she hadn't imagined it. "And where is 'here'?"

"The Witherlands, in a place my people called The Stretch. Two weeks east of my home village."

"What? We're in the north?" Again, Mica felt that deep craving for substance, for something to dull the edges of reality. "How is that even possible?"

Animkii's eyes, one a deep rich brown and the other a flickering array of lights and lenses, locked on Mica's face. In that questioning gaze were expectations for an answer Mica didn't have.

"What're you looking at me like that for? I don't know how it happened," she said, teeth chattering as she withdrew into the furs wrapped around her, like a beast burrowing into its den. Her mind raced, replaying the horrors of that day in Alpha, of dancing on the edge of madness before expecting to die like a gutted beast on some god's sacrificial altar.

Did her strange power over minds really bring them here?

Animkii's mouth tightened with an argument, but then softened. "I am sorry. It is difficult to fight an enemy that does not bleed," she said. One arm reached behind her back to pull off a bundle of blood-soaked hides. She unrolled the package onto the snow-packed floor. Three skinny fillets of meat tumbled onto the ground—just enough for one meal, maybe two—and the mod cut them into bite-sized chunks with a crude stone knife.

Mica eased back, watching the steel warrior set a clay pot over the flames and add the meat. Another wave of nausea washed over her, but she was determined in hiding her illness from Animkii. "I'm sorry too. I'm just... I'm not even sure how much of what I saw was real." She took a deep breath and, in the next few minutes, did her best to relay to the mod all she'd experienced in Alpha, from the time she'd first awakened in captivity to the manifestation of her new abilities.

"At first, I thought I was going mad," she said. "I could see inside people's minds, but there were so many I couldn't make sense of them—thousands of voices and pictures and feelings all jumbled together in my head." She looked down at her hands, clenching and unclenching them in an exercise of self-control, trying to keep her emotions from welling up. "And it turns out minds aren't the only things I can enter."

The remembered horror of the Other World froze the words in her throat, made her headache seem inconsequential as her memory filled with the terrible visage of that dark-winged monster. She drew her knees up to her chest unconsciously, a child at the mercy of nightmares, and exhaled a shaky breath.

"I saw the After Lord." In a horrified hush, she described all the things she'd witnessed in that unholy place until the story became a deluge of suffering and terror. Just speaking of it made her gut wrench with horror. "What the Cult believes isn't just some kind of story made up by delusional fanatics," she said. "He's real. And more terrible than you could ever imagine."

She felt like throwing up again.

"This After Lord must be some kind of evil spirit," Animkii said in her blunt machine voice.

Hysterical laughter bubbled up in her throat. She wanted to laugh at Animkii's words, dismiss them as some ludicrous Fire Bones fable, but humor died in the face of reality. She didn't know what to believe anymore. "I don't know *what* he is."

"Why is he after you?"

"The Cult believes my death will free him, allowing him to enter our world and destroy it."

"Mishibijiw," Animkii breathed in horror.

Mica's mind raced, recalling the name spoken by Ziiba in the mod's memories. Mishibijiw, the Great Lynx... She felt ill again, the lingering effects of withdrawal converging into a sharp pain behind her eyes.

Unaware of Mica's foray into her memories, Animkii hastened to explain, her metallic voice tinged with fear. "Mishibijiw is the monster that lurks at the End of the World's bottom. He seeks the destruction of all Creation."

"Children's stories," she muttered, the nausea thickening in her throat.

"No." The mod bowed her head, casting shadows across her biossteel face. "If this 'After Lord' is actually Mishibijiw and he emerges before we heal the Earth Mother, our entire world is in grave danger."

Something in her words chilled Mica. So convincing... She scowled. Why did Animkii always have to be so damn serious? "This is the part where you tell me I hallucinated the whole thing," she said, her voice thickening with misery. "Tell me it's just a bunch of lies. *Please.*"

"I cannot do that." Animkii's voice was a low rumble echoing in her steel throat. She kept staring into the fire, poking at it with a stick until the soup steamed, her machine-face impossible to read except for that tight-lipped mouth. "Even the place you brought us to is no longer safe. We are inside a rift."

Mica went cold. Thanks to Animkii's memories, she understood exactly what that meant: *Dreamers.* "These rifts you talk about... I think we've got them in Under-Alpha too, farther underground, way beneath the Old World cities," she said. "I bet that's where the hollow storms come from. No one's ever gotten close enough to find out, though. Most who go down that far don't come back out. I've probably gone farther than anyone else, and even I won't go down *that* deep."

"Why would you willingly enter such a terrible place?"

"There are loads of Old World artifacts down there, if you're brave enough to go deep. Back then, I'd do just about anything to put food on the table. Once you figure out which spots to avoid, it isn't so bad," she said, shrugging. "Besides, that's how I met my friend Samiel. He wanted to study the city ruins and hired me as a guide." An uncomfortable emotion burned in the back of her throat. "But so much has happened since then that when I think back, it's like—"

"Another person's life."

"Yeah." Mica studied the mod, catching the sudden distance in her voice, trying to reconstruct what her face must have looked like before her modification. It would've been a hard face, she decided, like her vessel's, dark and stoic and stern-mouthed, but the eyes would've been different. Kinder. "We've got to get out of here."

"We are too deep to climb out. We must head east and hope it comes to the surface."

"You said that your village isn't that far from here. Shouldn't we head there?"

"Firehome is gone. Destroyed." Animkii's voice strained with emotion. "It is where you first brought us. But it seems the Dreamers reached them first."

The wave of grief that hit her came as a surprise. All those people... Although she'd only been inside Animkii's memories for a short time, she'd formed a connection to the fierce warrior people. She struggled to find words of comfort for the other woman, but it wasn't in her vocabulary and instead she blurted out, "There must be survivors!"

"Snow covered any tracks, and Dreamers do not leave behind bodies."

She wished she could disappear under those penetrating eyes, but the best she could do was bury her face in the fur blanket as despair swelled inside her heart. "But you must want to search for them. Your clan. Ziiba and Niigaanii might still be alive—"

The moment the names left her lips, she knew she'd made a mistake.

***

For the first time since her freedom from the Alphaknot, Animkii was grateful that her machine-face lacked full expression, that Mica couldn't see the anger building inside her.

"Back in Alpha, you entered my mind too," she said in a flat voice.

Mica tucked her limp brown hair behind her ears, making the circles beneath her eyes, her sickly pallor, and the gauntness of her cheeks even more prominent. "I didn't mean to intrude," she said. "It was just like all those other memories that came flooding in, except I got stuck inside yours somehow. That's why I couldn't wake up. All that time, I was reliving parts of your life."

"How much did you see?" Her words were harsh.

"I don't remember much. Just flashes. Fighting Dreamers. Your vessel's death. The birth of your son. Other bits and pieces I couldn't make sense of."

Outrage sparked inside a heart normally stoic. How dare this outsider crack open her head and lay bare all her secrets and shames?! "You should not have done that."

"I didn't have control over it! I didn't want to be there, either!"

"What you did to me is the same as what the After Lord did to you when he invaded your thoughts."

Mica looked stricken. "I didn't think about it that way," she said, a deep shock wiping the lack of concern off her face, replacing it with horrified regret and none of her expected snark. A visible shiver passed through her body and her dark eyes turned hollow with an unspoken memory. "I'm sorry. I swear I didn't do it on purpose. I won't do it again."

Animkii nodded, though the uneasiness remained and gnawed at her forgiveness. "I know you did not choose these powers. The Technocrats have ruined us both. Just—try to control them. There are some things I am not ready to share."

Like Soulcleaver.

She looked back and found Mica staring at her. Ignoring the questioning gaze, she tipped the pot of squirrel meat onto a clay plate and handed it over. Though Mica acted with restraint, her dark eyes glistened with hunger. She murmured her thanks and took the plate, but Animkii saw her hands were trembling.

"Do not eat too fast." She felt a twinge of guilt that she hadn't been a better provider. These lands were too dead now.

Mica snorted softly at the warning, but didn't argue, blowing at a piece of steaming-hot squirrel meat until it was cool enough to pick up with her fingers. She chewed it slowly, thoughtfully, her expression guarded. "You know we have to return south, right?"

"It is too dangerous. We would not survive crossing the End of the World."

Not without Soulcleaver.

"Then I'll get us back the same way we came."

"No!" The word burst out of Animkii before she could stop herself, betraying her horror at using that unnatural power again. Whether forged from science, the workings of an evil spirit, or something worse, Animkii knew it was a wicked gift to have, stealing into people's brains and using what was there as a conduit across worlds. "It almost killed you," she said. "You may not wake up next time."

"You think we won't get killed if we stay here? If we can get back to Alpha, at least we have a chance."

"I would rather die in the lands of my people than become a slave to the Technocrats again."

"Okay, I get that," she said, "but what if there's another option? My friend Samiel knows all about Technocrat technology, and I mean the *high-level* stuff. I bet he can find a way to reverse your modification. If anyone can figure it out, it's him."

Animkii saw a flush creep into the other woman's cheeks. This Samiel was more than just a friend, wasn't he? She didn't give away her knowledge, but pondered Mica's words. More than anything, she wanted to believe she could become human again. Then she looked down at her left hand and saw the biosteel had spread down to her wrist. A sense of bleakness overcame her. Even before her stims ran out, it might be over for her. "It is too late. My modification is almost complete. I will find you a safe place to stay and then I—"

She'd walk into the storm to die.

As if on-cue, an eerie wail rose in the air outside their shelter and ice shot through her body. Animkii and Mica exchanged a look, and Animkii saw the horror she felt mirrored on the other woman's face. When she was in Animkii's mind, had she seen the Dreamers too?

"We have stayed too long. Attracted their notice," said Animkii, beginning to pack with urgency. "We must leave. Now."

"In this storm? Are you crazy? We won't even be able to see them coming!"

"Even in this cold, you will know if they are near."

Chapter Five

A nimkii packed their supplies with haste and strapped a protest-ing Mica to the sled, knowing they couldn't afford to slow down now. What lurked out there hungered for more than their flesh. From that moment, she spent every ounce of her energy moving blindly eastward, even when icy winds whipped up a snowstorm so thick, she had to activate her internal compass just to keep herself headed in the right direction. The howls of the Dreamers bayed in the distance.

Her body kept going, driven by machine long after her human body would've fallen. Night came too early and morning too late. There was no more stopping to sleep, to recalibrate, to warm up, to eat. Wordlessly she trudged through the snow, burning through her stims just to keep ahead of the distant howls.

It was one thing to die; another to have your soul stripped away by a Dreamer. Just the thought froze her to the core. Such souls would become Dreamers themselves, and only the intervention of the Creator could save them from an eternity of wandering the Earth as restless, soul-hungry wraiths.

Animkii's soul was just about the only thing she had left now.

With the Dreamers howling in her ears and Mica drifting in and out of restless slumber on the sled behind her, Animkii was conscious of blindly walking into a storm from which she might not return. Better hunters than her had lost their way and their lives in such weather. Her internal compass kept her oriented, but even her enhanced eyes couldn't pierce the wall of snow and she feared losing all senses just by staring into its void.

Another unearthly wail rose in the distance, awakening a surge of fear. It wasn't her imagination. The howling *was* getting closer.

"Are you okay?" Mica's voice drifted into her hearing.

Animkii shook her head. "We approach the Dead Lands. I had hoped to avoid these parts, but this rift is too deep."

"Dead Lands? Sounds ominous."

"Dreamers congregate there, drawn to the ruins. Few among my people ever entered voluntarily, except to offer sacrifices at the End of the World." Her tone darkened. "There were many sacrifices the year I left. Too many."

"Your own people would really kill you just for going into some old city?"

Glancing back, she found Mica watching her with unnerving intensity. Just how much of Animkii's past had she really seen? Did she know about her gravest sin? Did she know about Soulcleaver?

She weighed her words carefully. "Going into the city was reason enough for punishment, but it was the weapon I brought back that earned my death sentence. Our laws forbade touching anything belonging to the Ancients, but I believed my people would forgive me if I found a weapon powerful enough to destroy the Dreamers."

"You were wrong, I take it?"

"Very wrong."

Strange how the minor details of her own dread day of sacrifice remained so sharp in Animkii's mind. The last time she'd walked The Stretch, spring had poked green through the crust of snow, bristly stunted trees no higher than her knees struggled to reach the cold gray sunlight, and she'd watched a sharp-nosed fox chase a shaggy old hare across her entourage's morbid path.

Soon enough that same pathway had turned dark even in daytime, rot creeping over the earth as they'd entered the Dead Lands, that twisted landscape wrapping its arms around her and her somber companions, pulling them along a webwork of seething old rifts until at last they'd reached a crack so deep there was no bottom except blackness. *That* rift had led directly into the End of the World, the great crack that had severed Creation a thousand years ago...

Animkii stood at the edge of a cliff, staring downward into the terrifying face of her death, into the End.

From the void arose such a noise, the clamor of a thousand voices shrieking and moaning as the darkness stirred and came alive in anticipation of her blood. Even her fiercest kin couldn't hide their uneasiness, their jaws clenched in mute endurance as the deathly wraiths whispered their hungers into their minds. The putrid smell of rotten vegetation and old blood hung heavy in the mild spring evening as the silent group formed a half-circle behind her.

Animkii kept her gaze on the cliff's edge, grateful to be spared the condemnation in their watching eyes, if only for a moment.

The village Speaker, a sharp-nosed man with the voice of thunder, delivered her sentence:

"Animkii, warrior of the Fire Bones, daughter of the Bear Clan, you have violated the laws of Creation!" The holy man's wrath filled the air, his arm stabbing the air like a killing blade, his dirty face, spittle-covered lips, and tangled, peppered hair a framework for the zeal burning in his bloodshot eyes. "You walked among the forbidden lands and took from the Ancients that which is taboo. You have offended the Great Spirit and drawn the Dreamers' hunger down upon our entire people. Now we offer

you as a sacrifice, so that our people will not suffer the consequences of your sins!"

Animkii listened in grim silence, her spirit chained by her loved ones' judgement. When the Speaker had first ordered her seized, back at Firehome, she'd raged in her own defense, desperate to convince them that the weapon she'd brought back held the key to ending centuries of misery and death. But once the Speaker had condemned her to be a blasphemer, of breaking the Creator's covenant and bringing a curse down upon her people, no one would listen to her. Even the ones she'd loved best turned their backs on her.

When even Ziiba refused to speak out in her defense, Animkii lost all defiance. Shame replaced outrage. Her family's conviction of her guilt and her love for them had convinced her she was wrong after all—that some sickness of the mind must've overcome her senses for her to commit such a blasphemy. How else could she have been so arrogant, to think she could defy the Creator, that she alone could save her people? Unlike her faithless self, her people trusted the Great Spirit to bring them salvation when they were worthy.

In the end, she'd accepted the sentence. What else could she do? If she couldn't save them from the Dreamers, then at least she'd save them from the Creator's wrath.

"You who once shared our fire are now dead to us," the Speaker continued, his condemnation drawing a shudder from her skin. "We will erase your name from the Fire Bones' memories and your soul will walk with the Dreamers."

Her dearest mother made an awful choking sound then—grief strangled, contained, swallowed. Other family members and friends who'd once fought at her side, even Ziiba, remained as mute as stone. Facing forward, she never saw who pushed her into the chasm, just felt the shove against her back and the terrifying rush of the canyon's bottom rushing up to meet her, the explosive pain of hitting the ground and the cracking of her ribs. Seconds later, the reason for her exile came tumbling in after her, landing with a clatter a few feet away: an obsidian knife carved to resemble a raven.

She recoiled from Soulcleaver, despising the evil blade as the cause of all her misery. But when the Dreamers converged on her in a cloud of black terror, fear overcame shame and she took up that cursed blade and fought for a life no longer worth living...

Now, as the ghoulish cries rose in the distance, she wished she had it still. She cringed at her own blasphemy. How could she ever redeem herself when her will remained so weak, her soul so craven for life? She stared off into the gloom of the forest, reliving the shame and outrage and helplessness of her past.

"What are they, anyway?" Mica interrupted. "Dreamers, I mean."

"Our stories say they first appeared during the Sundering, that the Earth Mother's wounds gave birth to them," she replied somberly. "We call them Dreamers because they can only dream of ever being part of her wholeness again. So they hate everything that is alive and connected to the Mother. They prey on Her children and every human soul they corrupt weakens Her further."

"If your Creator's so powerful, why doesn't he just heal the Earth Mother and get rid of the Dreamers?" she asked, frustration seeping into her words. "Why does he make you suffer?"

"Humanity destroyed our Mother; it is humanity who must heal Her. Everything is interconnected. What we took, we must give back. That is the way of the Creator," she said. "We obey His covenant in order to heal our Mother before the Great Lynx rises from the End. With Her strength behind us, humanity will unite to defeat him and the Dreamers that follow in his wake. Together, we will usher in an age of renewal."

"And what if he wins?"

"The end of all things."

"Sounds like something a cultist would say. Always making up garbage to justify their awful beliefs."

"If we believe in nothing, then only nothing awaits us."

"Nothing sounds kind of peaceful to me."

Animkii side-eyed the woman and pitied her for her lack of belief, even while some insidious, blasphemous part of her whispered the same doubts. But she wouldn't succumb to those temptations ever again! The Technocracy would have its population believe in nothing but the rule of their law. And Mica's experience with the After Cult seemed to have damaged her. She'd never understand that the Creator's covenant was an act of healing, not cruelty.

The snowfall ceased after a few hours, replaced by a darkness that rolled over the land until it was night, even in the morning. No stars or moon lit their way. Even her tech-light couldn't pierce the distance farther than a few feet. This was no natural darkness and the chill that settled in was like that of a grave. The chunks of forest that had fallen into the rift were so thick in places that the pine needles scraped against her biosteel skin as she forced her way through the dense-needled branches, and while not a flake of snow fell, cold dread leaked into every part of her body.

Mica spoke. "This place..."

"Yes. The Dead Lands," Animkii said, her words ringing hollow in the dead air. Ahead of them, the forest was too dense to pull the sled through. "I will carry you on my back. There is no time to rest, not even for a few minutes."

Then she tore a bundle of limbs from a fallen pine tree to use as torches, keeping one out for immediate use and stashing the rest in the hide sack tied to her back. Pandora's hand lacked ignition points in the fingers, so Animkii exposed a corner of her weaponized chest and heated a firing chamber, holding a sap-coated branch up to it until it sparked to life.

"Normal weapons cannot kill Dreamers, but they are vulnerable to fire. If we keep the flame lit, they will avoid us until their hunger overtakes them."

"Then what?"

"We run."

"There must be another way out!"

Animkii shook her head. "I have looked, and our only choice is the Dead Lands. My body is not fully modified. I do not possess the tools we need to climb out: My human hand is too weak, and Pandora's arm lacks the required mechanisms."

"Great, so we're just going to walk into this nightmare and hope there's an end to it?"

"No. There *is* a way out," she said, drawing out the words, hesitant to voice her intentions. "There is an ancient city underground here. Its entrance lies about a day away."

Mica understood immediately. "That's where you found the weapon, isn't it?"

"Yes."

"Dammit."

Animkii shifted aside her backpack, crouching down to let Mica climb onto her back. She looped a sinew rope around the smaller woman's body to hold her in place and, once settled, Mica's arms laced tightly around the thick biosteel neck, her breath blowing warm against the warrior's flesh-cheek.

"I feel like a little kid, riding up here."

The warrior snorted, but Mica's words stirred the memory of her own child clinging to her shoulders, his shrieks of delight still ringing in her ears, the night before she'd left on her accursed quest. Grief dug into her heart with its merciless fingers. Niigaanii wouldn't remember that moment now, but it was one that Animkii would take to her grave.

"I wonder what they told Niigaanii about me," she said, her voice hoarsened with loss. "Do you think they told him the truth?"

Mica's answer was soft. "If they told him the truth, he'd think you died a hero."

Animkii bowed her head. She was no hero.

She pushed through the thickening evergreen forest with caution. A deathly chill rose from fissures hidden by the tangle of dead trees and a freezing mist swirled around their feet. The sky soon disappeared, blotted out by a canopy of broken tree trunks and other debris, the gaps filled by layers of filthy gray snow that turned orange in the torchlight.

"Feels like we're underground already," Mica muttered.

Their surroundings didn't improve much over the next day's travel, except for the dark turning to gray as daylight filtered through, just a little, past the clumps of snow and branches overhead. The shrieking in the distance was a constant reminder to keep moving. Animkii dared not slow down, not even for a moment, drawing on her precious stim repository to keep her mind focused and her pace quickened.

"The entrance can't be much farther," she told her passenger, who grumbled tiredly in response, but the reassurance was more for herself. In the firelight, she could see ruins poking out of the ground, remnants of walls that hadn't fallen into the Earth's belly with the rest of civilization but had spent a thousand years exposed to the elements.

This newest rift had torn through them, splintering the land anew and strewing the remains of the old city, obliterating any landmarks she might have remembered and leaving behind a stretch of devastation.

Another howl caused the pair to freeze.

"That sounded really close," Mica said. "What're we going to do?"

As Mica spoke the words, wispy shapes formed from the dark holes between trees. Animkii continued to move swiftly through the forest, thrusting the torch at the grasping shadowy hands that now crept between the branches and tried to reach into her soul. At the sight of her fire, the deathly spirits shrieked their rage and their loathing hit her with an almost physical force. She choked on it, staggering in the snow.

"Animkii..." A familiar voice drifted from the shadows.

Her heartbeat turned into a knife. Ishkode's voice.

She urged herself to ignore it, locking her jaw, keeping her eyes forward. Too many of her friends had fallen to these fiends' illusions, deceived into dropping their weapons and embracing a terrible death. Music didn't sound half as sweet as a Dreamer's voice. She glanced over her shoulder and met Mica's terrified expression as the shadows drew closer.

Why were the Dreamers hesitating? With one pitiful torch, Animkii was no match for these horrors. But no, it seemed these spiteful wraiths wished to torment them for a time, wanted to toy with their victims before consumption.

"I died to save our people." The cold, commanding voice of her long-dead vessel hissed from the darkness, awakening the pitiful, trembling dread of a child despised by its maker. "You made a mockery of my sacrifice by breaking our most sacred laws, and now you dare turn your face from me?"

Animkii refused to meet her tormentor's eyes. "Ishkode walks with the Creator. Her soul was never yours, Deceiver!" She swept out with the torch to force the shadows back, fighting the swell of emotion provoked by that voice. In her head, she replayed the last image of Ishkode walking into the flames, singing her funeral song until the fire consumed her last breath.

But this Dreamer did not flinch back in fear of the fire, as the others had done. Instead, it kept speaking, its voice warping, softening into another's.

"Do you really believe that, Ani?"

Ziiba. The name trembled on her lips, but she did not speak it. Brave, irreverent Ziiba, who'd kept all her blasphemies a secret until the very end, when she could no longer abide them. Animkii's heart tore in two and the sound of her lover's voice would've brought tears to her eyes if she'd still had the capacity for them.

But most heartrending of all, riding the icy wind that blustered around them, was the plaintive cry of a child.

Niigaanii.

Such a shiver went through her body that Animkii felt fully human for a moment. "I won't fall for your illusion, fiend!"

But she *was* falling for it. Her attempt to stay detached, to keep her head cool, was rattled by the desecration of her loved ones' memories. From the darkness the infantile cry grew louder, more intense, echoing the last memory she had of her son—of a stone-faced Ziiba handing her inconsolable child off to a village mother before joining the escort leading Animkii to her final judgement, to the End. Raging inside, she wanted nothing more than to launch every single weapon in her body at this Dreamer, even if meant her own demise.

But that would mean sacrificing Mica's life, too.

What could she do? Her torch light was faltering, struggling to stay alive against the wind and a new gust of snow. Animkii fought the doubts wriggling their way into her mind as fiercely as any battle.

"The Creator protects the faithful!" she said, wanting to scream, to hit something, to do anything but stand here and listen to this thing's lies.

"You left the Creator behind the day you walked into the forbidden city to meddle with things best forgotten." Darkness drew around her and the cold of winter seemed distant now, far away in another world.

Her hand tightened on the torch.

"Is that what this is all about?" she shouted, barking a laugh of disbelief. "Are you angry that I survived the End, you restless spirits? That I used that cursed blade to cut through dozens of your foul kind? Do you fear *me*?"

And now Animkii was a warrior once more. Every muscle tensed for the fight. Any power the Dreamers might've had over her dissipated the moment her laughter rang out, and she saw a shiver ripple through the shadows surrounding her as she activated her offensive systems, charged and ready to annihilate these fiends. Would the pyrolite burn through them like fire did? She was about to find out, her chest cavity opening up beneath her furs to expose rows of deadly missile ports. Once fired, the shots would burn her clothing right off, but what did a machine need clothing for?

She was still laughing when she saw the long, deathly fingers reach from behind her, through the branches, toward the figure strapped to her back. "No!" she said, twisting away.

"Let her go." The Dreamer's leader coaxed her with the voice of her absent lover, its deathly presence causing a crust of ice to form on her coat and boots. "Let her go and we will spare your soul."

It wasn't after Animkii; it was after Mica.

Even in the blizzard, she could see the shadows congregating, disembodied shapes drifting between the trees, drawn from the rifts in the ice, hungering for the life inside her, their very presence smothering her mind.

"No choice," Animkii growled, determination blazing through her steel body. She closed her eyes and prepared to let loose such a firestorm of missiles that not one of these evil things would survive. If she and Mica had to die here, let system burnout or the elements take them instead of these soul-devouring monsters.

She activated her weapons system and pyrolite erupted from multiple openings on her steel chest, evaporating the shadows standing in their way, ripping through their ranks with the same lethality of natural fire.

But there'd be more coming soon enough.

"We need to get underground," she said. "Hold on!" With Mica clinging to her back, she released another rush of stims and then ran with all her machine speed, smashing through overturned foliage in her haste to escape.

Behind them rose a chorus of voices. "We see you, Mica Stone. There's nothing for you in this world. All your family is dead. Your undercity friends have turned against you. Even Samiel's gone. Come now, and the After Lord will erase all your pain forever."

An awful noise choked from Mica.

"Don't listen to anything they say! They get into your head and—"

Animkii broke off, chilled by the similarity between the Dreamers' intrusion into her mind and Mica's powers, but it wasn't something she had time to worry about, not now. Fresh horrors amassed in the branches above them, blotting out the dim gray day, and she could feel their presence like an icy breath on the back of her neck as they closed in. This was it. She realized that she'd need to end them here, even if it meant draining her entire repository.

As she twisted to face their pursuers, though, her enhanced vision caught sight of a collection of toppled towers in the distance, obscured behind a massive thicket of fallen trees and broken debris. The city's entrance. Another hour and they'd make it.

They didn't have an hour.

The heat of pyrolite filled every available vessel in her body and she felt her offensive system hum in readiness. She lit up the sky with fireworks, tearing through the malevolent shadows as if through paper, her whole body shaking with the force of the energy she unleashed, the earth trembling beneath her feet, stones rolling and dirt slipping.

"Animkii, stop! The ground—"

As the air overhead flooded with fire, the forest floor opened up beneath their feet and dropped them into darkness.

Chapter Six

The straps tying Mica to Animkii's back broke. She felt the quick terror of falling through the wreckage of an ancient roof and the sharp pain of hitting bottom, cushioned from broken bones by a thousand years' growth of moss and rotten wood. Her pain was eased by the relief of hearing the enraged shrieks of their unearthly hunters growing distant and finally silent.

When she next opened her eyes, she saw Animkii climbing down through an opening in a lichen-covered roof, pushing aside fallen debris as she dropped farther down to the bottom level. A pale stream of daylight cut through the darkness, reflecting off a slow drift of snowflakes and ancient dust. It was just enough light for Mica to get a good, hard look at her hulking ally.

What she saw made her bite back a gasp, for the furs covering the mod's arms and torso had burned away to reveal the full and devastating extent of the biosteel's progression. Little organic remained: a few fingers on Animkii's left hand and the fading patch around her mouth.

At this rate, it wouldn't be months before the warrior was gone, but a couple of weeks, maybe days. An unexpected wave of sorrow rose inside her chest. Even Samiel would need more time than that to find a cure.

She cared more than she wanted to admit, as she wrestled with the realization that she was losing her only remaining friend. Her throat tightened with unexpected emotion. When had she started to see Animkii as a friend instead of a threat? Weary of loss and shaken by the sight, she sank her fingers into an ancient wall with pained determination and clawed her way back up to her feet, her breath hitching as old debris rolled under her feet.

"Do you think they'll follow us?" she asked, trying to keep the tremor from her voice. It had been terrifying enough to see such monstrosities through the eye of Animkii's memory, but to live it, to feel their presence invade her own body—that was something else entirely. Her legs trembled beneath the weight of her own body and gave way, sending her back to her knees. "How did they know—?"

"They always know." Animkii was at her side in a second, slipping a massive steel arm behind her back in support, lifting Mica back to her feet, the smell of hot metal and chemical afterburn wafting off her biosteel skin. There was a new metallic ring to her voice that hadn't been there before, just a slight hardening of her natural growl.

Mica tried not to think about what that meant.

"Dreamers can read your mind. If you listen to their words too long, you'll lose yourself," the mod said. "They'll corrupt your soul, and your body will rot away in an instant, leaving behind a shadow of what you were."

"Those we fought—"

"I only hope they were not from my village."

They shared a sober silence, looking down into the city beneath them. The entire scape had folded into the earth, a toppled map with broken foundations laid out sideways and upside-down. She recalled the stories of Animkii's people about the Sundering, when the Earth turned inside-out, swallowing whole cities into its belly and leaving little remaining on the surface.

Just like the ruins in Under-Alpha. Samiel had believed there were once thousands of cities like this, and that they'd covered every inch of the world. All buried now. Dead. If other lands had survived, they were beyond the Technocracy's reach thanks to the rifts and other dangerous anomalies bordering their lands.

"We're in a prison," he'd said, *"but the Technocrats refuse to see it."*

Mica's response had been flippant. *"So, if we're the prisoners, who's the prison keeper?"*

It was only now that she realized there might be a sinister truth to those words, that a greater evil existed—one that would make the Technocrats' rule seem like a marvel of benevolence.

What would Sam do if he were here? She gazed into the abyss that led farther downward, a treacherous staircase made of broken walls and chunks of fallen earth, exhaling a shaky breath. The stink of stone dust and damp earth rose from the void, filling her with apprehension.

Animkii spoke in her usual brusque fashion. "We must travel deep to reach the main city. From there, I can lead us back to the surface world. But we must hurry. The Dreamers will soon come."

"Pretty sure you incinerated the lot of them," she said, clamoring back aboard Animkii's back.

"There are always more."

They continued downward into the broken city, a sea of rubble spreading out before them. Animkii's artificial light caused shadows to dance across the ceiling of a massive cavern. Nothing here had survived its fall intact, leaving broken bits and pieces of the ancient world that shifted under their feet and sent them sliding downward more than once. When they reached the bottom of the hill of stone bones, the ground leveled out and they could see the skeleton of a city block.

Cracked pavement streets were littered with chunks of old brick and stone, and crumbled foundations outlined where buildings had stood a thousand years ago.

Throughout the ruined cityscape, tiny deadly fissures riddled the ground, exuding a terrible, unnatural cold, and they did their best to avoid these small rifts as much as possible. Though there were no Dreamers here yet, she could sense their chill on the fringes of this cursed place and it made her shiver.

One shot of angel's breath and she wouldn't have felt a thing. No pain. No fear. She shook her head, angry at her own powerlessness, at the grip this addiction still held over her, weeks after her last shot. Every part of her begged and pleaded for just a taste of that sweet release. She let out a tiny breath of longing.

Animkii misinterpreted her reaction. "You understand, now? They are here. They wait," she said in that grim metallic voice. "My attack outside caught them off-guard. They are wary, and they will wait until they have replenished their numbers. We need to leave this place quickly and get back to the surface world, outside their territory. They cannot survive long outside a rift."

"If they catch up to us, will you be able to fight them off again?"

"Until my stims run out."

Mica didn't miss the darkness in her tone. "Stims aren't the only problem, are they? I've seen the biosteel's progression. Every time you use stims, it speeds up your evolution."

"Yes." Her voice was soft.

Even with the expressionless mask that had replaced Animkii's face, even with that cold metallic voice, Mica sensed her friend's fear. The mod knew her time was running out.

"Look, don't worry about it, okay? Even if that damned biosteel spreads to your entire body, even if it takes your mind, I'll get you back to Under-Alpha. Samiel will find a way to reverse it."

"...thank you."

There it was. They'd both accepted the lie.

"I will try to reserve my stims," Animkii said, "but if the Dreamers attack us again, there will be no other choice. All that saved me the last time I walked these ruins was the weapon I took from this place."

This was the memory she was blocking, Mica realized. She could *feel* it, even without probing. Pictures flashed in her mind of this broken city, followed by a wave of dizziness so intense she had to lay her head against Animkii's back to steady her mind.

"Are you okay?"

"Just a little nauseous, that's all." The incessant exhaustion wouldn't leave her, and the limbs that clutched onto Animkii's back tingled with fried nerves. How much of what she felt was withdrawal and how much was damage from using that damn power?

If she was going to get through this alive, she needed to defeat both.

They kept descending farther into the city, following a crumbling road until it broke off and dropped fifty feet vertically into darkness, forcing Animkii into another perilous climb downward. Every inch of the earthen walls was slick with moisture and jagged with rocks, with razor-sharp scraps of steel and shards of broken glass poking out from the wall.

Though the mod said nothing, Mica could feel a fearful tension in her movement, a nervous energy that reminded her of when the pair had climbed through the ruins in Under-Alpha.

"You afraid of heights or something?"

Animkii shook her head. "The memory of this place is... not a pleasant one."

After a day of climbing and slipping through holes in the debris, the city leveled out.

"Looks a lot like the ruins beneath Under-Alpha," Mica said, setting her exhaustion aside out of an interest in her surroundings. The roads had cracked along stress lines and the buildings were on an unlikely slant, but otherwise everything was as if these ancient people had walked there yesterday, completely oblivious to what was about to transpire. Even the most perishable things looked as if they'd just fallen the previous day. A toppled trashcan littered the street with centuries-old food that hadn't rotted past the day the city died. Metal that should've rusted to nothing still gleamed silver. "The deeper-down you go, the less things decay. Except there are never any bodies. Not even animals. Not even insects."

Mica relived both the thrill and terror of her past ventures into Under-Alpha's own depths, of looking at what few above had ever seen, the fear of having a hollow storm strip the skin off your bones if you weren't prepared. Many ambitious explorers had entered those ruins, and as far as she knew, she and Samiel were the only ones who'd ever survived going as deep as they had. Luck, she used to say, though luck wasn't usually a friend of hers. It was her reputation that had attracted Samiel's attention to begin with.

Back then, she'd only cared about scavenging enough gear to buy her next shot of angel breath. She certainly hadn't expected to develop feelings for the pretentious and off-putting genius. No matter what Animkii said, once her strength returned, she'd get them back to Samiel.

"You never encountered any Dreamers during your trips?" Animkii asked.

Mica froze, and a dread built up from her gut. "No... There was something much worse down there—a winged giant, frozen at the bottom of a lake." A shudder rolled through her body as the creature's awful words came back to her in vicious whispers from the past.

"Everything you know is a lie to convince yourself this world is worth living in." *Its soft, menacing voice rasped against the walls of her psyche, filling the space with its darkness. Staring into the depths from the pool's edge, she was too distant to see whether the monster's lips moved at all; she only saw its unmoving form as an amalgamation of ice and shadow and nightmare.*

Still, she knew the source of those words.

A tremor coursed through her body as horrific images flooded her mind: the Earth collapsing in upon itself, oceans of black ichor flooding the land, streets cluttered with corpses torn apart by clawed hands... The monster's voice echoed from the depths of her mind. "Deep inside, you know your true purpose is to destroy it all."

"When it spoke," she whispered. "I saw the end of the world."

Animkii listened patiently, never questioning the horror she'd seen, never judging, and it gave Mica the courage to voice her suspicions out loud.

"I think that voice belonged to the After Lord." She heaved a shuddering breath. "But the giant didn't resemble the monster I saw in the Other World. Maybe the After Lord was using it as some sort of proxy. I don't know." Caught up in the terrible memory, she blinked and shook herself back to reality. "After seeing it, I refused to go back into the ruins again. I wanted to leave Under-Alpha entirely, but Samiel—" Her voice cracked. "We argued. I couldn't stay, and Sam wouldn't leave. So we parted ways."

"It is hard when the ones we love cannot understand what is in our hearts."

"Yeah." Mica rubbed her eyes, embarrassed by the mod's sympathy. "I guess you know how it feels."

Cluttered shops and restaurants lined the narrow sidewalks ahead of them. Clothing stores displayed statues wearing fashions from a forgotten age, ranging from ordinary black pants to puffy coats trimmed with fur to glossy white gowns with skirts like bells. The variety of materials and designs were mind-boggling for someone used to the formulaic apparel of the undercity. Synthread cloth could replicate many textures, but only the wealthy could afford designer cuts and colors. The rest of the population accepted the bland palette of gray, black, and brown included in the standard clothing allowance issued by the Technocracy.

Mica still remembered the first time she'd had enough money to buy whatever she wanted—she'd splurged on a knit sweater dyed a fiery red and fastened with real wooden buttons carved to resemble flowers. Here, there were a dozen stores with piles of sweaters and enough buttons to fill a transport.

Pulp paper was in abundance—flyers pinned to posts, pasted to windows, entire stores dedicated to books—something that was rare in the Technocracy, where infomatrix screens and holographic displays had long replaced the need for such physical documents. Registered under-citizens could also tap into the Alphaknot's public psy network to receive communications, while unregistered residents, like Mica, had to rely on illegal hacks to get the same information.

The dead society's prosperity was blatant in the many eateries they passed, with outdoor patios still cluttered with fallen chairs and tables holding half-eaten meals that waited for patrons who'd never return. There was a wondrous variety of Old World delicacies, things she'd never seen or eaten before—blocks of a spongy white material coated in wax and smelling of old boots, a myriad of sauces stored in glass bottles that ranged from sickly-sweet in smell to incredibly bitter, bowls of leafy greens and—

"Hey, what do you think this is?" she pointed out a bowl full of a jiggly red substance, climbing off Animkii's back to inspect it. She poked a finger into it.

"Stop! You do not know—"

Mica was already licking the digit clean. "Oh, wow, it's sweet. Like apples. Oh, there are chunks of fruit *in it* too!"

"You could poison yourself!"

"Nah. The food here's frozen in time like everything else. Sam and I had to survive off some of what we found beneath Under-Alpha. Here, try it."

"I cannot eat it, even if I wanted to," the mod said in that quiet, too-serious voice. "You were right. The biosteel absorbed my digestive system. I do not even feel hunger anymore."

Mica drew back, flushing with guilt. "I'm sorry. I didn't realize."

"Do not apologize. You were trying to be kind."

That only made her feel worse. "Yeah, I guess..."

She looked across the street to where dead brown grass covered a small yard in front of a play structure. Dozens of small footprints scuffed the sand, and a child's forgotten scarf still hung from climbing bars.

"I always wondered what happened to the people who used to live in the old city beneath Under-Alpha too. Whether they just picked up and left when the Earth broke apart. But look at this place. Whatever happened must've taken them by surprise. The Technocrats talk about *why* the Earth broke, shifting tectonics and broken physics or whatever, but they never talk about what happened to all the *people*. Why did they just disappear?"

Animkii tone was somber. "My people's stories speak of an affliction that preceded the breaking of the Earth, a sickness that consumed the host from the inside-out, feasting until there was nothing left behind. No flesh or blood or bone."

"Like what Dreamers do?" She gave the mod a side-eye.

"The stories say the Dreamers came afterward."

"Maybe the stories were wrong."

As they passed through the city, there were ancient signs everywhere, but the letters were no more comprehensible to Mica than a child's art—a language lost to time, reminding her of Samiel and his library of ancient texts. "You know, if Sam was here, I bet he could translate all this. He's a genius in so many other things, but the history of the Old World was his real passion." She gave a mental laugh, thinking that she really *did* miss Samiel if she was looking back fondly at his sleep-inducing discourses on Old World linguistics.

The pair came to a full stop in front of an ancient tech shop, and she looked through the broken glass window to see various tools hanging from hooks on the walls and scattered about workbenches. Mica recognized hammers and wrenches and screwdrivers as relics that had survived into the present era, but many others she had no names for. In the back, a rack hoisted a four-wheeled vehicle up into the air, and spare parts littered the floor.

Similar vehicles lined the streets outside, many with doors left ajar, as if their occupants had fled their approaching doom. When Mica glanced through one vessel's open doorway, she noticed that not a speck of dust had settled there. A set of keys lay tossed carelessly on what she assumed was the driver's seat by the steering wheel in front of it. A silly flower made from a curious, colorful material bobbed on the dashboard. There was a small seat strapped into the back of one of them, obviously intended for a child, its restraints still locked in place, as if a body had once been there and had just evaporated.

As the full horror of the scene set in, Mica could bear the silence no longer.

"Do you regret coming here all those years ago?" she asked, clenching her hands to still the tremors. "Do you ever wish you'd just accepted things the way they were, and stayed away?"

"Regret, yes. Accept, no," Animkii said in a slow, thoughtful voice. "I could never accept letting the people I love die. I wanted to protect my son's future. Maybe the path I chose was wrong, but I did not have a better one to take. I would do it again if I thought I could save even one soul from the darkness," she said, her metal feet scuffing the cracked pavement as they passed through the ghost city. The stillness of the place was eerie.

"Samiel and I, we wanted to change things too, back home," she said. "Sick of suffering under the Technocrats, letting them terrorize our lives, you know. And we're not the only ones—there are others like us, willing to fight for our freedom."

"Dissidents."

"Revolutionaries."

Animkii tilted her head and, though her lips were nearly gone, Mica imagined a faint smile there. "Do you really think your friend can help me?"

Mica grinned back. "Like I said, Samiel's a genius. That's why the Crats wanted him back. If he can't do it, then it's not possible."

"I cannot let you take the risk. That power will kill you."

"Let *me* worry about the dying part, okay?"

Animkii didn't answer. Though satisfied that the mod hadn't continued the argument, Mica couldn't ignore the disturbing reality of what that accursed power had already done to her. She could hardly walk a few paces without Animkii's support and whenever she tried to reach out with her mind, there was that sharp, terrible pain.

Was Animkii right? Was this power killing her?

***

"The city's center is just up ahead," Animkii said, her phantom gut twisting with very human apprehension. She'd imagined this possibility a thousand times since leaving behind her devastated village and had stored up all her courage for this unwanted confrontation with her past.

This part of the city she knew all too well. At first glance, it seemed to have changed little from the day it had first sunk into its grave, but as they trudged farther along the tangle of ancient streets, a new pattern of damage emerged. It was as if the city itself vanished before their eyes. Heaps of shattered brick walls and splintered wood supports were all that remained of most buildings. But this damage didn't look as if a fall from the surface world had caused it. It looked like something enormous had torn its way through—damage that had existed prior to the city's descent into the earth.

They walked across the field of debris, a desert of ruination that stretched a mile ahead, a vast ceiling of earth hanging above them. The cold sank into her steel bones as an unnatural wind rushed through the ruins, blowing up into a forceful winter gale so sudden that she had no time to brace herself when it slammed her back against a crumbled wall.

Mica let loose a cry of pain as she shared the impact. "Hollow storm! We have to take shelter!"

Even the worst winter storm couldn't match the strength and cold of this icy blast. A rime of frost grew on her steel skin so fast that she knew it wasn't natural, and she recognized it as a precursor to worse things. She bit down hard, resisting. Hollow storm? Yes, that was a good name for the chill that carved out your soul. But where to hide from it? This part of the city had been flattened, with nothing intact enough to offer shelter—just chunks of wall dotting the landscape. Mica's insistent pulling, hitting, yelling jerked her back to reality. She could hear her companion's breath coming in quick gasps.

It had been like this last time too. Freezing her in place. Until that monster's voice...

"Animkii, move! Now!"

Animkii turned her head, feeling the bound woman's frantic movements against her back as she fumbled with her bindings, her own movements untethered by the unnatural cold. Why wasn't she affected? But she obeyed the woman's voice, felt her mind release at the sound of it, just as the monster's voice had freed her all those years ago.

"If it's affecting you this bad, we're too close to the source of the storms." Mica dropped to the ground, still unsteady on her feet. Not a touch of frost appeared on her skin, while Animkii's was turning white with it. She grabbed the warrior's flesh-hand and tugged at it, an urgency in her movement. "Don't think about the cold. Just listen to my voice."

"Yes," was all she could manage.

The frost thickened on Animkii's arms and chest, but it wasn't the cold that paralyzed her—it was the insufferable psychic weight on her mind, the chill sinking so deep into her thoughts that it scrambled her mental circuitry.

The pair moved forward at an achingly slow pace, with Mica still not fully recovered from her own ordeal and struggling even to walk, her breath coming in shortened gasps, her gait clumsy. She often dropped Animkii's hand to steady herself against a wall or pile of rubble, but she never stopped talking, not even for a moment, her words empowering Animkii with movement, urging her to move forward even while her own face grayed with exhaustion.

For a time, they hunkered down inside a makeshift barrier of fallen walls and roofing, which sheltered them from the worst of the storm, but the wind chipped away at the ancient stonework while they crouched shivering in its shadow. "The same thing happens in Under-Alpha when people go down too deep," Mica said, sucking in a hard breath. "The hollow storms come, and people freeze, and then they die. Samiel thought I was exaggerating until it happened to him and his party. I saved him too many times to count."

"Why aren't you affected?"

"Don't know. I can feel the cold, but it just doesn't sink into my skin like it does for others."

Animkii's watchful eyes found a new webwork of cracks in the pavement, tiny but unnatural rifts that exuded the same burning cold found at the End of the World, spreading outward like a skin of ice breaking. Fear tightened her chest. "The rifts here are getting bigger. The Dreamers are coming. We cannot stay here."

As she spoke, Animkii caught a flash of movement across the field, a scurry of shadows between the expanse of ruins across from their shelter. Dreamers? But no, the movement was too erratic. An animal, maybe? Or something else. Her gaze remained fixed on the distant shadows, her senses on high alert.

"Did you see that?"

"See what?"

"Something is out there," she said. "Watching us."

Mica scoffed. "You're seeing things. Nothing can live out there while a hollow storm's raging," she said. "In all my years living in

Under-Alpha, I didn't meet a single person who could withstand a full hollow storm without my help."

"Your voice has power."

Mica flinched. "Back then, I just thought I had a talent for persuasion. But after all this business with the Cult, maybe it's something more." She closed her eyes, her dark hair cascading forward, veiling her emotions. "You'd think I'd be happy having these powers, like I could use them to do some great things once I knew how to control them. But all I think about is how this awful force inside of me is what got Reid killed and put the two of us on a cult hit list, when all I'd really like to do is just go home, take a few shots of angel breath, and have a good night's sleep."

There was an edge to her voice. A tremor shook her hands as she battled with a restless need. "But I have to stop thinking about it. Angel breath, dream-dust, euphoria, whatever... It only stops the pain for a bit, and it always leaves you needing more," she said. "And I'm so tired of feeling *tired*. I can't do it anymore, Animkii."

Animkii absorbed Mica's confession with shock. Now she understood that the tremors, the cries, the vomiting she'd seen over the last couple of weeks were not just the aftereffects of Mica's burgeoning powers, but something else.

After a thoughtful silence, she spoke. "There is a drug that my people use called wraith root. It is a sacred plant. Ingesting its juices grants visions. Among my people, there are those called dreamwalkers who use it to walk with our dead ancestors in the afterlife. But there are others it has a different effect on. It weakens their minds. They get stuck in the place between worlds and crave it over the real world. When this happens, we call it the 'empty sickness' because they are never full enough to stop taking it."

Mica put her head down, but Animkii could see the tears glaze over her eyes. "That's me," she whispered. "I'm empty. I've been empty since the day I was born. Every time I find something to fill myself with, it's taken away."

Animkii was stunned by this sudden vulnerability and didn't know how to react without provoking hostility. She shifted herself closer, not enough to touch, but enough to be present. "You are growing stronger," she said. "I have seen it. Even after all you have survived, you are still fighting back. You are a warrior, like me."

"No, that's not true. I've just spent my life tripping from one bad situation to another. Somehow I survived this long and I'm tired of surviving. I don't want to fight anymore. Maybe I should give up and let the After Lord win. Then all this suffering would be done with."

"If you feel that way, then why are you still here?"

"I don't know. I guess I just can't stand the idea of some self-proclaimed god walking into this world, trampling all over the little people like me. We didn't do anything wrong except hope happiness was possible in this messed-up world."

"The same reason you and Samiel tried to fight the Technocracy."

"Life's already hard enough without some tyrant coming along and making it worse."

"That is why I need to protect you. To make sure you keep fighting for this world when I am gone." Animkii stood up, steeling her will, facing the chilling wind of the hollow storm. There was no helping it. They'd have to pass through that fateful place, the place where her life had been forever altered. "It is time to go. We cannot stay here any longer."

"But where are we going? Even I can't keep you alive out there forever."

"To the place I found Soulcleaver."

Mica looked confused. "Soulcleaver?"

"The name of the weapon I brought back to my village. The one that damned my soul and sealed my fate."

"You're afraid, aren't you?"

"Terrified."

"Why?"

"You will see."

As Animkii led them down a path engraved in her memories, she fought the horror, the instinct to run away. Without thinking, she moved her fingers to trace a circle over her heart, a warding gesture meant to invoke the Creator's protection, but she caught herself halfway and cringed at her own blasphemy, of daring to ask for His blessing in this forbidden place. What was she doing, tempting fate by coming back to this accursed place?

But she'd gone too far now to turn back. She'd broken the laws long ago.

Fighting the hollow storm with every step, they finally made it across the broken landscape, following the trail of shattered buildings, resting only short periods, until at last they reached an artificial cave formed out of toppled towers and folded-over landscape.

"It told me it would give me the power to stop the Dreamers," Animkii said, moving toward the opening in the debris, to that graveyard.

"It?"

"Soulcleaver's maker."

"Wait. There was someone else down here?"

"Yes." She expanded her light, and the cave lit up. It was a burrow formed of fallen walls, with a ceiling held up by a web of wires and steel beams, all looking like they were seconds from collapsing.

And there it was, just as she'd left it, the monstrosity that had ripped through this city of stone and steel a thousand years ago, a gargantuan dead serpent sprawled out on its enormous back, its scaly coils woven in between huge chunks of rubble, its feathered wings broken beneath it.

Mica choked in horror. "The After Lord!"

Chapter Seven

No... This wasn't the After Lord....

This monster only resembled her adversary. Looking closer, Mica saw its coloring was different. Shimmering copper-bronze scales covered its massive reptilian form, and its broken, white-feathered wings were stained black with its own blood. Its belly was a mass of open wounds, spilling entrails that still glistened as if freshly released. Its neck had been severed clean through. A permanent snarl remained frozen on its mouth, its tongue lolling out, its whiskers curling around its snout like a cat's and its eyes staring wide-open at them.

She dug her fingers into Animkii's steel shoulders. "What the gore *is* this thing?!"

Animkii looked taken aback for a moment, but then her expression shut down. "Some kind of monster. When I came here, it was guarding Soulcleaver. It was in awful shape, dying, but unable to die."

Mica tasted the memory in the air, the one that Animkii had blocked, felt her struggle to resist it. "I don't know what's going on here, but this thing," she pointed at the corpse, "looks just like the After Lord. Coloring's different, but that's about it."

To think there might have been more monsters like the god who lived in her head made her sick to her stomach. Animkii *had* to know more than she was admitting to. She was hiding something, and if Mica could just peek into her mind... But she remembered her promise about staying out of the other woman's memories. Guilt battled with the need to know, to see what Animkii had seen. She felt the power inside her stir and ignored the pain it awakened. Just a little wouldn't hurt, would it? Animkii would never need to know.

As the impulse took over, Mica extended a psychic hand toward her friend's mind. A searing pain surged through her body, and a cry tore from her lips as the agony forced her to her knees. Animkii moved quickly to catch her as she fell, and in the moment their bodies touched, Mica leaped inside the warrior's psyche.

When she next opened her eyes, she had merged with the world inside the mod's mind, sinking into that warm pool of memories. Just like she'd done back in Alpha. Peering out through her friend's eyes as if they were her own, she once again found herself immersed in the other woman's past.

As she watched, the beast's eyes came alive. With each labored breath, its body rippled with copper-scaled muscles. The floor was sticky with tar-black blood and her eyes followed the trail back to its source. The gaping throat wound left its neck hanging on by a thread of sinew, unable to support the enormous head, which rested on a stack of broken planks.

No natural thing would still be alive with an injury like that.

Worse than the sight of the monstrosity was its sudden, jarring presence in their shared mind—the weight of its enormous pain and suffering and futile rage almost overwhelming to bear. Mind powers, like the After Lord. Mica's uneasiness grew. She felt Animkii grit her teeth against its influence, desperate to hide her confusion and terror as the dreadful voice sang into her head, urging her forward.

"Animkii, warrior of the Fire Bones people, daughter of the Bear Clan. I dreamed of you, and you came."

Mica's mind plunged into darkness once more as Animkii's shame and fear overwhelmed her. Unwilling to surrender, she clung tightly to her friend's consciousness, resisting the wave of emotion so fiercely that pain tore through her physical body in the real world, causing it to convulse. In the corner of her mind, she sensed the real-world Animkii trying to shake her free of the trance, but she refused to relinquish her grip on the memory, driven to see it through to its conclusion. Using her pain like a knife against the mod's closed psyche, she tore through the veil that hid her friend's terrible secret.

The real world disappeared completely now.

"What are you? How do you know my name?" Animkii demanded of the monstrosity, fear coarsening the young warrior's voice. Even years of fighting Dreamers hadn't prepared her for this confrontation; it shook her to the core. "Are you some kind of spirit?"

"Savior to some; destroyer to others," *it spoke into the warrior's head. The thing attempted a laugh, but the sound emerged as a gurgle from its nearly severed throat, quickening into a wheezing, agonizing noise that begged for mercy. A thick glob of black blood oozed out of the lethal wound as its voice slithered into her mind.* "For centuries, I have endured this half-life, trapped here inside this corpse of a body, unable to live, unable to die. Take the blade and end my misery. When I'm dead, it will give you all the power you need."

"Blade?"

One of its enormous, clawed hands spasmed, and all but one finger curled under its scaly palm, leaving the last to point to the far wall where an obsidian knife lay half-buried in the debris. The hilt was carved to resemble a raven. A shimmer of blue light danced on the ebony blade's edge, enough to illuminate the room, and she saw that the radiance pulsed in time with the beast's labored breathing. Compared to the monster, the size of the blade was insignificant—about the size of a skinning knife.

Couldn't Animkii feel it? Mica's mind prickled with power. The heat coming off that blade...

Animkii scowled, ignoring a nagging uneasiness. "A trinket," she said.

"No trinket. I forged Soulcleaver from a fragment of my soul and it carries my strength within it. Hurry!" *The voice in their shared mind urged her forward, barely audible, broken so that it was hard to piece together the words, the creature's sanity wavering as it wailed,* "I've endured so long, surrounded by these parasites, these aberrations, always hungering for my soul. You can't imagine the suffering!" *It sobbed then, the broken wailing of a child, which carried on until it faded back into incoherent mumbling.*

It was talking about Dreamers, Mica realized. The show of madness left her unnerved.

The pitifulness of the monster's state seemed to have the opposite effect on Animkii, easing her fears and reawakening the ambition that had driven her to this forbidden city. Her eyes fastened on the glowing blade, and she made her decision. She extinguished her torch. A knife was something she understood. A simple weapon, even when imbued with an alien power.

"Will it kill Dreamers? You say it will give me power, but will it help me free the Witherlands from those abominations?"

"It is what keeps the Dreamers from feasting on our souls this very moment."

Animkii's head snapped around, her keen eyes scanning the darkest corners of the cavern, following the trails of frost to where the quivering shadowy forms clung, the air rasping with their curses. The warrior could sense their loathing of this blade, how its very presence repulsed them, and smiled as her confidence returned. With her spear in one hand, she walked over to the glowing blade and the Dreamers stirred from the shadows.

With one swift motion, she pulled it free. Its light flared and the shadows surrounding her shrieked and shrank back against the walls.

The monster heaved a long, quivering sigh of relief. "Do it!"

Animkii did not hesitate. This was a mercy killing. Whatever apprehension she had, she shoved into the bottom of her heart and walked up to the head of the gargantuan beast. Its eyes tracked every movement right until she set the blade's edge upon the sinewy bundle of flesh that barely tethered head to neck.

"It is finished!" *The monster sighed its relief.*

With the ease of passing through water, the blade slid through leathery scales and muscle alike, and the head dropped free, its eyes closing forever as its whole body shuddered its way into death, the last of its life absorbed by the blade in Animkii's hand. Soulcleaver's light intensified, growing so powerful that every shadow fled shrieking before it. The eyes of the raven hilt flashed red for just one second before going dead again.

Animkii sucked in a horrified breath. She could feel it now, moving through the blade: a soul torn from its host, a living presence freed from the wreckage of its body, laughing in exultation in her head.

"You tricked me!" she roared.

"I gave you what I promised."

In horror, Animkii threw the weapon away from her, its light extinguished as it clattered against the far wall, plunging the total area into darkness. The second it left her hand, she knew she'd made a lethal mistake. Though her skin crawled at the thought of a weapon that devoured souls, she knew without its light she was a dead woman.

The howling of the Dreamers began picking up from behind the shadows. Though blind in the darkness, Animkii could sense the Dreamers closing in, hungering for the only real soul left here, and despaired at her own folly. There was no time to relight her torch, as if a single flame could hold off the ravenous numbers congregating at the edges of the cavern. Frost bloomed on her skin and clothes as the phantoms drifted out of their hiding places. She felt the tug of their hunger pulling on her soul, and exhaustion crept into her limbs.

Her mother's gentle face emerged from the darkness, midnight hair covering his shoulders like a cloak. Rounded cheeks bunched up in a sad smile. The wicked shade had even copied the tired crinkles at the corners of his eyes.

"Get away!" Animkii threw up an arm to cover her eyes.

"You were right to dispose of that accursed blade," the wretched creature crooned in Debwe's low, gentle voice. "Soulcleaver will bring you nothing but suffering. Why fight a losing battle when you can join our undying legion?" Its fleshless hand reached out to caress her, but she thrust out her spear to drive it back. She knew it wasn't real, that this abomination wore a false face, but it still fooled her heart just a little.

Seeing its illusion no longer had effect, the Dreamer dropped its guise and swept its arms outward in a sudden gust of wind, the deathly chill of a hollow storm sweeping through Animkii's body as countless ghostly shapes swooped down on her.

Animkii blindly threw herself against the icy shadows in an attempt to retrieve the weapon. Each one she passed through exacted a piece of her life with its chilling touch until she collapsed to the ground, uncertain whether Soulcleaver lay yards or inches away. She strained her arm out to reach it as the deathly frost crept up her limbs and her heart slowed to a crawl.

Mica could feel her friend dying. But this couldn't be how it ended... Animkii had survived!

Then, something changed. In her panic, Mica split from Animkii's dying dream-body. Instead of seeing through Animkii's eyes, she now saw the scene from across the other end of the ruined chamber. Unlike her dying friend, her vision was unhampered by darkness. She could clearly see Animkii huddled in a motionless heap, only feet away from the blade and covered in a swarm of Dreamers.

"Animkii!" she screamed. "Wake up! Soulcleaver's right there! You just have to reach a little farther."

Animkii's one eye snapped open, and she stared at the place where Mica stood, confusion and fear in her eyes.

She'd... heard?

Then the warrior's eyes rolled back, and the Dreamers feasted.

What could she do? With no other options, Mica rushed across the room, ghosting through Dreamers and rubble effortlessly until she was crouching beside Animkii. When she reached out to shake the fallen woman, she was startled to find her hand had turned solid, as if she'd become flesh.

Even without her modifications, Animkii was a large woman—tall, broad-shouldered, and thick with muscle. Long black braids lay coiled beneath her fallen form and her skin was a rich, coppery brown, decorated with innumerable black tattoos depicting stylized animals and geometric shapes, including one on her left shoulder that mirrored Ishkode's: the paw print of a bear engulfed in black flames. It was strange to see her friend as fully human, and a sadness swept through her at the loss.

"Come on! I don't know how this is possible, but if you can really hear me, get up!"

This was no longer just Animkii's memory; it'd become something else she couldn't define. Animkii was out cold, her body encrusted with ice as the Dreamers drew their cloak of death over her. Desperate, Mica lunged for Soulcleaver herself and the moment her fingers touched it, the blade burst with such light that it nearly blinded her.

The Dreamers exploded. There was no other way to describe their instant evisceration, only shreds of shadow left behind to float in the air until they too faded. Those few who'd survived shrieked in futile rage as they fled back into the surrounding rifts, taking with them the hollow storm and its icy kiss. The frost rimming Animkii's body melted, and she heard a moan from the woman.

What had she done?

Then the monstrous voice that had spoken to Animkii now spoke to Mica—and to her alone. Only this time the voice came from Soulcleaver, and all the madness in it was gone. It spoke with deliberate calm, though she sensed a lethal tension beneath the surface.

"So many futures I foresaw and planned for, but they were failures, every one of them, except for this very moment. I thought the blood-lines I left behind had weakened too much after all these centuries. Too much human blood in them. But it appears there was at least one of you strong enough to reach me..."

Mica gripped the blade tighter, swallowing her fear. "What are you?"

"I am Revan."

***

Animkii caught Mica as she fell, those empty black eyes staring into her soul.

"Mica! What are you doing? Are you—?"

Fear prickled the back of her head as she cradled her friend's unconscious body. Again, there was that sensation of being watched from a distance. Her eyes darted to the corpse of the great monster, half-expecting it to return to life, but it was still dead, still staring empty-eyed forever.

***

Revan? A dull, ugly feeling built inside Mica's chest. That name couldn't be a coincidence. Was this monster somehow her ancestor? But how? Revan wasn't even human. Her stomach tightened with revulsion and she swallowed the bile in her throat. "You're the one who imprisoned the After Lord?"

A small, bitter laugh echoed in her head. "My brother and I battled over this world a thousand years ago. The wound I gave him left him severed from Earth, trapping him inside his own creation—the nightmare realm you call the Other World, but which I know as 'Hul.' Even in his dormant state, he uses his dreams to poison this world. He slips on the skin of people's deepest desires and sells his lies to them. The people of this broken Earth have come to know him by many names: After Lord. Sleepless One. World Devourer. God. Creator—"

Mica sucked in a breath. "That means—"

The Creator and the After Lord were one and the same!

"Yes. He worms his way through the dreams of the hopeless, promising them paradise, when he gives only the gift of slavery to even his most valuable devotees—those he shall pervert and turn into daemons. A hundred worlds before yours he has consumed. This time I tried to stop him; it was for that purpose I forged Soulcleaver."

"I need to get back to the real world and warn Animkii!" Every instinct urged her to break free from this memory-that-wasn't-a-memory, but something even stronger held her tight.

"You must finish what I started," Revan said. "You must kill him."

"No chance! I don't want anything to do with this!"

"Now that my brother has awakened, he grows stronger daily," *he said.* "Take Soulcleaver. Walk into the dream. Slay him if you can. My mistake was believing he could be slain in this world."

"Even with your blood, I'm not strong enough. Look at me. I can hardly walk now, let alone fight."

Wearily, Revan answered, "Then he'll consume you, like he consumes everything else."

"This isn't real!" Her fingers loosened on the hated blade and its light flickered, the air growing instantly cold. "It can't be."

"Will you let your friend die?"

"This is just a memory. Animkii lived."

"She lived because of you. Because of Soulcleaver."

"That isn't possible!"

"It's possible because I made it possible. I put Soulcleaver in both worlds."

Revan implanted the knowledge in her mind. Soulcleaver had been waiting for her—or someone like her, a blood descendant—all this time. Whether willing or not, every time she closed her eyes to dream or walked through Animkii's memories, she was straddling the boundary of the Other World. Moreover, she now understood that the Other World was unlike any other. The After Lord had woven it from pieces of the worlds and souls he'd consumed. He'd already partially consumed her own world...

And her blood was the key to freeing him so he could finish the job. This was why the Cult and their master wanted her so badly.

"Yes, with my blood, you can break the Blood Gate I forged to stop my brother," *said Revan.* "But it also gives you other gifts, as you've discovered. One of these powers allows you to separate or join worlds together; with my blood, you can bring Soulcleaver back with you into your own material realm."

Her grip on Revan's soul knife tightened until she could see the white of bone beneath her skin. The light intensified, its brightness provoking howls of rage from the retreating shadows, whose hunger remained unsated, who waited for their prey's protector to withdraw. Animkii issued a loud groan.

"And what if I refuse?" she asked.

"Then your friend will never live to cross the End of the World. Without her interference, the After Cult will have their sacrifice, and your world will die."

Her blood ran cold. "You expect me to believe that what I do here will alter the past?"

"Do you want to risk it?"

Mica didn't know what to believe, but she'd spent enough time over the last several weeks treading the line between fantasy and reality, and she knew she wasn't willing to chance it.

"Fine. Save Animkii and I'll take Soulcleaver back with me to the real world. No promises on killing your brother, though," she said, tight-lipped.

She sensed the beast's ire, but knew he was helpless to do anything but accept the bargain. He was stuck inside that blade, and he needed her more than she needed him. She felt his reluctant acquiescence. "Agreed. Cut yourself with Soulcleaver and let your blood run. The worlds will join just long enough for the blade to pass through."

Crouching beside Animkii, she closed her friend's calloused fingers around the knife's handle. Then, gritting her teeth in anticipation, she ran the blade across the palm of her own hand, swearing as the flesh parted and blood as black as pitch poured freely.

A spark lit between this self and the other self in the real world.

One moment she was kneeling at Animkii's side inside this pseudo-memory; the next, she was staring up at the mod's tech-forged face, cradled in her big arms. Back from the past, she exhaled one huge breath and her whole body spasmed as if trying to expel something terrible from inside it, causing her to wheeze and flail against her friend's massive steel chest.

As quick as it came, the fit settled.

"Mica!"

Her breathing slowed. "I'm okay," she said, rolling out of Animkii's grasp.

But she wasn't. Her fingers were sticky with blood, and she felt something release, felt something burning-hot slide into her hand, the sensation breaking the remaining connection between her and Animkii's memories. She glanced down at her hand, shielding it from watching eyes, shaken to see the obsidian blade lying there, as real in this world as in Animkii's memories. Its glow had vanished, but she could feel Revan's power coursing through its gleaming black body.

Soulcleaver.

Fearing Animkii's reaction, she shifted her hand out of sight, concealing the blade with sleight of hand. The enormity of what she'd done came crashing down around her.

Back in Alpha, she'd reached into Father Dark's mind and seized control of his body with this power. Then she'd reached into Animkii's memory and transported them to these hostile lands. And now she'd reached into a memory and brought something back to the present.

What was she turning into? Her anxious gaze came to rest on the monstrous corpse before them, its scales a polished copper that reflected Animkii's optical light. She had this thing's blood in her.

Revan's blood.

The After Lord's blood.

She suppressed a shiver, cursing the ancestor who'd unwittingly entangled her in this mess. How could she tell Animkii the truth—that the Fire Bones' Creator was the same monster who haunted Mica's dreams, who lurked in the shadows of this broken Earth and waited to devour them all? And that the Cult believed Mica was his descendant. Telling Animkii the truth also meant admitting she'd gone into her mind again, that she'd broken her promise. But this was too important to hide.

"Animkii, I—"

But before she could speak, that now-familiar and terrible pain seized her body, and she clenched her teeth against it, smothering the cry, folding her body up to contain it. Liquid warmth ran from her nose, and she wiped away black blood. Brief though it was, her excursion into Animkii's mind had cost her more than she could afford.

Whatever happened, she needed to tell Animkii the truth! But a wave of exhaustion pulled over her head, pushing her to sleep despite the pain. Her bleary eyes drifted past the big warrior kneeling protectively by her side, past the makeshift shelter the mod had started building out of fallen timber, to a strange figure watching them from an archway made of fallen buildings. Its predator's eyes gleamed from beneath an antlered headdress.

A croak of warning was all she managed before the sea of darkness claimed her.

Chapter Eight

Animkii's head snapped around.

"Didn't I speak true, Brothers? See what the Creator has brought us?"

A light bloomed in the darkness and a woman's face materialized from the shadows. She wore a headdress with deer antlers on top, had skin the color and texture of birch bark, and lips painted black. Bird wing tattoos adorned her cheeks, but a deliberate blade had defaced the marks of her former people, leaving behind thick furrows of scarring that made her new allegiance clear.

Outlanders!

Animkii's fear heightened, not for herself but for Mica. Outlanders were wild people who belonged to no people or clan, but banded together to raid and assault settlements. She shifted her body out of a kneeling position, letting Mica's body roll to the ground, then stood protectively in front of it, baring her naked steel chest and activating her weapons.

From the shadows rippled murmurs of fear and awe. There was a flash of skin. A smear of warpaint. The curve of a bow stem. Then one figure emerged and another and another, stepping out of a dozen crooks and crevices in the ruins, fierce-faced warriors draped in colorful garb. Some held spears, but others had armed themselves with steel rods or metal crossbows. Knives hung from their belts, unsheathed. Like their leader, those with visible markings of their former people had carved them away in rejection of their former identities.

A mad laugh rang out from the crowd but was quickly stifled.

Considering the frailty of a human body and the northern people's inexperience with tech, Animkii wasn't concerned about being outnumbered in a fight, but she also couldn't guarantee Mica's safety during battle. She swept her gaze across the cavern, her optical light chasing away the shadows. In a fearsome voice, she addressed the gathered warriors in her native tongue. "I have no quarrel with outlanders. My friend and I only seek to return to the surface."

Their leader cocked her head to one side, her lips spreading into a too-wide smile and revealing a mouthful of sharpened teeth. She held up a hand to halt the warriors and shuffled toward Animkii, one hand holding a lantern that bobbed in time with her movement, the other clutching a beaded shawl around her bony shoulders. Her clothing was a bizarre mixture of current and Ancient styles: a tanned hide coat over a dazzling blue dress, strings of colorful plastic beads around her neck jangling alongside a set of bleached-bone talismans.

"The Creator sent you to us," she said in a girlish voice at odds with her worn face and old scars, her eyes obscured by the row of dangling bird bones threaded to the top rim of her headdress.

Animkii hid her impatience and studied the woman's tattoos. "You once belonged to the Severed Sky People," she said, keeping a steady gaze. "A Speaker."

"I am called Harvester and, yes, I once belonged to that doomed people."

Doomed? Animkii's uneasiness stirred. "I am Animkii, formerly of the Fire Bones' Bear Clan, and this is Mica, who belongs to no people or clan. We have traveled from lands far south of the End."

She waited for the woman's cry of disbelief, but instead there was a slightly disturbing smile, as if Animkii had confirmed something already known. Her odd mannerisms came as no surprise to Animkii, for Speakers treaded the line between worlds, acting as a mouthpiece for the Creator, and such a brush with the divine left its mark on the mind. But this Speaker was an outlander, and that made her even more unpredictable.

"You will accompany us back to our village," the woman said, her childish voice holding an authority that left no room for argument. She glanced over her shoulder at a long-nosed youth bundled in furs and jerked her head at him. "Carry the girl."

"We are not going anywhere!" Animkii's words boomed off the cavernous walls, ringing metallic, and startling the young man, who brandished a knife and bared his teeth.

These outlanders don't obey the taboos, she realized, uneasily watching the light gleam off the knife's steel blade. Steel was a creation of the Ancients. Forbidden.

"Stand down, Brother!" Harvester's order rang out. Then she turned to Animkii, and her voice softened again. "It is not safe here," she said. "Your friend is not well. I can help her, if you let me. She walks the Dream too deep."

"Mica is no dreamwalker. I doubt she has even seen wraith root," she said.

"But she *has* walked outside this world, hasn't she?"

Those words set Animkii's metal teeth on edge. "I have seen what Mica can do," she said in a rough defensive voice, "and dreamwalking cannot even compare." She thought of how Mica had used Animkii's own memories to move across space.

Harvester's smile widened, the points of her teeth gleaming white in the glow of Animkii's tech light.

Before Animkii could respond, the cavern's temperature dropped and the shadows thickened. The telltale frost of a Dreamer's presence began a slow creep over the ruins. An icy breeze turned rapidly into a cutting wind.

Not now! Animkii stooped to pick up Mica, knowing their time was short.

The outlanders' Speaker seemed undisturbed by the encroaching death. "The Dreamers are coming to collect the two souls who eluded them outside the city," she mused, that enraging smile never fading, her gaze never faltering. "I can sense their hunger. And their rage."

"You know about the fight?" Animkii bristled with anger, holding Mica's limp form against her protectively. "How long have you been watching us?"

"Long enough."

As the woman spoke, long fingers of deathly chill drifted through the cavern's entrance, ghostly shapes threading among the ruins, human only in shape, flickering in and out of view as the hollow storm behind them grew. The dread of their presence was like a knife twisting in her heart. The wind carried a breath of ice. Mica wasn't conscious, wouldn't be able to talk her through the paralyzing cold this time. She could already feel her will growing numb.

She turned to flee, but Harvester stepped in front of her and laid a cool hand on her shoulder. "The Dreamers will not bother us," she said in a maddeningly sweet voice, side-stepping Animkii to move toward the blackening storm.

"What are you doing? We have to get out of here!"

The shadows drew together and she could see human features materialize from the darkness, the faces of friends and family she'd once had, not knowing if they were alive or dead, all of them calling out to her, making promises they wouldn't keep. As always, part of her soul answered back, but just one look down at Mica, helpless in her arms, and she pulled away.

She opened her mouth to call the Speaker back to safety, but before a word left her mouth, Harvester's voice rang out with thunderous authority. "In the name of the Creator, I rebuke you! Be gone from this place, Dreamers!"

Animkii could only gape as the bone-rattling cold and smothering darkness fled instantly, taking with it the damned who'd brought it here, the shades shrieking their admonishment as some unseen force repelled them. The terror of their presence lifted so quickly it left her breathless.

"How—?"

Harmless wisps circled the suddenly empty air as the holy woman walked past Animkii.

"The Creator speaks and I listen," she said, as if talking to a child. "When you understand that, you will have no more questions."

***

Mica was awake and not.

"The Creator is the After Lord!" She tried to cry out to Animkii, but the words disappeared into the void.

Throughout her body, she felt a terrible pain, as if some force was meticulously tearing apart the very fabric of her being, down to the molecules. She remained conscious on some level, still tethered to the bag of bones that was her body, but she lacked the strength to either awaken or hitch her mind back to Animkii's memories. Held hostage between worlds, she drifted in blackness for what felt like an eternity, the cold current of the Other World coursing through her soul, trying to pull her into its depths. Her flesh vessel back in the real world was failing fast, but the Other World's dark god needed to keep her alive long enough to become a blood sacrifice on his altar.

"If I died right now, that'd spoil your plans, wouldn't it?" she managed to say through her pain.

A silvery laugh echoed in the darkness. *"You think I'd allow it?"*

The dreams came, as she knew they would: fleeting flickering images at first, of walking down the streets of her childhood, that same stage, same actors, same nightmare. But this time, she felt indifferent to them, an eerie calm blanketing her instead of that familiar and creeping spiral downward into dread and death. Her mind was sober. For years, she'd used any intoxicant she could get her hands on to dull the nightmares; instead, those chemicals had warped her mind and enslaved her will, until she'd given almost all her control to the Dream, to the Other World.

To think of all the years she'd wasted, all the opportunities crumbled, all the relationships ruined... The shame was agonizing. Even while sober, she'd allowed her addiction to taint her time with Samiel, constantly wrestling with the need for love over substance. She wished she'd realized back then what she'd done to herself.

Time to realize it now.

Mica was no longer a frightened child, winding through the chaos of the Festival of Masks, surrounded by leering shadows and hulking monsters hiding behind a masquerade. With a thought, she reduced them to what they really were—laughing children with paper masks and bags of treats. When the bodies of her neighbors fell at her feet with black blood trickling from their noses and ears, her mind wiped clean the gore and put them to sleep instead, their heads pillowed on the paving stones. Even the gaseous nether that poured from Pandora's lethal head wound was nothing more than an ill-placed shadow, and the corpses of her family... well, they were just gone, torn from her memory by her own desire to see their fates erased.

She was in control now. She was done with the nightmares, done with being afraid.

Making it real was as easy as picturing it in her mind. The portal to the Other World, with its terrible carvings of war and destruction, materialized on the street in front of her mom's dilapidated shop, while darkness swallowed everything else. Exhilaration thrummed her nerves and excited her blood.

So it was true. Somehow, she had power over this place, and even though her body was dying back in the real world, here she'd never felt so alive.

But as she stared at the portal doors, at the feather-winged serpents that swarmed the sky above a burning cityscape, old doubts resurfaced. Whatever power she had was miniscule compared to the After Lord's. Once she stepped past those cursed gates, *he'd* be the one in control.

Yeah, he was powerful, alright, but she'd gotten away last time, hadn't she? As long as her actual body was alive, she had the advantage. And now she had Soulcleaver too. The thought bolstered her confidence as she turned in a circle, her arms half-raised and her voice mocking. "Well? I'm here. This is what you wanted, isn't it? Aren't you going to invite me in?"

In reply, the doors swung open, but instead of the unholy pillared hall with its towering stone effigy, the entrails of a vast tree spilled out. Its roots writhed like a knot of snakes, braiding together to form a pathway leading upward, toward a blinding light.

A long hiss of displeasure sounded from the surrounding darkness. It seemed the After Lord hadn't expected this, either. She peered up the winding path with curiosity. Did *she* do this?

"That place is not meant for you," her oppressor warned.

"If that's what you believe, then all the more reason to go." Without further hesitation, she stepped through the gate.

***

Even with the Dreamers banished, the chill of the hollow storm lingered. Animkii and the outlanders departed the area, but the cold of the shadows' foul presence followed them, leaking from the cracks and crevices within the broken streets of the forbidden city. Another day's journey passed mostly in silence as Animkii followed the outlanders with a grim demeanor. Mica was nestled securely against her steel chest, her breath rising as mist in the cold tunnels, with Harvester keeping pace beside them.

"The Great Spirit truly speaks to you?" she asked the outlander in a quiet voice, reluctant to disturb the stillness of their passage.

Despite her outward appearance of frailty, Harvester had no problem keeping a brisk pace, her boots crunching along the gravelly pathway with a steady gait. Her small dark eyes peered back at Animkii from beneath her antlered headdress. "When did you lose your faith?" she asked, speaking with compassion and none of the condemnation Animkii expected from a Speaker.

Animkii opened her mouth to deny the words. Hadn't she defended her faith against Mica's accusations? Hadn't she trusted the Creator to show her a path of redemption? But her talks with Mica had left seeds of doubt in her heart, had caused her to question her maker's motivations. The same questions that had led her to seek Soulcleaver...

"It is complicated."

She nodded in sympathy. "The will of the Creator is difficult to understand. We experience suffering, but do not see the end that justifies it. Most people choose not to understand at all, but only obey the laws in hopes of salvation—they are not faithful, they are fearful. But there are others like you, like me, who seek answers. And what we find will either bring us true enlightenment and the power that comes with it, or it will destroy our very souls."

Animkii stared forward. "And what answer did *you* find?"

"That this world will soon be reborn, but as with all births, there will be pain, and that is why we suffer. What about you, warrior of the Fire Bones? What have *you* learned?"

A flash of something ancient and dead rose in her memory. Once more, she saw that terrible obsidian blade with its raven wings and aura of blue flame, and she remembered how quickly her last hope had died when she'd brought it home, when fears too old and engrained to uproot had extinguished her entire future.

"I learned that some people do not want to be saved," she said.

"That is the truth."

Animkii stared at the backs of the outlander warriors, now far ahead of them. Life had always been hard on the Witherlands, but these men and women looked as if they'd seen too many battles in too short a time, and laughter was something they'd left behind long ago. Behind the burden of scars, deep lines of suffering had aged them beyond their years. They were a mixture of outcasts from the Four Peoples, distinguished by their mutilated tattoos and ornamentations, warriors who'd once battled one another now united in their desperation.

A rattling noise, which might have been a sigh had she the breath left to make it, echoed metallically in her throat.

"You wonder about the fates of your own people." Harvester's antlered headdress jangled as she walked, a strip of sinew dangling a row of bird bones across her eyes. "We've not heard of a village that's been unaffected. No matter how far north or east or west we've gone, the rifts appear, and the Dreamers come."

"Are my people dead, then? Is that what you are saying?" She tried to keep the agitation from her voice.

A somber mood settled on the Speaker's shoulders. "Did you think they'd escape the Creator's wrath? The Earth Walkers, the Severed Sky, the Wave Carvers, and the Fire Bones... The Four Peoples were blind to any truth but their own. If they walk with the Dreamers now, then whose fault is it but their own?"

Animkii felt rage building. Lies! This outlander couldn't possibly know the truth, only wove stories out of rumors and speculation. The Fire Bones were a formidable people, accustomed to hardships. If the lands had split, they would've migrated north. There was no way the rifts could've swallowed the entire Witherlands. "You outlanders seem to have survived fine," she said in a hard voice.

Harvester's expression was a marvel of calm, seeming indifferent to her guest's outrage, speaking her truth with an ugly candor. "We live because we have kept the true faith. The Creator protects us and so we serve. You've seen the power He's granted me. Could any of *your* people's Speakers turn away the Dreamers with such authority?"

The knot in her steel gut made her want to scream.

"If you still do not believe me, you can ask the survivors yourself."

Her heart lurched. "What do you mean?"

"There is a place among us for those who accept our ways," she said, "but the Fire Bones, as you knew them, are no more. We are the Last People now. And together, we await the Creator's final judgement."

Chapter Nine

Mica balanced herself on the woven road. All around her and in the spaces between the roots and vines existed a darkness with no end. A sharp fear knifed into her heart, causing her to hesitate. What if she fell?

As if responding to her fear, the vines rose around her and entwined themselves into rails, the road beneath her shifting and reshaping itself, and the roots carrying her upward toward her destination without her making any movement. The gates behind her closed and she could no longer feel the After Lord's suffocating presence or his burdensome weight on her mind.

Was she in another world, then? As she rose up the stairs, she marveled at the living webwork of roots and vines, a tentative hope replacing the dread she'd felt earlier as the great white light encompassed her and swallowed both the darkness and pathway behind her. It was like she was flying now, invisible wings carrying her into a vast sea of whiteness, rising upward forever.

When at last the light faded, she found herself suspended in the air above a tree so enormous she was nothing but a flea in comparison. She felt dwarfed by it, diminished, and yet she felt a connection to it too; being near it brought her a sense of peace that eased the horror of these last couple of months.

At the tree's feet spread a carpet of wildflowers so fragrant that the wind carried their scent miles upwind and the colors dazzled her eyes, accustomed as she was to the dull grays and browns of undercity life.

The force that buoyed her flight released her gently, and after a slow descent, she stepped down onto the cotton-soft verdant field. The cool blades of grass tickled her bare feet. Above her, an endless golden canopy of leaves reached out, through which light gently filtered to the ground below. Gone were the threadbare jacket and pants she'd worn for weeks in unwashed filth, replaced by a dress spun of golden silk and seeded with pearls. New life flushed her sickly pale skin with the radiance of the sun. She felt cleansed and whole and no longer weighed-down by the bleakness of her mortality.

She blinked back tears of joy, overcome with emotion. A thousand times over, she'd imagined her own world looking like this—a realm untouched by the Technocracy's ruinous grasp. The closest she'd ever come to experiencing this feeling had been during Reid's mercantile expeditions to the far southern Fringe Lands. She'd been captivated by the sight of scrawny trees pushing through contaminated soils, and by the scraggly weeds with their heads of white and yellow, swaying beneath the pale gray light of day. She'd thought them the most beautiful things she'd ever seen. But this place was beauty on an entirely different scale.

Fragrances from uncountable blooms wafted across her senses, dazzling her with the sharpness and sweetness of their smell. A light breeze rustled the grass. No drug could be as intoxicating or addictive as this place. Now that she was here, she only wanted to lie down in this fragrant field and forget everything that came before. She belonged here.

Was she dead?

Was that why the After Lord had tried to keep her away from this place and why he couldn't follow? Was *this* the afterlife that Animkii's people believed in, the utopia where the Creator dwelled and called to him the souls of his fallen faithful?

But the Creator was a fraud. If Revan had spoken true, she couldn't imagine that an afterlife under the After Lord's control would look anything like this place. Still, the allure of a place to find solace after life's hardships tugged at her heart. Was it possible? Would she find her own dead loved ones here, waiting? The thought of seeing them again made her heart soar.

"You are not dead," a thousand voices chorused, their music filling the air, the sound of it so thrilling that it dulled her disappointment at discovering she was still alive. A warm breeze caressed her cheek and skimmed the tears from her eyes. "You are at the heart of what you call the Other World, the sanctuary called Hul."

Mica looked up at the vast smooth trunk of the massive tree, still marveling over how, despite its size, it cast no shade, but bathed her and the fields only in golden light. Though the voices came from all around her, she knew instinctively that this great mother tree was the source of them all.

"How did I get here?" she asked. "The last time I came through the portal, it was different." Different in a bad way.

The leaves shivered in reply. Despite the beauty of the golden foliage, she now saw that many leaves had withered, were torn and full of holes, with some branches stripped bare. Some kind of black rot had infested the tree's bark in places. A chill crept up her body. Up-close, the perfection was peeling away.

"Your blood called to us." The sound of their voices rippled like a breeze across the air. "Come, place your hand on us and let us look upon you."

There was no malice in their request, no demand, yet their curiosity made her uneasy. Too many people—*things*—seemed interested in her these days, and not one of them had shown any good intentions. She didn't move, but glanced around for exits, only to find golden fields that stretched on infinitely and a vivid blue sky that spanned the horizon.

"Is there a way back to my world from here?"

"There are always doors for those with the power to open them."

"Do *you* have that power?"

"We did at one time, but no longer." A branch bent down like an arm, gently draping itself around her shoulders, its leaves forming a golden shawl as it drew her forward. "Do not be afraid. We are simply curious to know how you came to this place, how you called to us, when only Janus and Revan have access."

The first name meant nothing to her, but the latter she recognized right away. "Revan is dead. Who is Janus?"

A tremor passed through the leaves, but before the voices could answer, a white-robed figure appeared at the base of the massive trunk. It was human by its shape, but its face was hidden in the shadows, the only shadows in this place. It laid a silencing hand on the peeling bark of the tree. A wind stirred the branches as they bowed in obeisance.

"That's enough of old stories, don't you think, Elder Tree?" His voice was soft, but his words carried across the wind as clear as a ringing bell—a sibilant sound she knew all too well, and that didn't belong to anything human at all.

The After Lord.

Mica bolted.

Through the endless grassy fields she ran, with no end in sight, just that beautiful blue horizon always in front of her and the golden canopy always above. *"There are always doors for those with the power to open them,"* they'd said.

"Then open up, dammit!" Her breath grew ragged with desperation. She was certain that a great clawed hand would snatch her from her flight at any moment. As if running could do anything in this place where space and time had no laws.

That thought brought a realization. She didn't need to run. Hadn't she already jumped between spaces and worlds? This was no different. Even if she didn't fully understand how, she knew she could do it again, just like she'd slipped into Animkii's memories and just like she'd summoned the portal. Only this time, she'd make this power take her where she *wanted* to go.

Clenching her teeth, she visualized the frayed tether of energy she now recognized as her soul and gripped it with the force of her mind, feeling the anchor of her real-world body pulling back. Still alive. Pain shot through her in both worlds as she yanked that spiritual umbilical cord with all her willpower.

She expected resistance from the After Lord and braced herself for an incoming psychic battle, but there was nothing. The Other World let her go without a fight, but in the air, she tasted the satisfaction of its god.

He *wanted* to let her go.

Why?

***

"We are the Last People now..."

Animkii continued to follow Harvester into the deepest reaches of the sunken city, the Speaker's words stirring a storm of emotion inside her, stealing her voice so that she couldn't speak. And when she regained her words, Harvester would speak no more, only tell her to wait until they arrived at their village.

Was it true? Had some of her people survived? She wondered at their fates, torn between joy and despair as she trudged the broken pathway. Had they really been so desperate that they'd joined out-landers?

Yet she'd seen Harvester's power, like nothing any Speaker she'd ever known possessed. Robbed of everything else, wouldn't it be tempting to follow someone like her? Wasn't Animkii tempted her-self?

In the days that followed, they traveled past toppled towers and ancient building complexes, over innumerable abandoned roadways and mountains of debris. When the hours grew too long, they took refuge in caves formed by fallen structures, a silent brooding group that huddled together around a small fire built out of broken crates, speaking little among themselves, but watching Animkii with a mix-ture of awe and fear and loathing. From Mica, there was nothing but the odd sigh or groan.

On the third day, they crossed an open plain of broken roadways and giant concrete bridges scattered across a vast field of long-dead grass. From there, they branched off into another collection of build-ings, most of them crushed beneath an enormous slab of earth that had fallen in such a way as to create a network of unstable tunnels.

The newest rifts had caused so much damage that it obscured this part of the city, obliterating the path she remembered from years before, though it hadn't erased one thing: As they emerged from one of the seemingly endless tunnels of debris, she could hear the familiar burble of an underground river.

"That river led me out of the city when I came here years ago," she said, relieved. "We must be close to the surface."

Harvester's eyes had a vague wandering look in them, as if she wasn't completely present, but her attention snapped back to Animkii. "Yes, the black snake's mouth opens to the sky. About a half-day's journey upward, but a treacherous climb to get there."

"How long have you lived down here?"

"Ever since the monster was slain, we've wintered in these tunnels."

"The monster..." Animkii bit back her words. "You mean the winged serpent back in the cavern?"

"Yes."

Was she imagining it, or was there a glimmer of knowledge in those eyes? Feeling uneasy beneath the outlander's gaze, she busied herself checking on Mica. Strapped to Animkii's back again, the woman's scrawny arms dangled over Animkii's shoulders while her head rested on her steel neck. Still alive.

What had Mica tried to do? Her worries chewed away at her. Had she tried to transport them again, even after Animkii's warning? Or was she trapped inside Animkii's mind again? Mica had promised to stay away from the closed door of Animkii's memories, but how much control over her abilities did she really have?

The tunnels of rubble finally opened up and her optical light illuminated a long corridor of broken streets enclosed on either side by towering brick buildings and crooked streetlights. A line of trees ran down a middle section, the leaves still impossibly green even in the dark, held in stasis by a force that defied nature. Farther up the street, she spotted specks of firelight dancing in the windows of the multi-storied buildings. On ground-level, the outlanders had built a large defensive wall, cobbled together from the sea of rubble. From behind that wall, she could hear the roar of the distant river echoing in the cavern beyond.

Whatever else happened, that river would lead them out of here.

A handful of grim, gaunt-faced guards kept watch at the wall's entrance, and when they saw what emerged from the shadows—Animkii, that nightmare of living tech—a thousand years of prejudice awakened, and their faces contorted with hostility. Three nocked their bows in preparation, while another loaded a metal crossbow, but before they loosed a single missile, Harvester called out to them. "Peace in the name of the Creator!"

The sound of her voice was like pouring cold water on a fever. The guards lowered their weapons. With no hesitation and to the last person, they obeyed this woman.

Animkii couldn't help but marvel at the Speaker's authority over these wild people. The outlanders she'd encountered in the past were violent even against their own kind, and prone to fits of madness, thought to be a consequence of spending too much time near rifts. But seeing them exert such self-control made Animkii question her prejudice.

Had her people not cast her into the End, might she have become an outlander too?

Yet even knowing their outlander status, there was something else unsettling about these people, a nagging feeling she couldn't shake. Close-up, the wear of hard times showed. Stains and tears marred the guards' caribou parkas, the once-pristine hides now worn thin, the quillwork torn. A woman's feathered headdress was missing most of its plumes. An older man, sporting a bright-yellow jacket, bore a face caked in dirt and old blood, with flakes of it littering the fur collar of his coat.

With their fear of Animkii extinguished, the emotion drained from their eyes, as if they had no more life in them than walking corpses. She shivered, not from the cold, which her body no longer felt, but from the creeping apprehension that followed her into this makeshift village.

If you could even call this a village.

There were no communal longhouses here. The outlanders had claimed many of the ancient shops and restaurants for shelter, and she saw their faces peering out of broken windows as they passed. At the street level, they'd cobbled together a collection of crude huts from concrete bricks, wooden planks, and sheets of hide. A group of cooking fires sat at the center of the motley encampment, where several grim-faced villagers went through the motions of making dinner, with none of the bustle or merriment of community.

It was too quiet here. Unnatural. Where were the songs? Where were the children?

Had the Dreamers left them so little?

At her approach, all heads turned, and she heard a rumble of discontent and suspicion from the shadows—the sound of weapons clattering, figures rising to fight. One woman let out an alarmed cry and dropped the clay pot she was holding into the fire, sending up a spray of sparks into the air. "Abomination!" The word hissed across the camp.

Animkii had become so used to the technology riddling her body that she hadn't much thought about how her own kind would view it until the last few days. To them, she was no longer human at all, but the living embodiment of the sins that had led to the Sundering, someone who'd broken their strictest taboos and whose very existence offended their god.

An abomination in need of killing.

She felt no fear at the realization, only a deeply entrenched shame. What had she expected?

Harvester was having none of it, raising a stern hand to silence the threats, her eerily childish voice as cutting as a knife and her eyes burning like embers sinking into ash behind the row of bone ornaments. "Do not fear," she said. "The Creator has spoken, has He not? I have told you this: The old ways are dead. It was not the Ancients' tech that corrupted us; it was our hearts. Did the Great Spirit not say, 'In the final days, the faithful will wear their souls as shining armor'?"

Dissent turned into murmurs of reverence and Animkii saw two dozen sets of eyes gleaming in the firelight, burning with fanaticism, their rapid shift of mood leaving her unsettled. The old ways were dead? What did that mean? And when Harvester recited that verse about wearing their souls as 'shining armor'...

Did Harvester think the Creator had made her like this?

Animkii wanted to argue that she was no fulfillment of whatever prophecy this mad Speaker had drummed up, but looking at the awestricken crowd, she knew she couldn't afford to antagonize them, not now when her stims were running so low and Mica still needed protection. But that wasn't the only reason she silenced her doubts. Seeing them huddled here, their faces gaunt with despair and their eyes bright with delusion, she couldn't bear to bring them more pain than what they'd already endured.

"Our new sister is not a stranger to all of us." Harvester's hands moved with her words, as if weaving a spell over them, her black-painted lips curving with a knowing smile. "She once walked among the Fire Bones as the warrior called Animkii."

"Not possible!" rasped a voice from the shadows. "That name was cursed and the one who owned it thrown off the End of the World."

Animkii's keen eyes picked out the speaker crouched by one fire, a sallow-faced man with long, filthy, ash-colored braids and a scar cut across his mouth. It took her a moment to absorb the shock.

Raak.

Her ruthless mentor's succession to the position of war chief had ushered in a new era of brutality and bloodshed for the Fire Bones, yet provided hope for a people desperate to recover their strength after the disastrous attack that had slain her vessel and so many other fine warriors. She cringed at the memory of how easily Raak had taken her youthful potential, her eagerness to please, and had twisted it to his own sadistic purposes. She'd blindly followed her mentor's lead up until her son's birth. After that...

Harvester's voice rose. "The Great Spirit has sent Animkii back from the End as a sign that we are *all* redeemed in His eyes," she said, stamping her booted foot to emphasize her words.

Animkii's machine body stiffened with denial. She couldn't let the lie pass this time and she opened her mouth to protest it. "No, I—"

But it was too late. Harvester's words ignited a mass hysteria among her followers. Clansmen began ripping their clothes and tearing at their hair and hitting themselves in awful acts of repentance. One woman clawed at her face until blood welled up from the scratches.

A wave of repugnance struck Animkii. This couldn't be what the Creator expected of them!

"Creator, forgive us!" Raak's shout stirred a wailing lament from the rest of the crowd. Her former mentor's expression had transformed, the cruel eyes squinting out from his weathered face now gleaming with the same mindless zeal that had once driven him into a battle fury.

Raak had always dealt a brutal hand to those he'd condemned as traitors to the Fire Bones. And yet he'd joined these outlanders. What did it mean? And where were the others?

The only other Fire Bones she spotted was another one of Raak's pupils—Tam, a timid boy who'd been only eight or nine summers old at the time of Animkii's exile. He sat in his mentor's shadow and rocked back and forth on his heels as if in some kind of trance. The boy's lips moved continuously, but Animkii's enhanced hearing picked up no words, and his liquid eyes stared into the fire with no emotion at all, as if someone had sucked free his soul and left behind a living doll.

Hope darkened into despair. Was this mad pair all that remained of the Fire Bones?

"Come, sit among us." Harvester waved a tattooed hand toward a central fire, acting oblivious to Animkii's distress.

Drawn by word of the newcomer's arrival, other outlanders soon arrived to gawk at Animkii's 'shining skin,' their expressions shifting from horror to veneration as their peers repeated Harvester's reassurances. It wasn't long before a crowd formed around the central fire and its guests, a sizeable group of maybe two hundred outlanders, though not packed so tightly that Animkii and Harvester weren't given a noticeable berth.

"I need to tend to my friend, Mica," she told Harvester.

"We will see to her needs."

The Speaker made a gesture and the same long-nosed youth who'd accompanied them to the village stepped forward to help unstrap Mica from Animkii's back. Animkii noticed his hands were shaking as they navigated the steel expanse of her skin to release the bindings. Whether from fear or awe, she couldn't tell.

Mica's body slipped into the youth's arms. As he held her, a woman hastened out of the crowd, laying an exquisitely embroidered hide blanket beside the fire. The young man carefully set his sleeping charge upon it, his eyes constantly flickering back to Harvester for approval.

Harvester made no acknowledgment of his obeisance, but curled her arm around Animkii's massive back, steering her to the fireside. Resigned to being a spectacle, Animkii shuffled across the cracked pavement with grim acceptance and sat cross-legged across from her motionless friend, trying to ignore the expectant eyes fastened on her every movement.

A hundred times before, she'd returned after a battle or hunt to enjoy the warmth of a roaring fire and the companionship of her kin and friends. Even though she no longer suffered the aches and pains of a long journey, it evoked memories of such experiences—of sharing tales around the fire, recounting epic battles, and weaving age-old legends dating back to the Sundering. But the stories she now carried in her heart would be the stuff of nightmares to these people.

Or would they? It seemed these outlanders had suffered their own nightmares.

Dinner was served—a stringy stew with tiny bits of dubious meat—but no dinner among any of the Four People had ever been as quiet as this one. Suffering had worked its way into the lines of every face here, and she wondered whether it was a mercy that more of her people hadn't made it this far. Filth and untended sores covered many of the outlanders, and even the smell of smoke couldn't conceal the stink of refuse left littering the dirt-packed floor. In the hours she sat among them, there were no visits between fires, just shadows huddled on benches. No mothers bustling back and forth with their children, and no warriors shouting out across the fires at one another. From the few children she spotted, there wasn't a peep, only eyes staring from the darkness. There was no life left in this bleak and joyless group, only a longing to see the promised end to their suffering.

As the others chewed on their grim supper, a young woman crouched next to Mica with a bowl of soup. The crossed-out footprint burned into the side of her neck marked her as a former member of the Earth Walkers Clan, the westernmost of the Four Peoples. She must've been pretty once, but now her eyes were ringed with dark circles, her long red hair matted with neglect and her lips cracked and bleeding as she murmured her encouragement to the unconscious woman. She lifted the rim of the bowl to Mica's lips and while the woman's eyes remained shut, her mouth opened to take in the liquid.

Mica was responding. That was something, at least.

Relieved, she turned her attention back to the question gnawing at her heart and, in the silence, spoke it. "I've waited long enough. I want to know what happened to my village." She looked directly at her former mentor, Raak, her unblinking tech eyes never moving from his face.

The pale light couldn't hide the twitch of his scarred mouth.

"Tell her," Harvester ordered him, and Animkii wasn't sure if she was more stunned that this woman would dare speak to the Fire Bones' war chief in such a way, or that Raak obeyed her without hesitation, giving the Speaker a curt nod of acknowledgment. The world had turned upside-down on Animkii, its contents dumped out and disordered so that nothing made sense anymore.

The aging warrior's voice sank deep into his chest, and he rose to his feet, a giant of a man withered by hardship and suffering. "The first new cracks appeared about a year ago, near our southernmost borders," he said, his dark eyes fixed on the flames of the fire, the light reflecting in them. The only other sounds came from the jangle of his hair pipe breastplate, the tubular beads clattering against one another.

No one dared move, his dark words compelling them to stillness. "At first they were small, scattered, barely rifts at all, but then they began to grow, spreading in every direction, too many to avoid. The Dreamers soon followed, so many that they blackened the horizon..."

Animkii saw now the empty shirtsleeve dangling at his left side and wondered what had taken the mighty warrior's limb. Had an enemy's hatchet severed it or had someone amputated it to halt the withering of a Dreamer's touch?

"Then the day of our undoing came... Just like in the stories of the Sundering, the Earth shook and broke apart, and those who couldn't flee decayed to nothing where they stood," he said. Now that he'd begun the tale, it was like a tsunami unleashed that would only end when it was complete. The pain of its telling swept away all who heard it. Even Animkii, who knew the deep sadism this man was capable of, found herself moved by the helpless agony in his eyes, the memory of having everything he'd built and lived for destroyed. "The Dreamers overran our outposts in a matter of weeks. Only a handful of us escaped."

Looking at the pale faces and hollow eyes of the outlanders gathered here, she wondered how many of their experiences mirrored the old war chief's. Harvester had said they were one people now. How many other villages had succumbed? How many of these outlanders were survivors? She recalled the terror of facing down the handful of Dreamers outside the city. To think her kin might've faced hundreds or thousands of them was an unimaginable horror.

"Enough to blacken the horizon..."

Raak wasn't one given to exaggeration.

His slow, deep voice filled the place with the darkness and dread of those times, describing the last brutal days of their people. "Without the outposts to slow the first wave of attacks, Firehome had little chance to defend itself," he said. "We arrived home just before the rift took the village into its belly. There was no time to recover from the fall. The Dreamers descended on us, feasting on the wounded and the dead first, then—"

Even Raak, ever-stoic, couldn't keep the horror from his voice.

"I saw the wreckage," Animkii said, her voice tight with grief and anger. It took all of her will not to grab him and shake the answers free. "What about my clan?"

He didn't answer, only lowered his head. "Some survived the collapse, but the Dreamers were tireless. Always at our heels. They chased us eastward until the weakest among us dropped dead from exhaustion, each death buying the rest of us more time to escape. Most did not make it." There was no sorrow in his eyes, only a deep simmering rage, the remembered humiliation of defeat. In the past, she'd often wondered whether he was capable of anything else. "Had Harvester not found us when she did—"

A shudder rolled through the once-great warrior, this man who'd raged through every battle, roaring his war song until his throat was hoarse from it. Dark days then. Dark days now. As his pupil, Animkii had learned how to hide her pain, had made herself as ruthless as Raak and Ishkode to survive the incessant, demoralizing wars against the Dreamers. But now, with the Fire Bones' demise, even Raak had faltered. Even Raak had broken. How much worse was it for the others? Ziiba, Niigaanii, Debwe, and so many more...

"Harvester called the Creator's wrath down upon the Dreamers, drove them away with her power, then convinced us to travel here," he said, his face darkening as he saw Animkii's expression at this admission of breaking their people's laws, and he repeated Harvester's words in a harsh tone, "The old ways are dead, and the Judgment is upon us. The Creator chose us to survive, so that we will witness the rebirth of our world. We made great sacrifices to prove our faith." The mad light in his eyes faded now and the youth beside him whimpered. "Great sacrifices."

Harvester's words slid across the silence, sand rasping against stone. "And we will sacrifice much more before the end is here," she said, "but the reward will be greater than the suffering."

"So speaks the Creator," the crowd rumbled in response.

Again, uneasiness crept over her, and Animkii couldn't shake the feeling that she was missing something important. "You said there were other survivors, but I don't see them here. Where are they? How many?"

"Fifty-two of us made it out of Firehome. Most continued on northward to join other survivors in our new village, Onehome."

"What about Ziiba? Debwe?" Her voice tightened. "Niigaanii?"

Without a word, he shifted his gaze, locking eyes with a group of drenched hunters who'd just entered the encampment.

All three were Fire Bones. She inhaled sharply, that old human habit, and her hand went automatically to her shoulder, to where her people's fiery mark had disappeared into the biosteel. These newcomers were like the others here, their faces starved and full of weary desperation, their sun-bronzed skin turned a leathery gray from hardship. But she knew all three: a red-faced man with the build of a bear, a scraggly, bearded old warrior missing half his face, and a young woman whose mouth had once been made for smiling.

But now, gazing into Ziiba's eyes was like looking into an empty grave.

Chapter Ten

Mica blinked, and it was dark; she blinked again, and she could see.

Someone had bundled her in a pile of warm, bug-eaten furs, leaving her with a fire blazing a few feet away. A dozen silent shadows huddled around those cheery flames, and when she inhaled, she caught the sweet fragrance of roasting meat. Her stomach tightened and groaned its hunger, but before she could make a sound, a young woman with sun-kissed skin swooped down on her with a bowl of soup. The anxious look on her face was enough to cause Mica to bark out a nasty laugh.

"Eat," she coaxed, lifting the bowl to Mica's lips, the music and rhythm of her native language now familiar to the southern woman.

Was she inside Animkii's head again? One glance around confirmed that she was back among the Witherlands' people, but she didn't recognize any of these grim faces from Animkii's memories. Her attendant propped her back against an ancient steel bench so that Mica could get a better view of her surroundings. This was no village, but an encampment enclosed on all sides by ancient brick and wooden structures.

She was still in the undercity then. So who were these people?

And where was Animkii?

Adjusting back to reality was always a slow process. She was still too weak to move without help and begrudgingly opened her mouth to accept the broth her caretaker offered. She savored the warm liquid that trickled down her throat, the taste of it carrying her between two worlds. All the while, her gaze wandered the gathering, searching for her friend.

What a gloomy crowd! She'd seen a man with his throat slit looking happier than this lot. Their vacant expressions reminded her of the times she'd spent prowling the drug dens of Under-Alpha. Hands moved to stoke a fire, a voice rose to still an unruly child, and a warrior practiced a spear-throw, but the ones performing those tasks had an absence in their eyes, as if their minds had disconnected from what their bodies were doing. It was an unnerving sight.

Right now, the crowd's attention seemed focused on an exchange taking place in front of a large, crude hut. She craned her neck to see past the press of bodies, curious, and glimpsed biosteel skin gleaming copper in the firelight.

Animkii! Relief flooded through her at the sight of her friend. She tried to rise, but the dark-haired woman held her back with a firm grip. "You mustn't interfere," she said, keeping her eyes averted.

"Interfere with what?" The language of Animkii's people rolled off Mica's tongue with startling ease. Looked like Soulcleaver wasn't the only thing she'd brought back from her trip through Animkii's mind.

The younger woman only shook her head at the question, unwilling to answer, so Mica returned her gaze to the hut and waited for the scene to explain itself.

***

"Thank the Creator you are alive!" Animkii lurched toward the trio, hearing the brokenness in her own metallic voice, raw emotion making her forget what she was.

All three Fire Bones brandished their spears, their faces dark with fear and loathing. "Stand back, Abomination!"

Her heart screamed its anguish. She'd rather have died a thousand times over than see such absolute hatred in Ziiba's eyes.

"I do not know why I thought you would recognize me, looking like this," she said in a subdued voice as she drew back, her broken heart oozing like an open wound. More than ever, she was self-conscious of her accursed machine body, the way it moved and scraped at the joints, how it felt sensations from a distance. "I do not even look human anymore, do I? How could I expect even *you* to know me? But it *is* me, no matter what your eyes see. I *am* Animkii."

The woman before her was a ruin, empty-eyed and gaunt-faced. Hair that had once been oiled and shining with care now hung matted with neglect, with more gray than black shooting through it. Her furs had worn away in patches and rot and dirt layered the leathers she'd once beaded and brushed with care.

Ziiba's eyes widened at the sound of Animkii's name. Wind-burned lips parted with surprise and a strange, pained light came into those drowning eyes. Then her mouth twisted downward.

"Whatever you are," she snarled, "you are *not* Animkii!" She sped forward and slammed the tip of her stone spear into Animkii's chest, jumping back in horror as the entire shaft splintered at impact, the crude weapon powerless against the armor.

Animkii didn't move an inch—just stood there, sinking into despair as the entire room gasped in unison. Her answering silence only seemed to confirm Harvester's claim that she was some kind of indestructible holy warrior.

The two hunters flanking Ziiba pulled her back, whispering fiercely to her, but her former friend and lover pushed them away, her voice shaking with anger as she leveled her wrath at the muttering crowd. "Why aren't you attacking it? Why are you letting it stand among you?!"

"She speaks the truth, Ziiba." Raak's rough voice called out. "Animkii returns to us, transformed by the Creator."

"That can't be!" Ziiba's expression warred between grief and rage. "Animkii is dead!"

"The Dreamers did not kill me," she said. The grief tightened inside her steel chest as she stretched her hands out in a pleading gesture, begging for understanding. "The End of the World is a bridge to an unfamiliar land, one far south of the Witherlands. Their scientists did this to me."

"If what you say is true, then you have robbed the Creator of your penitence; you are the one who brought His wrath upon us all! Everything that's happened since then is *your* fault!" she said. "I told you not to come to this place. I warned you not to break the taboos, but you didn't listen. You *never* listened!"

"I was trying to save our people! I could not let Niigaanii grow up like we did."

"No, you went into the Ancients' city because you couldn't ever let things just *be*. All you've ever done is make things worse."

"Enough!" Harvester's voice cut through the room as she stepped between the embittered pair, facing Ziiba and laying a soothing hand on the anguished woman's shoulder, her dark eyes flashing with that frightening authority. "All this was foretold. All this was necessary. The Great Spirit has chosen Animkii to herald the new world. Look how she is armored for the final battle!"

Ziiba's anger faded almost instantly and returned to a flat indifference. "You're right. Forgive me, Speaker."

Animkii watched her, mute with grief.

Then the holy woman turned to address the others gathered there and her voice heightened. "It was Animkii who slew the monster that guarded this city with the blade that broke the world. And it was the Creator's will that Animkii survive the End and usher in the new age. All that has transpired is part of His plan."

"Yes, yes!" The crowd stirred with zeal, their scattered affirmations rippling across space. "Aho, Great Spirit, your wisdom sustains us! In the Creator's light, we find our way! "

Animkii stared at her in horror. So that look Harvester had given her, back in the monster's chamber, hadn't been her imagination. She *knew* Animkii had killed it. And she knew about Soulcleaver too? How? Was she like Mica? Could she reach into someone's memories?

Only Ziiba's presence kept her rooted there when every ounce of her being screamed at her to leave. But no matter how much Harvester's knowledge disturbed her, no matter how much Ziiba despised her, she needed the answer to one last question. She looked her lost lover in the eyes.

"Tell me—is Niigaanii alive?"

An immeasurable pain shuddered across the other woman's face. "He is with the mothers and grandmothers. The Creator protects them, and so I serve the Creator."

She breathed in relief. "Where? When can I see him?"

But Ziiba answered with a cold indifference worse than hatred. There was no affection, no forgiveness, no love.

"When the Creator wills it."

***

Ziiba? Mica stared.

The cold-faced woman standing across from Animkii bore little resemblance to the teasing, carefree spirit that belonged to her friend's memories. Those merry eyes had turned dark and cold. Her suffering had written itself in the gauntness of her body and the filth of neglect that had accumulated on her clothing and person.

Mica's gaze drifted back to Animkii, who was standing there like a steel statue, her metallic voice ringing through these caverns, filling all who heard it with the pain of this reunion. Thanks to Pandora, Mica had grown to believe mods were incapable of genuine emotions, that any bond she formed with one would be nothing more than a programmed act of theater. Animkii had proven her wrong, time and time again, revealing a depth of emotion and humanity that Mica had never expected from one of the Technocrat's 'steel slaves.'

Animkii deserved to know the truth. She tried again to rise, but her legs wobbled beneath her and sent her back to the dirt. "Animkii!" Though rough, her voice carried over the crowd and turned the mod's head in her direction.

Animkii's patchwork face was all-but-gone, consumed by biosteel. She felt a pang of sorrow for the loss. Her once-mismatched eyes were now silver-irised twins, encased in a seamless band of biosteel, their precise inhuman gaze a stark contrast to the warm, brown eyes they'd replaced. Her face was no longer capable of expressing emotion, but the human habit of body language still survived. Mica saw her metal shoulders shift and settle in a release of tension.

"Mica!" The gratitude in the mod's voice sent a twinge of guilt through her, causing her to hesitate. Revealing the truth about their god would destroy these people's hopes. And what about Animkii? Unless Mica could conjure an impossible cure in the next few days, the mod would soon lose the rest of her humanity. What if Animkii's faith in the Creator, the belief in a paradise after death, was all that had kept her sane? She'd lasted weeks with no stims at all before she'd met Mica. Maybe that faith had saved her...

Maybe it was better to let her die without ever knowing the truth.

Animkii took a step toward her, but another body closed the gap, blocking the warrior's path. It was that woman who'd spoken earlier, the one wearing the antlered headdress. One of the others had called her 'Speaker.' A holy woman, then? Despite her diminutive size, her presence swallowed the room and she seemed to hold a frightening authority over these people. A small smile curled her black-painted lips, and her dark eyes stared straight at Mica.

A chill rippled through Mica as she recalled the Speaker's words. *"The Creator has chosen Animkii to herald the new world."*

Was that why they hadn't killed the mod on sight? Mica knew enough from Animkii's memories that these people should've seen her friend's modifications as the ultimate sacrilege. Instead, they thought Animkii was the bringer of some final holy reckoning?

Animkii's people believed that Mishibijiw was the great evil destined to rise against the Earth. What would they say if she revealed that their *Creator* was the true evil?

A cold clump of fear settled in her stomach. They'd kill her just like they'd tried to kill Animkii all those years ago.

She could hear the feverish whispers of the crowd, their manic eyes fastened on the Speaker and her herald, their faces lit with unwavering devotion. The older woman's lips moved and Animkii shook her head in response, raising an insistent hand toward Mica. Ziiba faded into the crowd behind them as Animkii finally broke from their confrontation to come to Mica's side.

Crouching beside her, the warrior lowered her voice, relief palpable in her tone. "Thank the Creator! When you lost consciousness again, I was worried."

Mica brushed aside her friend's concern, her mind preoccupied with a difficult decision. She needed to tell Animkii the truth, but the thought of revealing the Creator's true nature and her broken promise weighed heavily on her. "Never mind that," she said, steering away from uncomfortable questions. "Are all these people survivors from your village?"

"Only a few," the mod said, a tremor in her voice, a faint reverberation of sorrow within her steel pipe throat. "The Four Peoples have fallen. The rifts have spread throughout the Witherlands, destroying our villages and our people. Those few who survived have joined Harvester."

Mica followed Animkii's gaze across the space, to where the Speaker stood watching them with her predatory eyes. "You really trust that woman?" she murmured, conscious of listening ears. Although her unassuming caregiver seemed engrossed in feeding wood to the fire, Mica suspected every word spoken here would be relayed back to her leader, to this Speaker who held them all in thrall. It made no difference to Mica. She wasn't planning on staying long.

Animkii lowered her voice. "Harvester is an outlander. My people always despised her kind, but now I find they have turned to her for leadership. What am I to think? The Creator must have led us here for a reason."

"*I* brought us here to escape the After Lord. The Creator didn't do anything. And you should know—"

"I have seen Harvester's power with my own eyes, Mica."

Mica stopped, confession interrupted. She frowned. "Power?"

"She is a *true* Speaker. The Great Spirit has granted her the power to drive away Dreamers. He truly talks to her."

"I don't like it when people claim to talk to gods. Makes them think they can control what the rest of us do."

"What that cultist did to you is not the same!"

Mica tucked a hank of greasy hair behind one ear, unable to meet Animkii's reproachful gaze, her heart heavy with the burden she'd carried in silence. "I never told you, but Father Dark sent the collector that killed Reid," she said. "I saw it inside his mind."

But her confession didn't elicit the sympathy she expected. Instead, Animkii's expression shifted, suspicion clouding her inhuman features. "Back in the cave, when you blacked out," she said coldly, "were you inside *my* head again?"

"I knew you wouldn't tell me what really happened with that monster. I had to—"

"I trusted you!" Animkii's words burst out in a wave of humiliation, the thunder of her admonishment causing heads to lift, and Mica to flinch. She dropped her tone, though she couldn't hide the note of betrayal. "Those were private moments. You had no right to them!"

"You're right and I'm sorry, but there's something you need to know," she said, desperation leaking into her voice. "The Creator—"

"I have heard enough of your blasphemies." Fury crackled in Animkii's voice as she rose to her feet, towering over Mica. "Keep believing in nothing. Damn your own soul if you must, but leave mine alone."

"No, wait!" Mica struggled to stand, but her legs betrayed her again, and she tumbled back to the ground, stuck sitting in the dirt, unable to do anything but watch her former friend disappear into the undercity's ruined streets.

Chapter Eleven

"Your friend does not understand, does she?" Harvester said.

Animkii didn't even look up from the repair she was making to her snowshoes. "Mica comes from a land where people do not believe in spirits or gods. They believe in technology and the ones who gave it to them."

"As it was in the days before the Sundering, when humans put themselves above the Creator."

Animkii nodded, hoping that would be the discussion's end. Two days had passed since her argument with Mica and she had no interest in starting a new one with Harvester. Her anger was still too raw, the betrayal unforgiven. Her hands moved automatically, weaving rawhide laces in a crisscross pattern between the frame and crossbars of the snowshoe. Now that they'd merged with biosteel, Pandora's borrowed fingers moved as naturally as flesh ones, but even more dexterously. She found the exercise calming. Once she was done, she'd head up to the surface and hunt. It was an excuse to provide for her hosts while avoiding the reality of her people's ruination and the gnawing absence of answers.

Despite Harvester's talk of the Creator's mercy, all Animkii saw when she looked at the Four Peoples' sad leftovers were shells of what they'd once been. If she sat too long thinking about it, she'd lose her mind to despair. Instead, she focused on the one hope remaining—that she might reunite with her son before she died. Yet when she asked any of them when that would be, the answer remained the same: *"When the Creator wills it."*

And how could she argue with them, after all she'd done? Even the chance of a reunion was more than she deserved.

"They don't hate you," Harvester said. "Not anymore."

"They *should* hate me." She slipped her boot into one snowshoe, tying the bindings with her new biosteel fingers. She didn't want to have this conversation. "If I had stayed away from the Ancients' city, or if I had let myself die as a sacrifice in the End, maybe the Dreamers would not have risen up like they did."

"It was the Creator's will that you slew that monster."

Animkii laughed then, harsh, the sound of it like nails scraping metal. "And what good did that do? I could not even save myself in the end, let alone my clan or my people. I wish I had never laid eyes on this place or that accursed blade."

The Speaker's voice dropped to a covetous hush. "Your people spoke of Soulcleaver, but I knew its name long before they did," she said. "What became of it?"

"I do not know." Animkii didn't miss the way Harvester's voice grew craven or the way her eyes glistened as she spoke of the accursed knife. Mica's words came back to her: *"You really trust that woman?"* The memory made her tense. She kept her eyes on her handiwork, keeping her tone neutral. "The ones who pulled me out of the End took it," she said. "They likely destroyed it."

"Such a weapon is not easily destroyed."

"You seem to know more about it than I do."

Harvester drew her beaded shawl around her small shoulders and the wrinkles deepened around her small dark eyes. "In our oldest telling of the story, Soulcleaver was the blade used to break Mother Earth."

"No story I have ever heard."

"Time reshapes our stories. Humans forget, but the Creator does not."

Realization dawned. "You believe the beast I slew was responsible for the Sundering," she said, so incredulous that she would've laughed if not for the fierce look on Harvester's face. She straightened up, creaking with the movement like an unoiled joint, a steel goliath who towered over the tallest man here. However, neither tech nor stature intimidated Harvester. "But how?"

"Not how. *Who.* The monster you slew was the true form of Mishibijiw, the Great Lynx," the Speaker revealed. "The Creator's dark brother."

Animkii stared at her in disbelief. "The Creator has no brother. And even if that were true, Mishibijiw's rise heralds the final battle. There was no fight between us. His death was a mercy kill."

"Our ancestors were wrong. *We* were wrong!" The holy woman swept her arm dramatically, her bone bead bracelets jangling as her words rang out across the bustling encampment.

Then her voice dropped, so that only the two of them could hear the truth spoken. "Mishibijiw was the one who corrupted humanity. What we call the Sundering was the fallout from an insurrection he and his followers led against the Creator. He failed. He fled into the darkness, gravely wounded, too weakened to finish what he'd started. But the damage had already been done. The Earth Mother was left broken.

"When he realized that humanity had forsaken Him, the Creator withdrew from the physical world. Over the centuries, He has wandered the spirit plains, guiding the departed to their rest, awaiting signs the faithful had reembraced his teachings, and that they were prepared for the Mother's resurrection."

The zealot's eyes fixated upon her, a fervent burning inside them. "Your slaying of the Great Lynx was the first sign. Your passage through the End of the World was the second. Your return to this city was the third and final. Now that you're here, we can complete the Creator's work. We can resurrect the Earth Mother."

Animkii recoiled, torn between disbelief and longing for an end to her people's suffering. "Do the rest know?"

Harvester shook her head. "Not all of it. They are not ready to know the truth. Just as your people were not ready when you brought Soulcleaver back. The Creator chose you because you seek change, even as you fear it. We must break the old ways for a new world to evolve. Don't you want to create a safe place for your family?" Dried lips cracked a smile. "I've met little Niigaanii. So innocent, still untarnished by the horrors of this world."

Her heart burned. Of course she knew. Ziiba must've told her.

"I want it more than anything," she said. "Even if it is too late for me, I want *them* to be happy."

"It is not too late for you."

"It *is*." Animkii bowed her head. "My body is changing. In a few days, maybe a week, there will be nothing human left in me; I will be fully tech, with no control over my own actions. Before that happens, I must leave. Get far enough away that I cannot hurt anyone."

"Ah, but there are other ways." Her tattooed face was like a raptor's, with its sharp-beaked nose and tiny black eyes. Scraggly brown hair hung tangled over her slight shoulders, fragrant with sweet grass. "Ways to reverse what's happening to your body."

Animkii stared at her, stunned. Then she remembered the charlatan tricks of her own people's Speaker and the hold he'd had over the clans. He'd been the first to condemn Animkii to death. She shook her head, her tone brusque and dismissive. "No. There is nothing you can do."

"Not traditional ways," Harvester said, picking up on her indecision. She reached up with her hand to touch Animkii's biosteel shoulder, where the mark of her dead people once sat. "The Creator can make you human again."

Animkii jerked back. "How?" she demanded, *wanting* to believe but unwilling to trust. Yet she recalled that first encounter with Harvester, how this woman had sent the Dreamers fleeing back into the darkness with just the power of her voice. If she was a charlatan, she was one with actual power.

"A sacrifice is required, but no greater than what any other here has given." Her fingers curled up like claws and her smile was like a knife-slit in her face. "But I promise you, it's a small price to pay to save the ones we love."

"What is it, then?"

"It is sacrilegious to speak of its nature outside the ceremony," she said. "To commit to the sacrifice is a test of faith. To trust our Lord and do as He requires. In it you will find both redemption and salvation." Before Animkii could press her for more information, she held up her hand and shook her head, the beads in her hair rattling. "Tomorrow, all your questions will be answered."

"Why tomorrow?"

"We return to the surface for a celebration of the Creator's coming."

"I would rather have the answers now."

"The fire must first be tempered," she said dismissively. "There are preparations to attend to. But once the ceremony is complete, you can reunite with your son."

The emotion inside her swelled. To see Niigaanii again was something she'd only dreamed of. She opened her mouth to ask more questions, but the outlander turned her back to Animkii, ending all discussion and shuffling away toward a small huddle of men across the camp.

After all she'd done, all the laws she'd broken, would the Creator really cure her of this affliction? She didn't believe she was a herald *or* a savior *or* deserved to be saved. Was this truly her chance for redemption?

She'd do just about anything to become human again, to live the rest of her days with family, but even hoping for it brought her unwelcome anxiety and the expectation of disappointment. She thought she'd accepted her fate, but now...

It was the weakness of being human, this conflict when faced with decisions and choices. Had the Alphaknot still held control over her, the great machine mind would have figured it out for her, would have pieced together data with cold logic her mortal mind couldn't grasp. As it was, she only had her human brain to rely on.

One more day wouldn't make a difference, would it? If Harvester was lying, she'd know soon enough. And besides, she couldn't leave this place yet.

She cast a reluctant look across the encampment and found Mica sitting two fires down, propped up against a steel bench, gaunt-framed and hollow-eyed from her trials. But she was not alone. Two children sat across from her, their mouths stretching with mirth as she regaled them with tales of Under-Alpha.

It made her uneasy to hear her native language roll so effortlessly off the southerner's tongue, to know that Mica had stolen that knowledge from her mind. Her anger sharpened at the memory of her last words with Mica, but the softer side of her couldn't help but notice how Mica changed when speaking to these children. For the first time in their travels together, she saw a glimmer of genuine pleasure on Mica's long-suffering face. Her laughter rang out loudly as she stooped to draw pictures in the dirt, using them to describe sights the children had never imagined existing—buildings strung with netherlights, domed cities, and men built of metal. The children's dead eyes sparked, as if Mica's words had stirred them back to life.

Animkii didn't much like thinking about it, but for all of Harvester's claims about the survivors accepting a new path and putting their trust in the Creator, there was a sodden dreariness to this place and its defeated people. They were drowning on land. Life on the Witherlands was wretched at the best of times, with the Four Peoples constantly on the verge of annihilation, yet they had always persevered against hardship before, growing stronger from adversity. These people, though...

She dismissed her unease, stamping the ground with her snowshoes to test their fittings and then retrieving a spear from beside the fire, all the time watching the men and women who hadn't gone off to hunt prepare for the following day's celebration.

Craftsmen sat in silent circles around the various fires, finishing the beadwork on ceremonial garments or pounding minerals to make colorful pigments for ritual paints, their dour expressions and dark eyes avoiding Animkii's questing gaze. There was none of the chatter and laughter she'd grown up listening to, but there was still a frantic busyness to their movements as they made their preparations, an air of feverish anticipation. Not one of them looked up as she moved past them.

If she were human again, would they accept her as one of them?

Regardless of Harvester's reassurances, the ache in her heart told her it would be a bitter fight.

"—and one year at the Festival, Auntie Guen dressed up in a gown so big that my little brothers snuck in under the skirt of it and plundered about twenty apple tarts," Mica told her attentive audience. Her cheeks puffed out and her arms expanded as she described the skirt and then pantomimed her two brothers gobbling up the treats in record time after her mother discovered their hiding spot. For the first time since Animkii had arrived, the sound of children's laughter broke the silence, but it was awkward and terrible, like the act had interrupted something sacred.

One of the mothers scooped up the pair, her face marked with horror at their merriment.

"It's just a story!" Mica protested.

"My people see in your stories a world they have always feared."

Mica turned, her face lighting up at Animkii's arrival. "You're talking to me again?" she asked, scratching out the pictures she and the kids had drawn on the dirt with sticks. Mica was a gifted dirt artist, having drawn detailed pictures of common undercity structures and creatures: a rotund old lady selling pies from a stand, an alley cat curled up on a stair, and an automaton chasing a pair of children down a street of gawkers.

Animkii tried to smile, but there was no skin or muscle left around her mouth. "There is going to be a ceremony tomorrow," she said. "Afterward, I will leave this place to find my son."

"There's no way you'll make it. Look at you!"

"Harvester says there is a way to fix me, to make me human again."

Mica's jaw dropped. "Are you crazy? Your people are still using stone tools. You think she can concoct a magic potion to heal you? Please tell me you're smarter than that."

The blatant disrespect awakened an indignance in Animkii, and it took all her self-control to steady her voice. "You know nothing about my people and what they're capable of. A few days inside my head doesn't make you one of us!"

"Don't be an idiot! You're running out of time. Just give me a couple of days and I can transport us back to the south, right to Samiel. If anyone can fix you, it's him, not that hag."

"Harvester is our holy woman!"

"Our?" Mica repeated, her disbelief evident. "So, what, you've bought into their nonsense again? You think it's okay that they tried to sacrifice you, but now they think you're some kind of god-sent savior?"

Animkii felt anger pounding at her skull. "Who are you to judge? You, who believe in nothing but yourself!"

The woman's voice dropped to a murmur. "That's not all true. I believed in you too." She turned her face away, blinking rapidly. But in the next moment, her jaw tightened, her chin lifted, and her eyes flashed with determination. "Yes, what I did was rotten—entering your memories again—but you need to know the truth. Something important happened there." Her fingers twitched at her side, then reached down to touch her boot. Before she could complete her confession, though, her gaze caught something behind Animkii, and her expression soured. "Ziiba's coming over here," Mica said, withdrawing into herself. "Pretty sure it's not to talk to me."

Animkii felt her anger ebb, replaced by an adolescent smattering of nerves and apprehension. She turned to greet her former friend and lover after two days of silence between them.

"Would you join me on a hunt?" the woman asked.

If Ziiba had asked her to jump into a rift at that moment, she might've agreed to that too.

***

Mica scowled as she watched the empty-eyed Ziiba lead her friend away, a knot of worry tightening in her stomach.

"Dammit," she muttered, clenching her fists. Her attempt to warn Animkii had backfired again, leaving them both in danger. The burden of secrets filled her with anxiety. If Harvester found out that the After Lord was after Mica, they'd never get out of here alive. But Animkii wouldn't listen. She was getting sucked in by that witch's lies.

Mica had played along these last couple of days, hiding her suspicions and smiling with gratitude when they brought her food or helped her outside to take a piss. She was all too conscious that her survival relied on the hospitality of these beleaguered souls and their charlatan Speaker, but after watching her hosts between bouts of bone-deep exhaustion, she couldn't shake the feeling of being a prisoner. It wasn't that anyone tried to stop them from leaving, but there was always someone watching them, listening, waiting.

Why couldn't Animkii see it?

Mica couldn't fault her for wanting to reclaim the scraps of her old life. That's one thing they had in common—there wasn't anything they wouldn't do for the people they loved. Huffing an irritated sigh, she shifted her gaze away, only to find Harvester staring at her from behind a neighboring fire. The sight of that creepy woman with her tattooed face and evil black eyes caused her to shiver. Then a phantom breeze grazed the flames, sending the shadows around them dancing, and Harvester was looking elsewhere. Had Mica imagined that look? Was she becoming paranoid?

She didn't care what Animkii said. She didn't trust that witch. Telling Animkii that lie about being able to cure her...

Mica toyed with the hilt of Soulcleaver. She'd wrapped the blade in a bit of hide and tucked it down the side of one of her borrowed too-big boots. Her mouth twisted. She looked like one of them now, dressed in animal skins, and she'd grown accustomed to the smell of cooking fires and wet fur, though not so much the lingering decay that seemed to cling to everything in this place.

She'd heard enough by now to know that, if nothing else, Harvester was a fanatic. Her lofty promises were right in line with the crap spewed by the After Cult, that same 'new world rising from the ashes of the old' spiel, only mixed up with local superstition. Mica didn't look forward to tearing up Animkii's beliefs, but she couldn't let her friend keep thinking this 'Creator' was some kind of benevolent overseer.

She had to make Animkii understand before that woman got too far into her head.

Part of Mica hoped her suspicions were wrong, that they were nothing but the imaginings of her own broken mind. After everything she'd been through, this world, Animkii's memories, and that dark other place had begun to blur together. And she was just so tired all the time, so weak. That last excursion into Animkii's mind had sapped what little strength she'd regained.

Maybe she was wrong about these outlanders. Maybe they were as ignorant of their god's true nature as Animkii. Maybe she was looking for problems where there weren't any.

Still, the sooner they got out of this place, the better. Despite her brave facade and assurances of a swift recovery to Animkii, every movement sent tremors of weakness through her body. And it was always cold, even by the fire. Her nights were sleepless. Every time she closed her eyes, the After Lord's presence loomed like a relentless predator closing in on its prey, but she was too tired to stay awake...

"Your friend will make a fine, strong slave."

She woke up with a start at the sound of his voice. She'd dozed off again.

"What am I going to do? How are we going to get out of here?" she muttered, shivering uncontrollably. Maybe she should try transporting them out of here right now. Just one more time wouldn't kill her, would it?

But she wasn't so sure about that. She'd already tried reaching into the minds of the people here, to graze the thoughts of these empty-eyed sheep, and the pain had been so bad it'd nearly sent her back into unconsciousness. What little she'd managed to glean was useless. Animkii's return had both terrified and excited them, yet their zeal for the Creator overflowed their thoughts, consuming every moment, making it difficult to pick out anything else. Harvester had gutted their minds and turned them into fanatics.

Mica had no choice now. Once Animkii was back from talking to Ziiba, she'd have to tell her the truth, listening ears be damned. But when she looked around the see where her friend had gone, the mod was out of sight.

Bad timing for a romantic stroll. She blew at the air in exasperation and kicked at a piece of wood that had rolled off the fire. Unfortunately, her movement caught Harvester's attention. Those crow eyes fixed on her, and the holy woman grinned with a mouthful of sharp yellow teeth.

"If you're looking for Animkii, she's gone off with Ziiba," Mica said in a rough voice as the elder drifted over to her fire. "Not sure when she'll be back."

"It is not Animkii's time. It is *yours*." Those words! Harvester was speaking in the southern tongue, as fluent as Mica herself. Behind her, the shadows of other outlanders shifted in response to their leader's tone, closing in.

How could she speak a language from a land she'd never visited?

Harvester smiled, but her answer wasn't spoken aloud—it was inside Mica's head. *"I can walk dreams, just like you, Mica Stone. Well, not exactly like you. You're special, aren't you?"*

Startled by the sudden invasive presence in her mind, Mica stiffened, but fast recovered her senses to bark back a laugh. "You think so?" She felt the holy woman probing at the edges of her mind, but the invader's power was too feeble to penetrate, pitiful compared to what she'd already endured from the After Lord. It was as easy as flicking a finger at a gnat for her to block the witch's mind out of her own.

Harvester gasped as Mica expelled her psyche. "Such power!"

But it was nothing but a distraction.

Cursing her own overconfidence, she shrank back against the cold steel bench, eyeing two men approaching her from either side. A half-circle of outlanders formed behind them, zombie-eyed sentries that stood guard while Harvester watched, grinning as if she'd just won a magnificent prize. Around her neck dangled a silver charm fashioned into the shape of a serpent strangling an orb.

Biosteel?

Where the gore did she get *that* from? Was it possible someone else had bypassed the treacherous divide between the two halves of the world, a feat even the Technocrats with all their knowledge had failed? Father Dark's words came back to her from her captivity in Under-Zeta:

"Our efforts in the north are reaching fruition thanks to our new alliance…"

"Ah, dammit!" Mica reached down to pull Soulcleaver from her boot, but her movements were too sluggish, and one man grabbed her by the hand, disarming her with a twist of movement. The blade, still wrapped in its sheath of hide, spun out of reach. With no chance of defending herself against so many, she kicked the weapon away and saw it slide beneath Animkii's sleeping furs.

"Animkii!" she cried out.

Someone grabbed her by the hair and another man pried open her jaw, pouring a bitter liquid into it. All strength left her. What they'd given her wasn't angel breath, but its numbing effect soothed her fear just the same. The old craving for escape stirred, and she found herself yearning for more, longing to drown in its substance. Shame overwhelmed her. She'd come so far and fought so hard only to fall into this trap?

She crumpled to her knees, her vision blurring as her brain filled with the Other World.

***

Animkii studied Ziiba's back as they walked along the flat bank of the underground river, only a few minutes away from the encampment, bows and snowshoes slung over their shoulders. While stationed at the southern outposts, they'd often hunted together, looking for any excuse to catch what little alone time they could. But there was none of that companionable conversation now. No witticisms bantered back and forth.

Only silence.

"What is it like on the surface?" she asked. "Are the Dreamers—"

"The Dreamers do not bother us anymore. And we are not going on a hunt."

"Oh."

"I wanted to speak to you." Ziiba turned to face her, her expression so carefully controlled it looked carved from wood, yet weariness had etched every line on her face. "Harvester says you will join us at the ceremony tomorrow. That you will make the sacrifice."

"I told Harvester I would think about it."

Contempt flashed across her old lover's face. "Harvester has shown you the correct path to save our people *and* yourself."

Animkii wanted to scream, *"She hasn't shown me anything!"* But age and experience had tempered her passion. "She believes the Creator can make me fully human again. Is what she says true?"

She saw the wistfulness in her old lover's eyes, but she resisted reacting, unable to bear the inevitable rejection.

"The things I've seen Harvester do..." Ziiba's voice trailed off and she shook her head, as if arguing with herself. "When she says something will happen, it will. She is a *true* Speaker, Animkii. Not like the others. The Great Spirit has granted her miraculous power to do His will."

Animkii listened in surprise. She'd never heard Ziiba question the power of a Speaker before, not even when Animkii used to vent her frustrations about their own holy man's impotence against the threat of Dreamers. Ziiba had always rationalized his failures as a sign of their god's displeasure with the entire village, rather than blaming just one man. Even when Animkii broke the god's laws and brought back Soulcleaver, Ziiba had unwaveringly sided with their Speaker.

But Animkii found herself unable to resent Ziiba's betrayal. She remained cautious with her words, terrified of speaking the questions in her heart, not wanting to put any conflict between them, not now. "You were right about me," she said, her voice soft with remorse. "About never listening. I am sorry for everything."

Ziiba struggled with the apology. "Harvester says it was the Creator's will that you entered the dead city, and I mustn't question it. That I should forgive you," she said, her voice thick with emotion. "I am trying. But I can't be with you, Ani, not when you're like this. I can't even look at you." Her gaze faltered for a moment, and she took a deep breath. "Listen to me: This time, do what's right for your clan and our people instead of yourself."

Animkii felt the flicker of hope die within her. Ziiba wasn't speaking from her heart; she was reciting from a script.

"There are so few of us left," her former lover said. "It's the same everywhere, even in far-off lands we've never even seen. The Creator gathers the surviving faithful from east to west, in far greater numbers than we have here."

"And what of my kin?" she asked, her heart aching. "Raak mentioned a new village called Onehome."

Ziiba's expression turned vague. "Yes, Onehome... That's where they've all gone: Niigaanii, Debwe, and the others who made it out of Firehome. So many others didn't. Niigaanii was heartbroken. His favorite mother, Anang, perished when the village fell."

Anang. The name brought to her memory a sweet-faced youth who'd finished her motherhood trials just before Niigaanii's birth. A bit overeager. Talked too much. Emotion choked Animkii's words. "Was she—?"

"She was a good mother. Kind and patient. She would let me take Niigaanii on walks and teach him a few fighting moves." For a moment, the darkness in Ziiba's eyes cleared, and there was a tranquility there. Her beaded black hair fell across her sorrow-worn face and there was the suggestion of a smile on her lips. "He liked to think he was all grown-up. He'd get into anything and everything. Debwe said you were the same way, never accepting 'no' for an answer."

Animkii's heart broke. It was like she could hear Niigaanii's last cries again and her heart sobbed. "I wish I could have been there."

Ziiba leaned forward, her dark eyes burning with intensity. "Outlanders live by different rules than the Four Peoples," she said. "If you stay, you could be both warrior *and* mother to Niigaanii. Harvester has freed us from those restrictions, both the chains of the false covenant and the Peoples' laws. You and I and Niigaanii... We could have a family of our own."

The words hung in the air. Animkii couldn't move for a moment, paralyzed by overwhelming emotion. The idea of a family with Ziiba and Niigaanii awakened a terrible longing within her. Finally, she choked out her response. "I will do it. This sacrifice. If you say I can trust Harvester, then I will do what she says."

It was the oddest expression on Ziiba's face, more relief than joy, and Animkii didn't know how to read it, but then the woman embraced her, her body tiny against her towering steel form, and she no longer cared. It was an awkward embrace, and she mourned it was the machine sensors that picked up the warmth of flesh pressed against her. But that wasn't all she mourned.

Ziiba was lying to her with her body.

Animkii felt the sensation too late. A cool liquid entering her stim repository. How did she even know—?

The other woman smiled as she stepped out of her former lover's embrace, an expression reminiscent of carefree days.

"What did you do to me?"

"Harvester doesn't want to take any chances."

A heavy lethargy sank into Animkii's bones. No matter that her body was mostly tech, it hit her the same as if she were fully flesh, overwhelming organic and inorganic systems alike. Her biosteel limbs, once as light as paper, felt as though someone had just poured lead through them. Sleep hadn't been necessary since her modification and though she entered hibernation for periods to conserve her stims, now it seemed as if closing her eyes and drifting away was her only concern.

"You're exhausted," Ziiba said, guiding her back toward the encampment. "Let's return to the camp. We'll talk tomorrow, after the ceremony is complete."

It seemed a perfectly reasonable suggestion. *Thought-responsive drugs*, piped up a voice of alarm in her head. How was that possible? Where could Ziiba have gotten them from?

But she found her will restrained and her questions silenced. She could only obey this woman she'd once loved, who now betrayed her. In stupefied silence, she followed Ziiba's lead back to the fire she'd shared with Mica. Only Mica was gone now. A patch of haggard furs and shabby hides covered the dirt floor where she'd lain.

"Sleep now," Ziiba ordered, her voice softening with a sick sort of longing. "After tomorrow, you can reunite with your family, with Niigaanii. After tomorrow, all of our suffering will end."

Knees buckling, Animkii face hit the soft furs, and she sank into oblivion.

Chapter Twelve

M ica drifted between worlds, the intoxicant firing her neural pathways into a frenzy, and she was falling, falling forever through a dazzling starry night. There was no segue into the Other World this time, no stepping on pieces of her old, tortured memories to get there, no games, no doorways, no temptations. Even the gateway with its burning city and winged serpents made no appearance, and she wasn't exactly sure why. Could she now pass between worlds so easily that the gate was no longer necessary?

She blinked and found herself standing on the stone balcony of an enormous floating fortress, miles above the ground, shivering in a white dress made of delicate lace-like fabric. Far below was a city so vast it made Alpha look like a simple village, and yet the buildings were archaic in design, as if pulled out of one of Samiel's fantastical historical documents, from an age where the idea of machines hadn't yet touched on human thought.

It had never occurred to her that real people might live in the Other World under the rule of this sleeping god. Were the citizens as monstrous as their ruler?

She found her answer when she looked up. Above her, the minarets of the floating black citadel jutted into a blood-red sky, a vast crimson field swarming with winged guardians, terrifying creatures that looked as if someone had taken the human shape and distorted it. Some had enormous arms that bristled with spikes, some had extra eyes or limbs, others had appendages that resembled those of beasts.

Without having ever seen the outside before, she still knew it. This profane place she was standing in was the After Lord's palace, his house of worship, and at the center of it she'd find its master waiting.

And yet she was not afraid. She felt as if the Other World were welcoming her as a guest instead of an enemy, the same way she'd felt beneath the golden branches of the Elder Tree. Like she belonged.

As she stood there marveling, scenes from the real world bled through again and she had flashes of the outlanders dragging her half-conscious form back up to the surface world, out of the shadows of the undercity and into the face of a setting sun. Someone lifted her onto an altar made of sticks and bones bound with sinew and stinking of old blood, and she could feel the knobby ends of bone sockets poking into her back. There was no running away—the drug coursing through her had turned her limbs to liquid.

Just like in Zeta. She recalled her terrifying captivity in the Sixth City and shuddered. Different setting; same end.

In and out, back and forth, hours passed and night descended as she flickered between the Other World and the real world, stubbornly trying to hold onto the latter. *"Animkii!"* She reached out with her psychic fingers, only to find the warrior lost in her own stupor. They'd drugged her too.

Back on the earthly plane, a large river churned in the near-distance, throwing up chunks of melting ice, chafing at the rocky shore like an angry god against the backdrop of a black and dying forest. The altar was the gruesome head of a circle of ritual fires, the greedy flames surrounding it, sweet with the smell of human sacrifice. A child's leg bone poked out from a firepit and her stomach roiled at the sight, her belly too empty to vomit, her tears and screams used up hours ago when the children's agonized cries first chased her into the swallowing darkness of the Other World.

All night, the outlanders danced and sang within the ring of fire and blood, howling costumed warriors reenacting the Sundering with their strange contortions, their dead eyes turning manic in the throes of celebration. Self-inflicted wounds covered their bodies—personal blood sacrifices torn from their flesh with bone hooks and blades. The blood that covered the participants was their own.

Did they know that the new world they were trying to call forth would only consume and spit out the bones of the old?

Standing amid all the drumming and chanting and self-mutilation was Harvester, rocking back and forth, hooded with the head of a deer, her upper face obscured by a row of bone ornaments that dangled from the mouth of the dead beast. The rack of antlers gave her a height that made her stand out among the dancing outlanders. For hours, her lips moved in adulation to her god, the celebrations growing more and more frenzied as the participants blew their own minds out with ritual drugs, hacking off more of their own flesh, the blood flying. It all culminated with one mother throwing herself into a firepit to join the children she'd sacrificed earlier.

Finally, just as the morning sun peeked over the horizon, Harvester halted the celebrations and raised her hands.

"The Creator has spoken! Prepare the way! His Emissary approaches!"

The ground trembled at her words—barely noticeable at first, like a shiver across the skin—but the rumbles soon deepened and the quakes grew so violent that one outlander had to hold Mica's body onto the altar to keep it from spilling over. Even as he staggered and rocked back on unsteady feet, she saw his face was full of rapture.

Inside the ring of fires, the dancers stumbled and fell and leaped back up again, their song wavering at times and then growing stronger.

Panicked, Mica turned her head away from their mad movements and cast her gaze toward the distant river behind the altar, watching the waters lurch and swallow whole chunks of shore. Massive sections of land split apart. Pieces broke off to disappear into the gaps created. Her scream stuck in her throat, her lips unable to move, her legs unable to run, and she was helpless to do anything but watch in horror as the landscape shifted and tore apart before her eyes, a great rift forming and expanding as she watched it swallow the river and the forest beyond it in one massive gulp.

This couldn't be real. Maybe it was the drug they'd given her. It was strong, the chains on her mind too tight to throw off. Was this the wraith root that dreamwalkers used to walk with the spirits of their dead ancestors? Or something else?

Worse was to come. The wounded earth opened up and released the deathly chill of an oncoming hollow storm, which swept out of the abyss and covered all who had gathered, leaving traces of frost on everything it touched—except Mica. Ice blossoms froze on Harvester's tattooed cheeks and the warmth of her skin did not melt them, but the Speaker acted oblivious to the unnatural chill. Then Mica looked past the fanatic's frozen, manic expression and into the sky beyond, and despaired.

Riding the tail of the storm was a multitude of Dreamers, expelled from the rift in numbers too vast to count, faceless shadows that blackened the sky overhead. Anything living that had survived the overturning of the earth now began to wither and die. The needles on a nearby pine tree turned brown, then rained down as the trunk itself grew bent and brittle. A flight of birds winging overhead dropped dead midflight, their little bodies smacking hard against the stone ground. Even her captors seemed to diminish, their skin turning gray, their cheeks sinking against bone, their eyes growing hollow.

"Stop this!" she cried, breaking the drug's hold at last. *"Animkii! Wake up!"* Her cry carried across her psychic mindscape.

The outlander holding her down turned his head and shouted a warning to Harvester. "She's conscious!"

How the witch heard her subordinate's warning over the shrilling of the Dreamers and the rending of the earth, Mica couldn't guess, but the unholy woman hastened over to the altar, her face and deer-hide coat smeared with gore, her mouth pulling down with displeasure as she examined the prisoner.

"She's still fighting it. We'll have to give her another dose," she said, pulling a glass vial out of her hide pouch, the sight of the foreign object in this primitive place startling to Mica. "She must be ready for the Emissary."

Mica tried kicking out, but her leg wouldn't obey. Fighting? She couldn't even move.

A thick, dirty finger inserted itself into her mouth to pop it open, but this time she bit down hard.

"Animkii! Help me!" her mind cried out.

***

Another scream knifed into Animkii's skull, shaking her from the warm, heavy sleep of doped-up oblivion. But the darkness didn't want to let go, and it wrapped its arms around her, pulling her even deeper into its soothing depths, carrying her far away from all her troubles. *There's nothing I can do*, she told herself as the long sobbing wail again rose inside her head. Better to go back to sleep.

Her machine-senses were less sympathetic. They demanded immediate analysis of this new data. Her eyelids slid open and her gaze captured the glowing embers of abandoned fires. A sudden tremor shook the area. The surrounding buildings creaked and moaned, clay pots rattling together, and the fire beside her collapsing into itself, sending up sparks. When it was done, the silence that sat in the place of bodies was ominous.

Where had everyone gone?

The banshee cry rose again inside her mind and a chill shivered through her as she recognized the source.

Mica!

In an instant, her mind was fully awake, but she found the bulk of her body immobilized. With full consciousness came a terrible ringing sound in her ears, malfunction warnings issued by her besieged core pounding into her brain. Whatever Ziiba had contaminated her system with was potent enough to have knocked out her core system. How could she have known about Animkii's stim repository, let alone how to deliver an injection?

Being trapped inside her own body was like a slow descent to the bottom of an ocean, with the light of the surface always just out of reach. No matter how she tried, no matter how her mind clawed its way forward, she couldn't get closer to that distant crest. A feeling of claustrophobia closed in as frustration turned to fear, and fear turned to panic.

Stop. The still-rational part of her human brain barged in, shouldered aside the growing terror. Mica was depending on her. She mimicked taking a deep breath, and though it had no effect on her machine physiology, that simple human habit was enough to calm her racing mind.

She could purify her supply lines. To calculate the cost, she tapped into her neglected core. As suspected, doing so would use most of her remaining stims. But how much time left did she really have anyway, with how fast her modification was progressing? She marveled at how quickly the fear drained away, replaced by detached acceptance of her fate. There was no question of her own survival anymore.

<< REACTIVATE PERIPHERAL SYSTEM >>

> PHYSIO-OPTIMIZATION SUBSYSTEM ACTIVATED

> OFFENSIVE SUBSYSTEM ACTIVATED

> DEFENSIVE SUBSYSTEM ACTIVATED

> REGENERATION SUBSYSTEM ACTIVATED

> PERIPHERAL SYSTEM ONLINE

It was like releasing a pressure valve. The full power of a mod surged back through her body with an intensity that shocked her, igniting her network of artificial nerves, waking up her sleeping subsystems, and discharging her final reserve of stims to wash the contamination from her stim lines. The incredible high left her disoriented and, dismissing the incessant warnings about her low stim count, she lurched out of her bed of furs with the stagger of a drunk.

The outlanders' undercity encampment appeared deserted, not a soul in sight. Even the sentries guarding the wall had abandoned their posts.

Mica screamed again, a psychic cry that pierced through her skull, and Animkii instinctively moved to block ears she didn't have.

Animkii had spent four terrible years locked inside the Alphaknot's psy network. Did Mica's mind powers work the same way? Could she answer back, or would her words disappear into the void? She formed a tentative query inside her own head, *"Mica?"*

There was a bleak too-long silence and Animkii cursed herself as a fool for talking to herself until she heard a tremulous voice answer back, *"You can actually hear me?!"*

"Yes. Ziiba drugged me, but I'm awake now." The memory of that betrayal still stung. *"Where are you?"*

Mica gave a relieved sob. *"They took me outside the city. Just follow the river to the entrance but watch out—there are Dreamers everywhere. Harvester's planning on sacrificing me."*

Animkii felt sick. Was this the 'sacrifice' Harvester had spoken of? Was this what the outlanders believed they needed to do to appease the Great Spirit? *"The Creator would never condone harming an innocent!"*

Mica's pained voice resurfaced. *"Your Creator is an imposter,"* she said. *"He and the After Lord are one and the same. That's who Harvester serves. The monster you slew was his brother, Revan. He tried to stop the After Lord from destroying our world. And now the After Lord wants to come back to finish the job."*

Staggered by the revelation, Animkii stood there, paralyzed by the enormity of Mica's words. Had Harvester lied to her? Could the Creator she'd spent her life believing in, fighting for, and nearly dying for, be a fraud? Or was this a deception planted by the Great Lynx?

"It can't be true. That beast I slew was Mishibijiw!"

She felt Mica's desperation seething through their connection. *"If you don't believe me, then ask yourself: Which one of them is asking for blood sacrifices?"*

Her remaining faith crumbled. She felt it dying inside her heart, like the last mournful call of a loon before nightfall. All those years she'd struggled with it, questioning why the Great Spirit would allow her people to suffer, then loathing herself for betraying His covenant, blaming herself for the fate of her people. All along the After Lord had deceived them. Where then was the true Creator? Or had Mica been right all along, that there were no gods in this world except what humans invented?

"I'm sorry," Mica whispered into her mind, her words sodden with regret.

It wasn't just the death of her ideals, but the realization that she'd have to fight her own people to save Mica that came down hard on her. Even the strongest warriors had no chance against her armored skin and her advanced weaponry. It would be a slaughter.

But then there were the Dreamers. Another fight like the one coming into the city and there'd be nothing left of her. This would be a suicide mission, and she knew it.

"Use Soulcleaver."

Mica's words froze her heart. Was the other woman delirious? "You're not making sense."

"I tried to tell you earlier. I took it... from your memories."

"What do you mean?"

"Check by your bed."

Animkii's eyes flickered back to the stack of furs she'd passed out on earlier, scanning every inch of the floor with machine precision. Someone's discarded bowl. A pair of boots. A quiver of arrows toppled by the fire. A pile of clothing that matched the clothes Mica had worn in Alpha. Still reeling from all she'd learned, she walked over to retrieve the dirty garments, but as she bent over, a wave of heat rushed out at her from her right side. She crouched down and lifted back the pile of furs. An obsidian raven stared back.

It couldn't be!

The last time she'd seen it was at the Burning Wall, after the Technocrat's sentries had pulled her out of the End. Not quite willing to believe, she reached out with a tentative hand, her remaining flesh-fingers quivering in fear and apprehension. Animkii was no coward, but she despised this blade, this symbol of all she'd lost. As her fingers closed around its hilt and pulled it from its flimsy hide wrap, that immense, familiar heat crept up her tech-arm, causing her to almost drop it in surprise. There was no doubt now.

"How is this even possible?"

"Revan did it. Back when you took Soulcleaver, he put a copy in your memories."

She'd seen enough of the incomprehensible by now to accept it as fact. No matter how she resented the pain that Soulcleaver had brought into her life, she also knew that its power was real, that it could fend off those Dreamers outside like the ones she'd faced inside the End of the World. She didn't need to understand how; she just needed it to work.

"Hurry! Harvester said something about an 'emissary' arriving soon. I don't know what that means, but it can't be good. "

"Emissary?" she sent back the question, but there was no answer this time, just a wisp of a presence, a sigh that didn't have the strength to speak.

With no time to waste, her spear in one hand and Soulcleaver in the other, Animkii evoked her camouflage procedure, stripping the clothes from her back before racing toward the end of the village, to the rocky river edge with its churning black waters. Her naked biosteel skin took on the exact appearance of her surroundings and would shift according to the angle her enemies viewed her from. Mica's attackers wouldn't see her coming.

The path upward along the riverbank was a steep, two-hour hike. With a boost from her stims, she could easily cut the time in half, but would she make it before it was too late?

***

Mica was fighting a losing battle. Her arms ached with fatigue as she tried prying herself free from her guard's iron grip, the sweat and stink of him pressing against her as she squirmed and kicked and bit whatever she could reach. A great big hand clamped itself down on her nose, forcing her to breathe through her mouth, and that's when he jammed the vial past her lips and its foul contents slid down her throat.

The connection between worlds anchored and she felt herself slide back into the Other World. Once more, she saw the floating fortress standing black against the crimson sky.

Her body in the real world went limp and the man who'd drugged her hauled her up by one arm, rolling her back atop the altar, leaving her to stare up at the Dreamer-blackened sky, which flickered between bloody crimson and morning-pink as her mind switched between worlds. The foul-tasting drug stung her throat and worked its way through her body, enhancing what was already there, taking her beyond mere intoxication to a state of enlightenment.

Above her, she now saw the reality her human eyes had hidden from her. Silvery threads saturated the air, spinning a web that covered all she saw. In her own mundane world, the silver threads were sparse, dull, difficult to perceive even with this new sight, but in the Other World, they infused and entwined every inch of space, except for rare patches of blackness, spots of damage. Had this always been there?

"Nether," explained the After Lord's nefarious presence as it nestled back inside her mind, a serpent coiled to strike. Nether was the energy that the Technocrats used to power their tech.

"The Technocrats know about this?"

"They harvest it from hollow storms without seeing it or knowing its true nature."

She turned her head to stare at the young outlander guarding her, her mouth gaping loose as her physical body slowly lost muscle control to the drug. Floating in the place where the man's heart sat was a fist-sized golden ball of light, but she could see threads of silver wrapping around it, strangling it. Feeding off it.

"That's his soul, isn't it? The nether is feeding on it?"

"Transforming it," the dark god corrected her. *"Making it greater than it is."*

"You're killing them."

"Only their bodies."

Her gaze darted about the battlefield, confirming what she already knew. Nether was inside all of them.

And then she looked down at her own chest in alarm. If she had a soul left, it was impossible to distinguish it from the sea of silver that had replaced it. Strands of nether wound out from her body, as if she were some kind of alien creature, silvery veins of power throttling the world around her and stealing its life. She was a battery constantly recharging from that source. Instead of feasting on her, the nether was empowering her. She *was* the nether!

"You see it now. Nether is the true source of your power, as it is of mine. Your body and soul are infused with it."

"What have you done to me?!"

"I've told you before. You're being reborn. And when it's done, you'll understand that these mortals you feel such sympathy for are nothing but fodder. Can't you taste it in the air, the sweetness of his soul?"

"No!"

"Let me help you, then."

A disturbing new hunger awakened inside her as she watched the young outlander's soul writhe against the nether coiling around it. Her arm shot upward of its own accord, and without her ever touching him, he froze in place. His eyes bulged in pain as invisible strands of nether unwound from her own body to join what already entangled him, the tiny tendrils piercing his skin and digging down to feast on that golden core.

"Stop!" She tried to wrestle control back, but it was too late. The surge of power coursed into her failing body, filling her with a pleasure approaching orgasm. A ream of frost formed on the youth's skin as her parasitical touch sucked the life out of him, his own body withering, his sockets swallowing his eyes, his lips cracking with ice as his mouth opened for a last scream.

The After Lord's laughter rang in her head, fading as her horror only grew.

***

No sooner did Animkii emerge onto the surface, leaving the shelter of the broken city, than the frigid tempest of a hollow storm lashed out at her body, its deadly frost creeping over her artificial limbs. But even without Mica's presence to guide her through it, her machine-body moved unimpeded across the snow-covered grounds, the warmth of Soulcleaver in her hand warding off the worst of the cold.

So far, the only casualties were her remaining flesh-digits, which turned white, then black, in the space of a few minutes. Her core immediately sensed the damage and sped up regrowth, not repairing the injury with flesh but with biosteel. A brief sadness overcame her as the last outward sign of her humanity disappeared.

It was an emotion she had no time for. She heightened her senses to superhuman levels and immediately heard the distant pounding of feet and voices rising in a song that carried her on a wave of nostalgia. At first. But this was no Fire Bones celebration; this was something far more sinister.

When the next quake rocked the earth, she felt it seconds before it hit and leaped to one side just before the ground opened up beneath her feet. She raced ahead of the ruination, flattening herself against boulders and uprooted trees, until she could see the gathering.

What she saw left her shaken.

A massive rift stretched alongside the ceremonial grounds, creating a peninsula bordered by a bottomless trench that endlessly belched black mist and Dreamers. *Like the End*, she thought, terrified to see the rift widen as she watched, growing larger by the minute, swallowing everything it touched into its gorge. There was no river left, no shore, no forest beyond... only a shrinking piece of land that had once bordered the river, where now a blasphemy against everything the Four Peoples had believed in was taking place.

Harvester stood at the forefront of the twisted revelry, her back turned to a crude bone altar. Her hands lifted into the air and her antlered head tilted to the sky as she and the outlanders sang an eerie, wailing song to the Creator, asking for His deliverance. The land responded to their dark anthem, shuddering at the Speaker's feet while the Dreamers swirling overhead added their own unearthly voices to the call.

Laid out motionless on the bone altar was Mica. Animkii's artificial heart lurched in desperate terror at the sight. She had to get her friend away from this place, but how? A terrible groan issued from the land behind her, and she turned in time to see a portion of the ruined city sinking deeper into the ground behind her. Time was running short.

Her tech-enhanced eyes swept across the assembly of outlanders, calculating their threat. In doing so, her gaze zeroed in on the half-burned corpse of a woman hanging out of one fire, slumped over a neat pile of smaller bones. She strangled an outraged cry, tempering her rising emotions lest she give away her position. It wasn't just Mica they meant to kill. How many of their own kind had they murdered? And children among them! What sickness had so consumed her people that they'd sunk to committing such atrocities? A terrible thought struck her.

Ziiba... Was she part of this too?

She couldn't bear to think about it. Not now. It took all her self-control to keep from breaking stealth mode and rushing in to unleash her fury. There was nothing she could do to save the dead, but Mica was still alive. Watching from a distance, she saw her friend move, her head lolling, and heard a breathy scream that died in the wind.

A cold rage built within her. Harvester was the source of this destruction. If Animkii could stop her, then maybe the others would come to their senses.

Soulcleaver kept its light hidden as she crept forward, possessing intelligence that understood her need for discretion. The Dreamers hadn't yet sensed her but hung in the sky like a torn black shroud, their malice tangible even from where she crouched behind a withered stand of pine trees. The hollow storm pummeled her body as she fixed her tech-eyes on the corrupt Speaker. There was no time for mercy. She raised her left arm, reconfiguring the launcher for long-range assault. A small muzzle emerged, and she took aim, firing a single lethal shot at Harvester's head.

Her shot was perfect. It should've hit its target precisely, and yet Harvester somehow sensed the kill, and with a jerk of her hand, a younger woman stepped in front of her and took the shot instead.

The puppet's head exploded, spraying fragments of skull and gore everywhere.

Harvester had controlled that woman. Her jaw tightened. She was sure of it.

"It's time to make your choice, Animkii!" Harvester said without turning, her eerily girlish voice carrying over the revelry. "You stand on the edge of a new Creation. Will you join your brethren in renewal, or will you sink into decay with the rest of this world?"

The outlanders all stopped at once, their songs rattling off into silence as they scanned the grounds for the intruder.

There were few places to hide, and when she saw their attention shifting toward the concealing cluster of trees, Animkii slipped out of the shadows, her body's coloring switching from the shade of bark and shadows to mud-mottled snow. Outrage colored her cry, "Is this the sacrifice you were talking about?!" She jerked her spear toward the woman's smoldering corpse and its tragic company. "Are we to sacrifice our own people?"

Harvester turned then, her eyes obscured beneath the antlered hood, but her lips forming a blissful smile. There was a disturbing warmth and affection in her childish voice. "They sleep in the After Lord's endless dream and never again will they suffer in this world."

"If sacrificing my friends and family is what it takes to get back my humanity, then you can keep it!" Animkii plunged forward onto the field, kicking up chunks of snow and muck in her passage. Responding to her will, Soulcleaver exploded with light and the shifting dark things in the skies above shrieked and drew back, the solid black of their mass breaking up and revealing pieces of the morning sky.

At the sight of Revan's blade, Harvester's placid mask cracked and her voice shrilled with alarm. "Kill her!"

Chapter Thirteen

M ica was hyperventilating.

She could *feel* the man's stolen soul burning inside her as she lay there on the altar. As his corpse crumpled to the ground, a tidal wave of stolen energy surged through her, overwhelming the weak flesh that tried to contain it. A guttural moan escaped her lips as she instinctively curled her arms around her knees, seeking some semblance of control. Her skin turned translucent as the color drained away, revealing a network of thin black veins beneath its surface. Her heart hammered against her ribcage, protesting the strain on her mortal body as her skin cracked apart, the wounds filling with blood that froze as quickly as it ran.

Was she dying? Or was this something worse? As she struggled to comprehend this new horror, she heard Animkii's voice ring out, followed by Harvester's order to kill her. The threat awakened new terror—the thought that she'd be left alone with these deluded zealots. A group of outlanders closed in to restrain her and her fracturing body crackled with a terrible, white energy.

This feeling inside, this power... She'd first tasted it in Under-Zeta when she'd slain those cultists and again when she'd tried to kill Father Dark in Under-Alpha. She knew how to wield it. All she had to do was focus her feelings of rage, and pain, and helplessness onto these mad wretches. She licked away the blood trickling from her nose to her lips, and her guilt over the soul's theft vanished.

She had the power to end this.

With tremendous effort, she rose up from altar, her body weak but the power inside her only growing. "You're going to let me go *right now!*" she cried out, her voice shaking with a mixture of fury and newfound confidence.

Her fists clenched as she delivered an enormous psychic blow to the cluster of outlanders. Unlike in Zeta, this time she was in complete control. The ground exploded beneath their feet, hurtling them backward with such violence that two of them never got back up. The third fell too close to the rift and a ghostly black hand pulled him into the abyss. As she lay there panting with exertion, the horror of what she'd done warred with exultation.

Harvester alone stood against her attack, but even she dropped to her knees in the filthy snow, her clawed hands gripping her antlered head between them as black liquid poured from her mouth. Even while coughing up blood, the Speaker grinned with black-stained teeth, her small eyes gleaming with triumph from behind the row of dangling bird bones.

"It's all happening as He foretold," the unholy Speaker said, rising on shaky legs, taking a tremulous step forward, her hand outstretched and beckoning. There was no fear of death in her face, only a welcoming. "Come."

Mica's patience snapped. "I'm done with this! You want to make me into a monster? Then I'll show you what that means!" The threat caught in her throat as she shivered from fear and cold, her clothing soaked with blood and thawed snow, every inch of skin vibrating with the power that was killing it.

But she didn't want to be a monster.

"Finish it, then! Show me His power!"

Her taunt ignited a psychic bomb inside Mica. That man's soul... She could still feel him inside her. Flashes of his humble life passed before her eyes, and she saw a young widower who'd once defied his own clan to retire to motherhood after his lover's death. When the Dreamers came months ago and took his two daughters' lives, it had destroyed him, and he'd fled his village. Harvester had been the one to piece him back together, to fill that void with talk of a paradise where the dead walked again.

Her chest heaved with a heart that was desperate to break, and each breath was a knife in her lungs. Would she have done the same if she'd thought she could see her family again? She knew the answer, and the guilt was unbearable. Black spots danced in her vision as the agony she'd inflicted on her enemies returned tenfold onto herself, and she screamed herself hoarse. Her mind echoed her cries.

"Animkii! Where are you?!"

***

Answering Mica's call, Animkii sped toward the altar, skirting the ring of fire as the air filled with battle cries, dozens of outlanders abandoning their celebrations and coming at her from the left. Above them, the Dreamers churned like a storm, a few dark shapes separating from the rest and rushing at her only to be repelled by Soulcleaver's searing light. As one, the Dreamers let loose a vengeful howl.

Soulcleaver was keeping them away. For now.

Her feet pounded the slushy, slippery field. If she could reach Harvester first, if she could put down their leader, the other outlanders might stand down and this madness could end.

Her brainwashed brethren couldn't compete with her speed, but they were numerous enough to route her closer and closer to the rift's edge, until she could see the stretch of living blackness that was its bottom.

The soil beneath her feet loosened, and quick reflexes saved her from a deadly fall as she leaped to stable ground. With no other option for escape, she reversed her direction and charged straight through the oncoming wall of bodies, plowing through them. The stench of human neglect washed over her, putrid to her heightened sense of smell. Her camouflage was confusing to them. Each warrior saw a reflection of their own comrades when they looked at her, and their disorientation caused blows meant for Animkii to land often on their own allies.

She didn't want to kill them. Driven by mercy, she swung her crude spear in a sweeping motion, incapacitating her foes and clearing her path until her weapon's shaft splintered from the repeated blows. She discarded the broken pieces and jumped over the fallen warriors as others closed in to fill the gap. Their crude stone-and-wood weapons cracked and broke across her biosteel skin, not even scratching the impenetrable surface. Determined to free herself from the fray, Animkii rammed her steel shoulder into their midst and the force of her body was enough to break their line.

Harvester was only yards away now. So close!

Reaching the end of the crowd, she launched herself forward with a last burst of strength, only to find her path blocked.

Ziiba.

The sight of her former friend and lover stopped her charge dead. Ziiba's eyes were a stranger's, empty even of malice. At her side stood the old war chief, Raak, his lips rolled back in a snarl as he threw himself forward with a mindless animal savagery that erased all memory of the cold, calculating tactician who'd mentored her. She remembered the charred bones of children, and righteous rage poured over her. Her arm swung out with force. Bone crunched as her fist met his skull, but she kept her eyes on Ziiba. When the other two Fire Bones moved to flank her, she tossed them aside like they were nothing, stepping up to face Ziiba.

"Are you part of this too?" she demanded.

There was no reaction. Ziiba didn't even blink. "Harvester says the Creator chose you," she said in a dull voice. "And now, you must choose the Creator. All our lives, we've fought to survive, and now we can end it."

The pain in the heart she no longer had was tearing her apart. She wanted to weep and rage, and all those things human beings did when confronted with loss, but she felt only a terrible gnawing dread. All the time she was conscious of Harvester watching them from a distance, weighing the battle with her sinister eyes.

A final fleeting image of a younger Ziiba laughing flickered across her memory before fading to nothing. She locked eyes with the broken woman. "The Creator does not care about our people. He is using you to get Mica."

Ziiba's face twisted then, and she threw herself at Animkii with vicious intent, clawing a stone knife at her steel face. "What do *you* know? You weren't here!" she screamed, spittle flying. "We should have died with the rest of our people, but the Creator spared us for a reason. The sacrifices we've made have saved us *all!*"

Animkii's hand only tightened on her blade. "And who was *your* sacrifice?"

Ziiba's silence was all the answer she needed. She screamed her fury to the heavens. The sounds her steel vocal cords produced were guttural, more animal than anything human or machine, as she drove Soulcleaver right through her lover's unguarded middle. She tore the blade free and out poured a torrent of thick black blood.

She staggered back in shock and disgust.

"Don't you dare judge me!" Ziiba's face twisted with a snarl. "It was you who robbed the End of the World of its sacrifice and brought the Creator's wrath down upon our people. You can share my damnation!"

***

Mica drew a shuddering breath and moved away from the altar, her eyes locked on Harvester.

She couldn't see Animkii from her current vantage point. A horde of blood-soaked combatants had swarmed the mod, and it was only the psychic connection between them that assured her Animkii still lived. A nervous peek at the sky showed that the cloud of shadows still hadn't stirred, hadn't yet overcome Soulcleaver's light.

Revan's light.

Too late, she saw Harvester burst into movement, lunging forward at her with surprising speed given her grievous wounds, her bony fingers closing around Mica's upper arms and pinning her to the ground.

"You delusional witch! Get off me!" She pulled up against the false Speaker's bloody chest, breathing in those last wheezing breaths that stank of rotten meat. She saw the woman's foul soul writhing inside her body, entwined with nether. She could sense the power that the After Lord had infused it with, and it called to her like an addiction, so sweet that she wanted to feast on it, wanted to drain this wretch dry.

"Take it," Harvester's voice urged her from inside her mind. *"It is your right."*

Her right?

All desire to feed on Harvester's soul left her, a sick feeling inside her gut replacing hunger. She'd almost given in. She'd come so close to losing control. The ball of power inside her crumbled like sandstone as she released her hold on it. The rage that fueled it evaporated, replaced by a bone-aching weariness. "I don't need to do anything. You're already dead."

"Only in *this* world," the Speaker said, her grip on Mica weakening, then letting go, her eyes rolling back to look across the rift as she crumpled, her mouth fixing into a final terrible smile, her last words rattling with death. "The Emissary is here."

Lying in the snow, Mica turned her head in fear and followed the now-empty gaze.

Rising from the abyss was a man cloaked all in black, mounted on the back of a creature that resembled an elk, except this beast flew with giant bat wings and had a gleaming ebony coat and burning ember eyes. Mist billowed from the beast's sharp-toothed mouth.

The newcomer dismounted, his footsteps crunching the snow as Mica rolled over and started crawling to where Animkii fought in the distance, barely able to move as the pain and exhaustion swept back over her, her body burning all over.

A booted foot came down on the back of her knees, pinning her to the ground on her belly. She twisted her body around to see her new assailant and her gaze followed spotless black boots up past breeches threaded with silver and a luxuriant black fur coat. As he leaned over her, the morning light glinted off a mask of silver.

Father Dark.

***

"The Emissary has arrived," Ziiba said in a soft fanatical voice, clutching her abdomen as it gushed free her corruption. "You're too late to stop the sacrifice, Ani. The Blood Gate will soon open and the Creator will bring forth a new world out of the old."

Only now did it truly sink in for Animkii what Mica had told her about the Creator—that everything the Fire Bones believed in was a lie. This ritual was no normal sacrifice; it was meant to finish what Eleven and Father Dark had started back in Alpha. Despite all she and Mica had gone through to escape the foul god's designs, the After Lord had somehow still found them.

Mica's cry snapped her out of her despair, and she turned to see a man rising from the earth's gaping wound on the back of a monster.

Was this the Emissary? Where was Harvester?

The stranger's arrival quickened the battle. A club came smashing down on the back of her head, disintegrating into splinters at the impact and leaving no mark on its unmoving target. When another warrior charged at her side with a spear, she batted the weapon away with no more bother than shooing a fly. She focused only on Ziiba. Everything else was a blur in the background.

"If you wanted a new world," she said in a quiet, deadly voice, "there are better ways to get it!" She slammed into her former lover with all the force of her biosteel leg, heard her ribs crack and the ugly swish of bodily fluids dislocated to unnatural places as the force threw her backward.

What remained of the Last People was pitiful. Long after they should've fallen, the wild-eyed warriors threw their bloody, broken bodies at her, possessed by a battle rage that left them senseless to reason and foaming at the mouth. Their soft, unarmored human bodies broke like twigs beneath her armored fist. Everywhere, that awful tainted black blood spilled, proof that her people had sacrificed both their bodies and souls to the After Lord.

Even in her horror, she could not bring herself to use Soulcleaver against them.

Above them, emboldened by the Emissary's arrival, the Dreamers frenzied with excitement, a stormfront gathering, their deathly presence passing over the battlefield in icy gusts as several of them swooped down.

There was no way she'd give the Dreamers what they wanted. She thrust Soulcleaver into the air and its light cleaved through the opportunistic black mist that had gathered on the bloody field, chasing off the hungry ghosts attracted to the dying.

Then she turned toward the altar, her vision zooming in on the cloaked stranger's face as he dismounted from his monstrous steed.

That mask! But how could Father Dark be here when she'd last seen him back in Alpha, past the End of the World? A terrifying thought occurred to her. Was he able to transport himself across worlds like Mica? Or had he found another way to cross the End of the World? That monster he rode... Was it the result of some twisted Technocrat experiment?

One thing she *did* know: She couldn't let him get ahold of Mica.

Blind with panic, she raced through a final barrage of arrows and spear points, but what she didn't expect was Ziiba's sudden reappearance. Her lover was in a heap in the snow one moment. In the next, she leaped upon Animkii's back, her arm reaching around the steel chest to drive a knife into her face. The blade shattered. In desperation, Ziiba wrapped her hands around Animkii's throat and squeezed, not realizing that her former lover lacked the organic parts to make her attack effective, but catching Animkii so off-guard that she lost her grip on Soulcleaver.

The light blinked out in an instant and the Dreamers stirred from their stasis above her. They were coming for her.

***

A black cloud of death descended on the battlefield.

"It's over," said Father Dark, bearing the air of a conqueror as he stared down at Mica through the hollow eyes of his mask. A long red scarf trailed behind him like a swath of blood against a coat of black fur, and she noticed bitterly that not a spot of dirt touched the quilted white collar of his shirt. "The mod is dead."

Tears burned her eyes. *"Animkii?"* her mind called out, but there was no answer—just a distant buzzing in her head. What did it mean? A freezing wind cut across the grounds, carrying the moans of the dying as the Dreamers tore the outlanders' souls free. Was there still time to save Animkii? In vain, she tried to wriggle out from beneath her captor's boot.

"Don't bother exerting yourself. You're in no condition to win a fight against me."

"We'll see about that!" Mica twisted her body and flung out a hand, her face twisting with wrath as she willed her hatred into a psychic force that blasted out from her own mind like a missile. For one second, she had the satisfaction of feeling their minds meet, relished the short, sweet terror of him realizing she was inside his mind.

But it didn't last. Pain shot through every nerve in her body, breaking her focus. Pinned beneath the cultist's boot, she screamed and writhed and gasped, her heart pounding so hard it felt like it was tearing a hole in her chest, her hands clawing at the snow and frozen ground until her fingers were raw. Her skin cracked like parched mud and leaked black blood everywhere. Darkness closed in, forcing her to release her grip on the power inside her, and she despaired as it sputtered away into the snow.

"Your current body can't sustain your growing powers," he said, exhaling his exasperation. Even crippled by the pain of her failure, Mica didn't miss the relief in his voice. She wanted to laugh, but it came out as a sob as he continued. "The nether inside you is burning away your human shell. Without the After Lord's help, you will die an agonizing death. What our Lord offers you is a new life. Once we make the sacrifice, you will be reborn."

"As a slave to the After Lord?"

"We are all slaves to one power or another." His mask rippled between emotions, his voice softening with such compassion that it spooked Mica. "Our Lord will give you anything, if only you'll obey. He can ease your suffering in a way that angel breath never could."

"You don't know anything about me!"

"I know more than you realize."

Father Dark's fingers slipped beneath the edge of his serpentine mask and lifted it away from his face. Nightmarish, the memory roared through Mica's aching head. Once again, she saw the collector descend on a curtain of acid, its claws unfolding, consuming everything in its path. She drew back in denial, frantically shaking her head.

"You're dead," she said in a quivering voice. "I saw you die. The collector—"

"I'm sorry," he said gently. "The collector was mine; my 'death' borrowed from another. The trader we bought the transport off made a useful corpse. I sealed him inside my mask and then brought him out to use as a puppet for my show. With a few modifications, of course."

"This can't be real. This is some trick of the After Lord!"

The mask slipped from suddenly uncertain fingers. It struck the slushy ground without a sound, yet the drop deafened her with silence. Gone was his cool charisma. Shadows and pain pitted his face instead. "I meant for your transition to be quick and painless, but you resisted so hard. If you hadn't escaped in Zeta—"

"How long have you planned this?" Rage and bitterness rushed over her in a deluge of betrayal, tears flowing, collecting in the hollows of her cheeks before dripping down her chin. She could feel the nightmare power shuddering through her, and the world be damned if it killed her.

How, how, how? She stared at him, unable to articulate her agony, even while her mind screamed it:

How could you betray me, Reid?

Chapter Fourteen

R eid's face still struck Mica as too young for his age, that whimsical smile tracing his lips and a charming glint in his gold-flecked eyes, but now there something else there she'd never noticed before—a touch of madness.

Though he looked like her brother, he wasn't the brother she remembered.

It was like losing her family all over again.

He stood over her in judgment, taking in her appearance with a sweeping disdain—the unkept hair, filth-encrusted skin, and ragged hide tunic. "After everything we've suffered together, would you really rather stay here with that mod and live like a beast? Or go back to Under-Alpha and slave away for some gang and just hope the Crats find no reason to be interested in you?"

Behind him, the landscape continued to shrink. She could hear the crumbling of rock breaking away and the grating of the earth as it slid into the rift, audible even above the unceasing howls of the Dreamers as they consumed all that still lived on the battlefield. It would be so easy to let herself drift away on the current of annihilation...

"I don't understand you!" Reid's contempt built into outrage, clearly unable to fathom her reluctance to accept the glorious future he envisioned for both of them. "Why would you ever want to go back to that wretched existence, when you can live like a god in the Other World?!"

"Is that the crap he's been feeding you? You think he treats his slaves like gods? I used to think you were the smart one!"

"It's true that we all will serve Him, but He's chosen *you* for something much greater. Your bloodline, your powers ... You are more than human, Mica. He can make you like Him."

"What? You think I want to be like that monster?!" Her face crumpled with grief, the pain of her failing body nothing compared to the traitor's knife twisting in her heart.

"What, then? You still believe that you and Samiel can overthrow the Technocrats?" His laugh was scornful. "I thought I'd washed that idealistic garbage out of your head when I got you away from Alpha, but it appears I was mistaken."

Her heart shriveled at his words. Looking back now, who was it but Reid who'd first seeded her doubts in Samiel's love, who'd so readily supplied her with the intoxicants that had kept her sedated, who'd convinced her to settle in Sixth City Zeta, the seat of the After Cult's power?

It had all been there in front of her, and she still hadn't see the truth.

"Samiel was right about you," she said in a quiet voice. "He tried to warn me, you know, but I believed all your excuses. Your disappearances, your secrets... He knew all along there was something wrong with you." She closed her eyes and lay still in the snow even after he lifted his foot off her legs, pressing a cheek against the ground's icy bite. The fight had gone out of her, only to be replaced by an immense sorrow. "If you're really Father Dark, then that means you knew what the Cult did to me in Zeta. You were there."

"Yes." He held up his hand and peeled back the black leather to reveal the gruesome sleeve of burn scars she'd once accused him of hiding. "You're the one who gave me *these*."

She recoiled in horror. There was no denying it now. She felt sick, used, betrayed.

"Why didn't you just hand me back over and let them finish the job?"

He didn't answer immediately, sidestepping piles of rubble and puddles of viscera to reach Harvester's body, rolling it over with a shiny boot and lifting his eyes to survey the ruined battlefield with the displeased expression of an unhappy housekeeper. There were bodies everywhere. No longer warded off by Soulcleaver's light, the Dreamers had converged on the field with terrifying speed—vultures craving fresh carrion, picking away souls with voracious appetites now that they were no longer chained to Harvester's will. She closed her eyes and tried to filter out the terror and rage and fear that poured out in psychic waves from the dying outlanders. Soon the entire landscape disappeared beneath the shroud of shadow.

"I didn't take you back because you weren't ready," Reid finally said. "No matter what we tried, what we gave you, you were stuck inside *that* memory." There was a note of irritation in his voice, as if the devastating death of their family were nothing but an inconvenience to him. "Every time you entered your nightmare, you came back without reaching the Other World. We were certain Revan's blood would awaken in time, like it had with your father, and yet it never did. High Father Holy's impatience nearly ruined everything. But then you escaped and came straight to *me*, and I finally understood."

"Understood what?!"

"Your nightmares always ended as soon as I appeared in them. Don't you see? Your love for me chained you to this awful world; *I* was the barrier that kept you from reaching the portal to our Lord's domain. As long as I was alive, I kept you safe, not only in the real world but in your nightmares too."

Reid, who'd stood in the doorframe of her mother's shop all those years ago, her big brother arriving just in time to save her from the death that took the rest of their family.... Reid, who'd welcomed her home after her frantic dash for freedom from the Cult, sheltering her as he had when they were children hiding from their deranged father...

It wasn't until after Reid had 'died' that the portal had appeared in her dream that night at Lady Fang's. Was he right? Had her bond with him really kept her anchored to this world? It seemed a cruel joke that he would be the one to kill her now. "So, what? You engineered your death so you couldn't 'save' me anymore?"

"We needed your pain to break your connection to this world," he said. "You may not realize it yet, but I am saving you again. Saving us all."

Returning from his survey of the battle scene, he lifted her limp, unresisting body and replaced it gently atop the bone altar. Her head flopped against his shoulder. The smell of him was still familiar—a clean citrus scent that she'd once found comforting, but which was now mingled with the stink of smoke and blood. Silent tears streamed down her face as she turned her head to stare bleakly into the blackness that had swallowed her brave friend.

"Animkii? Are you there? Are you okay?!"

If Animkii answered, she couldn't hear it. The psychic connection between them had frayed, a tenuous thread, as if the cloak of Dreamers acted as a wall of interference.

"Did you ever care for me? Even a bit?" she asked her brother. Her throat was dry, her lips bitten raw, and every word spoken hurt. "Or was I always just a tool to you?"

For the first time, there appeared a crack in his veneer and his arrogant smile slipped. "How could you ask that?" he said in a wounded voice. "It was always the two of us against the world. Anything I've ever done, I did for *both* of us! Everything we ever dreamed about, the After Lord will make real. A world without the Technocrats, a world with unspoiled lands, luxuries we never could've imagined as children!" He argued with such passion that he almost convinced her, the seductions of a conman in every syllable. "The After Lord can even make Samiel love you again, if that's what you want."

"Only someone like *you* would think I'd be happy with that." Anger burned through the hurt in an instant.

"You're not the only one who's made sacrifices!"

"We have the same father, the same blood—Revan's blood—but I don't see *you* trussed up like a sacrificial lamb!"

He went coldly silent, and she knew she'd hit a nerve. "You know nothing."

"I know I mourned your death," she said. "And now that you're alive, I wish I'd never seen the day."

The sting of Mica's words was a slap across his face. Cold fury gathered in those winsome eyes and erased her brother again. "This is going to happen, Mica. You can either go quietly and it will end quickly, or you can struggle and prolong it. Either way, there's no escape this time."

***

As the army of Dreamers swarmed down from the sky, shrilling their victory, Animkii's world plunged into darkness—an unnatural night that blinded her tech-eyes, a bone-deep chill penetrating the battle and silencing even the most zealous warriors. Not a soul moved in those first terrifying seconds. Ziiba's grip on her neck slackened and her body slid off Animkii's biosteel back, landing with a thud that seemed thunderous in the void.

Then the screams began.

The Dreamers were turning on their own allies! Had Harvester lost control?

Before she could think on it further, the ravenous wraiths were upon her, their ghostly hands reaching into her body, covering her mind with a shroud of ice-cold that her sensory systems couldn't cope with. This was no physical cold, but one that penetrated the soul. A shocking weakness gripped her whole body as her mind succumbed, her biosteel body an ineffective defense without a coherent host to guide it. She fell to her knees in the snow.

She couldn't let it end like this! Not while Mica needed protecting. She calmed herself, focused, crawling forward on hands and knees, wresting control back from the darkness and activating her thermal vision. In an instant, the darkness lit with blurry red shapes, her sight capturing the warmth of those still living, and those—

Her hand landed on a body, and a groan issued from it.

Ziiba...

Grief gripped her heart and almost stopped her there.

No, Ziiba had made her choice and Animkii would make hers, like she always had, even if it tore her heart apart to do so. The woman she'd known was dead, had been dead for months, her soul blackened and sold to the After Lord, but Mica was still alive. No matter what it took, Animkii would reach Soulcleaver and stop the final sacrifice before these leeches sucked her dry.

A quick scan of the field found the blade right away, its heat so strong she could feel it from here, burning like a fire inside her mind. But even that heat couldn't stave off the cutting cold that clung to the dread things amassing around her fallen form, whispering seductions and curses in the same breath, besieging her mind while her machine-body crawled forward of its own volition.

Then she heard a child crying, its agonized wail drowning out all other screams, playing for her alone, heard it echoed back by Dreamer after Dreamer until it was all she could hear, and her resolve crumbled. If she hadn't gone after Soulcleaver, if she hadn't earned her exile, she might've been able to save her son. She threw a tormented look back to where Ziiba's body lay, only to find that her heat signature had faded to nothing.

Dead, then. As surely as Niigaanii was dead, and probably her mother, and all the other Fire Bones who hadn't been 'saved' by Harvester.

Pain blossomed into a need for vengeance. It burned through her, stronger than any stim. "You've only given me a reason to fight longer and harder!" she told the After Lord.

Through sheer will, she ordered her body to stand, switching controls to automation and programming her own body with the coordinates needed to retrieve Soulcleaver. So, while her mind sank deeper and deeper beneath the Dreamers' assaults, while her soul faded into nothing and she accepted she'd soon die, her machine-body kept moving until it reached the raven blade and picked it up.

Its light sheared the darkness away in one mighty swath.

***

Mica watched with elation as the explosion of light ripped through the darkness like a bomb, ripping the Dreamers into shreds of shadows that drifted away into the pink morning sky. "Haha!" she exhaled, giddy with triumph, still a little intoxicated by the drugs Harvester had forced on her.

Animkii was alive! But the realization that she was useless to help dampened her spirit.

Reid scowled. "That damned mod!" There was an edge of panic in his voice now as his expected victory came under the threat of being overturned. He pulled out the sacrificial knife he'd used in Alpha from beneath his coat.

She recognized it now as a counterpart to Soulcleaver. Unlike Revan's black raven, this one's ivory blade resembled a pale serpent with feathered wings. She couldn't help but feel a shiver run down her spine at the sight of it.

He saw her look.

"Magnificent, isn't it?" he said. "Carved from one of our Lord's own horns, a necessary piece to create a link between Him and His traitor brother's blood. But first, I need to be sure you won't cause any more trouble."

He slipped his free hand back beneath his coat and pulled out a syringe filled with a silver fluid.

Her fear sharpened. "What's that?"

"A guarantee," he said. "Revan's blood makes you resistant to normal doses of euphoria, but we can't let you keep bouncing between worlds, trying to elude us." He held up the syringe and the morning light glinted off the metallic liquid. His reptilian mask twisted to replicate a smile. "Eleven created this special concentrate just for you. It's enough to kill a human ten times over."

"You wouldn't! You need me to be alive when you spill my blood."

"You'll be alive long enough to complete the sacrifice."

He grabbed her arm, but before he could make another move, a furious behemoth of biosteel charged out of the dissipating darkness, roaring as she launched herself straight at the altar and its foul priest.

***

Animkii heard the crunch of Father Dark's ribs as her mammoth biosteel body plowed into him, sending him flying backward to the perilous edge of the growing rift.

But the things that lived inside the mouth of the abyss didn't attack the cultist, and he clawed his way free of the rift's gaping maw. The shock of seeing Reid's face in place of Father Dark's mask brought her to a startled halt. She'd only known the man a few days, but she'd never forget his last agonized screams.

Some kind of Dreamer trick? Her mind grasped for any kind of logical explanation. But Dreamers didn't bleed. But what kind of unnatural power could bring someone back from the dead? And why was he now their enemy?

"He's made some kind of deal with the After Lord. Faked his own death," Mica said in a mind-voice so weak she strained to understand. *"He's not my brother anymore. Stop him!"*

Animkii's attack should have pulverized the man, yet he climbed back to his feet with only a slight wobble while blood poured out from beneath his coat and pooled at his feet—blood as black as Ziiba's, as black as Mica's. He bent to pick up something in the snow, and the moment he touched it, a dark light shimmered down his body.

The same dark energy he'd wielded back at the Steel Fangs' headquarters.

Reid laughed. It was a maniacal sound that bellowed out over the sodden spring morning and echoed across the lip of the rift, his mouth stretching with the distortion of it, his body bending and waving back and forth as the dark humor spewed forth.

In his hand, he grasped his snake mask. Its biosteel surface swirled like liquid on his palm, rising from his hand, growing and beginning to weave itself into a new shape. Remembering too well the scene at Dathu's base and the strange violent energy he'd wielded there, Animkii didn't wait to find out the cultist's intentions, lunging through the snow and debris and aiming her launcher at him. She'd end him first this time!

But in those precious wasted seconds, the mask had ballooned to the size of a large shield, and her shots ricocheted off its shimmering surface, absorbed into the biosteel with no harm done.

Still laughing, Reid stepped back and released the shifting mask into the air, giving it room as it continued to expand, forming a large pool of biosteel from which emerged the head and shoulders of a towering reptilian monster, its liquid skin flowing over an enormous serpentine frame.

The collector that had 'slain' him.

Reid pointed at Animkii. "Kill."

***

A cry of anguish burned and died in Mica's throat as Reid released the collector.

Animkii...

Her brother staggered back to the altar, very much alive, his body covered in his own gore and every breath a liquid-filled wheeze, his right hand pressed against his chest, closed into a fist. How was he walking at all?! A faint smile drew across his lips as the fingers loosened and she caught the gleam of glass and silver.

"Don't do this, Reid. Please!"

He pinned her right arm down to the stone table and plunged the needle into her arm. The toxin hit her bloodstream like lightning and her whole body seized at once, the shock of pain causing her back to arch up from the bone table as her limbs went rigid. Fire chased every agonized breath, and she tasted blood in her mouth.

She couldn't speak, couldn't scream. It was like an immense weight was pressing down on her chest. A warm hand smoothed back the hair from her forehead, and she saw Reid's bleary face hanging over her, his words gentle. "I love you, Mica. This will all be over soon, I promise. And then you'll thank me."

In a blink, Mica stood again at the balcony of the After Lord's floating fortress, staring down at the sprawling megalopolis far below. A wave of intense pleasure washed over her body as euphoria excised her from the terrible pain of the real world, and she felt her fear and inhibitions slipping away into drugged oblivion. She became conscious that she was above all that existed here, that she was something greater.

A strain of music caught her ear, an invisible bow drawn across strings in a way that made her blood sing. Compelled by the power of this hallowed place, she left the balcony and drifted without resistance through the midst of a garden turned wild with neglect, passing through a set of paper doors painted with delicate golden flowers, to reach an empty ballroom.

Polished obsidian walls encircled the room with ornate reliefs depicting winged men and women in acts of revelry, attended and served by a myriad of different beings. Some resembled hybrids, with their mix of animal and humanlike features; others were so alien she didn't know what to call them. The pictures shimmered to life whenever she turned her eyes on them, and phantom music played as majestic couples swept across a carven dance floor. She swayed in time with them, wanting nothing more than to stay and join them, to lose herself in their merriment and forget everything else, but an unseen arm steered her from the picture-play and out into a gilded hallway.

Part of her knew she should fight back, but she was riding the bliss of euphoria, and why would she ever want to return to that filthy, pain-ridden place? Maybe Reid was right. Maybe the After Lord could give her what they'd longed for as children: a world without pain and sorrow.

What did she have left to lose, anyway? Back in the real world, her body was dying a tortured death, and her friend was engaged in an impossible battle against Reid's collector. Animkii was already dead; she just hadn't realized it yet.

Would it be so bad to die if what came after was so much better?

As she moved along the length of the corridor, she ran her hand along the marble wall, surprised to find it warm and pliant to the touch, like skin. There was a feeling of being watched, and once, she swore she heard faint laughter coming from behind her, but when she turned to search for the source, the hall was empty.

At last, she reached the After Lord's sanctum and the sight of it brought such joy that it swept her cares away. Where once the doors had images of a horrific battle engraved, they now depicted a circle of ten winged beings enthroned above a beautiful, thriving city, the artistry of the scene so intricate, she was certain a microscope would find details her natural eyes had missed.

The doors swung open and crimson light spilled onto the floor. At the end of the pillared pathway, on the dais where the altar once sat, stood the most magnificent man she'd ever seen. A long crimson robe hung from his shoulders, covered in symbols that she couldn't identify, and his bloodless, scaled skin gleamed as if lit by fire. There was no character to his face, not a wrinkle to betray age, not even the slightest crease of a laugh-line, not a pock mark or scar or blemish. He was neither handsome nor ugly, but exactly in-between in a way that made it difficult to tear her eyes away.

The air shivered as he rose, moving toward her like a wraith. Six ghostly black wings arched from his back, ethereal images that shimmered and vanished before she blinked an eye. Power haloed him in sickly green light that spilled on the ground like an apocalyptic sunrise.

This was the man she'd seen beneath the Elder Tree.

Janis.

The After Lord.

The enormity of his power choked her into submission, and she kneeled, groveling at his feet. When she tried to rise, his words halted her.

"Stay. That is your place now, Mica Stone. You will die. And then you will serve."

His words were like angel breath, poison so sweet that her mind and body craved it. But a fierce resistance rose inside her. Never again would she give up control, not to angel breath, and not to this otherworldly fiend! That moment of rebellion slipped through the euphoria, enough to open a crack between worlds.

The horror of that far-off battle between mod and collector poured into her consciousness, and Mica felt Animkii's desperation as the landscape washed away in a wave of acid, leaving the warrior to scramble for safety atop a pile of debris.

She saw it then—Animkii's plan—and felt her hesitate out of fear she'd kill Mica.

And in that brief break of lucidity, Mica had the coherency to scream into Animkii's head: "Do it! Please!"

***

There was no time to think, only move, as the collector sped across the snow-covered field, its coils gliding across the icy terrain, rolling over the dead and debris with fluid ease, its fanged mouth opening to release a torrent of acid.

Unable to maneuver around its bulk, Animkii dove for the ground, hearing the sizzle of acid against her biosteel skin. Unlike the last time she'd faced it, its corrosive attack did no harm; there was nothing organic left exposed to its bite. A pair of outlanders who'd survived the Dreamers' attack were not so fortunate. The poor wretches tried to leap away from the caustic air, but a chain of acid chased them across the snow and turned them into corpses. As quickly as she'd fallen, Animkii rolled back to her feet, unleashing a barrage of pyrolite against her foe.

Like Animkii, the collector could heal itself and in seconds it was like the attack had never happened.

Not good. She tried to peer around her monstrous opponent, checking if Mica was alright, but the collector didn't give her the time. It slammed its immense biosteel body against the ground so hard that it overturned the earth in front of it, throwing dirt and corpses high into the air and creating a field of rocky debris that hindered Animkii's full speed, impeding her path back to Mica.

She had no time to fight this thing. Her gunfire was useless. She didn't have enough fuel left to wear down its defenses. She tried to get around it, making gigantic leaps across the ruined terrain, relying on her enhanced senses to anticipate its attacks and avoid them, her only goal to reach Mica.

If she killed Reid, would his death disable the collector?

The monster was too fast; its serpentine form moved effortlessly across the rubble, positioning itself in front of her and readying another attack.

No chance this thing was going to let her get near Reid. What else could she do? She looked down at the blade, its glow still vibrant, and tightened her hold. Grasping its hilt with both hands, she ran toward the collector, harnessing the full extent of her machine-augmented strength into a final massive leap, propelling her body skyward to heights that defied the limitations of ordinary human legs.

Above the monster's scaly head, her descent began. Soulcleaver's light flared, its brilliance extending the knife's reach beyond its physical boundaries and transforming it into a massive, radiant blade. Using her downward momentum, she swung the blade across the collector's enormous neck, slicing through the biosteel scales as effortlessly as if parting water.

It had never done *that* before. Not even in the End…

The lack of resistance threw Animkii's balance off, and she stumbled as she landed back on the broken ground, the stones rolling beneath her feet and sending her to her knees. The collector's head landed with such weight that it cratered the ground, sending up chunks of debris, its mouth opening and closing, hissing and spitting, but cut off from the source of its acid attack.

In the distance, Reid chanted in a strange sibilant language. Animkii leaped up in alarm, hastening across the unsteady ground, trying not to fall.

"I'm coming, Mica!" she called out in her head, not sure whether the other woman was still there, scrambling to the top of the mound of overturned earth, her fear driving her forward as the altar and its unholy priest came back into view. Father Dark—Reid—was standing over Mica's immobile shape, holding a gleaming white knife up to the sky. But just as Animkii reached the heap's summit, a massive biosteel coil tore the ground out from beneath her.

The collector was still alive!

Even without a head, the body seemed to know its prey's rough location, whipping out at the hill of dirt and stone, causing it to landslide. Animkii clawed at the crumbling ground with her free hand, not daring to let Soulcleaver go, but the earth was too loose to gain hold of, and it piled in around her body, burying her as she watched her chance to stop Reid disappear beneath an avalanche of mud and rock.

She was out of time.

With another sideswipe of its monstrous biosteel body, the collector took out a whole chunk of landscape, tossing Animkii back into the air. She landed against a heap of rocks like a pile of old shop clutter. Her biosteel shell should've instantly absorbed and repaired the damage, but this time, hairline fractures appeared on the surface of her skin. She didn't have enough stims to both attack and heal.

She'd reached her end. But even in the face of her impending demise, her heart ached for her fallen brethren, whose souls the After Lord had ensnared. "Great Spirit," she whispered, desperate to believe the true Creator was still out there somewhere. "Walk us down the final path."

With a deep breath, Animkii sang her own funeral song, her voice rusty and discordant, a bitter reminder of her lost humanity. Memories of her fierce, fallen people flooded her mind: laughter around campfires, the scent of sweetgrass in the air, the raucous celebrations...

> *"My heart is a drumbeat*
> *that grows quiet.*
> *I can hear the voices of the ancestors*
> *in the whispers of trees*
> *and ancient firelight.*
> *They call out to my soul,*
> *'There is a place for you here*
> *with no chains.'"*

Her song carried on, echoing through the desolate landscape, reaching beyond the ruins and across the broken earth. Her soul poured into every verse. The Earth Mother seemed to respond to her call—the sound of distant rushing waters and the rustle of leaves through an absent forest thundered over the breaking of Her body, overcoming the agonized cries of the Last People. The world held its breath with her, and she hesitated.

What she was about to do would kill everything around her.

Mica's voice was static in her head. *"Do it! Please!"*

Animkii made her choice.

<<EXECUTE CODE WHITEOUT>>

Her whole body hummed as every single weapon, every piece of tech, turned red-hot as she released all of her remaining fuel at once and ran straight at the collector.

<<TERMINATE MOD D-2301>>

Chapter Fifteen

The last time Animkii had felt pain like this, it had been in the doomed city of Delta. Her brain was too human to turn it off and her tech too damaged to mute it. Every single artificial nerve in her body fired all at once. With no restraint, her system pumped out pyrolite in quantities impossible to contain, the remaining stims boiling inside her steel body as she pushed it past all limits, her chest and limbs ballooning as the pressure increased, building toward a massive explosion.

The resulting blast shook the land, uprooting what trees and earth remained. Human limbs and chunks of collector rained down on the battlefield. Animkii had just enough awareness left to see Reid throw himself over his sister's prone body as the surrounding landscape disintegrated, watching him take a lethal barrage of biosteel shrapnel as the altar beneath them shattered.

She couldn't even scream.

Then Mica's blood-soaked face emerged from beneath her brother's gruesome remains and a shock ran through her—Mica was alive!

But the other woman's mouth opened in a cry of despair as she met Animkii's gaze across the carnage.

Animkii knew it was bad. Real bad.

The last vestiges of her humanity began slipping away. Pain dissolved, emotions numbed, and her ties to this world grew faint. The machine-sentience within her didn't care that it was also dying—shutting down, being discontinued.

But as Animkii's life ebbed away, burdened by a broken world and the corruption of her people's souls, a distant drumbeat echoed within her fading consciousness.

Thump. Thump. Thump.

A vision emerged from the encroaching darkness of death—an elder woman with black hair streaked in silver, draped in soft deerskin robes, poised beneath a full moon in a star-spangled night sky. Holding a hand drum, she sang a mournful, wordless melody that reached into Animkii's lagging soul.

Who are you? Where am I? The words failed to reach her lips, fading into the silent void of her mindspace.

Starlight sparkled in the woman's eyes as she turned to face Animkii, her song falling silent. "My children, oh, how they've lost their way," she murmured, her voice carrying an unbearable weight of sorrow, her eyes glistening with tears. "But there might still be time for you to clear the path, Daughter." She extended a hand, wizened with age.

An immense warmth and all-encompassing love enveloped Animkii, the woman's words swimming in her skull as the world around her fell apart. She tried desperately to reach for that outstretched hand, longing for that motherly comfort, for that hope of a final chance, only to face a terrible revelation: there was nothing left of her to move.

***

Mica's abrupt return to the real world left her whiplashed. The After Lord's fury roared inside her head as he was once more robbed of his quarry, and the first things she saw as she resurfaced were Animkii's silver tech-eyes disappearing into a sea of fire and broken steel.

Something heavy pinned her to the ground, pressing her body into the jagged remnants of the broken bone altar, and it took her a moment to realize it was Reid's torso draped over her like a blanket of meat. The rest of his body lay in chunks around her—an arm flayed to the bone, a portion of his rib cage, and other smaller bits she couldn't recognize.

That awful and familiar grief rose as nausea in her throat. He'd protected her? She rolled out from beneath his body, hissing as the movement awakened a fiery pain in her left arm. Splinters of biosteel nettled the limb. The pain must've been what had brought her back from the Other World.

With agonizing effort, she propped her brother's remains up against the altar's ruins. The hatred she'd felt toward him waned and turned to regret.

How had they come to this? The pink had bled away from the morning sky, leaving behind a vast blue ceiling and its golden ornament. Looked like it was going to be a beautiful day...

Another seizure ripped through her failing body, the force of it causing a vein in her nose to pop and release a stream of black blood. She sank back into euphoria, carried away as the Other World, Hul, sang its sweet song in her head.

"There's still time to surrender," the After Lord offered.

Back in his world, Mica raised her eyes from the sanctum floor and steeled her will against the weight of that gaze. "You've lost," she said. "There's no one left alive to finish your damned sacrifice."

He smiled then, and it was a terrible thing to behold. "You can take your brother's blade and end it yourself."

"And why the gore would I do that?!"

"Because," he said. "I can give you back your family."

Melted snow froze Mica's back as she lay there, her heart pounding with disbelief. He was lying! But that old ache of loneliness crept back into her overburdened heart. If the possibility even existed… What had this world ever done for her, anyway? But as she thought it, as she approached surrender, a glint of silver caught her eye. Around Reid's broken neck hung a necklace with two rings dangling from it.

She drew a shaky breath, then caught the silver chain between her bloody fingers and tugged Sam's last gift free from her brother's corpse. She thought of her lost love, still alive someplace in this doomed world, still full of that damned fool idealism that Mica wanted so badly to believe in against all evidence to the contrary.

Sam would never forgive her if she let this monster into the world.

She stared across the field of smoldering debris that remained of the battlefield. Dozens of bodies lay strewn about, some shattered into pieces, others burned to nothing but bones. The foul stench of the collector's sulfuric breath still saturated the air and her eyes watered as a murky black haze of pulverized collector ash dusted the air. But she found what she was looking for.

Mica had seen a lot of messed up things in her life, but what remained of Animkii was the worst of it. Her friend's head lay yards away, still attached to its biosteel spine, with a chunk of its heart left dangling from a torn webwork of artificial vessels. But tucked beneath the twisted tailbone, she caught a glint of obsidian.

"What are you doing?" the god demanded.

"Dying. On my own terms."

Summoning every ounce of strength, gritting her teeth against the expected pain, Mica crawled on her belly across the mud and snow, every inch a battle against soul-destroying agony, her fingers bleeding and raw as they pulled her weight across plates of ice and stones sharpened by demolition. A terrible pain stabbed at the left side of her chest, and her head danced with darkness. Not now! Not when she was so close! She almost gave up then, but sheer tenacity drove her to keep going until she reached the sad remains of her friend.

She rolled over onto her back, panting for breath, an immense relief washing over her as she realized how close to the end she was.

"We won, Animkii," she whispered to the dead mod, her hand inching toward Soulcleaver's raven hilt. "World saved and all that. Can't say I ever liked this place, but I guess I don't hate it enough to destroy it." A grimace tightened her face, and she struggled for a breath against the oppressive weight on her chest. Her ears pounded with the erratic pulse of her swelling heart. "You know, maybe there *is* an afterlife for people like us, one that's far away from all this pain. If there is, I'll meet you there, okay? There's just one last thing I need to do first."

She turned her head to bid a last farewell to her dead friend and found the skull staring back at her with open tech-eyes.

Blink.

Blink.

It wasn't joy but horror she felt as the realization hit: Animkii was still alive in there!

Her plan crumbled in an instant. It was one thing to sacrifice herself, but if Animkii was still alive, if even the smallest bit of human consciousness rattled around inside that tin head, she couldn't leave her like this.

"I'll get you to Samiel! He'll fix you up, just like I promised," she said. "It's too late for me. My body's done with, but this power is just getting stronger. If I can keep myself conscious long enough—"

"No." The voice was disjointed, broken, inhuman. Yet *so* human. "Get. Away."

"I can get you out of here, just like I did in Alpha!"

Animkii's tech-eyes closed.

"Nonono, stay with me!"

"There's still time for me to save her," the After Lord said, offering a hand to his kneeling captive, his voice sweet with longed-for promises. "I could even make her fully human again. There's nothing beyond my power, if only you'll open the Gate."

But Mica was done.

"I don't need you. I'll save her myself!"

Her physical body was failing fast, her dying heart struggling to keep it alive, pushing her toward the dizzying edge of unconsciousness. She couldn't pass out yet. Her fingers snapped in place around Soulcleaver's hilt, and she felt its sentience awaken, the life of Revan pulsating in it.

"I'll be joining you soon, Ani." As she spoke the words, the blade flared to life, burning far brighter for her than it ever had for the mod, covering even the sun with its brilliance, syncing with the nether roaring through her blood, lending her its maker's power.

The last time she'd transported them, she'd used Animkii's memories. Could she do the reverse? Could she use her *own* memories?

She was about to find out.

Samiel. She clenched her jaw against the pain, reaching out an impossible distance with her mind, straining against all limitations, seeing red as her body began shutting down. Blood gushed from her nose and ears, dripping off her chin. She couldn't feel her toes anymore.

Out of her memories, she pulled an image of the man she loved.

Obedient tendrils of power unraveled from her mind, shooting off in search of that far off psyche, relying on emotion and memory to filter out millions of other minds in an instant. Her legs went numb. The fingers clutching Soulcleaver shook with the effort of her staying conscious.

She felt her power anchor on the other side, weaving a thread between this place and the other. Images of Upper-Alpha flashed through her mind, the domed city built of steel and plasticine, its subdued population moving through the immaculate streets like zombies, its sterile laboratories endlessly churning out monstrosities, mods floating in tanks of chemicals, vaults full of undercity plunder, and cages full of test subjects, all memories converging to meet in a single steel-walled cell.

Samiel's mind! Reid hadn't lied back in Alpha. He *was* alive!

A desperate longing filled her heart, and even though her whole body burned with the effort of maintaining the connection, she still wanted to linger, desperate for this long-awaited reunion with the man she loved.

But she couldn't afford to give in, not while Animkii's life depended on her. With unforgiving force, she broke into the mod's faltering psyche and pulled its consciousness into her own mind. *"Can you see my memories?"* she asked, growing frantic, every heartbeat plunging a knife into her chest. *"Do you see Samiel?"*

Animkii barely responded, so faint it was a whisper rasping against her mind. *"Yes."*

"It's going to be fine. See? I've got a hold of you. When you see him, tell him I'm sorry. Tell him I lo—"

"Let go!" The After Lord thundered into her mind, his force of will breaking the link between her, Animkii, and Samiel, the violent recoil of power hurtling her against the ground. But the blood bubbling from her lips couldn't stop a manic smile from forming. She'd done it!

With pure glee, she watched Animkii's remains dematerialize before her eyes. The gateway she'd opened between this place and Alpha slammed shut between them, but to the core of her nether-saturated soul, she knew her friend had made it across. Dark spots danced before her eyes and her life was quickly slipping away. She clutched Revan's blade against her breast in hands that had gone numb.

She recalled Revan's words: *"Take Soulcleaver. Walk into the dream. Slay him if you can."*

Time to end this for good.

The devastated landscape vanished, and she was once again back in the Other World, kneeling before its incensed lord.

"You stupid woman," he said. "I would've given you anything."

In the After Lord's sanctum, her fingers twitched against the floor, a familiar warmth filling her palm as Revan's blade slipped between worlds. "The only thing I want is for you to leave my world ALONE!" she screamed, leaping forward and slashing at his neck with Soulcleaver—

—only to be jerked back to reality as rough hands hooked beneath the armpits of her physical body and dragged it back across the snow. Her heart sledgehammered against her chest. Who was it? With a burst of panicked strength, she twisted her body away from that grip, staggered forward, and tried to run. She had to fight. Had to finish—

But a hand caught her from behind, and an ivory blade opened her throat.

Epilogue

“Who the gore are *you,* and how did you get in here?”

Animkii opened her eyes, startled by a man's voice. She found herself in a dimly lit prison cell built for one person. One person...

Sixty-two, she recalled blearily, her shock settling as she stared at the golden-skinned Technocrat.

No, not Sixty-Two...

“Samiel?”

Be sure not to miss the second volume of
H.S. Gilchrist's Primordial Engine series!

SEPARATE WORLDS
The End is Just the Beginning...

The sacrifice was made. A life taken. The Blood Gate has fallen, and Earth's breaking begins anew...

Amid a crumbling world, imprisoned Technocrat traitor Samiel finds an unlikely ally—a war mod's skull. Animkii's steel-encased brain still pulses with life, offering Samiel the key to escape and a chance to lead an undercity revolution against the dystopian Technocracy.

But as Samiel delves into Animkii's memories, a shocking revelation emerges about his lost love, Mica Stone, and her role in the world's unraveling. Animkii, however, is more than just a lifeless skull; the steel warrior's soul embarks on a journey through the spirit realm, seeking guidance from her ancestors and the spirits of the land in a desperate bid to halt the world's devouring.

With the sinister After Lord threatening Earth's annihilation, Samiel must transform his revolution against the Technocrats into a resistance against a greater evil. Can he and Animkii join forces to save Earth from its irreversible descent into ruin, or has humanity's final battle already begun?

**For order details, please visit the author's page:
https://hsgilchrist.com**

STEP INTO A WORLD ON THE BRINK!

Sign up now for Author H.S. Gilchrist's newsletter at

https://hsgilchrist.com!

Take an exclusive journey through the broken, dystopian Earth

of

THE PRIMORDIAL ENGINE series.

Be the first to access insider insights, the latest news, and

unique offers tailored for the adventure ahead!

VISIT OUR WEBSITE

hsgilchrist.com

LIKE US ON FACEBOOK

facebook.com/hsgilchrist

FOLLOW US ALL OVER THE PLACE!

Threads @hsgilchrist

Instagram @hsgilchrist

Twitter @hsgilchrist

Bluesky @hsgilchrist.bsky.social

Mastodon @hsgilchrist@mastodon.social

A WAR BETWEEN TWO WORLDS IS
BEGINNING... WHERE DO YOU STAND?

www.ingramcontent.com/pod-product-compliance
Lightning Source LLC
Chambersburg PA
CBHW051426190726
48289CB00001B/64